W9-DEC-551

alfred
HITCHCOCK'S
YOUR
SHARE
OF
FEAR

alfred
HITCHCOCK'S
YOUR
SHARE
OF
FEAR

Edited by
CATHLEEN JORDAN

The Dial Press
Davis Publications, Inc.
380 Lexington Avenue, New York, N.Y. 10017

FIRST PRINTING
Copyright © 1982 by Davis Publications, Inc.
All rights reserved.
Library of Congress Catalog Card Number: 76-43201
Printed in the U.S.A.

Grateful acknowledgement is hereby made for permission to include the following:

Haunted Hall by Donald Honig; first published in Alfred Hitchcock's Mystery Magazine; copyright © 1961 by H.S.D. Publications, Inc.; reprinted by permission of Raines & Raines. *Chinoiserie* by Helen McCloy; first published by Ellery Queen's Mystery Magazine; copyright © 1946 by Helen McCloy, renewed; reprinted by permission of the author. *The Billiard Ball* by Isaac Asimov; first published in the magazine If, March, 1967; copyright © Galaxy Publishing Corporation, 1967; reprinted by permission of the author. *The Bitter End* by Randall Garrett; first published in Isaac Asimov's Science Fiction Magazine; copyright © 1978 by Davis Publications, Inc.; reprinted by permission of Blackstone Literary Agency. *The Strange Children* by Elisabeth Sanxay Holding; first published in The Magazine of Fantasy and Science Fiction; copyright © 1955 by Mercury Press, Inc.; reprinted by permission of Harold Matson Company, Inc. *A Year in a Day* by Erle Stanley Gardner; first published in Argosy; copyright © 1930 by Frank A. Munsey Co., renewed 1958 by Erle Stanley Gardner; reprinted by permission of Thayer Hobson & Company. *The Peregrine* by Clark Howard; first published in Alfred Hitchcock's Mystery Magazine; copyright © 1965 by H.S.D. Publications, Inc.; reprinted by permission of Alex Jackinson Literary Agency. *Anachron* by Damon Knight; from THE BEST OF DAMON KNIGHT, Taplinger Publishing Co., N. Y., 1978; copyright © 1953 by Quinn Publishing Company, Inc., renewed; reprinted by permission of the author. *Change for a Dollar* by Elijah Ellis; first published in Alfred Hitchcock's Mystery Magazine; copyright © H.S.D. Publications, Inc., 1967; reprinted by permission of Scott Meredith Literary Agency, Inc. *Rest in Pieces* by W. T. Quick; first published in Isaac Asimov's Science Fiction Magazine; © 1979 by Davis Publications, Inc.; reprinted by permission of the author. *Play a Game of Cyanide* by Jack Ritchie; first published in Alfred Hitchcock's Mystery Magazine; copyright © 1961 by H.S.D. Publications, Inc.; reprinted by permission of Larry Sternig Literary Agency. *A Kind of Murder* by Larry Niven; first published in Analog Science Fiction/Science Fact; copyright © 1974 by The Conde Nast Publications, Inc.; reprinted by permission of Robert P. Mills, Ltd. *Confession* by Algernon Blackwood; from WOLVES OF GOD AND OTHER FEY STORIES; copyright © 1921 by Algernon Blackwood, renewed; reprinted by permission of A. P. Watt, Ltd. *The Adventure of the Intarsia Box* by August Derleth; first published in Alfred Hitchcock's Mystery Magazine; copyright © 1964 by H.S.D. Publications, Inc.; reprinted by permission of Scott Meredith Literary Agency, Inc. *A Question of Ethics* by James Holding; first published in Alfred Hitchcock's Mystery Magazine; copyright © 1960 by H.S.D. Publications, Inc.; reprinted by permission of Scott Meredith Literary Agency, Inc. *A Hint of Henbane* by Frederick Pohl and C. M. Kornbluth; first published in Alfred Hitchcock's Mystery Magazine; copyright © 1961 by H.S.D. Publications, Inc.; reprinted by permission of Frederick Pohl and Robert P. Mills, Ltd. *The Cold Equations* by Tom Godwin; first published in Analog Science Fiction/Science Fact; copyright © 1954 by Street & Smith Publications, Inc., renewed; reprinted by permission of Scott Meredith Literary Agency, Inc.

Introduction

The collection of stories brought together in this volume is, we think, a special one. It brings together a wide variety of very good authors, for one thing—from Conan Doyle to Isaac Asimov to Jack Ritchie, winner of the Mystery Writers of America's Edgar Allan Poe Award for Best Short Story of 1981. And for another, it shows the extraordinary range of the mystery story.

Compare, for example, M. R. James's eerie tale of a mezzotint that presented a strange new appearance almost every time its purchaser looked at it with Erle Stanley Gardner's "A Year in a Day" and with Elijah Ellis's "Change for a Dollar." All three are stories of crimes committed—murders, in fact—but each is handled very differently. The most traditional of them, the Gardner, involves straightforward detecting, with something from the future woven in. The Ellis story describes crime in the making, created bit by bit from events apparently insignificant in the great scheme of things but all fraught with anguish and with a nightmarish sense of inevitability; the evil that comes from evil is demonstrated almost clinically, but masterfully. And the James story partakes of the magical and the ghostly; it is full of darkness at every turning, from the deed itself to the nature of the mezzotint to its revelation of the shadowy past.

Crime can, it seems, be written about in almost any manner. Jack Ritchie's "Play a Game of Cyanide" is a light and playful story, as its title indicates. Helen McCloy's "Chinoiserie" is full of dreams from a vanished China. And Damon Knight's "Anachron" combines the sense of past, present, and future in so special and unusual a way that they almost become one.

Crime stories can involve, even if only peripherally, ghosts and robots and creatures like Clark Howard's peregrine. They can have to do with postulations from physics as well as foggy days in London; they can turn a criminal act inside out as James Holding does in "A Question of Ethics" or create powerfully the fear of what's-going-to-happen-next as Doyle does with his student of Egyptology, hidden in his room at Oxford. And they can raise interesting problems we have yet to face in crime solving, as Larry Niven demonstrates in "A Kind of Murder." Or for that matter, problems about crimes that still lie ahead of us, as Tom Godwin so movingly shows us in "The Cold Equations."

And among all these other matters, they turn on mystery. Mystery that brings with it a new puzzle, an unexpected and chilly touch, a share of fear. Best—and inevitably, with the mystery story—resolved snugly at home, rainy nights preferred (but not required).

We would particularly like to thank Gail Hayden, for her great help in selecting stories for this volume, and for her unerring sense of the spirit of the collection. In large part, she made it possible.

Cathleen Jordan

Contents

Haunted Hall

by Donald Honig

When I became owner and tenant of Cannon Hall in a small upstate New York town in 1902, I was the first person in almost forty years to live in the fine old house. Because the place unfortunately had been allowed to run down and because of some strange local superstitions about it, I was able to purchase the house quite reasonably. It was here at Cannon Hall, away from the bustling pace of downstate life, that I was able to withdraw into the quiet and solitude I needed to fulfill my ambition of writing a history of the Dark Ages, a scholarly work.

Cannon Hall (named for its previous owner, Horace Cannon, about whom I was to learn a great deal) was a rather forbidding place, three gloomy stories tall, with dormer windows along the top floor that looked like hooded eyes beneath their gables. The massive front door, appearing as sturdy and deathless as the oak from which it had been made, was a setting of elaborate scrollwork. Cannon Hall was surrounded by considerable acreage of once elegant grounds, all of which had been left to neglect, so that sullen weeds grew around the house tall enough to obscure the first floor windows, the nearby small pond had been allowed to become foul, and many of the old trees had died.

It took more than two months to give the old place a more agreeable aspect and to restore the grounds to at least a semblance of their original elegance. I had the weeds cut and the shaggy hedges which surrounded the house's upgrade approach trimmed. Still the house retained a morose, almost Gothic look as though it were haunted and cared not who knew. But I found myself developing a certain fondness for it nevertheless.

When I felt that the place had been made presentable (or as presentable as it would ever become, for you cannot efface a mood, an atmosphere, and there was indeed something stark and gloomy that lingered in the air), I decided to invite my nearest neighbor in for an afternoon's conversation.

This man, my neighbor, was Dr. Albert Morrison. I had met Dr. Morrison several times in the village and found him to be a rather charming old gentleman. Nearly eighty, he still retained a certain keenness and interest in his fellow man, after a lifetime of close observance of human behavior. When he heard I had bought and was restoring Cannon Hall, he sought me out one afternoon in the village and we had a brief chat on the porch of the general store. He seemed intrigued by my having moved into Cannon Hall. I felt he rather hoped I would ask him to stop by sometime, and when I sent one of my servants to his house with the invitation, the doctor's response was one of eager acceptance. Two days later, at the appointed time, he rode up the driveway in his buckboard.

"You've done a fine job here," he said when we'd settled down in the living room. He looked around at the large room, his bright blue eyes small and almost wistful. "I haven't been in this place since Horace Cannon's death—forty years ago. I never thought I'd ever be back, never thought anyone would open it again."

"Why not?" I asked.

"Because of the story."

I had heard the story, of course. A ghost had walked the floors of Cannon Hall and driven the master slowly insane—until he had finally hanged himself. There were countless variations of the details, and when you hear bits and snatches from so many different people, who have heard them from others, you naturally grow skeptical. I believe the doctor noticed my amused skepticism.

"Oh no, Mr. Howard," he said with gentle reproach. "It isn't as whimsical as you think. It only sounds that way, because no one knows the complete truth about it."

The implication was clear: Dr. Morrison knew "the truth about it."

"I would like to hear it," I said.

"No one has ever heard it before," he said, "because I've never told it. In the beginning I couldn't tell it, of course, and then as time went on I let it slip from my mind, the lapses becoming more frequent, deciding each time that it would be pointless to tell it. But now I'm an old man. Perhaps an old man shouldn't be going around telling ghost stories—people are always looking for excuses to call an old man senile, y'know. But as I say, I am an old man, so perhaps I should pass the story along to you and leave its further retelling to your own discretion."

"Fill your glass, doctor," I said.

10   DONALD HONIG

He poured himself half a tumbler of brandy from the decanter and took it in his soft, blue-veined hand. He looked around again at the high ceilinged room.

"Horace hanged himself from there," he said pointing up to the second floor balustrade. "I suppose this is an odd place to tell the story. If Horace's ghost is here, you'll hear a shriek of anguish when I'm through."

Cannon Hall was built by Horace Cannon's father early in the century (Dr. Morrison began) and passed on to the son when the elder Cannon died. Horace had always been a rather difficult person, first as a somewhat spoiled and headstrong youth and then as a morose man whose disposition seemed to grow more and more crabbed with each passing year.

My recollection of him goes back to when he was a young man just past his majority. He had designs upon the world then. He wanted to go to sea and travel to exotic places, but never did; he wanted to go to some university, either here or abroad, and learn all there was to learn, but never did. He was a creature of stops and starts, of sudden enthusiasms and of abrupt cancellations. He was moody and temperamental; he could be blackly uncommunicative sometimes and at others strenuously congenial.

Horace was married, briefly. She was a local girl, Helene. Their marriage did not last—it couldn't, I guess, since she was a girl of some character. When she left him, he became extremely lonely and bitter, his sense of failure more heightened than ever.

He spent his time riding about the grounds on a fine bay, when the weather was good, or down at the village talking with the men. When the weather turned bad he spent most of his time right here in this room, reading, before a roaring fire. He was quite fussy about his fire, it was one of his eccentricities. It had to be laid just right. This eccentricity was responsible for his downfall. But first let me tell you about Keever.

If Horace ever met his match in oddness of character, he met it in Keever. Keever was his manservant, officially. I say officially, for actually he was butler and handyman as well as gardener and hostler. He seldom spoke; his mouth was at all times shut as tight as a drum. He never came to the village—the cook, an old woman, did all the marketing. The first we heard of him was when the cook said one day, "We've a new man at the house."

We didn't see Keever until some months later when Horace, enjoying one of his lighter moods, invited some of us in for drinks. That was the first time I saw Keever. He was thin and wiry and like many men of that build, was stronger than he looked. Though he was as polite as could be, it was a sort of regal politeness, almost a condescension. His eyes surveyed you with contempt—he didn't try to disguise it. This contempt (that is what I called it at any rate) extended to Horace as well. Keever seemed to make private little comments, like a mime, whenever Horace spoke to him; you could see it in his face. But he was efficient; absolutely wordless, and efficient.

Horace had a curious attitude about Keever. He obviously didn't like him, but he seemed fascinated by the man's grim efficiency—he often spoke of it. Or perhaps he saw in Keever a nature darker and more unfathomable than his own. Whatever it was, Keever came and stayed.

Keever's background was unknown, and it remained unknown, for he wasn't the sort of person you put questions to. He was a widower; that much we knew. And he had two boys, Timothy and Henry, who lived with him here at Cannon Hall. Considering their father, their surroundings, their master, they were remarkably well adjusted and likeable lads. Henry was ten and Tim was twelve. They frequently came down to the village and played with the other boys and were quite popular. It was a pity such fine lads had to get drawn into so reprehensible an affair.

The trouble began one chilly winter's night. It was just after Helene had left him and Horace was then more than bitter—he was savage. He came into this very room, one dark chilly night, and found one of the boys laying the fire. For some unaccountable reason (it was probably only his own black temper that caused it) Horace decided the boy was not laying the fire properly—although how he was able to tell the difference I do not know since the room was quite dark. I suppose he was just looking for an excuse to vent some anger and he seized this opportunity. The boy was crouched before the hearth at his work and Horace stormed up from behind and said something and struck him on the back of the head. I doubt if it was a very hard blow, but it seemed to catch the boy off balance, and he fell to one side and struck his head on the hearthstone. Horace told him to get up, but the boy did not move. After prodding the fallen youth with his toe and getting no response, Horace went away.

On his way out of the room he encountered Keever in the doorway (that man seemed to be in every place at once).

"Something is wrong with your boy," Horace said, "I gave him a little

DONALD HONIG

push and he struck his head. You'd better see to him." Then Horace left the room and Keever went to the youth, who still lay, motionless, beside the fireplace.

A few minutes later Keever came quietly to Horace in one of the front rooms and said to him:

"Timothy is dead. My son is dead." Said it just like that, with no reproach, no accusation, as though he had come in to announce dinner.

"Dead?" Horace asked. "What do you mean? Are you sure? How can you be sure?" When Keever said nothing, Horace began to panic. "It was an accident, Keever," he said. "I merely tapped him and he fell. My God, I never wanted anything like that to happen." Then Horace lost all control. It had all been a terrible accident, he cried. He regretted it from the bottom of his heart. He would do anything in his power to make it up to Keever.

And then a very strange and unexpected thing took place. Keever agreed that it had been an accident, despite the fact he had seen what had taken place. To Horace's exclamations of sorrow and self-reproach Keever was stony. Then Horace abruptly changed his attitude. He forgot the sorrow and the self-reproach.

"But what will happen?" he asked, "How will we explain it?" he asked of the man whose son he had just killed.

"Timothy was my son," Keever said. "The explanation will come from me."

After leaving Horace, Keever returned to the living room and lifted the small body from the hearth and carried it to his room. That very night he placed the body in a wagon and with his other son drove off into the night. He reappeared at Cannon Hall three weeks later. To Horace's anxious inquiries he replied simply that Timothy had been buried next to his mother (which was the only time Keever ever mentioned a wife, a mother) and that he had seen fit to leave Henry with relatives. This last was quite a pointed action. Keever did not trust his master around his remaining son.

Just where Keever left Henry he did not say. Perhaps once in two or three months he would leave Cannon Hall for a few days and go somewhere. Horace assumed he went to visit the other boy. When he returned, he was as sullen and uncommunicative as ever.

I met Horace one evening in the village. I was sitting in the tavern smoking a pipe when he came in and sat beside me. He seemed to be concerned about something as he sat musing silently for a while. Then he said, out of nothing, as if to get it off his mind:

"Keever's boy Timothy is dead."

"Dreadful," I said. "How?"

"From a knock on the head. He fell. It was an accident."

"When did this occur?" I asked.

"Oh, some time ago," he said evasively.

"How much time?" I asked.

"Six months."

"And you haven't in all this time said anything?"

"What was there to say?"

"We could at least have sent condolences to Keever."

"He wanted it kept private. Took the boy to his people and buried him there."

"And Henry?"

"Henry is living with his people now."

"Keever must be terribly lonely."

"He has his work," Horace said.

That was the whole of that conversation. It was the first mention he'd made to me of the affair. Of course I'd been wondering about Keever's boys, they had come to the village so often and everyone liked them, but I had never thought of inquiring after them. I thought it odd that it took Horace six months to mention the tragedy, but then again, Horace was not the most accountable person in the world.

I next saw him about two months later. It was at my home. It was the first time Horace had ever come there, and he had come late at night, unbidden. I saw immediately that he was quite upset. He tried to be wry about it but his anxiety was plain.

"Do I seem like a rational person to you, doctor?" he asked.

"I've always thought you difficult, Horace, but never irrational."

"Do I look like a man who has hallucinations? Who sees ghosts?" He smiled as he said this, but it was a tight, humorless smile.

"No man who sees ghosts looks like a man who sees ghosts," I said. "And anyway there is no such thing as . . ." But he cut me off, grabbing my arm, suddenly in a panic.

"Then I've established a precedent," he said heatedly. But in a moment he regained his composure and sat back in his chair, somewhat abashed by his outburst.

14   DONALD HONIG

"Relax and speak slowly," I said, not knowing what to make of all this. He was clearly sober—if that is ever an indication of a man's rationality. If he had had a nightmare that was very real to him then I did not want to put myself in the position of taking him too seriously, but on the other hand if he had some valid disturbance neither could I permit myself to regard it too lightly.

He sat quietly for a few minutes, absorbed. I had the impression he was giving himself one last merciless interrogation on what was so deeply disturbing him before revealing it to me. Then he became quite calm, relaxed, and I thought for a moment he had explained it to himself to his satisfaction.

But he had not, for he began to tell me about it.

"I saw Timothy last night," he said calmly, looking at me, looking for some indication of condescension or incredulity; I tried to keep my face as passive as possible rather than to inhibit him with some skeptical reaction.

"Timothy Keever," I said.

"Yes."

"Where did you see him?"

He ran his hand over his face, covering his eyes for a moment. "I'm sure I saw him," he said. He let his hand fall and looked across at me almost defiantly.

"I'm certain it was him," he said.

"Where did you see him?" I asked again.

"There . . . at the hearth."

"What was he doing?"

"Standing there. Merely standing."

"Where were you?"

"Outside, coming from the stable. With Keever. Keever directed my attention to some silken threads that were lying on the shrubbery just under the window. When I went to examine them I happened to look up and saw him . . . standing at the hearth, as perfectly alive and upright as a living thing. I turned and called Keever, but when he got to the window the . . . boy was gone."

"What did Keever say to this?"

"Nothing. He said nothing . . . except to identify the threads on the shrubbery as being quite similar to the material of the shroud in which the boy was buried. . . ."

I felt I could not treat this incident lightly. For one thing, Horace had been most unnerved by it. Although he drank, I had never known him to do so to excess, and I had never known him to have hallucinations. At that time I had no idea as to why he should be the victim of such a scene. I learned this soon after.

Again Horace came to my house. It was about a week after his first visit. Now he was trembling like a man in fever, there was a bright ghastly look to him.

"Last night, doctor," he said, "I saw him again. I was walking across the dining room when suddenly I looked up . . . and there he was, at the head of the stairs, in the darkness, looking down at me with the most dreadful convulsion in his face . . . his head bent to one side, his tongue protruding like an idiot's, his eyes gaping. I almost had a heart seizure. I cried out and rushed to the kitchen, so alarming my old cook that she dropped a handful of silverware. I found Keever in his quarters and took him by the arm and brought him out. When we returned to the dining room he—Timothy—was gone. But he had been there, doctor, I know it, I know it. I saw him as plainly as I see you now."

Horace was in an incredible state of agitation. It took me close to an hour to calm him, to stop his pacing and hand wringing and muttering. When finally I induced him to sit down and have some hot tea, he told me the truth of how Timothy Keever had died. After telling this, he said, calmly enough, "I suppose then, doctor, these hallucinations are caused by my feeling of guilt."

"Perhaps."

"And that I might go on seeing them for the rest of my life."

"Can Keever offer no explanation?"

"No. You know Keever; he says nothing. And believe me, doctor, it's not the easiest thing for me to make mention of the boy, considering the circumstances. The subject is delicate enough without my aggravating it."

"I suggest you leave Cannon Hall," I said.

"That's absurd," he said. "What makes you think these hallucinations would be confined to Cannon Hall? They could well follow me around the world."

"Perhaps," I said.

"I call them hallucinations," he said, "but yet I see them as vividly as I see my image in a mirror."

DONALD HONIG

When Horace left me he was in a highly disturbed state. It is bad enough for a person to be seeing a ghost, but the ghost of someone you have killed . . . well, you can sympathize with Horace's state of mind.

I decided to pay a call at Cannon Hall; not, however, on Horace, but on Keever. I rode my buckboard up to the grim old place and around to the servants' quarters. There I found Keever at work in the yard stacking wood. He looked displeased at my approach. He was by far the most aloof and unsociable person I've ever known.

"I'd like a word with you, Keever," I said.

"Sir?" he said.

"I'm here in my capacity as Mr. Cannon's physician. I want to tell you that I'm quite concerned about Mr. Cannon's mental state. I suppose you know to what I'm referring?"

"I suppose I do," he said dryly. He had a way of speaking that was positively outrageous; the man had more pure insolence than the most pampered royalty.

"Is there any way you can account for these things he's been seeing?" I asked. Keever turned an impassive face towards me, coldly.

"I know nothing about it," he said.

"But he's mentioned them to you."

"I too, keep seeing my dead boy," he said.

"You do?"

"Yes. In my sleep, my dreams . . ."

"But never in the flesh."

"I'm sorry, sir," he said, turning away, "but this conversation has turned quite painful for me."

I asked him if he wanted to try and help his master. The wretch said nothing. He remained turned from me, with icy politeness waiting for me to leave. I laugh at myself now when I think of asking this man for compassion for Horace, for here, as I later was to learn, was one of the most diabolic and merciless minds ever fitted inside the human skull. I should have known then that any man who was able to exercise the restraint and self-control under the circumstances that Keever did, was not a man to be reached through the ordinary channels of human decency.

Several weeks later the ghost of Timothy Keever walked again in Cannon Hall. I happened to visit there the morning after it occurred, a gray drizzly morning. Much to my horror I found Horace lying in the driveway, lying face down on the gravel as if he had been shot in the act of running.

I jumped from my buckboard and went to him. He was alive. I lifted him up and carried him back to the house where I revived him. After several minutes of tortured breathing he was able to compose himself and tell me what had happened.

"I saw him again, doctor," he said. "Last night, I had just retired for the night and was nestling under my blankets when suddenly my door flew open and he was standing there in the entrance, in the blackness, his face illumined by a lighted candle; his face was white as marble and perfectly expressionless, his eyes staring pitifully at me."

"What did you do?" I asked.

"I cried out . . . then the candle was extinguished and he was gone. I heard running on the stairs. I leaped from the bed, dressed, and went running from the house—where I did not know, I simply had to get away. I must have tripped and fallen and struck my head in the driveway where you found me."

"You mean you lay there all night?"

"Yes. I must have."

"Where is Keever?"

"He's about, I suppose. I haven't seen him since yesterday afternoon. He was here at teatime."

I found Keever in the stable. He claimed to have heard nothing. When I attempted to question him further he simply walked away from me.

Horace Cannon continued to be haunted. Each time I encountered him—and now it was only in the village, for he never came to my house any more nor did I go to his—his appearance had become worse, more haggard, gaunt. His eyes appeared to be lidless, wide and staring with a fixedness that was appalling, a luster of almost saintly madness filling them. He became unapproachable on the subject of his hallucinations—that they continued to occur was obvious, but he would wave off the subject with his hand. He seemed resigned to some terrible inevitability.

And then one day about a year after the death of Keever's boy, I finally heard what I had known I someday would hear. Horace Cannon was dead. He had hanged himself, tied one end of the rope to the second floor balustrade and looped the other around his neck and thrown himself over. I examined the body after it had been cut down and it appeared to me that Horace had died in a state of agitation that amounted to a fit. He had been driven mad.

Soon after, Keever and the cook left and Cannon Hall was closed down.

DONALD HONIG

For a while many strange tales were told of moanings and wailings coming from behind the locked shutters, but gradually the people began to accept Cannon Hall for what it was, an old, un-lived-in house.

Needless to say, what had taken place inside its now silent walls continued to work upon my mind. I was not satisfied with the explanation that Horace Cannon had simply been seeing things. Perhaps toward the end, yes. But in the beginning he was as rational as you or I. It was true he had considerable feelings of guilt, but he was not the sort of man who would have let that kind of feeling prey upon him for very long. It was my conviction that what he had been seeing was in truth something less than supernatural.

One afternoon I ventured up to the old place. It was about six months after Horace's death. I was determined to give my curiosity at least the benefit of a look around. Of course my inquiry was confined to the house's exterior, all doors and windows having been securely locked and bolted, and I was not a person to force my entry. I walked around the grounds looking for something I sensed was there.

Much to my surprise I found the stable unlocked. I entered the dark and musty place and poked around the stalls. As I was about to leave I noticed a ladder against one wall. Climbing it, I found that it led to a loft. Here, to my astonishment, I found a cot and a chair. In addition there were evidences that someone had been living there. I found several dried crusts of bread and a half full jar of long-soured milk. I was surprised because I did not know anyone had lived there, for there were regular servants' quarters at the rear of the house, where Keever and the cook had lived.

Then about four years later I was on a holiday some hundred miles downstate. While there I became quite friendly with several of the local people. One of these, an elderly gentleman, suddenly died. Having been fond of the old fellow, I naturally felt an obligation to attend his funeral. While following the coffin to its resting place, my eye happened to light upon one of the headstones. The moment I saw this name I forgot about my old friend's funeral, for I knew immediately that I had found the answer to the ghost of Timothy Keever and the suicide of Horace Cannon.

I asked about in this town for Keever. Oh, yes, he was known there all right. Quite an odd duck, everyone agreed. After his wife's death he went to work as manservant somewhere upstate, they said. He'd had two sons and one had died in an accident and he had brought the boy back here for burial—here because this had been the home of Keever's wife. Then he had returned to his position and continued there until his master had passed away. After this, he had returned with his boy for a short stay and then gone away again, no one knew where, nor was he ever heard from again.

At this point in the old doctor's narrative I interrupted him.

"Just a moment, doctor," I said. "He returned *with* the boy? It was my understanding that—"

"That he had left the other boy, Henry, in this town? Yes, that was everyone's understanding, Mr. Howard. But it was not quite the truth. Henry Keever had returned to this town with his father, yes, though not to live there but to be buried there—for it was *his* name I saw on the tombstone in that cemetery, and name, age, and date of death coincided precisely with that of the youth who had died at Cannon Hall."

"Then you mean—"

"What I mean is . . . if you remember clearly, Horace Cannon struck the youth at the hearth in a dark room. Horace never saw the boy's face. Horace never saw the boy again. Keever told him it was Timothy; in the few minutes between Keever's looking at the dead boy and his returning to his master he had worked out in his mind the whole fantastic diabolic scheme which he pursued for the next whole year—that of driving his master insane. It was a plan of vengeance as fiendish as any ever calculated in the mind of a human being. He buried Henry and then returned with Timothy and secreted him in the loft in the stable, making him live there, bringing him out from time to time to do his—Keever's—unholy bidding."

DONALD HONIG

Chinoiserie

by Helen McCloy

This is the story of Olga Kyrilovna and how she disappeared in the heart of Old Pekin.

Not Peiping, with its American drugstore on Hatamen Street. Pekin, capital of the Manchu Empire. Didn't you know that I used to be language clerk at the legation there? Long ago. Long before the Boxer Uprising. Oh, yes. I was young. So young I was in love with Olga Kyrilovna. . . . Will you pour the brandy for me? My hand's grown shaky the last few years. . . .

When the nine great gates of the Tartar City swung to at sunset, we were locked for the night inside a walled, medieval citadel, reached by camel over the Gobi or by boat up the Pei-ho, defended by bow and arrow and a printed representation of cannon. An Arabian Nights city where the nine gate towers on the forty-foot walls were just ninety-nine feet high so they would not impede the flight of air spirits. Where palace eunuchs kept harems of their own to "save face." Where musicians were blinded because the use of the eye destroys the subtlety of the ear. Where physicians prescribed powered jade and tigers' claws for anemia brought on by malnutrition. Where mining operations were dangerous because they opened the veins of the Earth Dragon. Where felons were slowly sliced to death and beggars were found frozen to death in the streets every morning in the winter.

It was into this world of fantasy and fear that Olga Kyrilovna vanished as completely as if she had dissolved into one of the air spirits or ridden away on one of the invisible dragons that our Chinese servants saw in the atmosphere all around us.

It happened the night of a New Year's Eve ball at the Japanese Legation.

When I reached the Russian Legation for dinner, a Cossack of the Escort took me into a room that was once a Tartar general's audience hall. Two dozen candle flames hardly pierced the bleak dusk. The fire in the brick stove barely dulled the cutting edge of a North China winter. I chafed my hands, thinking myself alone. Someone stirred and sighed in the shadows. It was she.

Olga Kyrilovna . . . How can I make you see her as I saw her that evening? She was pale in her white dress against walls of tarnished gilt and rusted vermilion. Two smooth, shining wings of light brown hair. An oval face, pure in line, delicate in color. And, of course, unspoiled by modern cosmetics. Her eyes were blue. Dreaming eyes. She seemed to live and move in a waking dream, remote from the enforced intimacies of our narrow society. More than one man had tried vainly to wake her from that dream. The piquancy of her situation provoked men like Lucien de l'Orges, the French chargé.

She was just seventeen, fresh from the convent of Smolny. Volgorughi had been Russian minister in China for many years. After his last trip to Petersburg, he had brought Olga back to Pekin as his bride, and . . . well, he was three times her age.

That evening she spoke first. "Monsieur Charley . . . "

Even at official meetings the American minister called me "Charley." Most Europeans assumed it was my last name.

"I'm glad you are here," she went on in French, our only common language. "I was beginning to feel lonely. And afraid."

"Afraid?" I repeated stupidly. "Of what?"

A door opened. Candle flames shied and the startled shadows leaped up the walls. Volgorughi spoke from the doorway, coolly. "Olga, we are having sherry in the study . . . Oh!" His voice warmed. "Monsieur Charley, I didn't see you. Good evening."

I followed Olga's filmy skirts into the study, conscious of Volgorughi's sharp glance as he stood aside to let me pass. He always seemed rather formidable. In spite of his grizzled hair, he had the leanness of a young man and the carriage of a soldier. But he had the weary eyes of an old man. And the dry, shriveled hands, always cold to the touch, even in summer. A young man's imagination shrank from any mental image of those hands caressing Olga . . .

In the smaller room it was warmer and brighter. Glasses of sherry and vodka had been pushed aside to make space on the table for a painting on silk. Brown, frail, desiccated as a dead leaf, the silk looked hundreds of years old. Yet the ponies painted on its fragile surface in faded pigments were the same lively Mongol ponies we still used for race meetings outside

HELEN MCCLOY

the city walls.

"The Chinese have no understanding of art," drawled Lucien de l'Orges. "Chinese porcelain is beginning to enjoy a certain vogue in Europe, but Chinese painters are impossible. In landscape they show objects on a flat surface, without perspective, as if the artist were looking down on the earth from a balloon. In portraits they draw the human face without shadows or thickness as untutored children do. The Chinese artist hasn't enough skill to imitate nature accurately."

Lucien was baiting Volgorughi. "Pekin temper" was as much a feature of our lives as "Pekin throat." We got on each other's nerves like a storm-stayed house party. An unbalanced party where men outnumbered women six to one.

Volgorughi kept his temper. "The Chinese artist doesn't care to 'imitate' nature. He prefers to suggest or symbolize what he sees."

"But Chinese art is heathen!" This was Sybil Carstairs, wife of the English inspector-general of Maritime Customs. "How can heathen art equal art inspired by Christian morals?"

Her husband's objection was more practical: "You're wastin' money, Volgorughi. Two hundred Shanghai taels for a daub that will never fetch sixpence in any European market!"

Incredible? No. This was before Hirth and Fenollosa made Chinese painting fashionable in the West. Years later I saw a fragment from Volgorughi's collection sold in the famous Salle Six of the Hotel Drouot. While the *commissaire-priseur* was bawling, *"On demande quatre cent mille francs,"* I was seeing Olga again, pale in a white dress against a wall of gilt and vermilion in the light o ,hivering candle flames. . . .

Volgorughi turned to her just then. "Olga, my dear, you haven't any sherry." He smiled as he held out a glass. The brown wine turned to gold in the candlelight as she lifted it to her lips with an almost childish obedience.

I had not noticed little Kiada, the Japanese minister, bending over the painting. Now he turned sleepy slanteyes on Volgorughi and spoke blandly. "This is the work of Han Kan, greatest of horse painters. It must be the finest painting of the T'ang Dynasty now in existence."

"You think so, count?" Volgorughi was amused. He seemed to be yielding to an irresistible temptation as he went on. "What would you say if I told you I knew of a T'ang painting infinitely finer—a landscape scroll by Wang Wei himself?"

Kiada's eyes lost their sleepy look. He had all his nation's respect for Chinese art, tinctured with jealousy of the older culture. "One hears rumors now and then that these fabulous masterpieces still exist, hidden away in the treasure chests of great Chinese families. But I have never seen an original Wang Wei."

"Who or what, is Wang Wei?" Sybil sounded petulant.

Kiada lifted his glass of sherry to the light. "Madame, Wang Wei could place scenery extending to ten thousand *li* upon the small surface of a fan. He could paint cats that would keep any house free from mice. When his hour came to Pass Above, he did not die. He merely stepped through a painted doorway in one of his own landscapes and was never seen again. All these things indicate that his brush was guided by a god."

Volgorughi leaned across the table, looking at Kiada. "What would you say if I told you that I had just added a Wang Wei to my collection?"

Kiada showed even, white teeth. "Nothing but respect for your Excellency's judgment could prevent my insisting that it was a copy by some lesser artist of the Yüan Dynasty—possibly Chao Méng Fu. An original Wang Wei could not be bought for money."

"Indeed?" Volgorughi unlocked a cabinet with a key he carried on his watch chain. He took something out and tossed it on the table like a man throwing down a challenge. It was a cylinder in an embroidered satin cover. Kiada peeled the cover and we saw a scroll on a roller of old milk jade.

It was a broad ribbon of silk, once white, now ripened with great age to a mellow brown. A foot wide, sixteen feet long, painted lengthwise to show the course of a river. As it unrolled a stream of pure lapis, jade, and turquoise hues flowed before my enchanted eyes, almost like a moving picture. Born in a bubbling spring, fed by waterfalls, the river wound its way among groves of tender, green bamboo, parks with dappled deer peeping through slender pine trees, cottages with curly roofs nestling among round hills, verdant meadows, fantastic cliffs, strange wind-distorted trees, rushes, wild geese, and at last, a foam-flecked sea.

Kiada's face was a study. He whispered brokenly, "I can hear the wind sing in the rushes. I can hear the wail of the wild geese. Of Wang Wei truly is it written—his pictures were unspoken poems."

"And the color!" cried Volgorughi, ecstasy in his eyes.

Lucien's sly voice murmured in my ear. "A younger man, married to Olga Kyrilovna, would have no time for painting, Chinese or otherwise."

Volgorughi had Kiada by the arm. "This is no copy by Chao Méng Fu! Look at that inscription on the margin. Can you read it?"

Kiada glanced—then stared. There was more than suspicion in the look he turned on Volgorughi. There was fear. "I must beg your excellency to excuse me. I do not read Chinese."

We were interrupted by a commotion in the compound. A giant Cossack, in full-skirted coat and sheepskin cap, was coming through the gate carrying astride his shoulders a young man, elegantly slim, in an officer's uniform. The Cossack knelt on the ground. The rider slipped lightly from his unconventional mount. He sauntered past the window and a moment later he was entering the study with a nonchalance just this side of insolence. To my amazement I saw that he carried a whip which he handed with his gloves to the Chinese boy who opened the door.

"Princess, your servant. Excellency, my apologies. I believe I'm late."

Volgorughi returned the greeting with the condescension of a Western Russian for an Eastern Russian—a former officer of Chevaliers Gardes for an obscure colonel of Oussurian Cossacks. Sometimes I wondered why such a bold adventurer as Alexei Andreitch Liakoff had been appointed Russian military attaché in Pekin. He was born in Tobolsk, where there is Tartar blood. His oblique eyes, high cheekbones, and sallow, hairless skin lent color to his impudent claim of descent from Genghis Khan.

"Are Russian officers in the habit of using their men as saddle horses?" I muttered to Carstairs.

Alexei's quick ear caught the words. "It may become a habit with me." He seemed to relish my discomfiture. "I don't like Mongol ponies. A Cossack is just as sure footed. And much more docile."

Olga Kyrilovna roused herself to play hostess. "Sherry, Colonel Liakoff? Or vodka?"

"Vodka, if her excellency pleases." Alexei's voice softened as he spoke to Olga. His eyes dwelt on her face gravely as he took the glass from her hand.

The ghost of mockery touched Volgorughi's lips. He despised vodka as a peasant's drink.

Alexei approached the table to set down his empty glass. For the first time, his glance fell on the painting by Wang Wei. His glass crashed on the marble floor.

"You read Chinese, don't you?" Volgorughi spoke austerely. "Perhaps you can translate this inscription?"

Alexei put both hands wide apart on the table and leaned on them, studying the ideographs. " 'Wang Wei.' And a date. The same as our A.D. 740."

"And the rest?" insisted Volgorughi.

Alexei went on. " 'At an odd moment in summer I came across this painting of a river course by Wang Wei. Under its influence I sketched a spray of peach blossom on the margin as an expression of my sympathy for the artist and his profound and mysterious work. The words of the Emperor. Written in the Lai Ching summerhouse, 1746.' "

Kiada had been frightened when he looked at that inscription. Alexei was angry. Why I did not know.

Carstairs broke the silence. "I don't see anything mysterious about a picture of a river!"

"Everything about this picture is—mysterious." Kiada glanced at Volgorughi. "May one inquire how your excellency obtained this incomparable masterpiece?"

"From a peddler in the Chinese City." Volgorughi's tone forbade further questions. Just then his Number One Boy announced dinner.

There was the usual confusion when we started for the ball at the Japanese Legation. Mongol ponies had to be blindfolded before they would let men in European dress mount and even then they were skittish. For this reason it was the custom for men to walk and for women to drive in hooded Pekin carts. But Sybil Carstairs always defied this convention, exclaiming, "Why should I be bumped black and blue in a springless cart just because I am a woman?" She and her husband were setting out on foot when Olga's little cart clattered into the compound driven by a Chinese groom. Kiada had gone on ahead to welcome his early guests. Volgorughi lifted Olga into the cart. She was quite helpless in a Siberian cloak of blue fox paws and clumsy Mongol socks of white felt over her dancing slippers. Her head drooped against Volgorughi's shoulder drowsily as he put her down in the cart. He drew the fur cloak around her in a gesture that seemed tenderly protective. She lifted languid eyes.

"Isn't Lady Carstairs driving with me?"

"My dear, you know she never drives in a Pekin cart. You are not afraid?" Volgorughi smiled. "You will be quite safe, Olga Kyrilovna. I promise you that."

Her answering smile wavered. Then the hood hid her face from view as the cart rattled through the gateway.

HELEN MCCLOY

Volgorughi and Lucien walked close behind Olga's cart. Alexei and I followed more slowly. Our Chinese lantern boys ran ahead of us in the darkness to light our way like the linkmen of medieval London. Street lamps in Pekin were lighted only once a month—when the General of the Nine Gates made his rounds of inspection.

The lantern light danced down a long, empty lane winding between high, blank walls. A stinging Siberian wind threw splinters of sleet in my face. We hadn't the macadamized roads of the Treaty Ports. The frozen mud was hard and slippery as glass. I tried to keep to a ridge that ran down the middle of the road. My foot slipped and I stumbled down the slope into a foul gutter of sewage, frozen solid. The lanterns turned a corner. I was alone with the black night and the icy wind.

I groped my way along the gutter, one hand against the wall. No stars, no moon, no lighted windows, no other pedestrians. My boot met something soft that yielded and squirmed. My voice croaked a question in Mandarin: "Is this the way to the Japanese Legation?" The answer came in singsong Cantonese. I understood only one word: "Alms . . ."

Like heaven itself, I saw a distant flicker of light coming nearer. Like saints standing in the glow of their own halos I recognized Alexei and our lantern boys. "What happened?" Alexei's voice was taut. "I came back as soon as I missed you."

"Nothing. I fell. I was just asking this . . ."

Words died on my lips. Lantern light revealed the blunted lion-face, the eyeless sockets, the obscene, white stumps for hands—"mere corruption, swaddled manwise." A leper. And I had been about to touch him.

Alexei's gaze followed mine to the beggar, hunched against the wall. "She is one of the worst I've ever seen."

"She?"

"I think it's a woman. Or, shall I say, it was a woman?" Alexei laughed harshly. "Shall we go on?"

We rounded the next corner before I recovered my voice. "These beggars aren't all as wretched as they seem, are they?"

"What put that into your head, Charley?"

"Something that happened last summer. We were in a market lane of the Chinese City—Sybil Carstairs and Olga Kyrilovna, Lucien and I. A beggar, squatting in the gutter, stared at us as if he had never seen Western men before. He looked like any other beggar—filthy, naked to the waist, with tattered blue trousers below. But his hands were toying with a little image carved in turquoise matrix. It looked old and valuable."

"He may have stolen it."

"It wasn't as simple as that," I retorted. "A man in silk rode up on a mule leading a white pony with a silver embroidered saddle. He called the beggar 'elder brother' and invited him to mount the pony. Then the two rode off together."

Alexei's black eyes glittered like jet beads in the lantern light. "Was the beggar the older of the two?"

"No. That's the queer part. The beggar was young. The man who called him 'elder brother' was old and dignified. . . . Some beggars at home have savings accounts. I suppose the same sort of thing could happen here."

Again Alexei laughed harshly. "Hold on to that idea, Charley, if it makes you feel more comfortable."

We came to a gate where lanterns clustered like a cloud of fireflies. A piano tinkled. In the compound, lantern boys were gathering outside the windows of a ballroom, tittering as they watched barbarian demons "jump" to Western music.

Characteristically, the Japanese Legation was the only European house in Pekin. Candle flames and crystal prisms. Wall mirrors and a polished parquet floor. The waltz from *Traviata*. The glitter of diamonds and gold braid. Punch *à la Romaine*.

"Where is Princess Volgorughi?" I asked Sybil Carstairs.

"Didn't she come with you and Colonel Liakoff?"

"No. Her cart followed you. We came afterward."

"Perhaps she's in the supper room." Sybil whirled off with little Kiada.

Volgorughi was standing in the doorway of the supper room with Lucien and Carstairs. "She'll be here in a moment," Carstairs was saying.

Alexei spoke over my shoulder. "Charley and I have just arrived. We did not pass her excellency's cart on the way."

"Perhaps she turned back," said Lucien.

"In that case she would have passed us," returned Alexei. "Who was with her?"

Volgorughi's voice came out in a hoarse whisper. "Her groom and lantern boy. Both Chinese. But Kiada and the Carstairses were just ahead of her; Monsieur de l'Orges and I, just behind her."

"Not all the way," amended Lucien. "We took a wrong turning and

HELEN MCCLOY

got separated from each other in the dark. That was when we lost sight of her."

"My fault." Volgorughi's mouth twisted bitterly. "I was leading the way. And it was I who told her she would be—safe."

Again we breasted the wind to follow lanterns skimming before us like will o' the wisps. Vainly we strained our eyes through glancing lights and broken shadows. We met no one. We saw nothing. Not even a footprint or wheel rut on that frozen ground. Once something moaned in the void beyond the lights. It was only the leper.

At the gate of the Russian Legation, the Cossack guard sprang to attention. Volgorughi rapped out a few words in Russian. I knew enough to understand the man's reply. "The *baryna* has not returned, excellency. There has been no sign of her or her cart."

Volgorughi was shouting. Voices, footfalls, lights filled the compound. Alexei struck his forehead with his clenched hand. "Fool that I am! The leper!" He walked so fast I could hardly keep up with him. The lantern boys were running. A Cossack came striding after us. Alexei halted at the top of the ridge. The leper had not moved. He spoke sharply in Mandarin. "Have you seen a cart?" No answer. "When she asked me for alms, she spoke Cantonese," I told him. He repeated his question in Cantonese. Both Volgorughi and Alexei spoke the southern dialects. All the rest of us were content to stammer Mandarin.

Still no answer. The Cossack stepped down into the gutter. His great boot prodded the shapeless thing that lay there. It toppled sidewise.

Alexei moved down the slope. "Lights!" The lanterns shuddered and came nearer. The handle of a knife protruded from the leper's left breast.

Alexei forced himself to drop on one knee beside the obscene corpse. He studied it intently, without touching it.

"Murdered. . . . There are many knives like that in the Chinese City. Anyone might have used it—Chinese or European." He rose, brushing his knee with his gloved hand.

"Why?" I ventured.

"She couldn't see." His voice was judicious. "She must have heard—something."

"But what?"

Alexei's Asiatic face was inscrutable in the light from the paper lanterns.

Police? Extraterritorial law courts? That was Treaty Port stuff. Like pidgin English. We had only a few legation guards. No gunboats. No telegraph. No railway. The flying machine was a crank's daydream. Even cranks hadn't dreamed of a wireless telegraphy. . . .

Dawn came. We were still searching. Olga Kyrilovna, her cart and pony, her groom and lantern boy, had all vanished without a trace as if they had never existed.

As character witnesses, the Chinese were baffling. "The princess's groom was a Manchu of good character," Volgorughi's Number One Boy told us. "But her lantern boy was a Cantonese with a great crime on his conscience. He caused his mother's death when he was born, which the Ancients always considered unfilial."

At noon some of us met in the smoking room of the Pekin Club. "It's curious there's been no demand for ransom," I said.

"Bandits? Within the city walls?" Carstairs was skeptical. "Russia has never hesitated to use *agents provocateurs*. They say she's going to build a railway across Siberia. I don't believe it's practical. But you never can tell what those mad Russians will do. She'll need Manchuria. And she'll need a pretext for taking it. Why not the abduction of the Russian minister's wife?"

Kiada shook his head. "Princess Volgorughi will not be found until *The River* is restored to its companion pictures, *The Lake*, *The Sea*, and *The Cloud*."

"What do you mean?"

Kiada answered me patiently as an adult explaining the obvious to a backward child. "It is known that Wang Wei painted this series of pictures entitled *Four Forms of Water*. Volgorughi has only one of them, *The River*. The separation of one painting from others in a series divinely inspired is displeasing to the artist."

"But Wang Wei has been dead more than a thousand years!"

"It is always dangerous to displease those who have Passed Above. An artist as steeped in ancient mysteries as the pious Wang Wei has power over men long after he has become a Guest On High. Wang Wei will shape the course of our lives into any pattern he pleases in order to bring those four paintings together again. I knew this last night when I first saw *The River* and—I was afraid."

"I wonder how Volgorughi did get that painting?" mused Carstairs. "I hope he didn't forget the little formality of payment."

"He's not a thief!" I protested.

30   HELEN MCCLOY

"No. But he's a collector. All collectors are mad. Especially Russian collectors. It's like gambling or opium."

Lucien smiled unpleasantly. "Art! Ghosts! Politics! Why go so far afield? Olga Kyrilovna was a young bride. And Volgorughi is—old. Such marriages are arranged by families, we all know. Women, as Balzac said, are the dupes of the social system. When they consent to marriage, they have not enough experience to know what they are consenting to. Olga Kyrilovna found herself in a trap. She has escaped, as young wives have escaped from time immemorial, by taking a lover. Now they've run off together. *Sabine a tout donné, sa beauté de colombe, et son amour . . .*"

"Monsieur de l'Orges."

We all started. Alexei was standing in the doorway. His eyes commanded the room. "What you say is impossible. Do I make myself clear?"

"Of course, Alexei. I—I was only joking." Lucien sounded piteous.

But Alexei had no pity. "A difference of taste in jokes has broken many friendships. . . . Charley, will you come back to the Russian Legation with me?"

The Tartar general's audience hall had never seemed more shabby. Volgorughi sat staring at the garish wall of red and gilt. He was wearing an overcoat, carrying hat and gloves.

"News, excellency?" queried Alexei.

Volgorughi shook his head without looking up. "I've been to the Tsungli Yamen." He spoke like a somnambulist. "The usual thing. Green tea. Melon seeds. A cold stone pavilion. Mandarins who giggle behind satin sleeves. I asked for an audience with the Emperor himself. It was offered—on the usual terms. I had to refuse—as usual. By the time a gunboat gets to the mouth of the Pei-ho, they may agree to open another seaport to Russian trade by way of reparation, but—I shall never see Olga Kyrilovna again. Sometimes I think our governments keep us here in the hope that something will happen to give them a pretext for sending troops into China. . . ."

We all felt that. The Tsungli Yamen, or Foreign Office, calmly assumed that our legations were vassal missions to the Emperor, like those from Tibet. The Emperor would not receive us unless we acknowledged his sovereignty by kowtowing, the forehead to strike the floor audibly nine times. Even if we had wished to go through this interesting performance for the sake of peace and trade, our governments would not let us compromise their sovereignty. But they kept us there, where we had no official standing, where our very existence was doubted. "It may be there are as many countries in the West as England, France, Germany, and Russia," one mandarin had informed me. "But the others you mention—Austria, Sweden, Spain, and America—they are all lies invented to intimidate the Chinese."

Alexei was not a man to give up easily. "Excellency, I shall find her."

Volgorughi lifted his head. "How?"

Alexei shouted. The study door opened. An old man in workman's dress came in with a young Chinese. I knew the old man as Antoine Billot, one of the Swiss clockmakers who were the only Western tradesmen allowed in Pekin.

"Charley," said Alexei, "tell Antoine about the fingering piece you saw in the hands of a beggar last summer."

"It was turquoise matrix, carved to represent two nude figures embracing. The vein of brown in the stone colored their heads and spotted the back of the smaller figure."

"I have seen such a fingering piece," said Antoine. "In the Palace of Whirring Phoenixes. It is in that portion of the Chinese City known as the Graveyard of the Wu family, in the Lane of Azure Thunder."

"It is the Beileh Tsai Heng who lives there," put in Antoine's Chinese apprentice. "Often have we repaired his French clocks. Very fine clocks of Limoges enamel sent to the Emperor Kang Hsi by Louis XIV. The Beileh's grandmother was the Discerning Concubine of the Emperor Tao Kwang."

"An old man?" asked Alexei.

"The Beileh has not yet attained the years of serenity. Though the name Heng means 'Steadfast,' he is impetuous as a startled dragon. He memorialized the late Emperor for permission to live in a secluded portion of the Chinese City so that he could devote his leisure to ingenious arts and pleasures."

I looked at Alexei. "You think the beggar who stared at us was a servant of this prince?"

"No. Your beggar was the prince himself. 'Elder Brother' is the correct form for addressing a Manchu prince of the third generation."

"It is the latest fad amoung our young princes of Pekin," explained the apprentice, "to haunt the highways and taverns dressed as beggars, sharing the sad life of the people for a few hours. They vie with each other to see which can look the most dirty and disreputable. But each one has

HELEN MCCLOY

some little habit of luxury that he cannot give up, even for the sake of disguise. A favorite ring, a precious fan, an antique fingering piece. That is how you can tell them from the real beggars."

Alexei turned to me. "When a taste for the exquisite becomes so refined that it recoils upon itself and turns into its opposite—a taste for the ugly—we call that decadence. Prince Heng is decadent—bored, curious, irresponsible, ever in search of a new sensation." Alexei turned back to the apprentice. "Could the Beileh be tempted with money?"

"Who could offer him anything he does not already possess?" intoned the young Chinese. "His revered father amassed one hundred thousand myriad snow white taels of silver from unofficial sources during his benevolent reign as governor of Kwantung. In the Palace of Whirring Phoenixes even the wash bowls and spitting basins are curiously wrought of fine jade and pure gold, for this prince loves everything that is rare and strange."

Alexei hesitated before his next question. "Does the Beileh possess any valuable paintings?"

"His paintings are few but priceless. Four landscape scrolls from the divine brush of the illustrious Wang Wei."

Volgorughi started to his feet. "What's this?"

"You may go, Antoine." Alexei waited until the door had closed. "Isn't it obvious, sir? Your Wang Wei scroll was stolen."

Volgorughi sank back in his chair. "But—I bought it. From a peddler in the Chinese City. I didn't ask his name."

"How could a nameless peddler acquire such a painting from such a prince honestly?" argued Alexei. "Your peddler was a thief or a receiver. Such paintings have religious as well as artistic value to the Chinese. They are heirlooms, never sold even by private families who need the money. Last night, the moment I saw the marginal note written by the Emperor Ch'ien Lung I knew the picture must have been stolen from the Imperial Collection. I was disturbed because I knew that meant trouble for us if it were known you had the painting. That's why I didn't want to read the inscription aloud. It's easy to see what happened. The thief was captured and tortured until he told Heng you had the painting. Heng saw Olga Kyrilovna with Charley and Lucien in the Chinese City last summer. He must have heard then that she was your wife. When he found you had the painting, he ordered her abduction. Now he is holding her as hostage for the return of the painting. All this cannot be coincidence."

Volgorughi buried his face in his hands. "What can we do?"

"With your permission, excellency, I shall go into the Chinese City tonight and return the painting to Heng. I shall bring back Olga Kyrilovna—if she is still alive."

Volgorughi rose, shoulders bent, chin sunk on his chest. "I shall go with you, Alexei Andreitch."

"Your excellency forgets that special circumstances make it possible for me to go into the Chinese City after dark when no other European can do so with safety. Alone I have some chance of success. With you to protect, it would be impossible."

"You will need a Cossack escort."

"That would strip the legation of guards. And it would antagonize Heng. Olga Kyrilovna might be harmed before I could reach her. I prefer to go alone."

Volgorughi sighed. "Report to me as soon as you get back. . . . You are waiting for something?"

"The painting, excellency."

Volgorughi walked with a shuffling step into the study. He came back with the scroll in its case. "Take it. I never want to see it again."

At the door I looked back. Volgorughi was slumped in his seat, a figure of utter loneliness and despair.

Alexei glanced at me as we crossed the compound. "Something is puzzling you, Charley. What is it?"

"If this Beileh Heng is holding Olga Kyrilovna as a hostage for the painting, he wants you to know that he has abducted her. He has nothing to conceal. Then why was the leper murdered if not to conceal something?"

Alexei led the way into a room of his own furnished with military severity. "I'm glad Volgorughi didn't think of that question, Charley. It has been troubling me, too."

"And the answer?"

"Perhaps I shall find it in the Palace of Whirring Phoenixes. Perhaps it will lead me back to one of the men who dined with us yesterday evening. Except for the Carstairses, we were all separated from each other at one time or another in those dark streets—even you and I. . . . "

Alexei was opening a cedar chest. He took out a magnificent robe of wadded satin in prismatic blues and greens. When he had slipped it on he turned to face me. The Tartar cast of his oblique eyes and sallow skin

HELEN MCCLOY

was more pronounced than I had ever realized. Had I passed him wearing this costume in the Chinese City, I should have taken him for a Manchu or a Mongol.

He smiled. "Now will you believe I have the blood of Temudjin Genghis Khan in my veins?"

"You've done this before!"

His smile grew sardonic. "Do you understand why I am the only European who can go into the Chinese City after dark?"

My response was utterly illogical. "Alexei, take me with you tonight!"

He studied my face. "You were fond of Olga Kyrilovna, weren't you?"

"Is there no way?" I begged.

"Only one way. And it's safe. You could wear the overalls of a workman and carry the tools of a clockmaker. And stay close to me, ostensibly your Chinese employer."

"If Antoine Billot will lend me his clothes and tools . . . "

"That can be arranged." Alexei was fitting a jeweled nail shield over his little finger.

"Well? Is there any other objection?"

"Only this." He looked up at me intently. His pale face and black eyes were striking against the kingfisher blues and greens of his satin robe. "We are going to find something ugly at the core of this business, Charley. You are younger than I and—will you forgive me if I say you are rather innocent? Your idea of life in Pekin is a series of dances and dinners, race meetings outside the walls in spring, charades at the English Legation in winter, snipshooting at Hai Ten in the fall. Your government doesn't maintain an intelligence service here. So you can have no idea of the struggle that goes on under the surface of this pleasant social life. Imperialist ambitions and intrigues, the alliance between politics and trade, even the opium trade—what do you know of all that? Sometimes I think you don't even know much about the amusements men like Lucien find in the Chinese City. . . . Life is only pleasant on the surface, Charley. And now we're going below the surface. Respectability is as artificial as the clothes we wear. What it hides is as ugly as our naked bodies and animal functions. Whatever happens tonight, I want you to remember this: under every suit of clothes, broadcloth or rags, there is the same sort of animal."

"What are you hinting at?"

"There are various possibilities. You said Heng stared at your party as if he had never seen Western men before. Are you sure he wasn't staring at Olga Kyrilovna as if he had never seen a Western woman before?"

"But our women are physically repulsive to Chinese!"

"In most cases. But the Chinese are not animated types. They are individuals, as we are. Taste is subjective and arbitrary. Individual taste can be eccentric. Isn't it possible that there are among them, as among us, men who have romantic fancies for the exotic? Or sensual fancies for the experimental? I cannot get those words of Antoine's apprentice out of my mind: *this prince loves everything that is rare and strange. . . .*"

A red sun was dipping behind the Western Hills when we passed out a southern gate of the Tartar City. In a moment all nine gates would swing shut and we would be locked out of our legations until tomorrow's dawn. It was not a pleasant feeling. I had seen the head of a consul rot on a pike in the sun. That was what happened to barbarian demons who went where they were not wanted outside the Treaty Ports.

The Chinese City was a wilderness of twisting lanes, shops, taverns, theaters, tea houses, opium dens, and brothels. Long ago conquering Manchu Tartars had driven conquered Chinese outside the walls of Pekin proper, or the Tartar City, this sprawling suburb where the conquered catered to the corruption of the conqueror. The Chinese City came to life at nightfall when the Tartar City slept behind its walls. Here and there yellow light shone through blue dusk from a broken gateway. Now and then we caught the chink of porcelain cups or the whine of a *yuehkin* guitar.

Alexei seemed to know every turn of the way. At last I saw why he was Russian military attaché at Pekin. Who else would learn so much about China and its people as this bold adventurer who could pass for a Manchu in Chinese robes? When we were snipe shooting together, he seemed to know the Peichih-li Plain as if he carried a military map of the district in his head. Years afterward, when the Tsar's men took Port Arthur, everyone learned about Russian intelligence in China. I learned that evening. And I found myself looking at Alexei in his Chinese dress as if he had suddenly become a stranger. What did I know of this man whom I had met so casually at legation parties? Was he ruthless enough to stab a beggar already dying of leprosy? Had he had any reason for doing so?

We turned into a narrower lane—a mere crack between high walls. Alexei whispered, "The Lane of Azure Thunder."

A green tiled roof above the dun-colored wall proclaimed the dwelling

HELEN MCCLOY

of a prince. Alexei paused before a vermilion gate. He spoke Cantonese to the gatekeeper. I understood only two words—"Wang Wei." There were some moments of waiting. Then the gate creaked open and we were ushered through that drab wall into a wonderland of fantastic parks and lacquered pavilions blooming with all the colors of Sung porcelain.

I was unprepared for the splendor of the audience hall. The old palaces we rented for legations were melancholy places, decaying and abandoned by their owners. But here rose, green, and gold rioted against a background of dull ebony panels, tortured by a cunning chisel into grotesquely writhing shapes. There were hangings of salmon satin embroidered with threads of gold and pale green, images of birds and flowers carved in jade and coral and malachite. The slender rafters were painted a poisonously bright jade green and on them tiny lotus buds were carved and gilded. There was a rich rustle of satin and the Beileh Heng walked slowly into the room.

Could this stately figure be the same fellow I had last seen squatting in the gutter, half naked in the rags of a beggar? He moved with the deliberate grace of the grave religious dancers in the Confucian temples. His robe was lustrous purple—the "myrtle-red" prescribed for princes of the third generation by the Board of Rites. It swung below the paler mandarin jacket in sculpted folds, stiff with a sable lining revealed by two slits at either side. Watered in the satin were the Eight Famous Horses of the Emperor Mu Wang galloping over the Waves of Eternity. His cuffs were curved like horseshoes in honor of the cavalry that set the Manchu Tartars on the throne. Had that cavalry ridden west instead of south, Alexei himself might have owed allegiance to this prince. Though one was Chinese and one Russian, both were Tartar.

Heng's boots of purple satin looked Russian. So did his round cap faced with a band of sable. His skin was a dull ivory, not as yellow as the southern Chinese. His cheeks were lean; his glance searching and hungry. He looked like a purebred descendant of the "wolf-eyed, lantern-jawed Manchus" of the Chinese chronicles. A conqueror who would take whatever he wanted, but who had learned from the conquered Chinese to want only the precious and fanciful. . . .

Something else caught my eye. There was no mistake. This was the beggar. For pale against his purple robe gleamed the fingering piece of turquoise matrix which his thin, neurotic fingers caressed incessantly.

No ceremonial tea was served. We were being received as enemies during a truce. But Alexei bowed profoundly and spoke with all the roundabout extravagance of mandarin politeness.

"An obscure design of Destiny has brought the property of your highness, a venerable landscape scroll painted by the devout Wang Wei, into the custody of the Russian minister. Though I appear Chinese in this garb, know that I am Russian and my minister has sent me in all haste and humility to restore this inestimable masterpiece to its rightful owner."

Heng's eyes were fixed on a point above our heads, for, Chinese or barbarian, we were inferiors, unworthy of his gaze. His lips scarcely moved. "When you have produced the scroll, I shall know whether you speak truth or falsehood."

"All your highness's words are unspotted pearls of perpetual wisdom." Alexei stripped the embroidered case from the jade roller. Like a living thing, the painted silk slipped out of his grasp and unwound itself at the Beileh's feet.

Once again a fairy stream of lapis, jade, and turquoise hues unrolled before my enchanted eyes. Kiada was right. I could hear the wind sing in the rushes and the wail of the wild geese, faint and far, a vibration trembling on the outer edge of the physical threshold for sound.

The hand that held the fingering piece was suddenly still. Only the Beileh's eyeballs moved, following the course of Wang Wei's river from its bubbling spring to its foam-flecked sea. Under his cultivated stolidity, I saw fear and, more strangely, sorrow.

At last he spoke. "This painting I inherited from my august ancestor, the ever glorious Emperor Ch'ien Lung, who left his words and seal upon the margin. How has it come into your possession?"

Alexei bowed again. "I shall be grateful for an opportunity to answer that question if your highness will first condescend to explain to my mean intelligence how the scroll came to leave the Palace of Whirring Phoenixes?"

"Outside barbarian, you are treading on a tiger's tail when you speak with such insolence to an Imperial Clansman. I try to make allowances for you because you come of an inferior race, the Hairy Ones, without manners or music, unversed in the Six Fine Arts and the Five Classics. Know then that it is not your place to ask questions or mine to answer them. You may follow me, at a distance of nine paces, for I have something to show you."

He looked neither to right nor left as he walked soberly through the

        HELEN McCLOY

audience hall, his hands tucked inside his sleeves. At the door he lifted one hand to loosen the clasp of his mandarin jacket, and it slid from his shoulders. Before it had time to touch the ground, an officer of the Coral Button sprang out of the shadows to catch it reverently. The Beileh did not appear conscious of this officer's presence. Yet he had let the jacket fall without an instant's hesitation. He knew that wherever he went at any time there would always be someone ready to catch anything he let fall before it was soiled or damaged.

We followed him into a garden, black and white in the moonlight. We passed a pool spanned by a crescent bridge. Its arc of stone matched the arc of its reflection in the ice-coated water, completing a circle that was half reality, half illusion. We came to another pavilion, its roof curling up at each corner, light filtering through its doorway. Again we heard the shrill plaint of a guitar. We rounded a devil-screen of gold lacquer and the thin sound ended on a high, feline note.

I blinked against a blaze of lights. Like a flight of particolored butterflies, a crowd of girls fluttered away from us, tottering on tiny, mutilated feet. One who sat apart from the rest rose with dignity. A Manchu princess, as I saw by her unbound feet and undaunted eyes. Her hair was piled high in the lacquered coils of the Black Cloud Coiffure. She wore hairpins, earrings, bracelets, and tall heels of acid-green jade. Her gown of seagreen silk was sewn with silver thread worked in the Pekin stitch to represent the Silver-Crested Love Birds of Conjugal Peace. But when she turned her face, I saw the sour lines and sagging pouches of middle age.

Princess Heng's gaze slid over us with subtle contempt and came to rest upon the Beileh with irony. "My pleasure in receiving you is boundless and would find suitable expression in appropriate compliments were the occasion more auspicious. As it is, I pray you will forgive me if I do not linger in the fragrant groves of polite dalliance, but merely inquire why your highness has seen fit to introduce two male strangers, one a barbarian, into the sanctity of the Inner Chamber?"

Heng answered impassively. "Even the Holy Duke of Yen neglected the forms of courtesy when he was pursued by a tiger."

A glint of malice sparkled in the eyes of the Beileh's Principal Old Woman. "Your highness finds his present situation equivalent to being pursued by a tiger? To my inadequate understanding that appears the natural consequence of departing from established custom by attempting to introduce a barbarian woman into the Inner Chamber."

Heng sighed. "If the presence of these far-traveled strangers distresses you and my Small Old Women you have permission to retire."

Princess Heng's jade bangles clashed with the chilly ring of ice in a glass as she moved toward the door. The Small Old Women, all girls in their teens, shimmered and rustled after the Manchu princess, who despised them both as concubines and as Chinese.

Heng led us through another door.

"Olga!"

The passion in Alexei's voice was a shock to me. In my presence he had always addressed her as "excellency" or "princess." She might have been asleep as she lay there on her blue fox cloak, her eyes closed, her pale face at peace, her slight hands relaxed in the folds of her white tulle skirt. But the touch of her hands was ice and faintly from her parted lips came the sweet sickish odor of opium.

Alexei turned on Heng. "If you had not stolen her, she would not have died!"

"Stolen?" It was the first word that had pierced Heng's reserve. "Imperial Clansmen do not steal women. I saw this far-traveled woman in a market lane of the Chinese City last summer. I coveted her. But I did not steal her. I offered money for her, decently and honorably, in accord with precepts of morality laid down by the Ancients. Money was refused. Months passed. I could not forget the woman with faded eyes. I offered one of my most precious possessions. It was accepted. The painting was her price But the other did not keep his side of the bargain. For she was dead when I lifted her out of her cart."

The lights were spinning before my eyes. "Alexei, what is this? Volgorughi would not . . ."

Alexei's look stopped me.

"You . . . " Words tumbled from my lips. "There was a lover. And you were he. And Volgorughi found out. And he watched you together and bided his time, nursing his hatred and planning his revenge like a work of art. And finally he punished you both cruelly by selling her to Heng. Volgorughi knew that Olga would drive alone last night. Volgorughi had lived so long in the East that he had absorbed the Eastern idea of women as well as the Eastern taste in painting. The opium must have been in the sherry he gave her. She was already drowsy when he lifted her into the cart. No doubt he had planned to give her only a soporific dose that would facilitate her abduction. But at the last moment he commuted her

HELEN MCCLOY

sentence to death and let her have the full, lethal dose. He gave her good-bye tenderly because he knew he would never see her again. He promised her she would be safe because death is, in one sense, safety—the negation of pain, fear and struggle. . . .

"There was no peddler who sold him the painting. That was his only lie. He didn't prevent your coming here tonight because he wanted you to know. That was your punishment. And he saw that you could make no use of your knowledge now. Who will believe that Olga Kyrilovna, dead of a Chinese poison in the Chinese City, was killed by her own husband? Some Chinese will be suspected—Heng himself, or his jealous wife, or the men who carry out his orders. No European would take Heng's story seriously unless it were supported by at least one disinterested witness. That was why the leper had to die last night, while Volgorughi was separated from Lucien by a wrong turning that was Volgorughi's fault. The leper must have overheard some word of warning or instruction from Volgorughi to Olga's lantern boy that revealed the whole secret. That word was spoken in Cantonese. Olga's lantern boy was Cantonese. Volgorughi spoke that dialect. The leper knew no other tongue. And Lucien, the only person who walked with Volgorughi, was as ignorant of Cantonese as all the rest of us, save you."

Heng spoke sadly in his own tongue. "The treachery of the Russian minister in sending this woman to me dead deserves vengeance. But one thing induces me to spare him. He did not act by his own volition. He was a blind tool in the skillful hand of the merciless Wang Wei. Through this woman's death *The River* has been restored to its companion pictures, *The Lake*, *The Sea*, and *The Cloud*. And I, who separated the pictures so impiously, have had my own share of suffering as a punishment. . . . "

. . . Yes, I'll have another brandy. One more glass. Olga? She was buried in the little Russian Orthodox cemetery at Pekin. Volgorughi was recalled. The breath of scandal clung to his name the rest of his life. The Boxer Uprising finally gave the West its pretext for sending troops into China. That purple-satin epicurean, the Beileh Heng, was forced to clean sewers by German troops during the occupation and committed suicide from mortification. The gay young bloods of Pekin who had amused themselves by playing beggars found themselves beggars in earnest when the looting was over. Railways brought Western businessmen to Pekin and before long it was as modern as Chicago.

CHINOISERIE

Alexei? He became attentive to the wife of the new French minister, a woman with dyed hair who kept a Pekinese sleeve dog in her bedroom. I discovered the distraction that can be found in study of the early Chinese poets. When I left the service, I lost track of Alexei. During the Russian Revolution, I often wondered if he were still living. Did he join the Reds, as some Cossack officers did? Or was he one of the Whites who settled in Harbin or Port Arthur? He would have been a very old man then, but I think he could have managed. He spoke so many Chinese dialects. . . .

The scroll? Any good reference book will tell you that there are no Wang Wei scrolls in existence today, though there are some admirable copies. One, by Chao Méng Fu, in the British Museum, shows the course of a river. Scholars have described this copy in almost the same words I have used tonight to describe the original. But they are not the same. I went to see the copy. I was disappointed. I could no longer hear the song of the wind in the rushes or the wail of the wild geese. Was the change in the painting? Or in me?

HELEN MCCLOY

The Billiard Ball

by Isaac Asimov

James Priss—I suppose I ought to say Professor James Priss, though everyone is sure to know whom I mean even without the title—always spoke slowly.

I know. I interviewed him often enough. He had the greatest mind since Einstein, but it didn't work quickly. He admitted his slowness often. Maybe it was *because* he had so great a mind that it didn't work quickly.

He would say something in slow abstraction, then he would think, and then he would say something more. Even over trivial matters, his giant mind would hover uncertainly, adding a touch here and then another there.

Would the Sun rise tomorrow, I can imagine him wondering. What do we mean by "rise"? Can we be certain that tomorrow will come? Is the term "Sun" completely unambiguous in this connection?

Add to this habit of speech a bland countenance, rather pale, with no expression except for a general look of uncertainty; gray hair, rather thin, neatly combed; business suits of an invariably conservative cut; and you have what Professor James Priss was—a retiring person, completely lacking in magnetism.

That's why nobody in the world, except myself, could possibly suspect him of being a murderer. And even I am not sure. After all, he *was* slow-thinking; he was *always* slow-thinking. Is it conceivable that at one crucial moment he managed to think quickly and act at once?

It doesn't matter. Even if he murdered, he got away with it. It is far too late now to try to reverse matters and I wouldn't succeed in doing so even if I decided to let this be published.

Edward Bloom was Priss's classmate in college, and an associate, through circumstance, for a generation afterward. They were equal in age and in their propensity for the bachelor life, but opposites in everything else that mattered.

Bloom was a living flashlight; colorful, tall, broad, loud, brash, and self-confident. He had a mind that resembled a meteor strike in the sudden and unexpected way it could seize the essential. He was no theoretician, as Priss was; Bloom had neither the patience for it, nor the capacity to concentrate intense thought upon a single abstract point. He admitted that; he boasted of it.

What he did have was an uncanny way of seeing the application of a theory; of seeing the manner in which it could be put to use. In the cold marble block of abstract structure, he could see, without apparent difficulty, the intricate design of a marvelous device. The block would fall apart at his touch and leave the device.

It is a well known story, and not too badly exaggerated, that nothing Bloom ever built had failed to work, or to be patentable, or to be profitable. By the time he was forty-five, he was one of the richest men on Earth.

And if Bloom the Technician were adapted to one particular matter more than anything else, it was the way of thought of Priss the Theoretician. Bloom's greatest gadgets were built upon Priss's greatest thoughts, and as Bloom grew wealthy and famous, Priss gained phenomenal respect among his colleagues.

Naturally it was to be expected that when Priss advanced his Two-Field Theory, Bloom would set about at once and build the first practical anti-gravity device.

My job was to find human interest in the Two-Field Theory for the subscribers to *Tele-News Press*, and you get that by trying to deal with human beings and not with abstract ideas. Since my interviewee was Professor Priss, that wasn't easy.

Naturally, I was going to ask the possibilities of anti-gravity, which interested everyone; and not about the Two-Field Theory, which no one could understand.

"Anti-gravity?" Priss compressed his pale lips and considered. "I'm not entirely sure that it is possible, or even will be. I haven't—uh—worked the matter out to my satisfaction. I don't entirely see whether the Two-Field equations would have a finite solution, which they would have to have, of course, if—" And then he went off into his brown study.

I prodded him. "Bloom says he thinks such a device can be built."

ISAAC ASIMOV

Priss nodded. "Well, yes, but I wonder. Ed Bloom has had an amazing knack at seeing the obvious in the past. He has an unusual mind. It's certainly made him rich enough."

We were sitting in Priss's apartment. Ordinary middle class. I couldn't help a quick glance this way and that. Priss was not wealthy.

I don't think he read my mind. He saw me look. And I think it was on *his* mind. He said, "Wealth isn't the usual reward for the pure scientist. Or even a particularly desirable one."

Maybe so, at that, I thought. Priss certainly had his own kind of reward. He was the third person in history to win two Nobel Prizes, and the first to have both of them in the sciences and both of them unshared. You can't complain about that. And if he wasn't rich, neither was he poor.

But he didn't sound like a contented man. Maybe it wasn't Bloom's wealth alone that irked Priss; maybe it was Bloom's fame among the people of Earth generally; maybe it was the fact that Bloom was a celebrity wherever he went, whereas Priss, outside scientific conventions and faculty clubs, was largely anonymous.

I can't say how much of all this was in my eyes or in the way I wrinkled the creases in my forehead, but Priss went on to say, "But we're friends, you know. We play billiards once or twice a week. I beat him regularly."

(I never published that statement. I checked it with Bloom, who made a long counterstatement that began: "He beats *me* at billiards. That jackass—" and grew increasingly personal thereafter. As a matter of fact, neither one was a novice at billiards. I watched them play once for a short while, after the statement and counterstatement; both handled the cue with professional aplomb. What's more, both played for blood, and there was no friendship in the game that I could see.)

I said, "Would you care to predict whether Bloom will manage to build an anti-gravity device?"

"You mean would I commit myself to anything? Hmm. Well, let's consider, young man. Just what do we mean by anti-gravity? Our conception of gravity is built around Einstein's General Theory of Relativity, which is now a century and a half old but which, within its limits, remains firm. We can picture it—"

I listened politely. I'd heard Priss on the subject before, but if I was to get anything out of him—which wasn't certain—I'd have to let him work his way through in his own way.

"We can picture it," he said, "by imagining the Universe to be a flat, thin, superflexible sheet of untearable rubber. If we picture mass as being associated with weight, as it is on the surface of the Earth, then we would expect a mass, resting upon the rubber sheet, to make an indentation. The greater the mass, the deeper the indentation.

"In the actual Universe," he went on, "all sorts of masses exist, and so our rubber sheet must be pictured as riddled with indentations. Any object rolling along the sheet would dip into and out of the indentations it passed, veering and changing direction as it did so. It is this veer and change of direction that we interpret as demonstrating the existence of a force of gravity. If the moving object comes close enough to the center of the indentation and is moving slowly enough, it gets trapped and whirls around and round that indentation. In the absence of friction, it keeps up that whirl forever. In other words, what Isaac Newton interpreted as a force, Albert Einstein interpreted as geometrical distortion."

He paused at this point. He had been speaking fairly fluently—for him—since he was saying something he had said often before. But now he began to pick his way.

He said, "So in trying to produce anti-gravity, we are trying to alter the geometry of the Universe. If we carry on our metaphor, we are trying to straighten out the indented rubber sheet. We could imagine ourselves getting under the indenting mass and lifting it upward, supporting it so as to prevent it from making an indentation. If we make the rubber sheet flat in that way, then we create a Universe—or at least a portion of the Universe—in which gravity doesn't exist. A rolling body would pass the nonindenting mass without altering its direction of travel a bit, and we could interpret this as meaning that the mass was exerting no gravitational force. In order to accomplish this feat, however, we need a mass equivalent to the indenting mass. To produce anti-gravity on Earth in this way, we would have to make use of a mass equal to that of Earth and poise it above our heads, so to speak."

I interrupted him. "But your Two-Field Theory—"

"Exactly. General Relativity does not explain both the gravitational field and the electromagnetic field in a single set of equations. Einstein spent half his life searching for that single set—for a Unified Field Theory—and failed. All who followed Einstein also failed. I, however, began with the assumption that there were two fields that could not be unified and followed the consequences, which I can explain, in part, in terms of the 'rubber sheet' metaphor."

ISAAC ASIMOV

Now we came to something I wasn't sure I had ever heard before. "How does that go?" I asked.

"Suppose that, instead of trying to lift the indenting mass, we try to stiffen the sheet itself, make it less indentable. It would contract, at least over a small area, and become flatter. Gravity would weaken, and so would mass, for the two are essentially the same phenomenon in terms of indented Universe. If we could make the rubber sheet completely flat, both gravity and mass would disappear altogether.

"Under the proper conditions, the electromagnetic field could be made to counter the gravitational field, and serve to stiffen the indented fabric of the Universe. The electromagnetic field is tremendously stronger than the gravitational field, so the former could be made to overcome the latter."

I said uncertainly, "But you say 'under the proper conditions.' Can those proper conditions you speak of be achieved, professor?"

"That is what I don't know," said Priss thoughtfully and slowly. "If the Universe were really a rubber sheet, its stiffness would have to reach an infinite value before it could be expected to remain completely flat under an indenting mass. If that is also so in the real Universe, then an infinitely intense electromagnetic field would be required and that would mean anti-gravity would be impossible."

"But Bloom says—"

"Yes, I imagine Bloom thinks a finite field will do, if it can be properly applied. Still, however ingenious he is," and Priss smiled narrowly, "we needn't take him to be infallible. His grasp on theory is quite faulty. He—he never earned his college degree, did you know that?"

I was about to say that I knew that. After all, everyone did. But there was a touch of eagerness in Priss's voice as he said it, and I looked up in time to catch animation in his eye, as though he were delighted to spread that piece of news. So I nodded my head as if I were filing it for future reference.

"Then you would say, Professor Priss," I prodded again, "that Bloom is probably wrong and that anti-gravity is impossible?"

And finally Priss nodded and said, "The gravitational field can be weakened, of course, but if by anti-gravity we mean a true zero-gravity field—no gravity at all over a significant volume of space—then I suspect anti-gravity may turn out to be impossible, despite Bloom."

And I had, after a fashion, what I wanted.

I wasn't able to see Bloom for nearly three months after that, and when I did see him he was in an angry mood.

He had grown angry at once, of course, when the news first broke concerning Priss's statement. He let it be known that Priss would be invited to the eventual display of the anti-gravity device as soon as it was constructed, and would even be asked to participate in the demonstration. Some reporter—not I, unfortunately—caught him between appointments and asked him to elaborate on that and he said:

"I'll have the device eventually; soon, maybe. And you can be there, and so can anyone else the press would care to have there. And Professor James Priss can be there. He can represent Theoretical Science and after I have demonstrated anti-gravity, he can adjust his theory to explain it. I'm sure he will know how to make his adjustments in masterly fashion and show exactly why I couldn't possibly have failed. He might do it now and save time, but I suppose he won't."

It was all said very politely, but you could hear the snarl under the rapid flow of words.

Yet he continued his occasional game of billiards with Priss and when the two met they behaved with complete propriety. One could tell the progress Bloom was making by their respective attitudes to the press. Bloom grew curt and even snappish, while Priss developed an increasing good humor.

When my umpteenth request for an interview with Bloom was finally accepted, I wonder if perhaps that meant a break in Bloom's quest. I had a little daydream of his announcing final success to *me*.

It didn't work out that way. He met me in his office at Bloom Enterprises in upstate New York. It was a wonderful setting, well away from any populated area, elaborately landscaped, and covering as much ground as a rather large industrial establishment. Edison at his height, two centuries ago, had never been as phenomenally successful as Bloom.

But Bloom was not in a good humor. He came striding in ten minutes late and went snarling past his secretary's desk with the barest nod in my direction. He was wearing a lab coat, unbuttoned.

He threw himself into his chair and said, "I'm sorry if I've kept you waiting, but I didn't have as much time as I had hoped." Bloom was a born showman and knew better than to antagonize the press, but I had the feeling he was having a great deal of difficulty at that moment in adhering to this principle.

ISAAC ASIMOV

I made the obvious guess. "I am given to understand, sir, that your recent tests have been unsuccessful."

"Who told you that?"

"I would say it was general knowledge, Mr. Bloom."

"No, it isn't. Don't say that, young man. There is no general knowledge about what goes on in my laboratories and workshops. You're stating the professor's opinions, aren't you? Priss, I mean."

"No, I'm—"

"Of course you are. Aren't you the one to whom he made that statement—that anti-gravity is impossible?"

"He didn't make the statement that flatly."

"He never says anything flatly, but it was flat enough for him, and not as flat as I'll have his damned rubber-sheet Universe before I'm finished."

"Then does that mean you're making progress, Mr. Bloom?"

"You know I am," he said with a snap. "Or you should know. Weren't you at the demonstration last week?"

"Yes, I was."

I judged Bloom to be in trouble or he wouldn't be mentioning that demonstration. It worked but it was not a world beater. Between the two poles of a magnet a region of lessened gravity was produced.

It was done very cleverly. A Mössbauer-Effect Balance was used to probe the space between the poles. If you've never seen an M-E Balance in action, it consists primarily of a tight monochromatic beam of gamma rays shot down the low-gravity field. The gamma rays change wavelength slightly but measurably under the influence of the gravitational field and if anything happens to alter the intensity of the field, the wavelength-change shifts correspondingly. It is an extremely delicate method for probing a gravitational field and it worked like a charm. There was no question but that Bloom had lowered gravity.

The trouble was that it had been done before by others. Bloom, to be sure, had made use of circuits that greatly increased the ease with which such an effect had been achieved—his system was typically ingenious and had been duly patented—and he maintained that it was by this method that anti-gravity would become not merely a scientific curiosity but a practical affair with industrial applications.

Perhaps. But it was an incomplete job and he didn't usually make a fuss over incompleteness. He wouldn't have done so this time if he weren't desperate to display *something*.

THE BILLIARD BALL

I said, "It's my impression that what you accomplished at that preliminary demonstration was 0.82 g, and better than that was achieved in Brazil last spring."

"That so? Well, calculate the energy input in Brazil and here, and then tell me the difference in gravity decrease per kilowatt-hour. You'll be surprised."

"But the point is, can you reach O g—zero gravity? That's what Professor Priss thinks may be impossible. Everyone agrees that merely lessening the intensity of the field is no great feat."

Bloom's fist clenched. I had the feeling that a key experiment had gone wrong that day and he was annoyed almost past endurance. Bloom hated to be balked by the Universe.

He said, "Theoreticians make me sick." He said it in a low, controlled voice, as though he were finally tired of not saying it, and he was going to speak his mind and be damned. "Priss has won two Nobel Prizes for sloshing around a few equations, but what has he done with it? Nothing! I *have* done something with it and I'm going to do more with it, whether Priss likes it or not.

"*I'm* the one people will remember. *I'm* the one who gets the credit. He can keep his damned title and his prizes and his kudos from the scholars. Listen, I'll tell you what gripes him. Plain old fashioned jealousy. It kills him that I get what I get for doing. He wants it for *thinking*.

"I said to him once—we play billiards together, you know—"

It was at this point that I quoted Priss's statement about billiards and got Bloom's counterstatement. I never published either. That was just trivia.

"We play billiards," said Bloom, when he had cooled down, "and I've won my share of games. We keep things friendly enough. What the hell—college chums and all that—though how he got through, I'll never know. He made it in physics, of course, and in math, but he got a bare pass—out of pity, I think—in every humanities course he ever took."

"You did not get your degree, did you, Mr. Bloom?" That was sheer mischief on my part. I was enjoying his eruption.

"I quit to go into business, damn it. My academic average, over the three years I attended, was a strong B. Don't imagine anything else, you hear? Hell, by the time Priss got his Ph.D., I was working on my second million."

He went on, clearly irritated, "Anyway, we were playing billiards and

50   ISAAC ASIMOV

I said to him, 'Jim, the average man will never understand why you get the Nobel Prize when I'm the one who gets the results. Why do you need two? Give me one!' He stood there, chalking up his cue, and then he said in his namby-pamby way, 'You have two billions, Ed. Give me one.' So you see, he wants the money."

I said, "I take it you don't mind his getting the honor?"

For a minute I thought he was going to order me out, but he didn't. He laughed instead, waved his hand in front of him, as though he were erasing something from an invisible blackboard. He said, "Oh, well, forget it. All that is off the record. Listen, do you want a statement? Okay. Things didn't go right today and I blew my top a bit, but it will clear up. I think I know what's wrong. And if I don't, I'm going to know.

"Look, you can say that I say that we *don't* need infinite electromagnetic intensity; we *will* flatten out that rubber sheet; we *will* have zero gravity. And when we get it, I'll have the damndest demonstration you ever saw, exclusively for the press and for Priss, and you'll be invited. And you can say it won't be long. Okay?"

Okay!

I had time after that to see each man once or twice more. I even saw them together when I was present at one of their billiard games. As I said before, both of them were *good*.

But the call to the demonstration did not come as quickly as all that. It arrived six weeks less than a year after Bloom gave me his statement. And at that, perhaps it was unfair to expect quicker work.

I had a special engraved invitation, with the assurance of a cocktail hour first. Bloom never did things by halves and he was planning to have a pleased and satisfied group of reporters on hand. There was an arrangement for trimensional TV, too. Bloom felt completely confident, obviously; confident enough to be willing to trust the demonstration in every living room on the planet.

I called up Professor Priss, to make sure he was invited, too.

He was.

"Do you plan to attend, sir?"

There was a pause and the professor's face on the screen was a study in uncertain reluctance. "A demonstration of this sort is most unsuitable where a serious scientific matter is in question. I do not like to encourage such things."

I was afraid he would beg off, and the dramatics of the situation would be greatly lessened if he were not there. But then, perhaps, he decided he dared not play the chicken before the world. With obvious distaste he said, "Of course, Ed Bloom is not really a scientist and he must have his day in the Sun. I'll be there."

"Do you think Mr. Bloom can produce zero gravity, sir?"

"Uh . . . Mr. Bloom sent me a copy of the design of his device and . . . and I'm not certain. Perhaps he can do it, if . . . uh . . . he says he can do it. Of course"—he paused again for quite a long time—"I think I would like to see it."

So would I, and so would many others.

The staging was impeccable. A whole floor of the main building at Bloom Enterprises—the one on the hilltop—was cleared. There were the promised cocktails and a splendid array of hors d'oeuvres, soft music and lighting, and a carefully dressed and thoroughly jovial Edward Bloom playing the perfect host, while a number of polite and unobtrusive menials fetched and carried. All was geniality and amazing confidence.

James Priss was late and I caught Bloom watching the corners of the crowd and beginning to grow a little grim about the edges. Then Priss arrived, dragging a volume of colorlessness in with him, a drabness that was unaffected by the noise and the absolute splendor (no other word would describe it—or else it was the two martinis glowing inside me) that filled the room.

Bloom saw him and his face illuminated at once. He bounced across the floor, seized the smaller man's hand and dragged him to the bar.

"Jim! Glad to see you! What'll you have? Hell, man, I'd have called it off if you hadn't showed. Can't have this thing without the star, you know." He wrung Priss's hand. "It's your theory, you know. We poor mortals can't do a thing without you few, you damned *few* few, pointing the way."

He was being ebullient, handing out the flattery, because he could afford to do so now. He was flattering Priss for the kill.

Priss tried to refuse a drink, with some sort of mutter, but a glass was pressed into his hand and Bloom raised his voice to a bull roar.

"Gentlemen! A moment's quiet, please. To Professor Priss, the greatest mind since Einstein, two-time Nobel Laureate, father of the Two-Field Theory, and inspirer of the demonstration we are about to see—even if he didn't think it would work, and had the guts to say so publicly."

ISAAC ASIMOV

There was a distinct titter of laughter that quickly faded out and Priss looked as grim as his face could manage.

"But now that Professor Priss is here," said Bloom, "and we've had our toast, let's get on with it. Follow me, gentlemen!"

The demonstration was in a much more elaborate place than had housed the earlier one. This time it was on the top floor of the building. Different magnets were involved—smaller ones, by heaven—but as nearly as I could tell, the same M-E Balance was in place.

One thing was new, however, and it staggered everybody, drawing much more attention than anything else in the room. It was a billiard table, resting under one pole of the magnet. Beneath it was the companion pole. A round hole, about a foot across, was stamped out of the very center of the table and it was obvious that the zero-gravity field, if it was to be produced, would be produced through that hole in the center of the billiard table.

It was as though the whole demonstration had been designed, surrealist fashion, to point up the victory of Bloom over Priss. This was to be another version of their everlasting billiards competition and Bloom was going to win.

I don't know if the other newsmen took matters in that fashion, but I think Priss did. I turned to look at him and saw that he was still holding the drink that had been forced into his hand. He rarely drank, I knew, but now he lifted the glass to his lips and emptied it in two swallows. He stared at that billiard ball and I needed no gift of ESP to realize that he took it as a deliberate snap of fingers under his nose.

Bloom led us to the twenty seats that surrounded three sides of the table, leaving the fourth free as a working area. Priss was carefully escorted to the seat commanding the most convenient view. Priss glanced quickly at the trimensional cameras which were now working. I wondered if he were thinking of leaving but deciding that he couldn't in the full glare of the eyes of the world.

Essentially, the demonstration was simple; it was the production that counted. There were dials in plain view that measured the energy expenditure. There were others that transferred the M-E Balance readings into a position and a size that were visible to all. Everything was arranged for easy trimensional viewing.

Bloom explained each step in a genial way, with one or two pauses in which he turned to Priss for a confirmation that had to come. He didn't do it often enough to make it obvious, but just enough to turn Priss upon the spit of his own torment. From where I sat I could look across the table and see Priss on the other side. He had the look of a man in hell.

As we all know, Bloom succeeded. The M-E Balance showed the gravitational intensity to be sinking steadily as the electromagnetic field was intensified. There were cheers when it dropped below the 0.52 g mark. A red line indicated that on the dial.

"The 0.52 g mark, as you know," said Bloom confidently, "represents the previous record low in gravitational intensity. We are now lower than that at a cost in electricty that is less than ten percent what it cost at the time that mark was set. And we will go lower still."

Bloom—I think deliberately, for the sake of the suspense—slowed the drop toward the end, letting the trimensional cameras switch back and forth between the gap in the billiard table and the dial on which the M-E Balance reading was lowering.

Bloom said suddenly, "Gentlemen, you will find dark goggles in the pouch on the side of each chair. Please put them on now. The zero-gravity field will soon be established and it will radiate a light rich in ultraviolet."

He put goggles on himself, and there was a momentary rustle as others went on, too.

I think no one breathed during the last minute, when the dial reaching dropped to zero and held fast. And just as that happened a cylinder of light sprang into existence from pole to pole through the hole in the billiard table.

There was a ghost of twenty sighs at that. Someone called out, "Mr. Bloom, what is the reason for the light?"

"It's characteristic of the zero-gravity field," said Bloom smoothly, which was no answer, of course.

Reporters were standing up now, crowding about the edge of the table. Bloom waved them back. "Please gentlemen, stand clear!"

Only Priss remained sitting. He seemed lost in thought and I have been certain ever since that it was the goggles that obscured the possible significance of everything that followed. I didn't see his eyes. I couldn't. And that meant neither I nor anyone else could even begin to make a guess as to what was going on behind those eyes. Well, maybe we couldn't have made such a guess, even if the goggles hadn't been there, but who can say?

ISAAC ASIMOV

Bloom was raising his voice again. "Please! The demonstration is not yet over. So far, we've only repeated what I have done before. I have now produced a zero-gravity field and I have shown it can be done practically. But I want to demonstrate something of which such a field can do. What we are going to see next will be something that has never been seen, not even by myself. I have not experimented in this direction, much as I would have liked to, because I felt that Professor Priss deserved the honor of—"

Priss looked up sharply. "What—what—"

"Professor Priss," said Bloom, smiling broadly, "I would like you to perform the first experiment involving the interaction of a solid object with a zero-gravity field. Notice that the field has been formed in the center of a billiard table. The world knows your phenomenal skill in billiards, professor, a talent second only to your amazing aptitude in theoretical physics. Won't you send a billiard ball into the zero-gravity volume?"

Eagerly he was handing a ball and cue to the professor. Priss, his eyes hidden by the goggles, stared at them and only very slowly, very uncertainly, reached out to take them.

I wonder what his eyes were showing. I wonder, too, how much of the decision to have Priss play billiards at the demonstration was due to Bloom's anger at Priss's remark about their periodic game, the remark I had quoted. Had I been, in my way, responsible for what followed?

"Come, stand up, professor," said Bloom, "and let me have your seat. The show is yours from now on. Go ahead!"

Bloom seated himself, and still talked, in a voice that grew more organlike with each moment. "Once Professor Priss sends the ball into the volume of zero gravity, it will no longer be affected by Earth's gravitational field. It will remain truly motionless while the Earth rotates about its axis and travels about the Sun. In this latitude, and at this time of day, I have calculated that the Earth, in its motions, will sink downward. We will move with it and the ball will stand still. To us it will seem to rise up and away from the Earth's surface. Watch."

Priss seemed to stand in front of the table in frozen paralysis. Was it surprise? Astonishment? I don't know. I'll never know. Did he make a move to interrupt Bloom's little speech, or was he just suffering from an agonized reluctance to play the ignominious part into which he was being forced by his adversary?

Priss turned to the billiard table, looking first at it, then back at Bloom. Every reporter was on his feet, crowding as closely as possible in order to get a good view. Only Bloom himself remained seated, smiling and isolated. He, of course, was not watching the table, or the ball, or the zero-gravity field. As nearly as I could tell through the goggles, he was watching Priss.

Priss turned to the table and placed his ball. He was going to be the agent that was to bring final and dramatic triumph to Bloom and make himself—the man who said it couldn't be done—the goat to be mocked forever.

Perhaps he felt there was no way out. Or perhaps—

With a sure stroke of his cue, he set the ball into motion. It was not going quickly, and every eye followed it. It struck the side of the table and caromed. It was going even slower now as though Priss himself were increasing the suspense and making Bloom's triumph the more dramatic.

I had a perfect view, for I was standing at the side of the table opposite from that where Priss was. I could see the ball moving toward the glitter of the zero-gravity field and beyond it I could see those portions of the seated Bloom that were not hidden by that glitter.

The ball approached the zero-gravity volume, seemed to hang on the edge for a moment, then was gone, with a streak of light, the sound of a thunderclap, and the sudden smell of burning cloth.

We yelled. We all yelled.

I've seen the scene on television since—along with the rest of the world. I can see myself in the film during that fifteen-second period of wild confusion, but I don't really recognize my face.

Fifteen seconds!

And then we discovered Bloom. He was still sitting in the chair, his arms still folded, but there was a hole the size of a billiard ball through forearm, chest, and back. The better part of his heart, as it later turned out under autopsy, had been neatly punched out.

They turned off the device. They called in the police. They dragged off Priss, who was in a state of utter collapse. I wasn't much better off, to tell the truth, and if any reporter then on the scene ever tried to say he remained a cool observer of that scene, then he's a cool liar.

It was some months before I got to see Priss again. He had lost some weight but seemed well otherwise. Indeed, there was color in his cheeks and an air of decision about him. He was better dressed than I had ever seen him.

He said, "I know what happened *now*. If I had had time to think, I would have known then. But I am a slow thinker, and poor Ed Bloom was so intent on running a great show and doing it so well that he carried me along with him.

"Naturally, I've been trying to make up for some of the damage I unwittingly caused."

"You can't bring Bloom back to life," I said soberly.

"No, I can't," he said, just as soberly. "But there's Bloom Enterprises to think of, too. What happened at the demonstration, in full view of the world, was the worst possible advertisement for zero gravity, and it's important that the story be made clear. That is why *I* have asked to see *you*."

"Yes?"

"If I had been a quicker thinker, I would have known Ed was speaking the purest nonsense when he said that the billiard ball would slowly rise in the zero-gravity field. It *couldn't* be so! If Bloom hadn't depised theory so, if he hadn't been so intent on being proud of his own ignorance of theory, he'd have known it himself.

"The Earth's motion, after all, isn't the only motion involved, young man. The Sun itself moves in a vast orbit about the center of the Milky Way Galaxy. And the Galaxy moves, too, in some not very clearly defined way. If the billiard ball were subjected to zero gravity, you might think of it as being unaffected by any of these motions and therefore of suddenly falling into a state of absolute rest—when there is no such thing as absolute rest."

Priss shook his head slowly, "The trouble with Ed, I think, was he was thinking of the kind of zero gravity one gets in a spaceship in free fall, when people float in mid-air. He expected the ball to float in mid-air. However, in a spaceship, zero gravity is not the result of an absence of gravitation, but merely the result of two objects, a ship and a man within the ship, falling at the same rate, responding to gravity precisely the same way, so that each is motionless with respect to the other.

"In the zero-gravity field produced by Ed, there was a flattening of the rubber-sheet Universe, which means an actual loss of mass. Everything in that field, including molecules of air caught within it, and the billiard ball I pushed into it, was completely massless as long as it remained with it. A completely massless object can move in only one way."

He paused, inviting the question. I asked, "What motion would that be?"

"Motion at the speed of light. Any massless object, such as a neutrino or a photon, must travel at the speed of light as long as it exists. In fact, light moves at that speed only because it is made up of photons. As soon as the billiard ball entered the zero-gravity field and lost its mass, it too assumed the speed of light at once and left."

I shook my head. "But didn't it regain its mass as soon as it left the zero-gravity volume?"

"It certainly did, and at once it began to be affected by the gravitational field and to slow up in response to the friction of the air and the top of the billiard table. But imagine how much friction it would take to slow up an object the mass of a billiard ball going at the speed of light. It went though a hundred-mile thickness of our atmosphere in a thousandth of a second and I doubt that it slowed more than a few miles a second in doing so, a few miles out of 186,282 of them. On the way, it scorched the top of the billiard table, broke cleanly through the edge, and went through poor Ed and the window, too, punching out neat circles because it passed through before the neighboring portions of something even as brittle as glass had a chance to split and splinter.

"It is extremely fortunate we were on the top floor of a building set in a countrified area. If we had been in the city, it might have passed through a number of buildings and killed a number of people. By now that billiard ball is off in space, far beyond the edge of the Solar System and it will continue to travel so forever, at nearly the speed of light, until it happens to strike an object large enough to stop it. And then it will gouge out a sizeable crater."

I played with the notion and was not sure I liked it. "How is that possible? The billiard ball entered the zero-gravity volume almost at a standstill. I saw it. And you say it left with an incredible quantity of kinetic energy. Where did the energy come from?"

Priss shrugged. "It came from nowhere! The law of conservation of energy only holds under the conditions in which general relativity is valid; that is, in an indented-rubber-sheet Universe. Wherever the indentation is flattened out, general relativity no longer holds, and energy can be created and destroyed freely. That accounts for the radiation along the cylindrical surface of the zero-gravity volume. That radiation, you re-

ISAAC ASIMOV

member, Bloom did not explain, and, I fear, could not explain. If he had only experimented further first; if he had only not been so foolishly anxious to put on his show—"

"What accounts for the radiation, sir?"

"The molecules of air inside the volume. Each assumes the speed of light and comes smashing outward. They're only molecules, not billiard balls. so they're stopped, but the kinetic energy of their motion is converted into energetic radiation. It's continuous because new molecules are always drifting in, and attaining the speed of light and smashing out."

"Then energy is being created continuously?"

"Exactly. And that is what we must make clear to the public. Antigravity is not primarily a device to lift spaceships or to revolutionize mechanical movement. Rather, it is the source of an endless supply of free energy, since part of that energy produced can be diverted to maintain the field that keeps that portion of the Universe flat. What Ed Bloom invented, without knowing it, was not just anti-gravity, but the first successful perpetual-motion machine of the first class—one that manufactures energy out of nothing."

I said slowly, "Any one of us could have been killed by that billiard ball, is that right, professor? It might have gone out in any direction."

Priss said, "Well, massless photons emerge from any light source at the speed of light in any direction; that's why a candle casts light in all directions. The massless air molecules come out of the zero-gravity volume in all directions, which is why the entire cylinder radiates. But the billiard ball was only one object. It could have come out in any direction, but it had to come out in some one direction, chosen at random, and that chosen direction happened to be the one that caught Ed."

That was it. Everyone knows the consequences. Mankind had free energy and so we have the world we have now. Professor Priss was placed in charge of its development by the board of Bloom Enterprises, and in time he was as rich and famous as ever Edward Bloom had been. And Priss still has two Nobel Prizes in addition.

Only . . .

I keep thinking. Photons smash out from a light source in all directions because they are created at the moment and there is no reason for them to move in one direction more than in another. Air molecules come out of a zero-gravity field in all directions because they enter it in all directions.

But what about a single billiard ball, entering a zero-gravity field from one particular direction? Does it come out in the same direction or in any direction?

I've inquired delicately, but theoretical physicists don't seem to be sure, and I can find no record that Bloom Enterprises, which is the only organization working with zero-gravity fields, has ever experimented in the matter. Someone at the organization once told me that the uncertainty principle guarantees the random emersion of an object entering in any direction. But then why don't they try the experiment?

Could it be, then . . .

Could it be that for once Priss's mind had been working quickly? Could it be that, under the pressure of what Bloom was trying to do to him, Priss had suddenly seen everything? He had been studying the radiation surrounding the zero-gravity volume. He might have realized its cause and been certain of the speed-of-light motion of anything entering the volume.

Why, then, had he said nothing?

One thing is certain. *Nothing* Priss would do at the billiard table could be accidental. He was an expert and the billiard ball did exactly what he wanted it to. I was standing right there. I saw him look at Bloom and then at the table as though he were judging angles.

I watched him hit that ball. I watched it bounce off the side of the table and move into the zero-gravity volume, heading in one particular direction.

For when Priss sent that ball toward the gravity-zero volume—and the tri-di films bear me out—it was *already* aimed directly at Bloom's heart!

Accident? Coincidence?

. . . Murder?

ISAAC ASIMOV

The Bitter End

by Randall Garrett

I.

Master Sean O Lochlainn was not overly fond of the city of Paris. It was a crowded, noisy, river port with delusions of grandeur brought on by memories of ancient glory.

That it had been the seat of the ancient Capetian Kings of France, there could be no denying; that the last of the Capets had been killed in 1215 by Richard the Lion-Hearted and that more than seven and a half centuries had rolled past since then were equally true facts, but Parisians would have denied both if they could.

One of the very few places Master Sean felt comfortable in all that vast city was here, in the International Bar of the Hotel Cosmopolitain. He was wearing ordinary gentlemen's traveling clothes, not the silver-slashed blue that would proclaim him as the Chief Forensic Sorcerer for Prince Richard, Duke of Normandy.

It was four o'clock of a pleasant October evening, and the shifts were just changing in the International Bar, a barman and two waiters going off duty and being replaced by their evening counterparts. It meant a lull in service for a minute or so, but Master Sean didn't mind; he still had a good half-pint of beer in his mug, and the stout little Irish magician was not a fast drinker.

It was not the best beer in the world; in the Anglo-French Empire, the English made the best beer, and the Normans the second best. There were some excellent wines available here, but Master Sean usually drank wine only with meals. Distilled spirits he drank only on the rarest of occasions. Beer was his tipple, and this stuff wasn't really *bad,* it just wasn't as good as he preferred. He sighed and took another healthy swig.

He had time to kill and no place else to kill it. He had to catch the 6:05 train west for the ninety-odd mile trip to Rouen, which gave him two more hours of nothing to do.

On the floor at his feet was his symbol-decorated carpetbag, which contained not only the tools of his profession but, now, the thaumaturgical evidence in the Zellerman-Blair case, which he had come specifically to Paris to get from his colleague, the Chief Forensic Sorcerer for His Grace, the Duke D'Isle. Anyone noticing that carpetbag closely would immediately recognize Master Sean as a sorcerer, but that was all right; he was not exactly traveling incognito, anyway.

"Would ye be ready for having another one, sir?"

Master Sean lifted his eyes from his nearly empty mug and pushed it across the bar with a smile. "I would indeed," he said to the barman. "And might that be the lilt of County Meath I'm hearing in your voice?"

The barman worked the pump. "It would," he said, returning the smile. "Would yours be the north of Mayo?"

"Close you are," said Master Sean. "Sligo it is."

There were not many people in the International. Six people at the bar besides Master Sean, and a dozen more seated at the booths and tables. The place wouldn't be really busy for an hour or so yet. The barman decided he had a few minutes for a friendly chat with a fellow Irishman.

He was wrong.

One of the waiters moved up quickly. "Murtaugh, come here," he said in an urgent undertone. "There's something funny."

Murtaugh frowned. "What?"

The waiter glanced round with warning eyes. "Come."

The barman shrugged, came out from behind the bar, and followed the waiter over to a booth in the far corner. Master Sean, as curious as the next man if not more so, turned round on his barstool to watch.

The room was not brightly lit, and the booth was partly in shadow, but the sorcerer's keen blue eyes saw most of the detail.

There was a well-dressed man sitting alone in the booth. He was in the corner of the booth, against the wall, and his head was bent down, as though he were looking intently at the newspaper which his hands held on the table before him. To his right was a drinking glass which was either completely empty or nearly so; it was hard to tell from where Master Sean sat.

The man neither moved nor spoke when the barman addressed him. The barman touched one of his hands to attract his attention. Still nothing.

RANDALL GARRETT

Master Sean's common sense told him to stay out of this. It was none of his business. It was out of his jurisdiction. He had a train to catch. He had— He had an insatiable curiosity.

A magician's senses and perceptions are more highly developed, more highly trained, and more sensitive than those of the ordinary man. Otherwise, he would not be a magician. Master Sean's common sense told him to stay out of this, but his other senses told him that the man was dead and that this was possibly more complex than appeared on the surface.

Before the barman and the waiter could further disturb anything on or near the booth, Master Sean grabbed his carpetbag and walked quickly and unobtrusively over to the booth.

But he found that he had underestimated the sagacity and quickness of mind of his fellow Irishman. Barman Murtaugh was saying: "No, we don't touch him, John-Pierre. You go out and fetch an Armsman and a Healer. I'm pretty sure the feller's dead, but fetch a Healer all the same. Now move." As the waiter moved, Murtaugh's eye caught sight of Master Sean. "Please go back to your seat, sir," he said. "The old gent here's been taken a bit ill, and I've sent for a Healer."

Master Sean already had his identification out. "I understand. I don't think anyone else has noticed. The both of us could stand here while John-Pierre's gone, but that might attract attention, were you to be from your post so long. On the other hand, *I* can stand here and pretend to be talking to him, and no one will be the wiser. Meantime, you can get back to the bar and take careful notice if anyone shows any unusual interest in what's going on at this booth."

Murtaugh handed the identification papers back to Master Sean and made up his mind. "I'll keep me eye out, Master Sorcerer." And headed back to his station.

II.

The uniformed Men-at-Arms had arrived, made their preliminary investigation, and sealed off the bar. There were several indignant patrons, but they were soon quieted down.

The Healer, a Brother Paul, checked over the body, and after several thoughtful minutes, said: "It could be several things—heart attack, internal hemorrhage, drugs, alcohol. I'd have to get a chirurgeon to do an autopsy before I'd take an oath on any of them."

"How long would you say he'd been dead, Brother Paul?"

"At least half an hour, Master Sean. Perhaps as much as an hour. Call it forty-five minutes and you'd not be far off. Funny how he just sat there without falling over or anything, isn't it?"

Master Sean wished he had some official standing; he'd have his instruments out in half a minute and get some facts. "It's an old schoolboy's trick," he replied to the Healer's remark. "Surely you've done it yourself. You feel yourself getting sleepy, so you prop yourself up at your desk in such a way that you don't fall over—as he's done in the corner, there. Then you put your forearms on the desktop—in this case, tabletop—and put your reading material between them, so it looks natural. Then you let your head go forward. If you've done it properly, you can go right to sleep and look as if you're reading unless somebody notices you're not turning pages. Or gets at the right angle to see whether your eyes are closed."

"That suggests he felt the drowsiness coming on," said Brother Paul.

Master Sean nodded. "He'd not likely react that way to a heart attack. If a man's that full of alcohol, he usually doesn't have enough control or presence of mind to pull it off properly. A drunk just puts his head on his forearms and goes to sleep. How about internal hemorrhage?"

"It's possible. If the bleeding weren't too rapid, he'd begin to feel drowsy and might decide a little nap would be just the thing," Brother Paul agreed. "Certain drugs, of course, would have the same effect."

Around them, Men-at-Arms were taking statements from the patrons of the International Bar.

At that moment, the front door opened, and a smoothly-dressed, rather handsome man with a dapper little mustache entered, accompanied by another Man-at-Arms. He stopped just inside the door, looked all around, and then said: "Good evening, my sirs. I have the honor to be Plainclothes Sergeant-at-Arms Cougair Chasseur. I am in charge of this case. Where is the body?"

"This way, my sergeant," said one of the Men-at-Arms, and led the newcomer over toward Master Sean and Brother Paul. The Healer was wearing the habit of his Order, so Sergeant Cougair said, "It is that you are the Healer who was called?"

The Healer bowed his head slightly. "Brother Paul, of the Hospital of St. Luke-by-the-Seine."

RANDALL GARRETT

"Very good." The sergeant looked at Master Sean. "And you, my sir?"

The stout little Irish sorcerer carefully took out his identification, and with it the special card issued by the local Chief Forensic Sorcerer. Sergeant Cougair looked them over. He smiled. "Ah, yes. It is that you work with Lord Darcy of Rouen, is it not?"

"It is," said Master Sean.

"It is that it is a very great pleasure to meet you, my sir, a very great pleasure, indeed!" he bubbled. Then his smile faded and he looked rather dubious. "But is it not that you are a little out of your jurisdiction?"

"I am," Master Sean agreed. The atrocious Parisian manner of mangling the Anglo-French language had always set his teeth on edge, and the fellow's manner didn't help much. "I was merely being of some small assistance until you arrived. I have no further interest in the case." When talking to a Parisian, Master Sean's brogue vanished almost without a trace.

The sergeant's face brightened again. "Of course. But naturally. Now let us see what we have here." He turned his attention toward the corpse. "Without a doubt, dead. Of what did he die, Brother Paul?"

"Hard to tell, sergeant. Master Sean and I agree that the two most likely causes of death are internal hemorrhage—possibly of the cerebral area, more likely of the abdomen. And, second, the administration of some kind of drug."

"Drug? You mean a poison?"

Brother Paul shrugged. "Whether a given substance is a drug or a poison depends pretty much on the amount given, the method by which it was given, and the intent of its use. Any drug can be a poison, and, I suppose, vice versa."

"It is that it killed him, is it not?"

"We of the Healing profession, sergeant, use the word 'poison' in a technical sense, just as you do the word 'murder.' All homicides are not murder. Death caused by the accidental administration of an overdose of a drug is not poisoning any more than death by misadventure is murder."

"Ah, I see. A nice distinction," the sergeant said, looking enlightened. "What, then, of suicide?"

"There, if the intent was deliberate suicide, then it was intent to kill. That makes it poisoning."

"Most comprehensible. Very well, then; if we assume poisoning in your technical sense, is it that it is murder or suicide?"

"Why, as to that, Sergeant Cougair," Brother Paul said blandly, "I fear that is your area of expertise, not mine."

Master Sean had listened to all this in utter silence. He had no further interest in the case. Hadn't he said so himself?

But Sergeant Cougair turned to him. "Is it that I may ask you a technical question, Master Sean?"

"Certainly."

"Is it that it is at all possible that the deceased was killed by Black Magic?"

For what seemed like a long second, there was no sound in the room except for the murmur of voices from the patrons of the bar and the Armsmen who were questioning them. The question, Master Sean knew, was loaded—but with what?

He shook his head decisively. "Not possible. If Brother Paul's estimate of the time of death is correct—and I tend to agree with him—then I was in this room when it happened. There is no way a death-dealing act of Black Magic could have been perpetrated against the deceased without my knowing it."

"Ah. I presumed not," the sergeant said. "I presumed that had you known of such you would have mentioned it immediately. But it was my duty to ask, you comprehend."

"Of course."

Then he turned to the Armsman who had been standing unobtrusively nearby, taking down everything in a notebook. "Is it that the body has been searched?"

"But no, my sergeant. We awaited your coming."

"Then we shall do it immediately. No. Wait. Has anyone identified the deceased?"

"But no, my sergeant. The barman and the two waiters claim never to have seen him before. Nor do any of the patrons admit to any knowledge of him."

"They have looked at him thoroughly?"

"But yes, my sergeant. We marched them by while Brother Paul held up the head for one to view."

"And none of them knew him. Incredible! Well, to work. Let us examine his person and discover what we may."

Before they could move the body out of the booth, however, a uni-

RANDALL GARRETT

formed Sergeant-at-Arms came in through the door, spotted the Sergeant Cougair, and hurried over. "A word with you, Chasseur?"

"Yes."

The two of them walked to one side and talked for perhaps a minute in low tones. Even Master Sean's sharp sense of hearing could not make out the words. Psychically, all he could get was disappointment, frustration, and irritation on the part of Sergeant Cougair.

The uniformed sergeant departed and Sergeant Cougair came slowly, thoughtfully, back to where Master Sean and the others were waiting.

"A disaster," he murmured. "Most unfortunate."

"What seems to be the trouble?" Master Sean asked.

"Alas! A family entire have been wiped out by gas. The illuminating gas, you comprehend. A most important family they were, too—not titled, but wealthy. All dead."

"A disaster, indeed," Master Sean agreed.

"What? The deaths? Oy, yes; that, certainly. But that was not the disaster to which I referred."

"Oh?" Master Sean blinked.

"But no. I referred to the fact that foul play is suspected in the deaths of the Duval family, and our entire thaumaturgical staff has been called upon to aid in the apprehension of the perpetrators of this heinous crime. I have no forensic sorcerer to aid me in my work. My case is considered of importance so small that I cannot get even an apprentice for some hours yet. Delay! My god, the delay! And meanwhile , one's prime piece of evidence slowly but most surely decomposes before one's veritable eyes!"

Master Sean glanced at his watch. Five after five. He sighed. "Why, as to that, my dear sergeant, I'll cast a preservative spell over the body if you want. No problem."

The sergeant's eyes lit up. "By the Blue! How marvelous! I will at once take you up upon your offer!"

"Very good. But clear the rest of these folks out of here. I don't want a bunch of undisciplined civilians gawping at me while I do my work."

"But I cannot let them go, Master Sorcerer!" the sergeant protested. "They are material witnesses!"

"I didn't say let 'em go," Master Sean said tiredly. "I doubt if the Grand Ballroom of this hotel is being used this early in the evening. Get hold of the manager. Your men can keep them in there for a while."

"Admirable! I shall see that is done."

III.

Four men stood quietly in the echoing silence of an otherwise empty barroom. Three of them were Plainclothes Sergeant-at-Arms Cougair Chasseur and two of his Men-at-Arms. The fourth was Master Sorcerer Sean O Lochlainn. Brother Paul had, somewhat regretfully, returned to his duties at the hospital; having certified that the deceased was, indeed, deceased, he was no longer needed.

The three Armsmen stood well to one side, silent, unmoving. It is unwise to annoy a magician when he is practicing his Art.

Master Sean looked down at the body. The Armsmen had shoved a couple of tables together and reverently laid the corpse upon them as sort of makeshift bier. They had carefully undressed it, and, even more carefully, Master Sean had examined the late unknown. He was, the sorcerer judged, a robust man in his middle fifties. The body was scarred in several places; five of them looked like saber wounds which had been neatly stitched by a chirurgeon, four others came in pairs, front and back, each pair apparently made by a single bullet. The rest were the sort of cuts and scrapes any active adult might accumulate. All of them were years old. Master Sean marked the location of each on a series of special charts which he always carried in his symbol-decorated carpetbag.

Moles, warts, discolorations, all were carefully and duly noted.

There were no fresh wounds of any kind, anywhere on the body.

None of this preliminary work was necessary for a preservation spell. That sort of thing was usually left for the autopsy room. But Master Sean was curious. When a man dies of mysterious causes practically in your lap, as it were, even the most uncurious of men would be interested, and Master Sean, both by nature and by training, was more inquisitive than most.

When the superficial examination was over, Master Sean took from his symbol-decorated carpetbag a featureless, eighteen inch, ebon wand, half an inch in diameter.

That wand was not a glossy black. It was not even a dull, flat black. It was a fathomless black, like the endless night between the stars. It did not merely fail to reflect the light that fell upon it, it seemed to absorb

RANDALL GARRETT

light as though it were somehow *reaching* for it.

Under the precise control of Master Sean's right hand and fingers and arm, that wand began to weave an intricate pattern of symbols, series after series of them, above and around the dead man.

Those watching could sense, rather than see, that within and through the body, filling its every cell to the outermost layer of skin and hardly half a hairsbreadth beyond, a psychic field, generated and formed by the master sorcerer's mind and will, began to form.

There was no visible change in the body as that eighteen inch rod of light-absorbing night wove its fantastic spell, but every man there *knew* that the spell was having its effect.

When it was finished, the ebon wand slowed and stopped.

After a moment, Master Sean said, matter-of-factly: "There, now; he'll last as long as you need him to." And he put his wand away.

"Thank you, Master Sean," Sergeant Cougair said simply. Then, before he said another word, he took a couple of tablecloths from other tables and covered the body.

"I have seen that done many times, Master Sorcerer," the sergeant said then, "although never so quickly nor so gracefully. It has always seemed to me as a miracle."

"No such thing," said Master Sean rather testily. "I'm a thaumaturgist, not a miracle-worker. 'Tis simply a matter of applied science."

"Is it that I may ask what precisely happens?"

Sergeant Cougair did not know it, then or ever, but he had touched one of Master Sean's few weak spots. Master Sean O Lochlainn *loved* to lecture, to explain things.

"Well, now, that's very simple, Sergeant Cougair," he said expansively. "As you may know, matter is made up of tiny little particles, so small that they could never be seen under the most powerful microscope. Indeed, it has been estimated that a single ounce of the lightest of 'em would contain some seveteen million million million million of 'em. This theory of small particles was propounded first by a Greek philosopher named Demokritos about twenty-four hundred years ago. He called those particles 'atoms' and so do we, in his honor. His hypothesis has been confirmed by thaumaturgical theory and by certain experiments done by men learned in the Khemic Art."

"I comprehend," said the sergeant, looking as though he really did.

"Very well, then; these atoms are always full of energy; they vibrate and buzz about, which helps in their Khemic activity."

"Ah!" the sergeant, with a light in his eyes. "I comprehend! Is it that it is your spell which causes the cessation of all this—this 'buzzing about,' as you call it?"

"Good Heavens, *no!*" Master Sean fairly snapped. "Why, if I were to do such a thing as that, the body would freeze solid in an instant, and everything about it would likely burst into flame!"

"My god." The sergeant was instantly sobered by the thought of this phenomenon. "Continue, if you please."

"I will. Now pay, attention. These atoms react with each other to form conglomerates, and these conglomerates can react to form other conglomerates, and so on. All substances are composed of conglomerates of atoms, d'ye see. They react because each conglomerate is seeking a condition which will impose the least strain upon itself."

"A most natural desire," Sergeant Cougair commented.

"Exactly so. Now, then, in a living human being, these processes take place under conditions controlled by the life force, so that the food we eat and the air we breathe are converted into the energy and the substance we need. But these processes do not stop when the life force has departed; simply, they are no longer controlled. The body no longer has any resistance to microörganisms and fungi. The body decays.

"Even without microöganisms or fungi, these activities continue uncontrolled. That's why meat hung in a butcher's ice house becomes tender as it ages; the flesh digests itself, so to speak.

"Now, what a preservative spell does is make those atomic conglomerates *satisfied*. They wish to remain at their present energy levels, to maintain the *status quo* at the time the spell was cast. They are—*satisfied*."

"It is that it kills the microöganisms, is it not?" the sergeant asked.

"Oh, aye, They can't survive under any such conditions as that."

Sergeant Cougair gave a slight shudder. "I shudder," he said suiting words to action, "to think what it would do to a living man."

Master Sean grinned. "Nothing. Absolutely nothing. The life force of more highly organized beings resists the spell easily. Why, if yonder gentlemen has a tapeworm, I assure you the worm is alive. He may be getting pretty hungry, but I assure you the spell didn't kill him.

"The spell you see, is very unstable. It's a static spell, and so bleeds off in time, anyway, but—oh, too much heat, for instance, would break the spell. The conglomerates would be dissatisfied again."

"Such as in the tropics?"

"It rarely gets that hot, even in the tropics. But a very hot bath, say—almost hot enough to scald—would do the job."

Sergeant Cougair raised his hands, palms out. "I assure you, Master Sorcerer, I have no desire to give a corpse a hot bath—or any other kind." Then, more briskly: "And now let us discover what we may in and about the clothing."

There was the usual assortment of keys, a pipe, tobacco pouch, pipe lighter, coins in the amont of a sovereign and a half, forty-two sovereigns in banknotes, a fountain pen, and a brand-new notebook containing nothing but empy pages. The identification folder contained cards and papers showing that the bearer was Andray Vandermeer, a retired senior captain of the Imperial Legion. That, thought Master Sean, would account for the scars.

His present address was No. 117 Rue Queen Helga, Paris. An Armsman was instructed to go there and discover what he could.

"If there is a wife, or child, or other relative, break the news gently. You do not know the manner of his death. It may have been a heart attack. You comprehend?"

"But yes, my sergeant."

"Positive identification can wait until we have arrived him at the morgue. Go."

The Armsman went.

"And now, for *this* small object," the sergeant continued. He was holding an eight-ounce brown glass bottle full of liquid. "It has upon it the label of Veblin & Son, Pharamaceutical Herbalists. It contains, according to the same label, 'Tincture of Cinchona Bark'—now what would that be?"

"An alcoholic solution of vegetable alkaloids from a certain tree of New France," Master Sean said promptly.

"A poison?"

"Or a drug," Master Sean said. "Remember what Brother Paul said."

"Ah, certainly. But it may have been what killed him. If so, it was suicide, for we found it in his own pocket."

"What killed him didn't come from that bottle," Master Sean pointed out dryly. "It's still full, and the seal of the stopper is unbroken."

"What? Oh. You are quite right. But perhaps there is another bottle. Lewie, go into the Grand Ballroom and tell Armand to have all the suspects searched. Bring John-Jack back with you, and we will search his barroom."

"But yes, my sergeant." And off he went, leaving Master Sean alone with Sergeant Cougair.

"Sergeant," the stout little Irish sorcerer said carefully, "I would not presume to tell you your business, but while all this searching is going on, you might find out more about that medicine if you checked with the pharmacist who filled the prescription, and with the Healer who issued it. The stuff is taken for the cure of malaria, one of the few diseases a Healer cannot handle without such aids."

"That will be done in due time, Master Sean," said the sergeant.

"Why not now? Veblin & Sons is just across the arcade in this very hotel."

Sergeant Cougair jerked his head down and looked again at the bottle in his hand. "So it is! But yes! You are correct! I thank you for calling it to my attention."

"Think nothing of it." Master Sean looked at his wristwatch. "And now, if you'll pardon me I fear I must say goodbye. If I don't hurry, I shall miss my train."

The sergeant looked at him in astonishment. "But most certainly you shall miss your train, Master Sorcerer! You are a material witness and a suspect in a murder case. You cannot leave the city."

"I?" Master Sean was even more astonished. "*I?*"

"Certainly. It is an axiom of mine that the least likely suspect is the one most likely to have done it. Besides, I shall need you for the autopsy, to determine whether or not murder *has* been done."

Master Sean could only stare at him.

There were no words to be found for the occasion.

IV.

It is not wise to meddle in the affairs of wizards, for reasons well known to the *cognoscenti,* and when Master Sir Aubrey Burns, Chief Forensic Sorcerer for His Grace the Duke D'Isle, heard what Sergeant-at-Arms Cougair Chasseur had done, he definitely felt it was meddling.

Master Sir Aubrey did not hear about it from Master Sean. That stout little Irish sorcerer was perfectly capable of washing his own linen, but he had had to make a teleson call to Lord Darcy in Rouen to explain why he had missed his train, and he had used the offical Armsmen's teleson to do it. And the grapevine is almost as efficient as the teleson.

That Chasseur was well within his rights to have detained Master Sean is not debatable; whether he should have exercised those rights is moot.

Having decided that it was partly his own fault for sticking his nose into the case in the first place, and still beset by curiosity in the second place, Master Sean decided that he might as well go ahead with the autopsy and with the similarity analysis of the contents of the bottle and the dregs in the glass.

He didn't do the actual operation himself, of course; that was not his area of competence. The actual work was done by a husky young chirurgeon from Gascony who looked more like a butcher's helper than a chirurgeon, but whose fingers and brain were both nimble and accurate.

By half past seven, the body had been all sewn up nicely, and was ready to be claimed by the wife—if and when she actually identified it as being that of S/Cpt Andray Vandermeer, I.L., Ret. The Armsman who had been sent to No. 117 Rue Queen Helga reported that a servant had informed him that Goodwife Vandermeer was out shopping and was not expected to return until about eight.

Master Sean, meanwhile, pondered the data he had at hand.

The tentatively-identified Vandermeer had most certainly died of an overdose of some as yet unidentified drug. A similarity analysis showed that it was the same drug as that found in the dregs at the bottom of the glass found on the table near him. The prescription drug bottle had contained exactly what the label said it did, and was most certainly *not* the alkaloid that had killed Vandermeer.

Master Sean looked over the notes he had made during the autopsy. The internal condition of the body . . . the liver . . . the kidneys . . . those lesions on the brain. . . .

The whole picture rang a very small bell somewhere in the recesses of Master Sean's memory, but he couldn't quite bring up the data. He'd never *seen* a body in just this condition before, of that he was sure. No, it was something he had read or been told. But what? Where?

The beefy young chirurgeon rose from his desk across the room and came over to where Master Sean was sitting. He had a sheaf of papers in his hand. "Here's my report, Master Sorcerer," he said politely. "If there's anything you 'd like to add or change. . ." He let the sentence trail off and handed the magician the papers.

Master Sean read the report carefully, then shook his head. "No changes, Dr. Ambro, and the only thing I'd like to add is the name of the poison. Unfortunately, I can't as yet." He smiled up at the younger man. "By and by, I should like to compliment you on your skill and dexterity with a scalpel. I've never seen a neater job. There are some pathologists who feel that just because the—er—patient is dead, any old hack work will do."

"Well, Master," the chirurgeon said, "I feel that if a man lets himself get sloppy with the dead, he'll soon get sloppy with the living. It generates bad habits. I owe a great deal to the Healing Art, and I feel that as a technician I should do my best to repay that debt. If it weren't for a great Healer, I wouldn't be a chirurgeon at all."

"Oh? How's that, Dr. Ambro?" Master Sean was curious.

Dr. Ambro grinned. "As a lad, I had my heart set on being a chirurgeon. I felt it was a useful and rewarding trade. Then I found I wasn't cut out for it—no pun intended."

"Really?" Master Sean raised an eyebrow. "You seem singularly apt at the work to me."

Dr. Ambro chuckled. "I couldn't stand the smell. I couldn't even operate on the practice cadavers. Fresh blood nauseated me. Opening the abdominal cavity was even worse. And the dead? Forget it. And it *was* the smell. Nothing else. I couldn't even stand the odor of a raw steak or side of pork."

"Ah, I see," said Master Sean. "An unusual phenomenon, but by no means unique. Pray continue."

"Nothing much to tell, Master. A fine old Healer, Father Debrett of Pouillon, cast a mild spell on me. Now I find the scent pleasant enough—rather like roses and lilies, if you follow me."

"Oh, certainly. A well-known procedure," the sorcerer said. "Well, I'm glad it was done; it would have been a shame to let your skill be wasted."

"Thank you, Master Sean; thank you very much."

There was a knock on the office door, and it opened. A massive, totally bald head with a smiling face and bushy black eyebrows appeared around the door. "Hullo, chaps. May I come in?" the intruder asked in a pleasant baritone.

"My dear Sir Aubrey!" said Master Sean. "Of course! Do come in!"

RANDALL GARRETT

Master Sir Aubrey Burns, Chief Forensic Sorcerer for His Grace D'Isle, came the rest of the way into the room. He stood perhaps a hair under six feet, and was massive, not fat. He had been wrestling champion for Oxford University in 1953 and '54, and had kept himself in trim ever since.

"I didn't know if anyone connected with this office would be welcome," he said. "I'm frightfully sorry about all this, Master Sean."

"Come, come," said Master Sean. "Not your fault, my dear fellow. How has your gas poisoning case come out so far?"

"The Duvals? Sad case. Two brothers and their wives having a little party. Got a little drunk out, I'm afraid. The two men brought a keg of beer up from the cellar at one point, banged it against a gas line. Cracked the line. The servants had all been told to go off to the other wing and leave them alone, you see. By the time they had drunk a good part of the keg, plus assorted other inebriating beverages, the room was full of gas. They were too blotto to notice. By the time the servants smelled the gas and took alarm, it was too late. We're bringing in the bodies for autopsies to clinch the evidence, so Dr. Ambro will have more work to do, but there's really no question about what happened. Death due to misadventure." His smile came back. "How's your case doing?"

Master Sean told him, then added: "But I wish you wouldn't call it *my* case. Your Sergeant Cougair can have it."

"That consummate ass!" Master Sir Aubrey said with a scowl. "Well, well, what's done is done. The thing to do is for us to find out who did it and clear the thing up. I wish Lord Varney were here; our chief investigator's the man for this sort of thing. Unfortunately, he's laid up in the hospital, as I told you earlier today."

Master Sean nodded. "Aye, How's he coming, by the bye?"

"Well as could be expected. He's a good investigator, but I don't think I'll go mountain climbing when I'm his age."

"No, nor I," Master Sean agreed. "Not even at my age. The African elephants may have crossed the Alps with Hannibal, but Irish elephants like meself stay on level ground."

Master Sir Aubrey chuckled. "And English elephants the same."

"Elephants?" said a voice from the door. "What is it that the elephants have to do with the case?"

It was Sergeant-at-Arms Cougair Chasseur.

"Nothing whatever, sergeant," Master Sir Aubrey said coldly. "We were not discussing your case."

"No, indeed," Master Sean said smoothly. "We were discussing the case, two years ago, of the elephant theft from the Maharajah of Rajasthan in Jodhpur."

"Someone stole an elephant?" the sergeant asked in some surprise.

"Eight of them," said Master Sean. "Eight white elephants."

"My god! And how is it they were recovered?"

"They never were," Master Sean said solemnly. "They vanished utterly, without a trace."

"It seems hardly possible," Sergeant Cougair said in awe. Then his eyes narrowed and he glanced at Sir Aubrey, then back to Master Sean. "The solution is most obvious to the deductive mind. The elephants were stolen by a sorcerer. You may depend upon it."

"I wish," said Master Sir Aubrey, "that we could have assigned you the case."

"But of course," the sergeant agreed. "I dare say I should have found them easily. Elephants are very large, are they not? Not easily concealed. Well, it is of no consequence. I have a case at present to solve."

"How are you doing so far?" Master Sean asked.

"Indeed, I shall tell all," said the sergeant, "but first, is it that it is permitted that I ask the results of the autopsy? Is it that it is indeed a case of poisoning?"

"It is," said Master Sean, and proceeded to give the results of his labors.

Sergeant Cougair scowled. "Then it is indeed murder. No bottle or paper or box that could have contained the poison has been found. It has disappeared as if by—" his narrowed eyes glanced covertly at Master Sean, "—as if by magic."

He let his eyes relax and looked down at his hands. "It is sad that we do not know what the poison was."

"I'm working on it," said Master Sean dryly.

"Most of a certainty," the sergeant said agreeably. "Now, as I promised, I shall tell you how we have progressed ourselves.

"We have thus far found no motive whatever. The twenty-two customers who were in the establishment have been released to their business or homes, but forbidden to leave the city. I have a list of them here, should you care to peruse it. The two waiters and the barman we are keeping for a while, since it is apparent that it is more likely that one of them poisoned the drink than any other. Equally, we have apprehended

RANDALL GARRETT

for questioning the two waiters who were on duty before the changing of the shift at four of the clock. We are still looking for the barman; he is a bachelor and has not yet returned home.

"We have questioned the Goodman Jorj Veblin, who is the 'Son' of Veblin & Son, and he has deposed that the Senior Captain Vandermeer has appeared at his establishment every Tuesday for the past three months with a prescription from the Reverend Father Pierre St. Armand, Healer, for a week's supply of the medicine.

"We spoke to the Father Pierre, a venerable old gentlemen, who deposes that the said Senior Captain Vandermeer did, indeed, suffer from the malaria, as you conjectured. He appears to have obtained this disease while serving with the Imperial Leion in the Duchy of Mechicoe, upon the northern continent of the New World, New England."

Master Sean sighed. He needed no one to tell him that Mechicoe was in New England, nor that the New England was the northern continent of the western hemisphere. Next the sergeant would be explaining that the square of seven was forty-nine.

There was a short silence, broken at last by Master Sir Aubrey. "Well? What else?"

The sergeant spread his hands and shrugged. "Alas! I greatly fear me, Master Sorcerer, that that is all the information we have obtained so far."

"Who benefits by his death?" Master Sean asked.

"So far as we have determined, his wife only. He has no children of record. But there was no woman in the barroom during that time."

"She might have disguised herself," said the Irish sorcerer.

"It is possible, but we have a description of her. She is young—not yet thirty—with very long black hair, very tanned skin, and dark eyes. She is adjudged very beautiful, with a slim waist and a full figure— a *very* full figure. Such a one would be difficult to conceal; it has been a warm day, so she could not have worn a cloak without attracting attention. Still, we shall, of course, check her every move during the afternoon. She is reported to be shopping. If so, we can find out where and at what times, do you comprehend."

"She might have paid someone to do it for her," Master Sean pointed out.

"Again, it is possible, but it has been my experience that a paid assassin does not poison his victims. The knife, the club, the pistol are his tools. Or, for some of the more clever, the accidental-seeming death. Poison is more the tool of the amateur."

Master Sean had to admit to himself that, for once, Sergeant Cougair was very likely right.

"The problem is," Sergeant Cougair continued, "that *anyone* could have done it. Distract a man's attention but for a few seconds, and the drink is poisoned. Our sole hope, I fear me much, is to find the poison container, for which we are even now searching diligently." He looked at his wristwatch. "I go now to search out the whereabouts of Cambray, the missing barman. It was, after all, he who mixed the deceased his drink, and perhaps he has information for us. With God, my sirs." And he left.

Master Sean stared at the door that had closed behind the sergeant for two full seconds before he said: "Now let me see. Cambray, the barman, poisons Vandermeer, goes off duty, drops the poison container into the Seine, takes the 4:22 to Bordeaux, and can be in Spain in the morning, safely away from extradition. But *he* may merely be able to give information, while *I* am a suspect. I admire his reasoning powers for their depth and complexity. No merely intelligent man could reason in that manner."

"I told you he was a consummate ass," said Master Sir Aubrey.

V.

Sergeant Cougair had been right about another thing: The late senior captain's wife was beautiful, and had a *very* lush figure. In addition, she stood no more than five feet tall. No, Master Sean thought, it would not be possible for her to go into a bar and not be noticed, no matter what she was wearing.

There was another possibility, however. Did the woman have the Talent? If so, there were several ways she could have gone into that bar without attracting attention. The Tarnhelm Effect, for one. It did not, as popularly supposed, render a person invisible; it was merely a specialized form of avoidance spell. Anyone using the Tarnhelm Effect remained unnoticed because no one else looked in that direction; they would avoid the person with their eyes; they would look anywhere except at that person.

Mary Vandermeer had come in with three other people to identify the

RANDALL GARRETT

body: the late senior captain's manservant, Humfrey; the pharmacist, Jorj Veblin; and the Healer, Father Pierre. Humfrey was an old Vandermeer family retainer; he had helped bring up the child who was to become Senior Captain Andray. His old face was lined with worry wrinkles, as though the job had been far from easy.

Master Pharmacist Jorj Veblin was a competent looking man in his early thirties, with regular, rather pleasant features and mousy brown hair which he brushed straight back and kept cut somewhat shorter than the current style.

Father Pierre looked, as the cant phrase had it, "ninety years older than Methuselah." He was taller than Master Sean, but very thin and frail looking. His face had few wrinkles, and a benign smile, but the skin was tightly drawn over the facial bones, and the few white hairs on his skull looked like an aura in the gaslight.

One by one, separately, they were led into the room where the de l man lay. One by one, separately, they identified him as Andray Vand meer.

Old Humfrey had tears in his eyes. "Bad, very bad. The captain had a good many years in him yet, he did."

Goodwife Mary choked up and could say nothing but: "That's him. That's Andray."

Master Jorj looked both grim and sad. "Yes, that's Captain Andray. Poor fellow." He shook his head sadly.

Father Pierre looked long and carefully. "Yes, that's poor Andray," he said at last. Then, turning to Master Sean: "Has he been given the last rites?"

"He has not, Father," the sorcerer said. "And there is no thaumaturgical reason why he should not be given them. We have all the evidence of that kind we need."

Senior Captain Andray Vandermeer was given the last rites of Holy Mother Church. The wife, the valet, the pharamacist, and two Armsmen were present at the ceremony. Master Sean and Master Sir Aubrey were in another room, constructing a subtle trap.

Perhaps "subtle" isn't exactly the right word, but no other will quite do. In form, it was about as subtle as coming up behind a person who is pretending deafness and shouting "*Boo!*" in his ear. But in practice, it was such that only one person would be aware that anything out of the ordinary had happened, and then only if that person possessed the Talent.

The spell itself is simple and harmless. As Master Sean had once put it to Lord Darcy: "Imagine a room full of people, each one with a different kind of noisemaker—a rattle, a drum, a horn, a ball of stiff paper to crackle, a hissing though the teeth, every sort of distracting noise you can imagine. What would you do if you had to think?"

"Put my fingers in my ears, I should imagine," Lord Darcy had replied.

"Exactly, me lord. And there's not a Talented person alive who wouldn't do the psychic equivalent of just that, if that distraction spell were cast on him. A person with little or no Talent just becomes distracted and loses his train of thought. He hasn't the least notion that it came from outside his own mind. A person with a good but untrained Talent will recognize the spell for what it is, but won't know what to do about it. A Person with a trained Talent will block it instantly."

"Can't the response be feigned?" his lordship had asked.

"It can, me lord, but only after the initial blocking. In order to think out a lie, a false reaction, you need at least a fraction of a second of peace. Which you can't get without putting up the block, d'ye see."

"How could that be detected by a sorcerer who's putting out all that mind noise?" Lord Darcy had wanted to know.

"He couldn't," Master Sean had explained. "That's why it takes two to spring the trap. One to say *Boo!* and the other to see if the victim jumps."

This time, Master Sir Aubrey would cast the quick-shock spell, and Master Sean would watch the victims.

"Fat lot of good it did us," Master Sir Aubrey said half an hour later. "I noticed no reaction from any of the three." They had not tested Father Pierre; there was no question about a Healer having the Talent.

"Master Jorj and Goodman Humfrey haven't got a trace of the Talent, Master Sean said. "The young woman has a definite touch of it, but it's undisciplined and untrained. If there's any magic involved in this killing, we haven't uncovered it, and we haven't found a magician, either."

Master Sir Aubrey looked at the wall clock. "Fifteen of nine. You should have been in Rouen by now."

Master Sean scowled. "And now I can just twiddle my thumbs. There's nothing left for me to do. Except think. I wish I could remember what there is about that poison. . . ."

"See here, old friend," said Master Sir Aubrey, running a palm over his smooth pate, "we've got a room upstairs, with bed and bath, for important visitors. You are a visitor, and you are the Chief Forensic Sorcerer for Normandy. You are, *ergo et ipso facto*, qualified to use that room. A good shower will make you feel better. Or have a tub, if you like."

"My dear Sir Aubrey," said Master Sean with a smile wreathing his face, "you have made yourself a deal. Let's see this room."

The big sorcerer led him up a flight of stairs to a narrow corridor on the upper story. He took a key from his key ring and unlocked a door.

The room was small, but comfortable, like those of a good country inn, with the added attraction of an adjoining bath.

"I couldn't ask for better," Master Sean said. "Fortunately, I always carry a change of underclothes in me carpetbag."

He put his symbol-decorated carpetbag on the bed, opened it, and rummaged around until he came up with the underclothes. "Socks? Socks? Ah, yes, here they are."

Master Sir Aubrey was looking at the bag, using more senses than just his eyes. "Interesting anti-tampering spell you've got on your bag," he said. "Don't think I've ever come across one with quite those frequencies and textures. What's the effect, if I may ask? I detect the paralysis component, but . . . hmmm . . ."

"A little invention of me own," said Master Sean, a bit smugly. "Anybody opens it but meself, he immediately closes it again, then sits down next to it and does nothing. He's in a semi-paralytic trance, d'ye see. If anybody else comes along before I get there, the man who tried to open me bag will jump up and down and gibber like a monkey. That attracts attention. Anyone seeing a fellow behave like that in the vicinity of a sorcerer's bag will know immediately there's something wrong."

Master Sir Aubrey laughed. "I *like* it! I won't ask you for the specs on the spell; I'll try to work out one of my own."

"Be glad to give 'em to you," Master Sean said.

"No, no; more fun to work it out myself."

"Whatever you say. Look, I'll freshen meself up, and I'll see you in, say, half an hour. Is there somewhere we can get a bite to eat? I haven't had a morsel since noon."

"Do you like German food?"

"With German beer?"

"With German beer."

"Love it."

"Good," said Master Sir Aubrey. "I know a fine place, I'll be waiting downstairs. Here's the key to this room. You can leave your bag here, if you like. Just shove it under the bed and lock the door. I'll post notice that the room is yours, and nobody but a fool would disturb it."

"Right," said Master Sean. "I'll see you at—say, twenty past nine?"

VI.

The *Kölnerschnitzel* at Hochstetter's was delicious, and the Westphalian beer was cool and tangy. In fact, the beer was so good that, after packing away the *Kölnerschnitzel*, the two magicians had another stein.

"Ahhh!" said Master Sean, patting himself three inches below his solar plexus. "That's just what I needed. I feel so good that I'm not even angry with Sergeant Cougair any more."

"Speaking of whom," said Master Sir Aubrey, "the sergeant came into the office while you were bathing. I didn't want to bother you with anything until you'd eaten."

"Oh? Is it something that should bother me?" Master Sean asked.

"Not particularly. More data. I just didn't want you to be trying to piece everything together until you had a cold beer in your hand and enough fuel inside you to power your brain."

"I see. What is it?"

"He finally found the barman who went off duty at four this afternoon. Fellow named Cambray. He knew the deceased by sight and name. Seems the captain came in every week, had a few drinks and left."

Master Sean nodded. "I see. Came in every week to get his prescription filled and then had a few snorts at the bar before going home."

"Precisely. Regular as clockwork, it seems. Now, here's the peculiar thing: he always ordered the same drink, which is not peculiar in itself, but what he drank was a Mechicain liqueur called *Popocotapetl*. It's not much called for, and it's rather expensive, since it's imported from across the Atlantic."

Master Sean nodded. "I've tasted it. A former pupil of mine, Master Lord John Quetzal, gave me a few drinks from a bottle his father, the Duke of Mechicoe, sent him. It's a semi-sweet liqueur made from some cactus, I think."

"This wasn't semi-sweet," said Master Sir Aubrey.

RANDALL GARRETT

"No. Sergeant Cougair impounded the bottle—the only bottle they had, by the way—and tasted it, the idiot. He reports that the drop on his fingertip was as bitter as potash."

Suddenly several things came together in Master Sean's mind. "*Coyotl* weed!" he snapped.

The other sorcerer blinked. "What?"

"*Coyotl* weed," the Irish sorcerer said more calmly. "I was told about it by Lord John Quetzal while he was studying forensic sorcery under me. It's an alkaloid extract of the weed, actually. Been used as a poison in Mechicoe for centuries. Lord John Quetzal said it has no pharmaceutical uses, at all. I doubt if we could get a sample of the stuff to do a similarity analysis with. The Mechicains used to use it for poisoning rats, but since they've got trained sorcerers now to handle that problem, the stuff has been declared illegal except for research purposes. So someone put it in the bottle of *Popocotapetl*, eh?"

"Yes, and that makes the whole case crazier than ever," Master Sir Aubrey said. "It could have been put in there *any* time previous to the murder—days before, even. And it would have killed anybody who drank it. *Anybody*, not just Captain Andray Vandermeer."

Master Sean said: "We might be dealing with a psychotic individual. Or, possibly, someone who wants to ruin the reputation of the International Bar or the Cosmopolitain Hotel. Your Sergeant Cougair has his work cut out for him."

"Oh, the sergeant has his theories," Master Sir Aubrey said dryly. "You see, since the barman and waiters agree that nobody came behind the bar except for themselves, then whoever put the poison in the bottle must have been invisible. According to the sergeant, I mean. And that means a sorcerer, and that means you."

"*Me?*" Master Sean managed to keep his voice under control—barely.

" 'Least Likely Person Theory,' he calls it," the big magician continued. "But I think it's more than that. This case really has him baffled. He can't understand what happened—can't see how the trick was done. The more data he comes up with, the more mysterious it gets, and the more confused *he* gets. Not his type of case, really."

"What *is* his type of case?" Master Sean asked. "Nursery riddles?"

"No." Master Sir Aubrey chuckled. "Nothing that complicated, Street killings, bar killings, brawls, that sort of thing. The knife drawn in anger, the sudden smash of a club. Such things are usually pretty much open-

and-shut. But this one is beyond his mental equipment. And instead of admitting it, he's trying to bull it through. If it weren't for your presence there, he'd probably have already rushed off and arrested the widow as the *most* likely suspect."

"What's my presence got to do with it?" Master Sean said irritatedly.

"To him," said the English sorcerer, "if there's no obvious answer at hand, then there's sorcery afoot. And you're the sorcerer. He still can't find that bottle of poison, and he thinks you magicked it away somehow."

With great care, Master Sean lifted his beer stein and drained it slowly without stopping. He put it down. "I will not," he said calmly, "let that blithering jackass upset me digestion. Let's get back to the station and see what new developments have come about, if any."

They paid their bill and strolled leisurely the quarter mile back to the Armsmen's station, discussing several subjects that had nothing to do with the murder case.

It was twenty-five of eleven when they went into Master Aubrey's office.

Lord Darcy was waiting for them.

VII.

Lord Darcy, Chief Investigator for His Royal Highness, Richard, Duke of Normandy, looked up from the book he was reading and took his pipe from his mouth. "I trust you gentlemen had a good meal," he said in a mild voice.

"Me lord!" Master Sean's voice showed a touch of surprise. "When did you get in?"

"Fifteen minutes ago, my dear Sean," said Lord Darcy, with a wry smile on his handsome face. "When you informed me that the Parisian authorities had you in open arrest, I took the next train east. We have to have that evidence on the Zellerman-Blair case in court on the morrow. How are you, Master Sir Aubrey?"

"As well as could be expected, my lord. And you?"

"Well, but impatient. Whom do I see to get Master Sean released on his own recognizance?"

"Justice Duprey keeps late hours. When he hears Master Sean's side of the case, against Sergeant Cougair's, he'll release Sean on the instant.

RANDALL GARRETT

But *you'll* have to bring the motion; *I* can't, naturally, since I'd be going against the . . ."

"I understand," Lord Darcy cut in. "Nor could Master Sean without representation. Very well; we'll have this Cougair and Master Sean up before the Justice as soon as possible. The problem is that nobody around here has seen Sergeant Cougair for the past hour, and nobody seems to know where he is. Naturally, he'll have to appear to tell his side of the story or the Justice won't hear it."

"Oh, I'm sure he's around somewhere," Master Sir Aubrey said. "Wait a little. When's your train back to Rouen?"

"There's a slow one at two-five," Lord Darcy said. "We'll have to be on it. The express doesn't leave until five-twenty, and it will get us in very late for a six o'clock court.

"However, I'm sure we can make it. Would it be asking too much for you two to tell me what this farrago is all about?"

"Aye," said a voice from the door." 'Tis a story Ah'd like tae be hearing', masel'!"

The tall, lean, well-muscled man in the doorway looked rumpled. His black and silver uniform was neat enough, but his thick thatch of dark, curly hair looked as if it hadn't seen a comb for weeks, his firm, dimpled jaw was bluely unshaven, and his deep-set, piercing blue eyes looked rather bloodshot beneath their shaggy brows.

All three of the men in the room immediately recognized Darryl Mac Robert, Chief Master-at-Arms for the City of Paris. They gave him a ragged chorus of: "Good evening, Chief Darryl."

Chief Darryl grinned but shook his head. "Nae, 'tisna that. Ah was oop a' the nicht last nicht wi' the Pemberton robbery; nae sleep this morning because o' the Neinboller swindlin' case; oop a' the afternoon wi' the Duval gassing. Ah try tae get soom sleep o' the evening, and Ah find that a routine death in a bar has snowballed as it if were rollin' down the Matterhorn. Nae, lads, 'tis nae a guid evenin'. But 'tis guid tae see ye lairdship."

"I quite sympathize with you," said Lord Darcy. "Well, do come in and sit down, my dear chief. Master Sean, would you begin at the beginning and proceed therefrom to the present?"

"Glad to, me lord."

The telling of it took nearly three quarters of an hour, but every detail, every nuance had been told when Master Sean was through. When it was over, Lord Darcy thoughtfully smoked his pipe in silence. Chief Darryl looked grim. "It looks," he said, "as if we hae us a madman loose i' the City."

Lord Darcy took his pipestem from his mouth, "I disagree, Chief Darryl. This was carefully planned and carefully executed murder aimed solely at one man: Senior Captain Andray Vandermeer."

"D'ye ken who did it, then?"

"The evidence we have points in one direction. If my theory is correct, we only need a little more data, and the thing will be quite clear."

"Then let's *get* it, mon! Ah need the sleep!"

"Well, it's hardly my place to tell your Sergeant Cougair how to conduct his own case," Lord Darcy replied carefully.

"As o' this moment, Ah'm takin' charge o' the case masel'," Chief Darryl said firmly. He looked at Master Sean. "And ye'll nae have to take Chasseur before the Justice. He'll drop the charges."

"I'm afraid, however," Lord Darcy said, "that we shall have to trouble the Justice after all. We need two search warrants."

"Ah'll get 'em. For what places?"

"One for the residence of the late Captain Andray, and another for the pharmacy of Veblin & Son."

Chief Darryl was making notes on a pad he had taken from his uniform belt. "Wha' are we tae search for, yer lairdship?"

"A bottle of *Popocotapetl* that hasn't been opened, and a bottle of poison that has."

Chief Darryl murmured to himself as he wrote. "Liqueur at Andray's home. Poison at pharmacy."

"No, no!" his lordship said sharply. "There will undoubtedly be a few bottles of liqueur at Andray's home, and there are poisons galore in any pharmacy. No, it's the other way round; liqueur at pharmacy, poison at Andray's."

"Verra well, me laird. Anything else?"

"Find out who sold the *Popocotapetl* to the International Bar, and pick him up. I want the man who made the delivery, not the merchant, unless they are one and the same."

"Och, aye. Anything else?"

"One more thing. Bring in Mary Vandermeer, Jorj Veblin, and following Sergeant Cougair's theory of the Least Likely Suspect, I fear you must bring in Father Pierre."

"Surely *he* couldn't have had anything to do with this murder, me lord!" Master Sean said in astonishment.

"I assure you, my dear Sean," Lord Darcy said solemnly, "that without Father Pierre's Talent, this murder could never have happened—at least, not in this way."

"Ah'll get some men on it," Chief Darryl said heavily.

VIII.

Midnight. Three men stood in the thaumaturgical laboratory at Armsmen's Headquarters.

Chief Darryl put two bottles on the lab table. "There they are, just as ye said, yer lairdship. Item—" he picked up a pint-sized, stoppered brown glass bottle, "—a bottle found in a closet in Goodwife Mary Vandermeer's bedroom. Three-quarters empty, it is." He put it down and picked up the other, a tall quart bottle full of golden yellow liquid. "Item, a bottle of *Popocotapetl*, seal unbroken." He put it down. "And we got the woman and Veblin in holdin' cells. You wanted to see Father Pierre and the spirits man?"

"Not just yet. I want to be sure that what is in that brown bottle is what killed Vandermeer. Will you make a similarity analysis, Master Sean?"

"Aye, me lord, I'll have to go up and get me bag."

"No need," said Master Sir Aubrey, coming in through the door. He held Master Sean's symbol-decorated carpetbag in one hand. "I took the liberty of fetching it myself."

"Ah, fine. Thank you. If ye'll excuse me, gentlemen, I'll get about me work."

Lord Darcy and Master Sir Aubrey followed Chief Darryl out of the lab, down the hall, and into the chief's office.

"Sit ye doon, gentle sirs," he said with a wave toward a couple of chairs. He planted himself firmly behind his desk. "Ah'd like tae know, ma laird, why ye eliminated the barmen as suspects, if ye dinna mind."

"Because the bottle itself was poisoned," Lord Darcy said promptly. "If the barman wants to poison a customer, he can put the stuff in just one drink. He wouldn't have to poison a whole bottle of good liquor."

"But suppose he were a madman who didn't care whom he killed?"

Master Sir Aubrey asked. "If he wanted to kill a lot of people, wouldn't poisoning a bottle be easiest?"

"Possibly. But in that case, he'd poison a bottle of brandy or ouiskie, something that was called for regularly, not a rare liqueur that's little called for and very expensive. And certainly he would have chosen another poison than the *coyotl* weed extract. No, that poison was intended for Vandermeer and none other. He was the only customer they had who drank *Popocotapetl*."

"But, ma laird," the chief objected, "anyone could ha' coom intae the International and ordered the stuff. Some Mechicain micht hae come in, for instance."

"True," Lord Darcy said, "but he would be in very little danger of being poisoned. Consider: one usually sips a semi-sweet liqueur, especially an expensive one. One doesn't just knock it back against the tonsils as if it were cheap apple brandy. One sip of that stuff, and the customer would spit it out and complain loudly to the barman. It's a very bitter substance."

There was a pause. Suddenly, Master Sir Aubrey said: "Then why, in God's name, did *Vandermeer* drink it?"

"Aha! That's precisely the question I asked myself," said Lord Darcy. "Why should—"

He was interrupted by the entrance of Master Sean. "No doubt about it, me laird," he said firmly, "that's the stuff that killed the captain."

"Excellent. We progress. Chief Darryl, will you have one of your men bring in Father Pierre?"

Father Pierre, looking benign but somewhat puzzled, was led in by a uniformed Armsman a minute later. Chief Darryl said: "Ah'm sorry to have inconvenienced ye, Reverend Sir, but we hae a most heinous crime tae clear oop."

"Oh, that's all right, I assure you, Chief Darryl," the old priest said. "I am happy to be of any assistance that I may."

Master Sean was mildly pleased to hear that the priest's Parisian accent had been smoothed and made less harsh by time, travel, and education.

"Verra well, Reverend Sir. Ah thank you. Lord Darcy here would like tae ask ye a question or two."

"Of course." Father Pierre turned his soft eyes on the chief investigator. "What is it, my lord?"

"You were treating the late Captain Andray for malaria, I believe,

88   RANDALL GARRETT

Father?" Lord Darcy asked.

"Yes, I was, my lord."

"Do you know where he contracted the disease?"

"In Mechicoe, while he was serving with the Imperial Legion."

"And you were treating him with a herbal prescription?"

"Yes, my lord. Tincture of Cinchona. It is a specific for the disease."

"How did you get him to take it regularly, Father? It's rather bitter drug, is it not?"

"Oh, yes. Very bitter." The priest glanced at Master Sean and Master Sir Aubrey. "You sorcerers are acquainted with the spell, I am sure. It's a matter of shifting modes of sensory perception."

"Aye," said Master Sean. "I was talking to a man a few hours ago who had had this sense of smell subtly altered so that an otherwise nauseous smell would smell sweet to him."

"Just so." Father Pierre looked back at Lord Darcy. "I cast a similar spell over the captain, so that the bitterness would register as sweetness, you see. Mixed with a little lemon juice and water, a spoonful of the tincture became quite a pleasant drink—to him."

"Would that apply to just the tincture, or to anything bitter?" Lord Darcy asked.

"Oh, anything that was bitter would taste sweet to him. No getting around that. I'd warned him of it. He was not to accept anything as being sweet unless he knew for a fact that it *was* sweet, unless he knew that it actually contained sugar or honey. He was a very careful man, was Captain Andray."

"A lesson one learns in the Legion," murmured Lord Darcy. "Thank you very much, Father. I think that's all for now. Thank you again."

When the Healer had gone, Lord Darcy looked at the others. "You see? Of all the many people who might have come into that bar and ordered *Popocotapetl*, only Captain Andray Vandermeer would have sat there and quietly sipped that bitter potion without raising a fuss. He knew the liqueur was supposed to be sweet, and never noticed the *coyotl* extract."

"But why use a bitter poison like that?" Chief Carryl asked. "Wouldna it ha' been easier to use something more palatable?"

Lord Darcy shook his head. "That poison has one very important quality. Master Sean, you said it was used as a rat poison. Why?"

"Because it's painless," Master Sean said. "It puts the victim quietly to sleep before it kills. Rats are pretty smart creatures; if they know a bait is poisoned, they'll avoid it, and they know if it kills a few friends in agony. For some reason, the bitter taste don't bother 'em if the stuff is mixed with bran and a goodly dollop of sugar-cane syrup."

"And how did the poison get i' the bottle i' the first place?" the Chief Master-at-Arms asked.

"That worried me, too, for a few moments," Lord Darcy admitted. "How could an unauthorized person get behind the bar, poison a bottle of expensive liqueur, and leave, without being seen?" The International never closes, so it couldn't have been a burglary job. Otherwise, then, the bottle, when it was brought into the bar, *was already poisoned!*" He waited while they absorbed that, then said, "Chief, will you have the liquor man brought in?"

The man who delivered potable spirits to the International Bar was a rotund, red-faced man named Baker who looked as though he smiled a lot when he was not caught up in the hands of the law.

"Master Sean," Lord Darcy whispered to the sorcerer, "would you go fetch that bottle of *Popocotapetl?*"

Master Sean nodded and left without a word.

Again Chief Darryl went through the preliminaries and then turned the questioning over to Lord Darcy.

"Goodman Baker," his lordship began, "I understand you make deliveries of spirits regularly to the Cosmopolitain Hotel."

"That I do, my lord." Baker spoke Anglo-French with as pronounced an English accent as Lord Darcy did, but it was pure middle class London.

"To what other establishments do you deliver besides the International Bar?"

"Well, my lord, of the usual drinkin' spirits, that's the only place."

"You say 'the usual drinking spirits.' What other kind do you deal in?"

"Well, there's the high-proof clear spirits, what I delivers to the pharmacy of Veblin & Son. They uses 'em to make medicines, d'yer see. And they also takes the special medicinal brandy."

"I thought as much. Now, I want you to think hard— *very* hard—about my next question. Did anyone at Veblin & Son order anything out of the ordinary in the past few months?"

"Don't have to think too hard on that one, yer lordship," Baker said with a self-satisfied air. "He bought—young Master Jorj, that is—he bought a quart of that Mechicain stuff, the Popey-cott-petal. Very dear it is, yer lordship, and as we being the only importers of it in Paris, I remembered his buying of it."

"And when was this?" Lord Darcy asked.

"Four weeks ago Friday last."

"And when was the last time you made a delivery to Veblin & Son?"

"Friday last."

"How very gratifying," Lord Darcy murmured with a pleased smile. "And did you deliver a bottle of *Popocotapetl* to the International Bar on that day?"

"I did, my lord. I suppose they told you that."

"As a matter of fact, they did not. I deduced it. I shall make a further deduction: that you always and invariably make your deliveries to Veblin & Son *before* you make your deliveries to the International."

"Why, that's true as Gospel, my lord! I always park my delivery wagon to the rear of the hotel and my helper holds the horses while I takes the deliveries in on a hand cart. From the rear door, the first place you comes to is the pharmacy, so I makes my delivery there first."

"Bringing your hand cart in with you, I presume?"

"Oh, indeed, my lord. Leave it out in the corridor, and likely there'd be a bottle or two missing when I came out."

"And you carry the delivery into the rear of the pharmacy, leaving the hand cart in the front room?"

"I do. Master Jorj keeps an eye on it for me. He'd not steal from it himself, nor let anyone else do so."

"I dare say not," Lord Darcy agreed. "Then you go on to the International and deliver their orders."

"I do, my lord."

By this time, Master Sean had returned with the bottle of *Popocotapetl*. Lord Darcy extended a hand, and the little Irish sorcerer handed him the bottle. Lord Darcy put it on the desk in front of Baker. "Is this the bottle you sold to Master Jorj Veblin four weeks ago Friday last?"

Baker looked at the bottle. "Well, now, I couldn't swear as to that, my lord. Them bottles are all pretty much alike, and . . ." Suddenly he picked up the bottle and looked more closely at it. "Wait a minute, my lord. This ain't the bottle I sold him."

"How do you know?"

Baker pointed at some small figures written on the label. "The date's wrong, my lord. This is from the shipment we received from Mechicoe two weeks ago."

"That's a stroke of luck!" said Lord Darcy. "Master Sean, bring in the bottle we found in the bar."

Master Sean returned within a minute, bearing the poisoned bottle. Lord Darcy took it, and without letting it out of his hands, showed the label to Baker. "What about this bottle?"

"Well now, I can't positively identify it as being the one I sold to Master Jorj, but it's got the proper date on it."

"Very well. Thank you very much for you help, Goodman. You may go home now."

When Baker had gone, Lord Darcy picked up his pipe and lighter, and puffed the pipe alight before speaking. "And there you have it, gentlemen. I daresay, Chief Darryl, that a little probing into the activities of Mary Vandermeer and Jorj Veblin over the past several months will reveal a greater intimacy between them than has heretofore been suspected. Vandermeer was much older than his wife, and it may be that she decided to dispose of him in favor of a younger man—Veblin, to be exact. If the captain was like most Legion officers, he left her a small, but comfortable, fortune."

"I'm afraid I don't quite see the whole picture," said Master Sir Aubrey. "Exactly what happened?"

"Very well. Some years ago Captain Andray married his present wife—rather, widow—who was a woman of Mechicain descent. He probably married her over there. At any rate, he brought her with him when he retired. And she brought with her a bottle of *coyotl* extract. We can't be certain why, at this time; perhaps she was planning his murder even then.

"Exactly how she met Veblin, and how they made their arrangements, is something you'll have to get your men to dig out, Chief Darryl, but that's routine legwork."

"But how did ye know 'twas them?"

"Who else knew that he was under a Healer's spell that would make bitter things taste sweet? He undoubtedly told his wife, and the pharmacist would certainly guess it.

"At any rate, she gave Veblin the poison. She knew of the captain's taste for *Popocotapetl*, and so informed Veblin. Veblin thereupon bought a bottle of the stuff, laced it with poison, and waited until Baker delivered a fresh bottle to the International Bar. Then, while Baker was unloading the medicinal spirits in the back room, Veblin switched bottles so that the poisoned bottle was delivered to the bar. Then it was simply a matter of waiting until the following Tuesday—today—" he glanced at the clock. "Yesterday," he corrected himself, "the captain comes in, orders his drink as usual, and that's that."

"But why did he keep the good bottle after the switch?" Master Sean asked. "Why not get rid of it?"

"Because he knew that eventually the investigators would find the poison in the bottle and check with the importers. They would inform us, as they did, that he had bought a bottle. It was his intention to say, 'Oh, yes, I did, and I still have it.' He didn't know that the importers of spirits put the date on the goods when they are received."

"It seems tae me," said Chief Darryl, "that a pharmacist would have plenty of poisons on hand withoot having' tae use a special import frae Mechicoe."

"That's just the point," said Lord Darcy. "If he had used any of the normal pharmaceuticals, any competent forensic sorcerer could have identified whatever poison he used, which would increase his chances of being found out. He was hoping that there wouldn't be a man in Europe who could identify *coyotl* extract. Any other questions?"

Chief Darryl thought for a moment, then shook his head. "That aboot covers it, ma laird. Since we know how it was done and who did it, the rest is simple." He looked up at the clock on the wall. "Where the De'il is Sergeant Cougair? Ah hae a few words to say to that wee mon."

"Why, as to that," Master Sir Aubrey said, almost offhandedly, "the last time I saw him he was in the upstairs bedroom."

Chief Darryl shot to his feet. "What the hell is he doin' oop there?"

"Sitting. Just sitting."

"Armsman Stefan!" bellowed the Chief Master-at-Arms. The door to the corridor popped open, and a Man-at-Arms stuck his head in.

"But yes, my chief?"

"Go oop the stair tae the visitor's bedroom and fetch me Sergeant Cougair Chasseur."

"But yes, my chief!" The door closed.

Master Sean looked at Master Sir Aubrey. Master Sir Aubrey looked at the ceiling. Lord Darcy looked puzzled.

Man-at-Arms Stefan returned. It was obvious from the contortions of his face that he was attempting to control a giggle. "My chief, it is apparent that the Sergeant Cougair has taken leave of his senses. When one speaks to him, he leaps up and down and gibbers like a monkey."

"He does?" Chief Darryl headed toward the door. "We'll see aboot this. Coom wi' me!"

In half a minute, there were loud voices and laughter coming down the stairwell.

Master Sean sighed and opened his carpetbag. He took from it a small, four inch wand made from a twig of the hyssop plant. "I'll go up and remove the spell," he said. "You didn't by any chance tell him the poison bottle was in me carpetbag, did you, Master Sir Aubrey?"

"Of course not," the sorcerer said indignantly. "Quite the contrary. I absolutely forbade him to look there at all."

Master Sean left. Lord Darcy said nothing; he had the Zellerman-Blair case to worry about, and he had no wish to meddle in the affairs of wizards.

RANDALL GARRETT

The Strange Children

by Elisabeth Sanxay Holding

Marjorie Smith sat up very straight in the car. When they swerved sharply round a corner, it sent her lurching against the side wall; when they made a sudden stop, it jerked her forward.

And it seemed to her that this was as it should be. Her blue corduroy raincoat was bulky, the collar rubbed her chin, and to her stern young conscience, this was right. Right and fitting to be uncomfortable, when you were doing something that you knew was wrong.

It *is* wrong, she told herself. I've always said I'd never do it. Never go to sit with children I hadn't met. It's not fair to them, or to yourself. If anything goes wrong, if they wake up, and call, it's a shock for them to see a complete stranger. And you can't do your best for them, if you don't know them at all.

But this Mrs. Jepson had been so insistent on the telephone, a few hours ago. Do *please* help us out, Miss Smith! We're more or less obliged to go to this thing at the country club; we engaged a table there, and invited these people to a late supper ages ago. And Katie, the maid who's been with us for years, was suddenly called away to a sick sister. Do, please, manage it somehow, Miss Smith! I've heard such wonderful things about you from Myra Williams. At half past eight?

I'd like to come earlier, to meet the children before they go to bed, Marjorie had said. But, my dear, the chauffeur's gone on an errand. I couldn't send the car for you until eight. I'll take a taxi, Marjorie had said. But, my dear, it's not *necessary!* Mrs. Jepson had cried. It's a perfect maelstrom here, without Katie. I'll have to get some sort of dinner for my husband and myself, and then we'll have to dress. . . . Really, it's not necessary. The children *never* wake up at night.

You never know when they may, though, Marjorie had said. And if there was a stranger there . . . My dear! Mrs Jepson had said, my children don't mind strangers the least bit! They're the friendliest children—almost *too* friendly, I sometimes think.

And then she had said, Miss Smith, my husband and I both realize how bothering this is for you. Being asked at the last moment, and such a bitter cold night, and not knowing us, and so on. We're going to make out a check for twenty-five dollars. . . .

No, thank you! Marjorie had said. It will be my usual rate. If I come.

Oh, well! We can argue about that later, Mrs Jepson had said. There are stacks of new books here, my dear, and magazines, and Katie's left all sorts of things in the icebox—cold chicken, and chocolate cake, and salad. . . .

Then she must have realized that she was off on the wrong track, and getting nowhere. The chauffeur says he can get this woman he knows, she had gone on. But I've seen her once, and I hate the idea of leaving the children with her. I'm quite sure she drinks, and suppose she set the place on fire, with a cigarette? That's always my great terror. Do, please, manage to come, Miss Smith, so that I won't have to get that woman.

I was a fool to say yes, Marjorie told herself. This woman who drinks might very well be just an invention of Mrs. Jepson's, to get me there. But if she wasn't an invention then I don't think much of this Mrs. Jepson. No matter how important her engagement was, to leave her little children with someone she didn't trust.

But people do things like that. You read about them in the newspapers. If I do decide to marry Johnny, and we have children of our own, I don't see how I could ever bear to leave them with anyone, unless it was Mother, or my own sister, or some old friend. . . . Because—I like children.

The car turned off the highway into a side road that seemed to plunge into a forest, black and frozen. The bare trees creaked in the wind; here and there stood a big old house, some with a light in a window, some in darkness. I suppose it's mostly a summer place, Marjorie thought. They always look rather forlorn in the winter.

Then, as they turned a corner, she saw ahead of them a bungalow, brightly lighted, trim and cheerful as a little launch in a harbor among grim old freighters. The car stopped; the chauffeur, who had not said one word, had not once turned his head, jumped out nimbly and opened the door of the car. Marjorie got out, went along the path and up the two shallow steps to the veranda. I'm glad the house is like this. It's cosy.

She rang the bell, and the door was opened almost at once by a big,

ELISABETH SANXAY HOLDING

heavy man in shirtsleeves and braces.

"Miss Smith?" he said. "I'm Jepson. Carl Jepson. This is very good of you. Very good."

His big shoulders sloped, his arms hung down in front of him, giving him a clumsy air. He was handsome, after a fashion, with butter-colored hair slick on his skull, good features, but marred by a curious expression of unhappy and almost stupid confusion. He looked at Marjorie, his light brows drawn together.

"You're very young. . . . " he said, in a loud tone.

"I'm twenty-two," she said, a little nettled at what she thought a criticism. "And I've had quite a lot of experience with children."

"Ralph, *darling!*" cried a gay, clear voice. "Let poor Miss Smith come in and get her coat off, do!"

It was the voice Marjorie had heard on the telephone that afternoon, a lovely and very persuasive voice. And Mrs. Jepson herself was like that: dark-eyed, slender, and tall, she persuaded you with a glance that she was your friend, your wellwisher, that you would be happy in her company. She wore a black dinner dress, a necklace of shining silver leaves and earrings to match, and she was charming.

"Ralph, darling, hurry up and finish dressing!" she said. "While I brief Miss Smith." She raised her arms in a gesture of shoving him away, and led Marjorie into the long, softly lit sitting room. "It's a weird little house," she said. "The children's rooms are down here, those two doors. And here's their bathroom. And here's the kitchen. You'll find lots of things in the icebox; just please take anything you like. And there's a radio, and a television, and a phonograph, and stacks of records. And don't worry about waking the children. *Nothing* bothers them. And here are books, and magazines, and cigarettes. And here's the telephone number where you can reach us, and the doctor's number. Will you be all right?"

"Yes, thank you," said Marjorie, a little stiffly. For, in her New England fashion, she found Mrs. Jepson a little too nice, too eager. "And the children's names?"

"There's Ronald; he's seven, and Jean, five. We won't be very late, Miss Smith. *Au revoir!*"

When she had gone, and the door closed after her, it was as if some fresh breeze had suddenly died, leaving the air stagnant; the little house was very still. The wind blew against the windows; an electric clock ticked, with a sort of purr; the refrigerator buzzed and whirred for a moment, and then was silent.

Ronald and Jean, Marjorie said to herself. Two little children here, in my care, and I've never seen them. If they don't wake up, I suppose I'll go home without having seen them, and they'll never know I've been here. I don't like it.

She took up a magazine, but she could not read. She was waiting. For the sound of a car going by outside, for the telephone to ring, for the icebox to start up again? For a board to creak, for a tap to drip, for a rustle, a sign? But there was only the wind, and the rain outside.

And then she heard it, a sound that should not frighten anyone: a low chuckle of laughter. It's one of the children, she thought. Still asleep, probably. And then a soft murmur, another soft laugh. She rose, and as she stood by the chair, she heard the patter of bare feet running. They're up, she thought. I'll have to see.

She went to the nearest door and turned the handle gently. But the door was locked. She tried the next one, and that, too, was locked. She knocked.

"I'm Marjorie Smith," she said. "I've come to see you. Open the door, will you?"

"No, thank you!" answered a little boy's voice, very resolute. "Go away, please."

"Go away!" echoed a little girl's voice.

"I just want to come in and say good evening—"

"No, thank you!" said the little boy. "We *never* let *anybody* come in at night, *never*."

"Just for a moment."

"Go away!" cried the little girl.

Marjorie stooped, and looked through the keyhole. The light was on in there; she could see a pink wall, a bed on which a little fairhaired girl in a blue dressing gown was sitting beside a darkhaired young man in a gray suit.

"Let me in!" she called, knocking more loudly.

"Go away!" said the little boy.

The young man in there said nothing, did not stir. I'm afraid! Marjorie thought. Who is he? What is he doing there? How did he get in? *I'm afraid*.

All right! Be afraid, then. It doesn't matter. Those children are in my care, and I'm going to get into that room. I'm going to find out who that man is. And I'm going to get rid of him."

She put on her raincoat; she fixed the front door on the latch and left it held ajar by a telephone book. Better to let the house grow chill than for her to take any chances of being shut out, away from the children.

The cold caught her by the throat, took her breath away. If only the house next door had one lighted window; if only there were some sound from the street, a car going by, a radio; if only there were someone . . .

The light from the children's room shone across the gravel path; she went close to it, and looked in. A dark little boy in a plaid dressing gown sat on the floor, hands clasped round his knees; the little girl still sat on the bed, and now the young man had his arm about her shoulders. Both the children were looking up into his face; they were listening to him.

With an effort, Marjorie pushed up the window from the bottom.

"Who are you?" she cried.

He turned his head and looked at her, with desperate, dark eyes. And then he was gone. He had not risen, or moved, but he was gone.

For a moment she held tight to the window sill, and it seemed to her that the wind went roaring through her head, so that she could see nothing, hear nothing. But the little girl's voice came to her, high and wild.

"Georgie! Georgie! Come back! Come back, Georgie!"

She climbed in over the sill; she stood in the room, dripping wet, her hair blown across her forehead.

"That's a fine way to treat me!" she said, laughing. "The very first time I come to see you, too. Making me go out in the pouring rain and climb in the window."

She had struck the right note.

"Well, you see," the little boy said. "Georgie won't stay if anybody else comes. Even Mommie. He doesn't want *any*body to see him but us."

"Katie sawed him, and she went away," said the little girl.

"Do you like him?" Marjorie asked.

They both looked at her, surprised, wondering.

"We like him the *best*," said Ronald. "He tells us stories, and he sings songs."

"And he stays here in the dark, too," said the little girl. "You go away now, and he'll come back."

"I can't go away," said Marjorie. "I promised your mommie I'd stay with you till she came home."

"We'd rather have Georgie, thank you," said Ronald.

"Some other time," said Marjorie. "I thought we'd all go out to the kitchen, and make some cocoa, have a little party."

It was nearly two hours before she could get them back to sleep. She made cocoa for them, and toast; she read to them, she played the phonograph records they wanted; she told them stories. They were, she thought, unusually attractive children, intelligent, reasonable, mannerly, and the little girl was beautiful, with great dark eyes and thick, fair hair, as fine as silk. But they were, both of them, curiously tense and excited; again and again they would turn their heads, they would look, they would listen.

"I thought it was Georgie," the little girl said.

Marjorie ignored that. She asked them no questions; she tried, in every way she could, to distract their attention from Georgie, to quiet them. When they had fallen asleep, she opened both their doors, and sat down in the living room. I got chilled when I went out, she told herself. That's why I'm so cold. The heat's not very good in this house. It's—there seems to be a draft somewhere. A very cold draft.

Almost all children invent imaginary playmates who seem absolutely real to them. When they're pretending they're one of these imaginary creatures, their voices change, and their expressions. If *they* feel absolutely sure they see one of those imaginary creatures, it might . . . Thought-transference? People can be made to believe they've seen things, and heard things. . . .

No, I did see him. I did hear him. And he—vanished. Is it my duty to tell Mrs. Jepson? Oh, how *can* I?

"Please don't be frightened," he said. "I'd very much like to come and talk to you for a few moments, but if you'd rather I didn't, I'll stay away."

The comfortable lamplit room was empty, but the voice was near.

"Where—are you?" she asked.

"I'll clear out, if you'd rather."

"*Where are you?*" she demanded, so loudly that she felt a sudden worry about waking the children.

"Well, I'm here," he said. "If you want to see me, I can fix it. But if you don't—"

She was silent for a moment, trying not to breathe so fast, so loudly.

"Yes. I do want to see you," she said.

Then he was there, standing at the other side of the table. He was

ELISABETH SANXAY HOLDING

young, and he was handsome, in a way, but his gray suit was shabby, and he looked tired to exhaustion, his dark eyes hollow.

"Who—are you?" she asked.

"My name is George Stewart," he said. "Or it was. But, you see . . . It's hard to explain. . . . You see, I was murdered five years ago."

"No!" Marjorie said. "Things like that—aren't true."

"I didn't believe things like this, myself," he said, "until it happened to me. It's—you can't think how bad it is."

"Then why do you do them? Why do you—come back?"

"Well . . . " he said, in his gentle, tired voice, "we don't 'come back,' you know. We've never been able to get away. When you've been murdered, when you die—*at the wrong time*—you're caught here in this world."

"You mean—you're alive?"

"No," he said. "Not alive. And not dead."

"I don't understand," she said curtly.

"I don't think anyone does, quite," he said. "Some of the others like me have worked out theories—"

"You mean other ghosts?" she asked, and because of the dreadful confusion within her, she spoke in a scornful, sneering tone she had never used before in her life.

"That's what you call us," he said. "I've gone to see others I've heard about, in England, Ireland, Hungary. They'd all been murdered, even though sometimes it wasn't suspected. And one woman who'd been in a castle in Ireland for four hundred years told me it was because if you're murdered, it's not the *right time* for you to die. So that you *can't* die. You can't go on to the next world."

"And what's the 'right time' to die, may I ask?"

"This woman believed it was all predestined. You're born, she thought, with a natural lifespan, whether it's one day, or ninety years, depending upon the constitution you've inherited. Your inherited constitution will determine what diseases you'll avoid, and what ones will finish you."

"What about accidents?"

"She thought they were predestined, too. And it's true that if you go to a place where there's been some great disaster, a flood, a volcanic eruption, a train wreck, anything of that sort, no ghosts have ever been heard of there. No. It's only murder that makes us—as we are. Because murder, she said, doesn't *have to* happen. Nobody is born destined to be murdered, because nobody is born obliged to become a murderer."

"So if you've been murdered, you stay on earth, and try to hurt and terrify people?"

"I've never found a genuine case of anyone's being really hurt by a ghost," he said, with a faint sigh. "If people are terrified at the sight of us, that's not our fault. We go on and on, in a sort of despair, and nobody will listen to us, nobody will help."

"Why do they want people to listen to them? What sort of help do they want?"

"We want to be killed," he said.

"But you *have* been killed!"

"No," he said. "It wasn't the right time for us to die, so we couldn't."

"And when is this 'right time' supposed to come again?"

"Any time after we're murdered," he said. "We're ready then. Our life here is finished. We're longing, every minute, to get out of this world, and on to the next one."

"Well? Can't ghosts kill themselves?"

"I don't know," he said. "But they never do. They never even try. It's—I couldn't tell you how bad—how shocking the idea seems to us. No. We wait. We feel we *must* wait. Until we're taken."

"What do you mean by 'taken'?"

"We're killed," he explained, earnest and patient. "A building collapses, there's a stroke of lightning, a fire; in the war, some of us were killed by bombs. But often it's a long time. Such a long time . . . That's why we're always looking for someone who'll be merciful enough to set us free. Even to listen to us, as you're listening to me."

"Why should the murdered people, the victims, be punished, and not the murderers?" she demanded.

"I don't know what happens to the murderers," he said. "But I'm certain that our waiting isn't meant as a punishment. I suppose—" He paused for a moment. "I suppose," he went on, "that if life is eternal, one hundred years, five hundred years, of waiting hasn't much significance. The way I see it, it's part of a plan, an order of things that we can't grasp. But . . . If you'll help me . . . If I give you the gun . . . "

"No! I couldn't! I couldn't! What happened to you, to turn you—into this?"

"Nella killed me," he said, casually.

"Nella?"

ELISABETH SANXAY HOLDING

"Mrs. Jepson."

"*What!* What are you saying?"

"I was her lover," he said. "I suppose that's the word for it. Anyhow, that autumn, five years ago, she was sure Jepson suspected what was going on, and she wanted to get rid of me. She tried to bribe me—with Jepson's money—to go away somewhere. When I wouldn't do that, she got into a panic. She believed I was going to make a scandal, ruin her, make her lose Jepson's money, her social position, everything she valued."

"Were you going to do that?"

"No," he answered, simply. "I've never been like that. Never wanted to injure anyone. But she couldn't believe that; literally *couldn't*. She thought everybody was vindictive—and dangerous. She asked me to talk things over with her, and we drove in her car up to the lake. She was very quiet and serious; more reasonable, I thought. She'd brought along some drinks in a thermos, and she poured out one for each of us. I don't know how she managed it, but mine was poisoned. I wasn't watching her, particularly. I was smoking. I was looking out at the lake, at the autumn leaves floating on it. I was starting to tell her, once more, that she needn't worry, but that I wasn't going to give up my job here, my friends, everything, and go to Seattle, as she wanted, when the pain came.

"It was—like a thread spinning up and up, round the blade of the sharpest knife. Then it was cut into ribbons, and it was over. . . . She'd got me out of the car, onto the ground, when Jepson came. I don't know what made him come, or how he knew. But he was—overwhelmed, that's the word. Sick, with horror.

"Nella was stunned, for a moment. But only for a moment. Then she had her story for him. She said she'd never imagined the stuff she gave me would be fatal. She said she'd only wanted to knock me out for a few moments, so that she could get back some foolish letters she'd written to me. I'm sure Jepson didn't believe her. But he helped her. He tied a heavy stone on my ankles and another round my neck, and together they dragged me down to the lake and into the water, where it was deep.

"I stayed there, at the bottom of the lake, for a while, two or three days. But I knew, all the time, what had happened to me. I knew I could get out when I wanted."

"But how?" Marjorie cried.

"I don't know how to explain it," he said. "It doesn't seem strange to me. I can be anywhere I want, and it's no trouble, no effort. I can be here, or not here."

"You can disappear?" she said, unsteadily. "Vanish?"

"It doesn't seem like that, to me," he said. "To me, it's simply going away, somewhere else. It's hard for me to realize that I frighten anyone. I don't eat or drink, of course, because we don't need to. Nothing in us breaks down or wears out; nothing needs building up. But I'm just what I was, five years ago; the same blood, and bones, and muscles, the same mind. I can see, I can hear, I can speak. Why am I—terrible?"

"You're not!" she said, and it was true; all her cold horror and confusion had gone. "But why do you come back here? Is it to—make them remember what they did?"

"No," he said. "I don't care about Nella any more. And I'm only sorry for Jepson. He doesn't need any reminding. He's never got over it. He's—you can see it in his face, poor devil. . . . No, I've never let him see me here. No. It's Jean. You see, she's my child."

Marjorie began to cry, and that seemed to trouble him.

"I'm sorry," he said. "But I don't know where else to turn. It won't take a moment. If I give you the gun—"

"I couldn't! I couldn't! Please don't ask me! Can't you stay here—with Jean?"

"But don't you see?" he cried. "That's the worst of it. If anything should happen to her, if she should die, she'd go on, to the next world. And I couldn't. She'd be gone, and I couldn't find her. I beg of you—!"

The wind shook and rattled the front door; a freezing blast streamed in as it opened and Jepson stood there. Marjorie's lips parted, but before she could make a sound, there was a streak of yellow light, the crack of a shot, and George Stewart fell at her feet.

"I saw the whole thing from my window," said the woman who lived across the street. "And I called up the police at once. I saw Mr. Jepson go up on the veranda and look in at the window. I saw him open the door and when he was in the room, I saw him take out his gun and fire."

"I didn't mean to," said Jepson. That was what he had said to Marjorie, over and over, before the police came.

"Sure," said the police lieutenant. "You didn't know the gun was loaded. Only how did you get rid of the body so fast? Or was there a body? Did he—"

"No, he was dead, lieutenant. There wasn't any doubt." said Jepson.

"This time," he added.

"Yes," said the woman from across the street. "I can identify the dead man. His name is George Stewart, and I used to see him here—" she paused. "A *lot*," she said, with malicious significance.

"Did you see Mrs. Jepson?"

"Yes. She got out of the car, and she went into the house right after he did."

"Mrs. Jepson, will you tell us . . . ?"

"No," said Nella Jepson. "I have nothing to tell you. I'm not obliged to give evidence against my husband."

She could not have said anything more fatal to him, and, thought Marjorie, she knew that, and intended it to be so.

"I didn't mean to," said Jepson. "I didn't think he was . . . I didn't think there was anyone here."

"Do you wish to state that you did not see this man, when you fired a shot directly at him?"

Jepson wiped his forehead with a handkerchief. His heavy face was dazed and stricken.

"I didn't know I *could* see him. . . . I've thought about him, night and day . . . I thought he was—gone."

"Come now, Mr. Jepson. Pull yourself together. Do you admit that you fired that shot?"

"Yes, I did. But I didn't think it would—do any harm."

"Why did you think that?" The police lieutenant waited. "Come now!" he said. "Why did you think it wouldn't 'do any harm' to fire a bullet in the man's back?"

Bear witness to the truth. . . . Marjorie was saying to herself. Never mind about your pride. Never mind what people will think of you. Never mind how hard it is. Mr. Jepson *can't* say it. But I can. I must.

"The man was dead before Mr. Jepson came in," she said.

"Why, he was not!" cried the woman from across the street. "I saw him, with my own eyes, standing there, talking to you!"

"He was a ghost," said Marjorie, with an effort that made her voice husky and deep.

Jepson turned to her, his blurred eyes brightening with gratitude.

"Yes!" he said. "Yes! You're—very kind. . . . "

"McGraw," said the lieutenant, "take Miss Smith home in your car."

"I'd rather stay—"

"You're not doing any good here, Miss Smith," said the lieutenant. "We'll want to ask you some questions, later on. *Will* we want to ask you questions! Perfect eyewitness testimony to a murder, plus a virtual confession—and no body to tie it to. The corpus delicti without a corpus . . . You're the one who should be able to straighten it out; but just now you're—overwrought. Drive her home, McGraw."

"Overwrought," Marjorie said to herself. Hysterical, does he mean? Or crazy? Raving? She could imagine the spiteful woman from across the street telling this story with delight. A *ghost*, that Smith girl said. *Imagine!* The story would spread through the little suburban town; perhaps it would reach the ears of people who liked her and respected her, but wouldn't want to leave her in charge of their children any more.

She could not save Jepson. His wife would not help him. He was doomed. He would go from here to a jail, if he was quiet, or a madhouse, if he insisted on the truth. She looked at him, and he smiled, and the blurred misery in his face had gone. It was as if his monstrous burden had at last been lifted, and he was at ease.

"Thank you!" he said, again.

ELISABETH SANXAY HOLDING

A Year in a Day

by Erle Stanley Gardner

1.
The Invisible Death

Of the five men who sat in that palatial room, Carl Ramsay had the gift of dramatic expression. He thought in blurbs, talked in motion picture subtitles.

The hour of midnight chimed from the expensive clock on the mantelpiece. Somewhere a cuckoo clock sounded.

"A New Day," said Carl Ramsay.

Tolliver Hemingway, multimillionaire, stirred uneasily.

"The day I am to die," he said, and forced a laugh.

Nick Searle of the *Star* scraped a match along the sole of his shoe and grunted.

"One chance in a thousand."

Inspector Hunter glowered about him, and his eyes were a challenge.

"One chance in ten thousand. One chance in a million," he said.

No one contradicted him, but Carl Ramsay of the *Clarion* uttered another subtitle.

"The Death Day Dawns," he murmured.

Arthur Swift surveyed the men in the room with curious eyes.

It was his first experience with men of this type. Inspector Harrison Hunter, forceful, driving, alert; Tolliver Hemingway, multimillionaire, suave, polished, dignified, yet somewhat nervous beneath the external polish; Nick Searle, veteran reporter of the *Star*; Carl Ramsay, of the *Clarion*, who had been aptly described as "the man with the tabloid mind"; and, himself, a young teacher of physics in the state university. It had been Searle who had called him in, to cover the case for the *Star* from a scientific angle.

Yet Swift could see nothing to cover.

The room was locked, guarded. The five men were to keep a constant vigil for twenty-four hours within that locked room. Every bit of food they were to eat during that time had been hermetically sealed in cans. It would be consumed immediately after the cans were opened. Every bit of liquid they were to drink was contained in bottles that had been sealed and certified.

The room was on a third story. The windows opened out upon magnificent grounds, landscaped, cared for, and guarded. The side of the house was perfectly blank, devoid of any projection up which a man might climb. Searchlights played about the grounds. Floodlights illuminated the side of the building. A hundred armed deputies patrolled the place.

Such precautions seemed so elaborate as to be absurd. Under ordinary circumstances they would have been. But these were not ordinary.

Six of the richest men in the city had received letters on a single day. Those letters had been uniform in their terms. The men were to signify their willingness to pay a certain sum of money, which sum varied in each instance, or they were to die.

None of the men paid the slightest attention to those letters, save to turn them over to the police.

Then I. W. Steen, the millionaire head of a publishing company which included several magazines and two newspapers, one of which was the sensational *Clarion,* received a second letter.

That letter announced the day and the hour of his death in the event he did not comply with the request. Steen turned that letter over to the police and took precautions against attack.

The precautions were in vain.

Seated in his private office, in conference with the heads of his various publications, a sickening sweet odor became noticeable in the room. Ten seconds later Steen was dead. No other occupant of the room suffered the slightest inconvenience, the slightest sensation of discomfort, although all of them noticed the peculiar odor.

Two days later C. G. Haymes received a summons through the mail. It was in the nature of an ultimatum. He was to signify his willingness to comply with the terms of the man who signed himself "Zin Zandor," or he, too, was to die.

The hour of his death was not given. But the day of the death was announced.

ERLE STANLEY GARDNER

C. G. Haymes had been frankly worried. He had placed himself in the hands of the police. They had isolated him in his home, surrounded the place with guards. He, too, had become good "copy," and the newspaper reporters who enjoyed the confidence of the administration had been permitted to cover the case. They had done it with an air of boredom. Steen's death had been due to fright, they felt; the autopsy disclosed no organic lesion. There was no chance that coincidence would repeat itself.

Yet, while the reporters were lounging about at ease, while the police cordon surrounded the place, while even the servants had been excluded, C. G. Haymes died, and the manner of his death was as the other's. A sickening sweet odor that had been noticed by the other occupants of the room, yet had not seemed to affect them in the least, a cry of anguish from the millionaire, a sudden spasm, and death.

Three of the remaining millionaires had capitulated.

They had followed the routine indicated in the letter for showing their willingness to pay. And they were paying, transmitting the money to the dreaded Zin Zandor by means which they refused to divulge. For Zin Zandor had made it apparent that any information given to the police would result in death.

Tolliver Hemingway alone of the remaining men who had been threatened refused to be cowed. He hurled forth his defiance, and the mail had brought him the information that he would meet his death on the twenty-fourth day of June.

Now midnight had struck on the twenty-third of June, and the clocks clacked off the seconds of the fatal twenty-fourth.

"Well, we might as well have a drink," said Inspector Hunter, pouring himself a stiff jolt from some of the prewar whisky the millionaire's cellars had furnished.

"None for me," said Hemingway. "I think I'll go easy on the drink. One can't tell . . . "

The inspector snorted.

"Don't be foolish. You're absolutely safe here. Every bit of food and drink in this room has been checked by two police chemists. I wouldn't even waste the time to sit here with you, only the public are in a panic over this Zandor fellow, and we've got to show them how powerless he is in the face of adequate precautions. In the meantime, our paper and handwriting experts are at work on those letters. They were all written on a Remington typewriter, and all on the same machine. The stationery has been traced to a job lot that went to one of the big stationery firms. It's a cinch."

He drained the whisky.

Carl Ramsay scribbled a sentence in a notebook, and, as he wrote, read aloud the words he jotted down for future reference.

"The Man Who Dares Not Eat," he intoned. "We'll run a picture over that."

Nick Searle snorted.

"You've got a cinch with that yellow journal of yours, Ramsay. Wish I had things as easy."

Arthur Swift stirred in his chair uneasily.

"You both have a snap compared to me. What am I supposed to do?"

Searle laughed.

"Look wise and feel foolish. Along about nine o'clock we'll cook up a column or two for you to write about the scientific angle of the thing. I'll dope out what I want, you can stick in a couple of high-sounding scientific terms, something about metabolism and the oxidation of tissue. We'll run your picture at the head of the column. There'll be a catchy headline, 'Noted Professor Explains Hysteria,' or something of the sort. The idea will be that there was something akin to hypnotic suggestion in the minds of the men who died."

Carl Ramsay lit a cigarette.

"Better headline than that," he said: " 'Scientist Pits Skill Against Death.' "

Searle stretched, yawned.

"You ought to have the city editor I've got to go up against," he said gloomily.

And Arthur Swift, watching Ramsay, suddenly saw a peculiar thing. The right hand of the reporter seemed to vanish. He rubbed his eyes. The hand was back in place.

But, for a split fraction of a second, the right hand of the tabloid reporter had simply vanished. It had not only dissolved into space, but the right arm, almost to the shoulder, had ceased to exist.

It could hardly have been a mere freak of the imagination. Neither could it have been an optical illusion. For Arthur Swift had been able to see everything else within that room clearly and with normal vision.

Tolliver Hemingway, the millionaire, was taking a cigarette from a gold case. Searle was biting the end from a cigar. Ramsay was smoking. His left hand was conveying the cigarette from his lips. Inspector Hunter was finishing the last of the generous drink he had poured.

Everything was entirely normal, save and except for that sudden disappearance of Carl Ramsay's right hand. It had happened that Arthur Swift was watching that right hand. He had seen it suddenly become nothing. He had blinked his eyes, and the hand was back, reaching for a notebook. It could not have been more than a tenth of a second that the hand was gone, perhaps not half that long. Yet it most certainly had disappeared.

"Look here," said Swift, "did you fellows notice anything just then?"

They looked at him, and as their eyes saw the expression on his face, they snapped to rigid attention.

"What?" asked Searle.

"Shoot," said Inspector Hunter.

"Your hand," said Swift, addressing himself to Ramsay, "it seemed sort of—er—well, sort of funny."

And then a strange thing happened.

Ramsay opened his lips to make some reply, and the sounds that came forth were not words. They seemed a peculiar rattle of gurgling noise that beat with consonant harshness upon the eardrums, rattled against the intelligence with such terrific rapidity that they were like static on a radio receiver.

"What?" asked Swift.

Ramsay drawled slightly, in his normal irritating tone of voice, as he reached for the pencil and scrawled a line across the notebook.

"Guard Goes Goofy," he scribbled, and said: "That'd look fine under your picture. It shows what hysteria will do. Sort of fits in with a general theory. Get a man to believe that a sickening sweet odor will produce death upon him alone, and then fill the room with such an odor, and the man who believed it would be fatal would kick off. Good thought that. I'll write it up with a by-line by Professor Somebody-or-other: Scientist Suggests Solution."

Inspector Hunter snorted. "Foolish to have amateurs in a place like this."

Searle frowned. "One of the first things you've got to learn, Swift, in a situation of this kind, is to see things and see them accurately. Don't go letting your imagination run away with you. Now all the *Star* wants is the use of your name and some scientific terminology. Maybe you'd better curl up and take a nap."

But Tolliver Hemingway, accustomed to appraising character with unerring accuracy, leaned forward.

"Tell us what you saw," he said.

Arthur Swift turned red. Under the rebuke of the reporter who had employed him, he realized how absolutely foolish it would sound for him to mention that the right hand and arm of a man had disappeared—had become simply as nothing.

"Why—I guess—"

The steady, keen eyes of the multimillionaire bored into the young man's face.

"Yes. Go on. Nothing's too absurd to be given careful attention."

"Well," blurted Swift, "if you've got to know; it sounds sort of goofy, but—"

He broke off as a cry of alarm burst from the lips of Carl Ramsay.

"The odor!" he cried.

And there could be no doubt of it. The room was filling with a peculiar odor, a something that was like orange blossoms, yet was not like orange blossoms. It was too sickeningly sweet to be pleasant, yet so cloyingly rich that it was not unpleasant.

Tolliver Hemingway was on his feet, his gray eyes snapping.

"All right, boys; don't think I'm afraid, and don't think any hysteria is going to get me. Inspector, I've one request. If anything *should* happen, search every man in this room, from his skin out. I have an idea this—"

He paused. A look of surprise came over his features. He clutched at his throat.

"I . . . am . . . not . . . afraid," he said, thickly, speaking slowly as though paralysis gripped the muscles of his throat.

"It . . . is . . . "

And he swayed on his feet, lurched forward, flung out a groping hand. The hand clutched the rich cloth which adorned the table on which Inspector Hunter had set his empty glass, and on which the whisky bottle reposed. The cloth came off. The glass crashed to the floor. The bottle rolled across the room.

Tolliver Hemingway crashed to the floor.

He was dead by the time they managed to open his collar and take his limp wrist in their fingers.

Inspector Hunter rushed to the window.

Outside, the searchlights played silently across the darkness of the grounds, their beams interlacing, bringing trees and shrubs into white brilliance, casting shadows which were, in turn, dispersed by the rays of other cross-lights, flickering and flitting. The whole side of the building was covered by floodlights, and the inspector had no sooner thrust his head from the window than a voice from below called up.

"All right, inspector?"

"Anybody come near here?"

"No, sir. Of course not, sir. Our orders were to shoot on sight."

"Who's there with you?"

"Laughlin, O'Rourke, Maloney, and Green."

"One of you sound the alarm. The others wait there. Shoot any stranger on sight."

Inspector Hunter whipped a service revolver from his belted holster, and fired two shots from the open window, signal to the various guards. Almost immediately a siren screamed forth the agreed signal of death.

Inspector Hunter turned back to the room, then suddenly snapped his revolver to the level.

"Get your hands up, Searle!"

The surprised reporter, in the act of shooting the bolt on the door, regarded the inspector with a puzzled frown.

"I've got to get to the paper. I can handle this so much better on the ground than I can over the wire. We'll get out an extra—"

There was no mistaking the cold calm of Hunter's voice.

"Get away from that door or I'll shoot you like a dog. You know what this means. It's the beginning of a reign of terror. This is once that the news comes second. You men will remain here. The murder will be kept absolutely secret until we've exhausted every possible clue.

"And every man in this room is going to be searched from the skin out. Everything in this room, including the very air, is going to be analyzed. Damn it, I'm going to get at the bottom of this!"

And Nick Searle, white-faced in his rage, slowly turned back from the door.

"The *Star* will break you for this," he said, in a low tone, vibrant with anger. "You can't pull a stunt like this and get away with it."

"The hell I can't," said Inspector Hunter, his cold eyes glittering over the barrel of his service revolver. "Get back in the corner, and take your clothes off. Every damned one of you take your clothes off."

He turned to the window.

"Green, send up some doctors, and two of the chemists. Let no one else come into the grounds or the house. Let no one leave. Keep your mouth shut. Have two men come up here and knock on the door. Let them have their revolvers in their hands. Let them shoot to kill at the first sign of disobedience to my orders."

And then Inspector Hunter slammed down the window.

The sickening sweet odor was still in the air, but it was not as noticeable as before.

"Boys, take off your clothes and stand over there in the corner, naked as the day you were born."

Ramsay sneered. "Inefficient Inspector Insults Interviewer."

Searle added another thrust: "Police Inspector Drinking at Time of Tragedy."

Hunter whirled on him.

"You'd use that? After my pulling the wires to get you in here so you'd have an exclusive?"

"I'd use anything," said Searle, his face still white. "The news comes first. You can't hush this thing up, and you can't stall it. The *Star* will get scooped by every paper on the street."

Inspector Hunter shook his head, slowly.

"It won't get out."

"Aw, hell. It's getting out right now. There were reporters watching the house, watching the grounds. Think they heard those shots and the alarm siren without putting two and two together? They'll have extras on the streets within an hour announcing the death, and they'll make a pretty shrewd guess at what's happened afterward."

Hunter lowered the gun slightly.

"The department will issue flat denials. We'll deny the death. We can't let this get out. It would rock the city. It would start a reign of terror. This means the police are powerless."

"You can't hush it up. Your denials will only get you in bad at the start, and give the other papers that much more prestige when you finally have to admit the truth."

Hunter shook his head.

"This is an emergency the like of which has never faced the city before."

He jerked up his revolver as one in whom the last vestige of indecision has vanished.

"Get over there and get your clothes off."

"Hunter Has Hysterics!" rasped Ramsay. "Intoxicated Inspector Incarnate Inefficiency!"

"Get your clothes off!" yelled Hunter.

There was a double knock at the door.

His eyes squinting over the barrel of his revolver, Hunter threw open the door. Two uniformed policemen with drawn guns stood gaping on the threshold.

"Boys, see that these men strip!"

Nick Searle moved slowly, reluctantly.

"You'll strip, too, damn you," he said, "or I'll write an article accusing you of the murder."

"Examiner Evades Equal Examination," sneered Ramsay, moving, however, toward the corner indicated by Hunter.

"No. I'll join you. That's fair. That's what I wanted these boys up here for," said Hunter, throwing down his gun, and taking off his collar and tie as he moved to the corner.

The police chemists found four naked men and a corpse in the room. They made a minute examination of every article in the room. They analyzed every single thing that they fancied might have played a part in the tragedy. They examined even the tobacco in the cigarettes, the paper with which they were tipped. They found nothing.

Dawn found the men working frantically.

It also found extras on the streets, intimating that there had been a tragedy despite the vigilance of the police. It found a crowd surging about the streets which bordered the grounds of the millionaire's mansion.

Noon found Hunter throwing up his hands in helpless despair.

Three o'clock found him pleading with the reporters to be reasonable and give him a break. But Searle and Ramsay, insisting upon the right of the press to print the news, were obdurate.

They were released from custody at three fifteen.

Searle took Swift to the *Star* offices. There they wrote frantically. Swift was given a rewrite man. He gave a few scientific terms covering possible causes of death, made some comment upon atmospheric poisons, and then read the proof of an article that was more wildly speculative than any thoughts he had dared to formulate or utter.

"Celebrated Physicist Hints at Atmospheric Poisoning," he read, then, lower down, in smaller type: "Mysterious Ray Penetrates Walls and Locked Doors. Possibility That Radio May Act as Transmitting Medium. Scientist Confirms Report That Intoxicated Inspector Delayed Transmission of News to Eager Public."

The cashier handed Swift a check that was three times the amount of a month's pay at the state college.

"We'll want a follow-up tomorrow. You'll get the same rates," he said.

"In the meantime?"

"Do anything you want. Keep in touch with the office."

Swift bowed, reached for his hat.

At that moment the telephone shrilled sharply. One of the men barked excitedly as he listened to the sounds that rasped through the receiver.

Another reporter came in, breathless.

"Here's a photo of the letter," he said, and rushed to the darkroom.

"Better stick around, Swift," said Searle. "Hell's to pay."

2.
Trailing an Evil Genius

Events of the next two hours were crowded.

Six new letters had been mailed. Five had been to wealthy men. The sixth had been to none other than the President of the United States of America. Five of the letters contained a demand for money. The sixth letter demanded that the nation accept Zin Zandor as dictator.

The penalty in each case for refusal was death.

The millionaires were to begin paying tribute immediately. The government was given thirty days within which to comply with the demand. At the end of thirty days the President was to die, first of a series of martyrdoms only to be ended by surrender.

But sheer luck had given the law a break.

Post office employees had been instructed to note anything unusual in the mail, particularly anything unusual in the mail addressed to wealthy or prominent people.

One Steve Roscin, a mail carrier, driving to a mailbox to pick up the mail, had noticed rather a striking figure striding away from the box.

It was a man well over six feet tall, thin, slightly stooped. The figure was muffled in an overcoat, despite the fact that the day had been oppressively warm. There was a long black beard which concealed the lower part of the face, dark glasses over the eyes, and a crush hat, pulled well down.

But the postman had caught a good look at the right hand. It was a peculiar ring on the third finger that had caught his eye. He described the ring as being carved in some grotesque fashion in the shape of interlaced triangles of white against a background of red.

The postman insisted that the ring was fully as large as a twenty-five cent piece, perhaps larger where it bulged out into a circle of mingled gem and design.

At the time he had paid no great attention to the man, noting only the overcoat, the beard, and the unusual ring. But when he had opened the green box, his eye had alighted upon six letters at the top of the pile of mail. The uppermost letter had been addressed to the President of the United States of America. The other five letters were addressed to people of prominence in financial circles.

The postman had acted quickly. He had slammed the mailbox shut, jumped into his car and whirled about in pursuit of the strange figure.

At the corner he was in time to see the man climb into a red roadster of speedy design, whose make the postman had been unable to determine. In the gathering dusk, the roadster had shot away from the curb and easily outdistanced the lighter car which the postman was driving.

He had abandoned the futile pursuit, and had telephoned to headquarters at once. Experts had appeared, examined the letters for fingerprints, opened them, found their terms, and had immediately started a search for the tall man in the red roadster who wore a peculiar ring and who wrote his letters on a Remington typewriter.

The police predicted an arrest within twenty-four hours, stating they would make a house-to-house canvass of the city if necessary.

Arthur Swift, caught in the excitement of the investigation, remained at the *Star* offices until nearly midnight.

By that time the telephones were ringing constantly, giving new clues, cases of arrest of suspects. Garages were combed for red roadsters, people were asked to report any tall figure with beard and overcoat that had been seen at or about the time.

The police adopted the theory that the beard was a disguise, that the overcoat was merely to prevent recognition, and that the man probably did not live anywhere near the place where the mailbox was located, but had written the letters, then driven to some isolated section to mail them.

By midnight there were no fewer than fifty tall suspects incarcerated at police headquarters, awaiting a complete check of their activities for the day.

Arthur Swift caught Nick Searle for a short conference.

"Look here, Searle, there's one thing about this business that's strange."

"Meaning?"

"The time those letters were mailed."

"What of it?"

"They must have been already written, held ready for mailing, but the mailing was to be at a certain definite time."

"The time?" asked Searle, smiling rather patronizingly.

"The time was when the person who did the writing was certain the death of Tolliver Hemingway had taken place."

Searle continued to smile, the smile of calm superiority.

"Wrong, Swift. The time was when the writer knew that the people had been advised of the death of Hemingway."

Swift shook his head.

"No. You see, it would have taken the letters twenty-four hours to be delivered at the very least. Therefore, had the writer been absolutely certain of Hemingway's death, he would have mailed the letters, knowing the press would have the facts long before those letters were read by his victims."

The smile melted from Searle's features.

"By George, there's a thought there! Then you mean the person who committed those murders wasn't absolutely certain the murders had been committed. He only released certain agencies of destruction, knowing that they *should* work, but those agencies were not sufficiently certain to make him positive of their success."

Swift, knowing that he now held Searle's attention, nodded.

"That," he said, "is one possible explanation. The other is harder to comprehend, but yet, in some respects, more logical."

"Shoot," said Searle.

ERLE STANLEY GARDNER

"That the person who ordered the mailing of those letters was one of the persons who were in the room with Hemingway, and was, therefore, unable to communicate with his accomplices until after Inspector Hunter had released him."

Searle dropped into a chair, as though his knees had suddenly weakened.

"Not that, Swift. That would make four of us suspects—and you, being of scientific training, would be the first they'd go after. They'd slam us in cells and start giving us third degrees that would make us wish we'd never been born. Why, we've been panning the inspector, calling him intoxicated and all that. Lord, how he'd delight in having some legitimate excuse to get us thrown in the jug and work us over."

Swift nodded.

"I hadn't thought of it from exactly that angle, but I was wondering about Ramsay."

"What about him?"

"You remember I mentioned seeing something just before Hemingway's death?"

"That's right, you did."

"Well, I'm going to tell you what that something was. It sounds incredible, but for a split fraction of a second, Ramsay's hand vanished. The hand and the biggest part of the arm just melted into space."

Searle knitted his brows.

"Listen, son, you haven't batted around the way I have, and you don't realize what tricks nervous strain will play on a man. They sometimes kick about the reporters being so hardboiled and calloused, but a man ain't worth a damn as a reporter until he does get calloused. You were all worked up, and your eyes just started playing tricks on you. Even if they didn't, how could anybody have managed to bring about the death of Hemingway without leaving any clue at all?"

Swift was stubborn.

"Somebody did. And it must have been done by unusual methods. Therefore, anything unusual—"

Searle surrendered the point. "All right. Let's drop around and see Ramsay. We'll ask him what he knows about it. That'll convince you. Ramsay's on the square."

They got hats and coats, went out into the velvety midnight. They found Ramsay's room, knocked on the door, got no answer, walked in.

Searle turned on the light.

Swift stood by the door.

The click of the switch showed a scene of confusion. Drawers were pulled from the dresser. The mattress had been slit in a dozen places, and the stuffing pulled out, strewn over the floor. The bedclothes were wadded into a knot. A suitcase had been cut open. The clothes closet showed a pile of garments, the pockets pulled wrong side out.

A letter file had been dumped in a chair, and the wind from the open window had sifted various letters about the room. All over the floor, even on the walls, were drops of blood, and those blood drops were scarcely dry.

Searle made a wry face.

"Another victim," he said.

Arthur Swift made a hurried examination of the various letters and papers while Searle was telephoning the police. Among some of the more recent letters he found a bit of paper which contained a single word: "Tonight."

That bit of paper was undated and unsigned, but, in the lower right hand corner was the imprint of a seal, an affair of interlaced triangles, the impression of which was visible only when the paper was held at an angle to the light.

Swift laid the letter or note back in the pile of papers.

"Know anything about rings?" he asked Searle.

That individual impatiently shook his head.

"To thunder with all that hooey. The thing that we've got to find out is the method of death. Then we can guard against it. And we've got to trace each individual victim. Imagine what it means when some individual can inflict death at will upon any certain man he may select, regardless of the precautions with which that individual is surrounded! Then he writes a letter demanding certain things of the government, threatening to take the life of the President.

"And he can do it, too. Make no mistake about that, Swift. I've seen 'em come, and I've seen 'em go. I know the work of the fanatic and of the bluffer. But this man is different. He works too efficiently, too damned efficiently. Imagine picking a time right after midnight to bump off Hemingway! He picked the very time when everybody was the most alert.

He did it to show how little he cared for us or our precautions."

"Maybe," responded Swift. "But you've got to admit that ordinary measures get us nowhere in this case. Now there were rings made along in the fifteenth century that were known as poison rings. They were large, made especially to hold a quantity of poison, and I have a hunch such a ring figures in this case. I'm going to find out."

"How did the murderer get the ring in contact with Hemingway?" asked Searle.

"Perhaps he poisoned him with a slow moving poison that was implanted in his system days before."

Searle grinned. "Wrong again. He gave Hemingway the option of avoiding death at any time by simply paying out money."

Swift made for the door.

"Anyway, I'm going to beat it before the police arrive. After the way you've been panning Inspector Hunter it'll be only a question of hours until he figures out a scheme for getting you on the inside. I don't want to be around."

And he walked out, went to a nearby hotel, registered under an assumed name, took off his clothes, and sank into deep slumber.

By morning he was ready to run down his theory. He called on certain antique ring dealers and made known his wants, a poison ring of large capacity, answering a general description.

There were five prominent dealers in such jewelry. Three of them gave him blanks. But the fourth scratched his head, consulted his books.

"It is possible we might get you such a ring. We sold one a little over sixty days ago to a man who makes a hobby of rings. He buys, holds for a while, then sells or trades."

Swift whipped out a pencil.

"Give me his address. I'll pay you a commission if I make a deal."

"Marvin is the name," said the dealer. "I'll give you the address in a letter of introduction."

Marvin was at home, genial, cordial. He was a little man with puckery eyes and perpetually smiling lips. He was hardly the type one would have picked as a murderer.

Swift broached the subject of rings, gradually leading the way around to various poison rings.

"I had a magnificent specimen a couple of months ago," said the collector. "But my physician took a fancy to it and I gave it to him."

Art Swift nodded, as though the information were of but casual interest, talked for half an hour, purchased a small antique ring, and finally announced an obscure physical ailment which had been bothering him for some time.

Marvin suggested a good physician.

"Don't know any," remarked Swift.

"Try mine. Dr. Cassius Zean."

Swift yawned.

"Thanks, I may look him up. Well, I've got to be going. It's been a pleasure to chat with you. Good morning."

Dr. Zean! The name filled him with curiosity. The man whose name was Zean might well have adopted a name such as Zin Zandor.

He called a cab, went at once to the doctor's office.

An office girl was busy at a typewriter. Swift moved over so that he could see the make of the machine. It was an Underwood. A white-uniformed surgical nurse bustled in and out of the outer office. She had Swift fill out a card with his name, address, and occupation.

The doctor, it seemed, was in, but would see no one that day. It would be necessary to make an appointment. Art Swift made an appointment for the latter part of the week, but insisted upon an immediate interview. The nurse withdrew to take the message to the inner office. She was gone for some time. Swift felt the uncomfortable feeling which he experienced at times when he felt people were talking about him.

While he was sitting there, twisting his fingers, his brain racing with thoughts and conjectures, he heard the telephone on the desk at his elbow give a series of clicks.

The desk, he saw, was one where the surgical nurse held forth when not busy elsewhere. He wondered if the telephone was merely an extension of the telephone in the private office and if the clicking of the bell clapper denoted a conversation starting by the removal of the other receiver.

Casually, he half turned in his chair. The girl at the desk was clacking out letters on the typewriter. Her eyes seemed to be entirely occupied. Stretching forth an arm, moving with the air of one who is bored and restless, Swift inserted his hand under the receiver, cupped the palm, and gently lifted the receiver so that the spring tension on the hook caused a contact.

Instantly he heard the metallic raspings from the receiver which showed a conversation was being carried on over the line. Swift was sitting in a chair which brought his ear not very far from the level of the desk. He managed to work a book under the receiver, holding it up a half inch or more from the hook. Then he slumped down until his ear was but an inch or two from the edge of the desk.

The conversation became faintly audible.

"Send a messenger after it right away. We need some . . . "

"Can't let you have it for half an hour."

"All right. They're raising hell, making a house-to-house search of the city. Better be careful about mentioning that ring. Somebody may ask you about it."

"No chance of that. Send a messenger directly to room 920, knock once, then pause and knock twice. Will I know this messenger?"

"No, this will be a new one."

"All right. G'by."

"G'by."

There was a series of clicks from the wire. Swift slipped the book out from under the receiver. The girl at the other desk continued tapping the keys of the typewriter.

The surgical nurse appeared, frowning, to communicate the doctor's refusal to see any one except by appointment. Swift acknowledged defeat and left the office.

His mind fairly reeled with the information he had received. The telephone conversation doubtless referred to the search that was being made for the tall man with the odd ring. It was very possible that Dr. Cassius Zean was none other than the mysterious and sinister Zin Zandor.

Swift debated whether to call up Searle, finally decided to do so. He went to a public telephone, called the newspaper office, and found that Searle was out. He left a message for him.

"Tell him I've got something hot. I'll call again in half an hour. If he comes in, have him wait."

3.
Unchained Lightning

As he hung up the telephone, a daring thought possessed Swift.

Why not stroll up to room 920, knock once, pause, and then knock twice? The voice over the telephone had said the doctor wouldn't know the messenger!

The thought had no sooner entered Swift's mind than it crystallized into action. He sprinted for the elevator, was whisked to the ninth floor, and walked the corridor upon nervously impatient feet.

At 920 he paused, contemplated the plain door for several seconds, was painfully conscious of the throbbing of his pulse, and knocked. He paused, knocked twice.

There was a vague shadow flitting over the ground glass square. Then the shadow took bulk and sharpness of outline. Swift had visions of a tall, sinister figure with a cold eye, and was absolutely unprepared for the short, stumpy man with fleshy jowls who glared at him.

"Well?"

"Messenger. Told to get somethin' here," said Swift, slurring his words together to disguise his nervousness.

The doctor glowered at him from eyes that were as twin chunks of polished ebony. "Come in," he said. "You're early."

"Am I?" asked Swift, striving to appear casually unconcerned. "I was told to come in half an hour. I walked around for a while, didn't have my watch."

The doctor grunted.

Swift noticed that he was slow and lagging in his movements, that his lips were a sickly blue, that the flesh sagged down in flabby pouches. There were pouches beneath the eyes, pouches below the cheek bones, a pouch below the chin, and a sagging pouch at the belt. The doctor was wheezing from the effort of walking toward the door.

He went to the door on his right, which Swift surmised must lead to the reception room, and locked it. Then he turned toward a door enameled a pure white.

"Just making a final test," he said.

Art Swift got a glimpse of a long, well-lighted room. There were white tables, chairs, a long sink, a battery of test tubes, bottles, retorts, microscopes, and a cage full of canaries. These canaries sang in nervous, chirping voices, fluttering restlessly from perch to perch.

Dr. Zean left the door open as he entered the room.

"Sit down," he wheezed over his right shoulder. "You must be the man that's detailed to cover Washington."

Swift resolved on a bold stroke.

"I am," he said. "The chief sent me down here to get my stuff and get started."

"Know how to use it?"

"Only generally. I understood you were to give me instructions."

The doctor turned, frowned. His ebony black eyes bored into Swift's features. The blued, flabby lips quivered.

"All damn foolishness trying to— Oh, well, you aren't to blame."

He reached in the cage. The birds fluttered their protests at the invading hand, flung themselves against the gilded bars. At length the fat fingers closed about a slim, yellow body. The bird gave a shrill cry of alarm, then was pulled from the cage, wings fluttering and flapping, occasional feathers drifting to the floor.

Dr. Zean raised a hypodermic, jabbed the needle into the fluttering bird. Almost instantly there came a rapid change. The fluttering wings began to move more rapidly. They gave forth a low humming sound.

"Watch," said the doctor and liberated the bird.

The wings were moving so fast now that it was impossible to see them. They were like the wings of a humming bird, giving forth a low, droning sound. The canary hung for a split fraction of a second, poised in the air, then zipped into flight. Such a flight it was!

The bird seemed like a yellow streak, moving with incredible speed. Swift turned his head to follow the flight, turned it back again. Try as he would, he could not keep the bird in sight. Neither could he lose sight of it. The canary was merely a flash of yellow.

So rapidly did it move that the eye could see it only as a swift flicker of motion. Like an electric spark, it was impossible even to tell the direction of its flight. One time the bird seemed to be going in one direction, yet almost immediately it appeared in the opposite side of the room.

No direction in which Swift could direct his eyes but what that droning yellow streak zipped across his field of vision with such rapidity that it seemed there must be half a dozen of the birds in the air at once. In fact, there were several occasions when there seemed to be three different birds flying in opposite directions at the same time.

Swift rubbed his startled eyes.

The husky voice of the doctor took up a brief explanation, a word of warning.

"Time," he said, "is an illusion of the senses. Space is an illusion. If there's anything in infinity as an established fact, then there can be no limit to either time or space. To think of something that has no limit, yet has an existence, is absurd. Our finite minds place a limit on everything. So does existence.

"Therefore, the limitation of space and of time are the limitations and fallacies of the mind. It's like a single tube radio set. It has a limited range. That doesn't mean the radio waves that it receives are limited to that field. Same way with the human mind.

"Now some organisms live much more rapidly than others. Their concept of time is so radically different that the life energy is used up in a few hours.

"Naturally, if one could determine the particular gland which controls that time element it would be possible either to speed up life or slow it down. The dog uses up his allotted life energy in seven or ten years, the horse in a longer time. And there are cell organisms that live but a few hours.

"There's no time for details. You wouldn't understand them, anyway. But the point I'm making is that the extract I am able to furnish doesn't do anything to give new energy. It simply directs the speed with which the existing energy is burned up. So you've got to be careful of the dosage. It's barely possible that one could take a sufficient dose to live up a whole lifetime in five minutes.

"The effect of this extract is to speed up everything. It wears off as quickly as it takes effect. The muscles, the nerves, the brain, the heart, all function according to the new scheme of things. And your strength is multiplied accordingly.

"We don't know what strength is. Take the elbow, for instance. It's a fulcrum for the forearm. The raised forearm is a lever of the third class. The power is applied but a few inches from the fulcrum. Yet a strong man can raise a fifty- to eighty-pound weight in his hand without difficulty.

"Take a pencil and paper, calculate the moments of force, and you'll see that this calls for an utterly incredible amount of power to be applied to the forearm. In fact the bone wouldn't stand such a strain. Take the forearm of a cadaver, put such a weight in it and raise it by mechanical means, and the bone snaps.

"Therefore strength has something mental about it. The mind acts on the molecular structure in some way. Gravitation is the tendency of the molecules of all matter to draw together in proportion to the mass. Because of the greater mass of the earth, it attracts an object many millions of times more than the object attracts the earth."

The doctor ceased speaking and glared at Art with a look of hostility.

"Damn it, your mouth has flopped open as though the whole thing was strange to you. I've repeatedly warned those who sent you to see that this preliminary ground was covered first. I can't be running a kindergarten here!

"Now here's a box. That box contains two dozen little capsules and one big capsule. The little capsules contain enough of the extract to speed up your physical and mental processes at the rate of one hundred to one. Each capsule terminates in a hollow needle. When you are about to make use of a capsule take a deep breath, insert the needle, squeeze the capsule.

"Within the space of three deep breaths you will find your processes speeded up. You will move, think, breathe, talk one hundred times faster than normal. The small capsules last for about thirty seconds. Then the effects wear off. During that half minute you have lived fifty minutes of your normal life at a rate one hundred times as rapid as ordinary. Remember that your fast motions will be utterly invisible to ordinary eyes. If you talk, your speech will be unintelligible.

"It will be advisable to take two or three preliminary doses so you can accustom yourself to your new rate of life, and be able to gauge your motions accordingly.

"Now the big capsule is to be used only in the event of a major emergency. Every man is similarly equipped. It will speed up your life at the ratio of five hundred to one."

There was an imperative pounding at the door which led to the reception room. Dr. Cassius Zean stifled an impatient exclamation, and wheezed his way to the door.

"I'm busy," he said.

The girl's voice that drifted through the panels contained some note of alarm. Art Swift could not hear the words. The doctor shot the bolt. The surgical nurse appeared in the crack of the open doorway. Art Swift kept his back turned.

There was the hissing of a sibilant whisper.

"Very well. I'll attend to it at once," said the doctor.

The nurse turned, paused, swung back. Art Swift could feel her eyes upon him.

"Turn around!" she cried.

Art turned, and, as he turned, he took a swift step toward the pair. The girl's eyes burned into his own. Her lips parted in a screamed warning. "He's a spy!"

Dr. Cassius Zean flung a hand toward his hip.

The girl jumped into the room and kicked the door shut. Her face was chalky white, the lips a thin line of grim determination.

"A knife!" she cried. "No noise!"

But Dr. Zean was lugging a heavy revolver from his hip pocket.

Art Swift was unarmed. The girl was coming toward him, fury blazing from her eyes. The doctor was raising the revolver.

Art made a wild leap.

The girl went through the air and tackled him with outstretched arms, a tackle that would have done credit to a football star. Despite himself, the surprise of the attack, the weight of her hurtling form, threw Swift from his feet. He staggered, tried to catch his balance, and crashed to the floor.

"Crack him!" he heard the girl say.

He saw Dr. Zean's arm upraised, bringing down the weapon in a crushing blow, and flung up his knees, swung to one side.

The blow missed.

"Then shoot him, quick!" yelled the girl. "He's breaking my grip!"

Even as she screamed the words, her hands slipped from the struggling body, and Art Swift lunged out with a circling arm, caught the ankle of the pudgy doctor, and gave a jerk. The foot slipped, the ankle gave, and the huge bulk came down with a thud. The girl's hands had been busy. She was scratching at his face, biting, kicking.

Art rolled over, got to one knee, heedless of the fury of the nurse. He swung his right arm. The fist connected with the purpled jaw, but, even as he struck the blow, Swift realized that something was wrong. The flesh he hit was the color of fresh putty. The lips were blued, parted, gasping. The tongue protruded. Dr. Zean's heart had given out, the excitement proving too much.

There remained the girl.

Swift flung his arms about her, held her helpless. He grabbed a roll

ERLE STANLEY GARDNER

of bandage that had become tangled in his feet and whipped it about her hands. She tried to scream then, but he stifled the sound, thrust the roll into the parted teeth. There followed a subdued gurgle. He tied the gag in place, endured the white-hot fury of her eyes, finished binding the wrists and ankles.

There was a closet opening from the room. He pushed her in there, gave a final inspection to the knots, closed and locked the door.

Then he turned to the doctor. He was dead, this pudgy physician who had isolated the extract that governed the tempo of conscious life.

As Swift started to search his pockets, there sounded a knock at the door of 920. A pause, two knocks. It was the messenger!

Art Swift grabbed the coat collar of the inert clay and dragged the pudgy form along the floor to the door of the laboratory. He pushed the man inside, closed the door, and walked toward 920. His fist was clenched. He was ready to strike the instant the man walked across the threshold.

He slipped the bolt, threw open the door.

"Come in," he said, and then gasped his astonishment.

The figure that entered the room was that of a young woman, well-formed, beautiful. She smiled at him graciously.

"You are Dr. Zean? I was to receive certain things. Doubtless there is no explanation necessary," and her lips parted in a smile.

Art Swift floundered in a confused greeting, invited her to be seated.

Should he tie and gag her? But she was so smiling, so innocent in appearance, so refined in her manner. Violence was unthinkable!

Then, as he hesitated, another thought flashed across his mind. Why not give her that which she sought, send her away, and follow? She would lead him to the rest of the gang.

He bowed deeply.

"If you'll excuse me a moment," he said, and went toward the door of the laboratory. He was careful to open it in such a manner that she could not see the corpse, and promptly closed it behind him.

He searched shelves, finally found that which he sought, a little pile of metal boxes in which were capsules similar to the ones the doctor had shown him.

He took a box of the extract, returned to the girl, and gave her as much of the doctor's talk as he could remember.

"You look as though it was all news to you!" he stormed, just as the doctor had stormed at him. "I can't run a kindergarten here. Why can't they explain these rudimentary preliminaries to you before you come? Take this box and go."

"Hadn't I better try a capsule?"

He grunted, still keeping in the part of a testy scientist, impatient at having to explain fundamentals to an ignorant woman.

"I don't care what you do!"

She flashed him a smile, opened the box, took out a capsule, took a deep breath, jabbed the needle into her arm, squeezed the capsule.

Then Art Swift realized that he, too, must test this diabolical extract of some nameless gland, or the girl would be able to vanish, moving a hundred times more rapidly than he could.

He grabbed a capsule from the box she held in her hand.

"I'll take one with you," he said, and took a deep breath.

The girl was breathing deeply. Her cheeks were flushed, her eyes were brilliant with excitement and with the stimulus of this strange substance.

Swift felt the bite of the needle, felt his blood tingle with the sting of the extract, and glanced at the clock on the wall. It was precisely two fifteen. The second hand of the mechanism was tick-tocking around its smaller circle. The minute hand pointed at the figure three, the hour hand at two.

The girl's potion took effect first.

He suddenly saw her start to get up. Then it was as though she became a blur of motion. She walked, and her feet moved so rapidly the eye could scarcely follow. She talked, and her lips showed only as a filmy substance. The sound of her words was as the clatter of a watchman's rattle.

She made toward the door, moving so fast that she was as a streak of whizzing speed, and then something clicked in Swift's brain. Just as he was trying with leaden feet to move and intercept her, he suddenly saw her moving at normal speed, her hand on the door knob.

"Well, I guess I'll be going," she said.

Swift wondered if the effect of the extract had worn off so quickly.

"Just a moment," he said, sparring for time.

"Yes?" she asked.

"You felt the effect of the extract?" he wanted to know, curious as to her feelings.

"Just a slight dizziness. When does it take effect? It seemed to make you almost unconscious. You must have sat motionless for nearly five

ERLE STANLEY GARDNER

minutes. I talked to you and you didn't answer. You seemed sick. I was alarmed."

A sudden explanation flashed upon Art Swift. He looked at the clock. It was three seconds past two fifteen. The second hand seemed to have stopped in its motion. But there was a low-pitched sound coming from the clock, a long-drawn rasping of some sort of slow-moving mechanism. He listened, attentively.

"T . . . O . . . C . . . K," said the clock, and the second hand moved an infinitesimal fraction of an inch of crawling motion.

He pointed toward the clock.

"Can't you see? You're under the influence of the extract now."

She regarded him with startled eyes, then moved toward the clock.

As she walked, Art watched her clothing. It was flattened against her figure as though pressed by some invisible hand. Then he remembered a strange, whizzing sound that had been in his ears as she had moved.

The girl modestly pulled at her skirt. It remained plastered against her limbs.

Swift laughed.

"The atmospheric pressure remains the same," he said. "You are moving just one hundred times more rapidly than normal. Naturally, your speed through the atmosphere forces your clothing against you. There's no use struggling with it. You'd have to remain still for some apparently perceptible interval to give the air currents a chance to adjust themselves."

The girl laughed, a nervous, throaty laugh.

Swift found himself keenly interested in the various physical phenomena which surrounded them.

"Do you mean to say we've speeded up our lives so we live fifty minutes while that second hand clacks through thirty seconds?"

He nodded.

"And when I'm in the room," said the girl, "and take the drug, then what do I do?"

Of a sudden, Art Swift knew exactly what she was to do.

"Simple," he said. "Train yourself to sit absolutely still. Remain motionless with your body for minutes on end. Move only your right arm. That will enable you to put the poisoned cigarette in the hand of the victim without being detected. The motion of the hand will be far too swift for ordinary senses to detect. If any one should happen to be looking directly at you he will see your right hand apparently disappear. So be careful not to make the motion until every one is looking in some other direction."

"But what if they should flash me a quick glance?"

"Quick?" He laughed. "The quickest glance they could flash you would be so slow that you would see their eyeballs move as though by slow clockwork."

"And the cigarette?"

"Will have the extreme end of it filled with the poison. The victim inhales it fully into his lungs and dies. The other occupants of the room sense only the greatly diluted odor of the poison gas as a sickening sweet smell."

"Goodness!" she exclaimed. Then, her eyes filling with some sort of emotion he could not fathom: "I must be going."

She moved toward the outer door.

"I'll see you to the elevator," said Swift, and opened the door, taking care to slip a metallic box of the capsules into his hip pocket.

The outer office looked just as it had when Swift had first seen it. The furniture, the windows, the rugs. But as he opened the door he seemed pulling against a great weight, and he noticed the sudden vacuum swirl the rugs into bulging ripples of slow motion.

He understood then what he had done. He had jerked that door open with a motion one hundred times as swift as the ordinary opening of a door. It had disturbed the atmospheric equilibrium of the room.

Alarmed, he glanced at the stenographer to see if she had noticed it, to see if she would sense anything unusual in a strange man's emerging from the private office, escorting a young woman to the door.

As he looked, she was about to glance up from her typewriter. She was striking the letters of the machine, glancing toward the door. Swift pressed the arm of the girl.

"Notice the mechanics of alarm," he said.

They watched.

Slowly, the girl's eyes swung upward. The lips sagged open in what was doubtless to be a gasp, but it was so ludicrously slow that they both laughed. The right hand pressed down on one of the keys of the typewriter. They saw the type bar slowly move upward to strike the paper.

The bar struck the paper, remained pressed against it for what seemed seconds, then slowly began to drop back. The carriage started a sluggish movement to make way for the next letter which was already being pressed, and still the girl's eyes had not fully raised to the two figures who were watching her.

"Let's move and see if she can follow us," said Swift.

He grabbed the girl's arm, darted to one side.

The typist's eyes were raised now, but they stared in wide-eyed, frozen alarm at the place where they had been and not at the place where they were.

4.
Outlawed from Mankind

They darted to the outer door, tugged it open, slipped into the outer corridor.

"I didn't get your name," said Swift.

"Louise Folsom."

"You're the Washington agent?"

"Er—yes, the Washington agent."

She jabbed a forefinger to the button of the elevator.

They waited for a short time in silence; then, suddenly, Swift burst out laughing.

"Foolish. You can't get an elevator."

"Why can't I?"

He pointed to the glass door through which could be seen the cables controlling the cages. The strands were crawling at such a slow rate it seemed the cable was hardly moving.

"We're speeded up too fast. You'll have to wait for what'll seem a very long time, or else take the stairs."

"Nine flights?"

"Nine flights."

"How long will it seem to me if I go down on the elevator?"

"Nearly ten minutes."

She paused, uncertain.

"I rather think I'll wait. Nine flights is a long way."

This gave Swift the opportunity he was looking for.

"All right. But be careful when you get in the cage. Move so slowly that you seem to be fairly crawling. Try to take eight or ten seconds to get into the elevator. Don't try talking with anybody until the effect of the extract wears off. You've got your box?"

She nodded.

Swift turned and left her, walking down the corridor.

He noticed a red light flash on over the elevator door, saw the bottom of one of the cages come creeping into view and slowly crawl to position before the door. This was the break for which he had been waiting, and, as the girl concentrated her attention on the elevator, Swift darted for the stairs.

He went down the nine flights with such speed that his coat streamed straight out behind him. He beat the elevator to the ground floor and was waiting when the door opened and the girl came out.

She had forgotten his admonition, and was rushing at a rate of speed a full hundred times faster than that of the average pedestrian in a hurry. Open-mouthed spectators stood frozen in motionless surprise as she whizzed by them. Then, as she gained the street, they seemed not to see her at all, so rapidly did she move.

Swift followed her, and emerged from the office building into a strange world.

Automobiles barely crept along the street. Even the noise and confusion of the city had been toned down until it sounded as a hollow boom of slow noise, low-pitched, almost inaudible. Hurrying pedestrians seemed standing upon one leg, their feet almost motionless. Their swinging arms were held at grotesque postures. A newsboy crying his wares stood for seeming minutes with his mouth open, a queer, rattling sound slowly emerging from the throat. A paper being waved in front of a passing pedestrian seemed utterly motionless; one corner, fluttering in the wind which whipped down the street, was barely moving.

Swift followed the girl, keeping well behind her, swinging his way between other pedestrians as though they had been inanimate figures, bunching on the sidewalks for purposes of ornamentation.

No use to take a car or cab. Walking at a rate of speed that seemed painfully slow, the atmosphere whipped his garments until it seemed they would be torn to ribbons. The girl's short skirt streamed and fluttered, flapped and blew, whipped and skirled. Her hair came out from under her hat and streamed back of her head. She was exerting her every ounce of strength to fight against the wind caused by her rapid progress through the air.

Swift figured they were walking at a rate of speed that would ordinarily have taken them two miles an hour. Now, multiplied a hundredfold, that speed of two hundred miles an hour caused the terrific rush of air to threaten to tear their clothes off their backs.

He felt his coat whip and slat into a ripping tear. He slowed his speed still further, noticed that the girl's skirt was coming off, saw her stop to adjust it. Yet it seemed several long minutes before it ceased its fluttering.

During all of this time the street traffic seemed barely crawling along; the wheels of the automobiles hardly moved in their slow revolutions.

The girl resumed her pace. She was walking more slowly now. A man standing at the window of a store, apparently engrossed in the display within, seemed vaguely familiar to Swift. As he glanced for a second look, he saw the girl was approaching him. She put her hand on his arm.

The man started what was evidently intended to be a swift whirl. To Art Swift it seemed to be but a slow motion picture of a slow motion picture. After an interval of what seemed seconds he had his eyes telling more than his ears, for the two were gazing at each other, and the man was Nick Searle of the *Star*.

The girl was talking. Swift could see her chin move, see the lips opening and closing. Searle was trying to talk, but the slow, drawling sounds which issued from his leisurely lips were nothing the girl could wait for. Her eagerness to impart her information made her pour out a torrent of sound at top speed.

Swift wondered how much longer the drug would act, and, even as he wondered, saw the phenomenon happen before his eyes. The girl suddenly became a sluggish replica of her former self. She had started a gesture with her right hand. That gesture slowed in its motion until the hand barely crawled toward the lapel of Searle's coat.

Swift knew then that the drug had worn off. He remembered also that he had taken his drug just a second after the girl had taken hers. That would give him the advantage.

He moved forward, walking as swiftly as he dared, the wind whipping at his garments.

So rapidly did he move that the eyes of the two never faltered from each other. Not by so much as a glance did they see this man who was circling them at a rate of speed which made him almost invisible.

There was a pillar of concrete supporting an alcove, almost directly behind Searle, and Art Swift made for this place of concealment. He wanted to hear what the girl was saying, and he wanted to warn Searle that the girl was in reality one of the gang of crooks that bade fair to terrorize the country.

He leaned forward. The girl was speaking. Her slow words drawled with such exasperating languor that it seemed to take fully half a minute to drag out a word.

The traffic continued to crawl. Noises were as a low-pitched clack of sound, overlapping at times, but hardly audible. And then, right in the middle of a sentence, Swift's ears snapped back to normal. There was a brief period of dizziness as his functions returned to normality.

Of a sudden the traffic resumed its customary rumbling roar and shot past the store. The girl's voice was shrill with hysteria. The words ceased to drawl, but beat upon Swift's ears as the patter of a torrential rain on a tin roof.

"I have some of the drug. He never questioned my identity at all."

Searle's voice was also rapid, fierce in its intensity.

"Could you recognize this man?"

"Of course."

Searle pulled a photograph from his pocket.

Art Swift, crouched behind the pillar, cast about for some way by which he could warn Searle of the identity of the girl, of the danger of being trapped. But the reporter handed her the photograph.

"Why, yes. It's this man, the third from the end."

"Great Scott! Why, that's Art Swift!"

"I can't help who it is. It's the man that gave his name as Dr. Zean."

Swift's mind whirled. What was this all about? He started to step forward.

"Then we'll have to kill him on sight," snapped Searle's voice. "He knows too damn much!"

Swift sank back against the support of the cold concrete.

Searle, then, was the real arch-villain in the whole affair! He had been the one to bring about the deaths of the millionaires. He had been the one to send the letters to the unfortunate men who had attracted his attention.

As Swift turned this matter over in his mind, Searle and the girl moved

ERLE STANLEY GARDNER

away.

Swift waited a few minutes, thinking, then moved out into the stream of pedestrians. A chance fragment of a passing man's conversation came to his ears.

"Something whizzed right in between us. It must have been a cannon ball or something. It went so fast I could feel the air tugging at my clothes, but I couldn't see a damned thing. I'd have thought I was dreaming or drunk, but Roberts felt the same sort of a sensation."

Swift moved away. His senses were reeling. He looked at his watch. It was exactly sixteen minutes past two o'clock. All of this frantic action had taken place in just about a minute.

He thought of the dead doctor, the nurse imprisoned in the closet. He must arrange for the arrest of the nurse, and he must arrange to have Searle arrested.

A sudden drowsiness overtook him. He went to his room in the hotel, telephoned police headquarters, and asked that a detective be sent out to interview him. Then he fell asleep.

The newsboys were crying "Extra!" on the street when he awoke, and someone was pounding on his door. Swift turned the key, instinctively knew the square-toed man who hulked on the threshold was a detective.

"You had a tip an' wanted a man from headquarters?" asked the man.

"Yes," said Swift. "Come in."

The detective entered the room, whirled, swung out a hand. By sheer luck Swift was able to dodge that grasping hand.

"What—" Art began, dodging another fist, and then the detective was on him in a lunging attack.

The very bulk of of the man made him clumsy. Yet his charge knocked Swift to a corner. He saw it all, then. This could be no detective, but an agent of the crime ring, sent out to kill him. Fear and desperation gave him strength.

The other was pulling a revolver from his hip. Swift swung a chair. There was the crashing of wood as the rungs slivered, and then Swift saw the man staggering back, slumping to the floor.

Swift ran from the room to the foot of the stairs. A newsboy thrust out an extra of the *Star*. Swift grabbed it, and, to his horror, saw his own features staring forth at him, just underneath the words: KILL THIS MAN ON SIGHT!

A YEAR IN A DAY   137

Then followed an article about the identification of Art Swift as the arch-killer, the greatest blackmailer, the scientific wonder who had used his genius to undermine civilization.

Swift stared at it, stupefied. Was it possible Searle was so daring as to hope he could prevent discovery by making a counter-accusation? The idea had merits, particularly as the *Star* argued that the scientific knowledge of the criminal made him immune to arrest and necessitated his being shot as a mad dog would be dealt with.

Swift read the article. To his surprise, it exposed the secret of the extract which speeded up the human metabolism to such an extent that life was lived a hundred times more rapidly than was possible under normal conditions.

The article claimed that Searle had solved the mystery with the aid of a female assistant who had tricked the arch-criminal into explaining the details of the crime to her.

That might have been correct. The girl might have been an assistant. Then Searle would not be the real criminal, but just what he appeared, a reporter. Yet, suppose this was merely a trick? Suppose Searle was so clever he had planned for this all along?

Swift wanted to think it over. He clutched the newspaper to him, started for a taxicab. There was the crash of glass, a bellow of rage, the shrill of a police whistle.

The detective had smashed out the glass of the hotel window, was frantically blowing his police whistle. As men looked up in startled surprise, the detective opened fire.

Swift ducked behind a parked car. The bullets from the detective's gun crashed into the metal, spattered the glass from the door windows, but failed to find their real mark.

Swift realized, however, he was trapped. It would be all right if he had a chance to tell his story. But how about the hysteria of the police? Would they get rabid and shoot on sight as the *Star* requested them?

He thought then of the box he had in his pocket, the rubber capsules that would speed up his body so that he could escape. He slipped the cover from the box.

And just then a burly form catapulted around the corner of the car. Swift had only time to thrust the box back in his pocket. The cover clattered to the sidewalk. A great bluecoated figure swung a club. Swift tried to dodge, but to no avail. He felt the impact, felt a great wave of nausea and engulfing blackness. Dimly, he realized that the thing that smacked him between the shoulders was the cold pavement. He felt the bite of handcuffs at his wrists, and then lost all consciousness.

5.
In a Frozen World

Searle's voice was in his ears when he regained consciousness. There was a tang of jail odor in the air. His form was stretched on a prison pallet and the steel contained a single bright incandescent, which stabbed his throbbing eyes.

"From the looks of this telephone number, we figured it might be a lead. I got Louise Folsom to give a ring and stall along for information, and the conversation sounded promising, so I sent her up.

"She ran onto this Swift. Of course, she didn't know him at the time. He was merely a certain Dr. Zean. But he proceeded to explain to her just how the murders had been committed and—"

He broke off as there was a commotion near the door.

"We knocked over that office and found a nurse tied and gagged in the closet, and a dead man in the laboratory. Looks like there's hell to pay. Somebody had been in the place and cleaned it out, busted up bottles, pulled out drawers, and raised hell generally." A red-faced sergeant was speaking.

There was the scraping of chairs.

Swift struggled to a sitting posture.

"Can't you understand, you fools?" he asked.

Hands grabbed his coat, jerked him forward.

"All right. Let's hear your story."

Swift kicked with his feet. "Take these handcuffs off."

A clock, clacking off the seconds, pointed to three minutes to four o'clock.

"Leave him with a guard and let's go see the office and the dead man," said one of the officers.

"Triple handcuff him, then," said Searle, "because he's the man who pulled the murders. There's no doubt of that in my mind."

"It was Ramsay," said Swift, striving to be patient. "I blundered on to this Dr. Zean, and—"

"Save it!" snapped one of the officers.

"No, no, let him talk."

Art Swift told his story. The officers looked at one another, incredulity stamped on their faces.

"There's a chance," said Searle, speaking judiciously, "just a chance that he's right. But, Swift, how did you know about the idea of switching cigarettes, the mechanics of the murders? You told Louise just how to go about it."

"Pure deduction, putting two and two together," said Swift.

One of the men clicked a key in the lock of the handcuffs.

"Stand up here and we'll make a search," he said.

Swift moved to stand up, and, as he did so, felt as though a hundred needles were shooting into his hip. He jumped, gave an exclamation, then as it suddenly dawned on him what had happened, he frantically plucked at his hip pocket.

"The capsules!" he exclaimed. "They've spilled from the metal box, and I jabbed myself with them!"

He pulled out of his pocket the crushed capsules. He had given himself a terrific dose of the extract. Nearly all of the capsules were crushed. The extract had penetrated to his blood. Even the big, five-hundred-to-one capsule had discharged its contents.

Men moved toward him.

"Maybe it's a s . . . u . . . "

Searle was talking, but midway in the sentence, his mouth ceased to make sounds. The extract had taken effect, and Swift was speeded up to a terrific rate of activity. The men before him were arrested in mid-motion. One of the officers had been in the act of jumping forward. His feet, Swift noticed, were both off the ground.

Art amused himself by walking around the officer, bending down and inserting his hand beneath the officer's foot. He couldn't feel the foot even moving.

He waited patiently for what seemed seconds, waiting for the situation to change. It remained unchanged. Men remained as they had been, their eyes staring, their mouths open. Every possible expression of surprise was depicted upon the frozen faces.

Swift realized that there was no use spending hours in that jail waiting for these men to dawdle through their slow motions.

ERLE STANLEY GARDNER

He walked to the door.

Even when he walked as slowly as possible, the wind tore savagely at his garments. He knew then that he was speeded up many times faster than when he had taken his first, experimental capsule. He was living at a ratio of at least five hundred to one, perhaps much faster.

He worked his way through the jail doors.

At the outer door a guard was stationed and the officer who sat on a stool on the other side of the door was peering intently through the bars. The door was locked.

Swift reached through the bars, grabbed the guard by the coat collar, pulled him forward. He pulled so slowly that it seemed hours before he had the man against the bars. Yet he noticed even that slow motion was about to jerk the head of the officer from his neck.

He had to reach out with his other hand and pull the head of the guard so that it followed the body. Otherwise he would have broken the neck of the unfortunate man.

He searched the pockets, found the key, fitted it to the lock from the outside, manipulated it with the tips of his fingers, and heard the bolts shoot back.

He pushed open the door.

The guard was as he had left him, but, as Swift watched, he fancied he detected the faintest possible motion of an eyelid, the beginning of a slow flutter.

Swift waited for what was, as nearly as he could judge, five minutes, watching that eyelid. There could be no question of it, it was slowly moving.

"Evidently he started to wink when I grabbed him," said Swift to himself, interested in the scientific aspect of the phenomenon. "It only takes a man around a fiftieth of a second to wink his eye, but I can't even see the blamed thing move. I must be speeded up so fast I whiz like a bullet!"

That thought made him wonder how a bullet would appear. Could he see it leave the gun?

He took the revolver from the officer's belt, pointed it at the steel wall of the jail and pulled the trigger.

Nothing happened.

He waited, watching, his wrist braced for the explosion.

"Something wrong," he said, and lowered the weapon, put it back in the holster of the officer. As he did so, something unusual about it caught his eye. The hammer of the weapon was only halfway back.

"Must have forgotten to cock it, but thought I did," he mumbled, and took it once more from the holster.

Then an explanation dawned upon him. The hammer was descending, ready to fire the shell. But that split fraction of a second which elapsed between the pulling of the trigger and the exploding of the shell was so multiplied by his speeded-up senses that it seemed an interval of minutes.

He looked around the jail for a while, watching the postures of the men who remained as living statues, motionless. Here was a man who had been about to sit down. Now he was suspended in mid-air, his body jackknifed, the weight on his heels.

Swift watched him for a while, then returned and took up the revolver. The hammer was just about to contact the shell.

Swift moved to a place where the light was good, pointed the weapon, waited.

There was a faint jar, a slow impulse up his wrist. Then he saw something mushroom from the mouth of the weapon. It was the bullet, propelled by a little mushroom of fire and smoke.

He was able to follow the progress of the bullet from the time it left the gun until it struck the wall of the cell. He could even see it flatten against the steel and start dropping to the floor.

He knew it must be dropping because he could see that nothing supported it. But it remained in one position so long he was unable to detect motion.

He returned the weapon to its holster, walked back to the cell where the officers had been interrogating him. The men all remained in the same position. The officer who had been jumping forward still had his feet off the floor.

Swift turned and walked from the jail, out into the late afternoon sunlight.

The atmospheric conditions bothered him more than any other thing. There was a perpetual shortness of breath. It seemed as though his laboring lungs simply couldn't suck enough air into his system. It was only when he was walking that he could breathe comfortably.

It must be that the rapidity of his progress forced the air into his lungs. But when he walked the wind pressure against his body was terrific. It tore his coat to tatters, and it was a physical impossibility to keep his hat on his head. He had the unique sensation of walking at a rate of speed that seemed to him to be somewhere around one mile an hour, and having the air pressure whip his hair straight out while his garments were torn.

And he was isolated in the midst of a busy world.

The street was crowded. People were starting for home. Street cars were jammed. Vehicular traffic was at its peak. The sidewalks were a seething mass of jostling humanity frozen into rigid inactivity.

Everywhere were people. Yet nowhere was motion. There was no sound. The universe was as silent as the midst of a desert. Occasionally there would be a faint buzzing sensation in Swift's ears, and he realized that this was probably caused by sound waves which were too slow for him to interpret as sound.

He walked across the street, threading his way through traffic, and wondering how long this strange sensation was to continue. He thought of the words of the dead scientist that it might be possible for one to live his entire life in a space of five minutes.

What a terrible fate it would be to be left to go through an entire lifetime without any contact with other people, to go from youth to middle age, middle age to doddering old age, all the time in a city that was suspended in the rush hour of its traffic.

If the scientist had been right, it would be a horrible fate. There was a man getting in a taxicab. It might be that Swift would be an old man before that fellow had traversed the length of the block. He could amuse himself for a year, then come back and find the taxicab just starting; perhaps the cabbie would be in the act of closing the door.

When Swift got to be an old man he could come hobbling back to the corner and find that the traffic signal had changed and that the man in the cab was halfway across the street.

It was an appalling thought.

But Swift was glad he had not been imprisoned in a cell. He might even have been held in a dark dungeon. He paused to think of what it would have meant. He would have had no food or water. He would have starved to death in what would, to the ordinary mortal, have been but half a dozen seconds, perhaps not that long.

The air tugged and whipped at his garments. He crawled painfully along, thinking over the events which had led up to the strange position in which he found himself.

A YEAR IN A DAY 143

6.
Among Living Statues

Art thought of Carl Ramsay and of how Ramsay would undoubtedly have summarized the situation in headlines. "Time Ticks Tediously," or some such alliterative expression, And, thinking of Ramsay, he suddenly thought of the murders, and knew that he must apprehend the real criminal.

He had unlimited time at his disposal. He could cover all trains, all means of escape. It only remained to walk where he wanted to go. Any form of so-called rapid transportation was out of the question.

One mistake he made. He jumped over the wheel of a machine that stood between him and the curb. The trip up in the air was quite all right. In fact he felt like a feather. Had it not been for the atmospheric resistance it would have been simple. But the rush of air held him down somewhat.

Even so, he jumped faster, farther, and higher than he had intended or thought possible. This was doubtless due to the fact that his strength had multiplied with his ability to speed up the muscular action.

But when he wanted to come back to the sidewalk he found that he could not do so. He was held a prisoner, floating in mid-air. The force of gravitation was so slow that it seemed he wasn't even drifting toward the sidewalk.

Finally he managed to claw his way along the side of a building, find a projection, use this to give him a handhold, and push himself toward the sidewalk.

He walked for fully a quarter of a mile before a strange pressure seemed to strike the bottoms of his feet. Then he knew that he was normally just alighting from the jump he had made. The force of gravitation had just taken hold.

That very element made it difficult for him to get about. He found that he dared not trust to any jumps, but must keep at least one foot on the pavement; if he made any sudden motion, there was not enough friction engendered by the force of gravitation to give him a foothold.

Altogether, it was a strange world, one in which every physical law seemed to be suspended. This was due, not to any change in the world itself, but merely to a change in the illusion of time. To express it in another manner, it was due entirely to the fact that Art Swift could think

ERLE STANLEY GARDNER

more rapidly.

The rate of thought, then, controlled environment.

It was a novel idea to toy with, but he couldn't wait for speculation. He had work to do. He must solve those murders, apprehend the real criminal.

He started with Carl Ramsay.

Undoubtedly Ramsay had been the point of contact for the murders. He had taken some of the drug, diluted so the tempo of living became a hundred to one. He had switched the cigarette Tolliver Hemingway was about to take from his cigarette case, for a poisoned cigarette in which the first half inch of tobacco had been prepared with some poisonous drug.

The millionaire had inhaled that drug with the first puff of the cigarette. Then, when he exhaled the smoke, the other watchers in the room had been able to get the odor. But Hemingway had received the full force of the concentrated gas.

It had been simple.

But Ramsay had grown careless. He had made his substitution when Swift's eyes were upon him. Swift hadn't been able to detect what was going on, but he had been able to see the sudden disappearance of the fast-moving right hand and arm, and then, when he had talked to Ramsay, Ramsay had tried to answer before the drug wore off.

That was the reason those first sounds which came from Ramsay's lips had been so unintelligible. Doubtless they had been words, perfectly formulated. But the sounds had been so rapid that it had been impossible for the eardrums of his hearers to split those sounds into words.

Then something had happened to Ramsay. Either he had planned his disappearance because he knew he would be suspected, or else he had actually been abducted after a struggle.

Swift determined to find out which.

He battled his way against the ever-present roar of the rushing atmosphere to Ramsay's room and took up the trail from there.

The police had combed the room, and had taken every article that might be of value. Yet Swift made a search of his own, going into every nook and corner. He found nothing.

He wondered if he should make an attempt to cover trains, and thought of Dr. Zean's office. He might find something there, and he could drop into the Union Depot on the way.

He walked down the stairs to the street, and suddenly jerked himself upright with an exclamation. A strange sight met his eyes.

The street was frozen into arrested activity. He had grown accustomed to that spectacle. A horse was trotting, and but one foot was on the ground. On his back was a mounted policeman. He had evidently been swinging his club. Now he was like a mounted statue. A taxicab was cutting over on the turn, and the tires on the outside were flattened by the weight of the car. There was not the slightest motion in either wheels or tires.

But that which arrested Swift's attention was the peculiar sight of a man walking casually through the tangled mass of arrested traffic.

The man's coattails were whipped out behind. His hair was streaming. His hat had gone, and he walked with the peculiar pavement-shuffling gait which Art Swift had found so necessary to cultivate.

Here, then, was a man, the tempo of whose life was some five hundred times plus that of other men. Here was a man who must be inoculated with the mysterious extract which Dr. Cassius Zean had discovered. By that same token, he must be one of the outlaw gang.

He carried a suitcase, and the suitcase had been streamlined to make it offer less resistance to the air. He walked like a man with a certain fixed purpose, and he seemed perfectly at ease, confident in his own power.

Watching him, Swift became convinced the man was an old hand at this rapid life. He seemed to show no interest in the strange phenomena of the frozen world where motion had been stilled. He walked calmly, sedately.

And Swift, slipping behind a parked automobile, watched him curiously, wondering what strange errand had caused this man to speed up his life at a ratio of five hundred to one.

The other slithered his way across the street, paused before the door of an imposing edifice. There was a fleshy woman leaving the door of that building, and Swift had noticed her prior to seeing the other man.

She was tugging at the door, one foot stretched out, ready to step to the pavement. Her mottled face was flushed with dark color. Her glassy eyes were staring straight ahead. Her mouth was open. Probably she was gasping for breath, but it would have taken seeming hours for her progress to the place she was going, minutes for the first intake of her breath to be apparent.

Swift realized now that he had no mere five-hundred-to-one ratio in his life tempo. The cumulative effect of the dosage he had taken when several capsules jabbed their contents into his blood stream had given him a much faster rate of life than that. He had no means of knowing just how fast.

The man he followed walked directly to the door out of which the woman was emerging. He ducked under her arm, brushed against her, and entered the lobby of the building.

Swift followed.

Once the man turned. By the simple process of freezing into complete immobility, Swift defied detection. All about were the figures of men staring with glassy, unseeing eyes at what was going on about them.

There was a policeman standing at a marble table in the center of the flagged floor. All about were counters, wickets, gilt cages.

Swift realized he was in one of the big banking establishments. The man he followed walked to one of the cages. He took a key from the inert hand of a guard, unlocked the cage door, pulled it open, entered.

There were piles of gold on the counter, stacked up in glittering spheres of coin. The man scooped them into the suitcase. Then he left and went to another cage. Here he repeated the process. Here, also, there were several piles of large-denomination currency. The man scooped these in with the gold.

When he had selected the cream of the plunder, he closed the suitcase and turned toward the door. Swift became stockstill, standing with one foot out and up, as though in the act of taking a step. The man passed within three feet of him. When he had gained the street, Swift followed.

His quarry led him to a corner a block away. Here he set the suitcase down, right beside a traffic policeman who was in the act of blowing his whistle.

He had left thousands of dollars in stolen gold and currency unguarded, right within reach of a policeman's hand. Yet he was perfectly safe in doing so. No one could move fast enough to pick it up.

The bank bandit shuffled into a jewelry store, selected several diamonds, dumped them into his pocket, returned to his suitcase, bowed his head to the policeman in ironical thanks, picked up the bag, and crossed the street.

Swift followed.

The man walked as rapidly as the air resistance would allow. He seemed intent upon reaching a certain destination as quickly as possible.

He turned into an alley. A truck was standing there, motor running. The suitcase was tossed into the truck. There were more suitcases there, all of the same general design.

As Swift watched, another figure came around the corner, walking in the same pavement-shuffling manner, carrying a suitcase. He tossed this upon the truck, paused to speak with the man Swift had been following.

Then the two turned and came directly toward Art Swift.

Once more he froze into immobility. They passed close to him. One of the men stopped.

"Say, I've seen this guy before. Who the hell is he?"

Swift remained motionless, one foot reaching out as though taking a step. Yet he knew there was something different in the studied balance of his pose from that of the other men who were caught in arrested motion.

"Never lamped him," said the second man. "Come on. We've got work to do."

But the man Swift had been following wasn't so certain.

"I'm telling you there's something funny about this guy. He stands funny, he looks funny. I've seen him before. I think he was standing in the bank I frisked. Let's go through his pockets and see who in hell he is."

"Aw, forget it. We got no time to be pulling all the funny stuff. That newspaper gave the whole show away, Doc Zean is croaked, and we ain't goin' to be able to get no more of the stuff. We gotta work fast and make a cleanup while the getting is good."

They moved away. Swift heard the man he had followed fling a final comment.

"When we come back we'll see which way he's walking and what he's got up his sleeve. He looks off color to me."

The men reached the mouth of the alley and turned away.

Swift started for cover, and, as he approached the place opposite which the truck was parked, saw a swirl of motion at the opposite end of the alley.

He adopted his usual expedient of standing absolutely still.

Two men, loaded down with suitcases, came into the alley. One of them stopped.

148   ERLE STANLEY GARDNER

"Say, that guy wasn't there last trip!"

"What do we care? He couldn't do anything."

"Yeah, but he might be stallin'."

They set down their suitcases, walked with quiet menace directly toward Art Swift.

Then Swift caught sight of something else. Another man glided swiftly into the alley. There was something familiar in the posture of that man. He gave a swift glance and found that it was Nick Searle of the *Star*.

In some manner the reporter had speeded himself up so as to get into the game. Art thought of the metal box the girl had received, a box containing a complete assortment of the rubber capsules. Probably Searle had secured possession of that and had injected sufficient of the serum to take part in the strange game which was being enacted.

The two bandits approached Swift. Searle was not far behind.

"Hey, you, what you doing here?" asked one of the men, pausing before Swift.

Swift endeavored to keep his face entirely devoid of expression. He fixed his eyes upon distance, and held his breath.

"Aw, he's all right," grumbled one of the men. "Just some poor mutt that strayed into the alley and we didn't notice him the other trip."

"The hell we didn't," insisted the more suspicious of the two. "He just wasn't here, and if he wasn't—"

He moved his hand in a swift gesture, directly toward Swift's eye.

"If he's on the up-and-up, we can stroke the eyeball," said the man.

Involuntarily Art blinked.

"Ha!" exclaimed the bandit, and jumped forward, his fist swinging in a terrific uppercut.

Art sidestepped, jerked his head back to dodge the blow, and shot out a straight left.

He found that the atmospheric resistance slowed his punches somewhat, but the superior strength which had come to his muscles with the speeding-up process largely overcame that. It was his clothes that suffered most.

As he launched that straight left, the resistance of the air held his coat sleeve stationary. He had the peculiar sensation of feeling his sleeve peeled back from his arm, and the bare arm flashed forward in a quick punch which connected.

But the second man was busy. He swung a slungshot, and only missed

Swift's head by a matter of inches.

"The damned spy!" yelled the man who staggered back under the impetus of Swift's punch.

Art knew he was no match for the two men, and jumped to one side, hoping to get where he could have his back to the wall. But they understood his maneuver and closed on him from different angles.

He ducked, caught a punch on the back of the head, felt his stomach grow cold as a fist landed in the solar plexus, and dropped to his knees. He flung out his arm, reaching for the legs that sought to kick him in the face, caught an ankle, jerked it, and had the satisfaction of seeing the man go down.

7.
The Man Who Mastered Time

With a roar Nick Searle joined the conflict.

That was the determining factor. The men had hardly expected an equal battle. Having Swift down and getting ready to knife him was one thing; having that wiry young man on hands and knees grabbing at their ankles while another man swung lusty fists was quite another.

It took but four punches to decide the battle. The two bandits sprawled on the cement.

Swift was still on hands and knees, writhing in pain. But he had managed to tackle both of his adversaries with groping hands which had kept them from doubling up on Searle.

"Hurt?" asked Searle.

Swift made a wry face, gasping for breath.

"Wind—knocked—out."

Searle helped him to his feet.

After a few seconds Swift got over the temporary paralysis of the diaphragm which had been induced by the blow he had received, and gave a wry grin.

"How'd you get here?" Art asked the reporter.

"Took some of the serum and started out. Found I wasn't hopped up enough, so I put half a dozen of the small capsules into effect all at once.

"How did you know you weren't hopped up enough?"

"Because of the way things were whizzing by me. I tried to follow a

ERLE STANLEY GARDNER

man, and I might as well have tried to follow an express train. I figure we are living right now at a ratio of around three thousand to one." Searle seemed awed as he said the words.

"Not that fast."

"Mighty near it."

"The girl?" Art demanded.

"You mean Louise Folsom?"

"Yes."

"That's what worries me. They've managed to get her somehow, and they've carried her off. This looks to me like the final blow-up. The exposé in the *Star* has broken a lot of their power. . . . You'll forgive us for jumping at the conclusion you were the mysterious scientist who was at the head of the thing? Tell me how you got into it—but first let's get these two chaps tied up nice and tight and see if we can't locate where they were going."

Swift nodded.

"There's some rope on the truck. I'll tell you the story while we truss 'em up. And I think I know about where headquarters are."

"What truck? This one?"

"That's the one. You'd better be careful with those suitcases. They're all loaded with money and gems."

"What?"

"Fact. They've lost their power to terrorize the nation and make the big executives bow to their will, but they still have their power to rob without the victim's being able to guard against it. They're stripping the city."

"Humph. And there's only two of us," commented Nick Searle, as he trussed up one of the bandits. "Guns any good?"

"None whatever. The bullets could be dodged, and it takes forever and a day for the hammer to explode the shell. If we wanted to shoot one of these men when he broke loose, we'd have to start shooting the gun now. Then we could go about our business for a while, come back and see if the man had got the knots untied, and, when he did, trust the explosion of the revolver would happen somewhere along about that time."

Searle laughed.

"You paint a gloomy picture."

"It's almost that bad. Notice the truck is backed up to a cellar. I have an idea that cellar is of some importance. Let's explore in it a little."

"Suits me. What'll we do with the men?"

"Drag 'em in . . . Look out! Here come another couple! Lord, there are two more. Four of 'em. We've got to hide here in the truck, and when we start hostilities we've got to work fast. There's a couple of stakes that'll make good clubs."

Swift crouched behind a pile of the strangely streamlined suitcases. Four men appeared, laden with loot. They called a greeting, started for the truck.

"Look out!" yelled one. "Somebody's hiding here!"

"Let's go!" shouted Art Swift.

The young scientist and the reporter got into action.

One of the outlaws, doubtless forgetting the uselessness of the weapon, pulled an automatic from his pocket, leveled it, and pulled the trigger. Then he dashed it to the ground when the weapon failed to explode.

Two of the men had knives. One climbed on the side of the truck, the other tried the rear.

Thud, thump sounded the clubs, and the men drew off, one of them with a broken arm.

"Let's go!" yelled Swift, for the second time, and they charged.

It happened that the two men had chanced upon the most deadly weapon available. Knives were limited as to range. Guns were of no use. Clubs, swung with terrific speed and force, were bone-breaking instruments of destruction.

Apparently these outlaws had never encountered resistance in the time-plane upon which they had learned to function. They had never experimented with various weapons, and the futility of their guns, the limited efficiency of their knives, left them helpless before the onslaught of the two men armed with clubs.

Searle surveyed the sprawled figures, grinned at Swift.

"Looks like a good job. Do we tie these up?"

"Sure thing."

"How about headquarters?"

"Let's investigate."

"Attaboy! Better keep that club. We'll probably run into some more trouble."

They lowered themselves into a cellar, pushing themselves down the stairs because the force of gravitation was too slow to function, felt their way along a passage, and emerged into a lighted room.

A man sat in this room with telephone receivers clamped to either ear. He was tall, gaunt, dominating. His eyes held a restlessness that seemed unclean, unhealthy. The thin lips were compressed into a single razor-blade slash that cut from cheek to cheek. His jaw was bony, determined.

On the third finger of his right hand gleamed a ring of interlaced triangles. He glanced at the two men, looked at their clubs, half rose from the chair.

"Mr. Zin Zandor, I presume," said Swift.

The restless eyes snapped to his face.

"So?" rasped the man, and fumbled beneath his desk.

"Stop him," shouted Searle, and made a wild leap forward.

Swift lowered the point of his club and launched it through the air like a lance with every ounce of force of which he was capable.

At the same instant he became aware of a sickening sweet odor which permeated the room.

Zandor tried to duck. The hurtling club caught him on the forehead as he lowered his head, cutting an ugly gash, sending him staggering back.

His right hand flashed up. It held a sort of gas mask, which he tried to raise to his nostrils. But the impact of the blow had dazed him. His hands seemed to function uncertainly. He turned half purple in the features as congested blood mottled the skin.

"He's holding his breath," shouted the reporter, quick to grasp the situation.

Swift whirled. Together they fought toward the door, holding their breath, the sickly-sweet odor seeming to constrict the muscles of their throats.

Behind them they heard a peculiar scraping sound. They turned for one last look.

Zin Zandor was clawing at the top of the desk. The poison gas had got him now. His features were distorted, his mouth open. Even as they looked he went limp, and apparently remained suspended in mid-air.

"Dead and falling," said Swift as he dragged his companion into the passageway, out to the open air.

They sucked in great lungfuls, feeling strangely dizzy.

"The girl!" cried Searle.

Without an instant's hesitation, Swift turned and led the way back into the passageway.

"Take a deep breath and we'll try for her. Probably the gas rises. Keep your head near the floor."

They dived down and crawled along the floor. The sickening sweet odor was in their nostrils. At the corner of the desk, inclined at an angle of almost forty-five degrees, was the form of the man who had signed himself Zin Zandor. He was falling to the floor, and the force of gravitation was so slow, compared to the speeded-up life forces of the two men who watched him, that he seemed to drift downward with hardly perceptible motion.

There was a door to the left of the desk. Swift took a deep breath, reached upward, turned the knob. The door opened; they scrambled into the inner room.

Here was a Remington typewriter, doubtless the one upon which the blackmail letters had been written. Here, also, was stored great treasure, gold coins, currency, gems. And here they found the girl who had posed as messenger. She was bound hand and foot, gagged—Louise Folsom, captured, doomed to die.

Her eyes stared straight up at the ceiling of the room. She made no move when they entered.

"Living at a normal rate. Can't see us," said Searle.

He drew a knife and cut the ropes. Even then she did not move. They watched her anxiously. The closed door was shutting out many of the poison fumes. But there was a chance she had already inhaled too many of them.

Searle reached out and gently touched the eyeball with the tip of his finger. The lid gradually—very, very slowly—commenced to droop.

"She's alive," said Swift.

The girl's lips moved with such slowness that the motion was hardly perceptible.

"She knows we're here, trying to talk."

Searle nodded.

"We've got to get her out of here. That gas, you know."

"The door's closed. Remember, it disperses quickly. It takes a concentrated dose to produce death. He probably had it in the ring. He intended to liberate the gas from the poison ring and fill the room with it. Then he was going to put on some sort of a gas mask."

ERLE STANLEY GARDNER

"Yeah. Your blow with the club got him groggy, and he sucked in a mouthful of the concentrated gas before he knew what he was doing."

"How about getting the girl out?"

"Let's try to carry her. But pick her up gently or we'll jerk her to pieces, and we'll have to stop easy like or—wait a minute—I'm feeling queer!"

At that same moment Art Swift felt a peculiar sensation at the pit of his stomach.

"The gas!" he exclaimed.

"No," said Searle. "We're coming back to normal!"

There was a brief spell of vertigo, and then, of a sudden, things were normal.

The girl's eyes were blinking; her lips were forming words.

Beyond the door that led to the other room something crashed—the body of Zin Zandor, just falling to the floor.

The girl's rapid words rang in their ears.

"Hoped you would come. They were planning to make this the day of the big clean-up. They had all their men ready to bring on a new reign of terror, and they were going to kill me."

Swift pointed to a door that opened from one side of the room. He picked up a chair, crashed it through one of the panels.

"Let's get out of here!"

They felt the tang of fresh air upon their faces, saw the street roaring with the busy life of a rush hour. The noise burst upon their ears. In the alley, motor running, was the truck, filled with the strangely shaped suitcases. Sprawled just inside the door, where the two adventurers had dragged them, were the bodies of the unconscious bandits, tied hand and foot.

There was no traffic in the alley, but the street just beyond was filled with activity.

"Load 'em in and start for headquarters," said Searle, and grinned.

The girl climbed into the driver's seat.

"I can handle the truck."

They struggled with the men, got the inert figures into the truck.

"Let's make a good job," said Searle.

Swift caught his drift and grinned assent.

They returned to the cellar. The fumes of the deadly gas had dispersed.

There remained only an odor, something like that given off by orange blossoms. The dead form of Zin Zandor sprawled on the floor.

They carried it to the truck. Then they loaded the stored treasure. Then they started the truck.

"Go to the *Star* office," Searle called to the girl. "We were the ones to blacken Swift's character, and we might as well be the ones to laud him to the skies as the hero who saved the country."

The girl flashed him a smile.

"Scientist Saves Day!" she said.

"That reminds me, where do you suppose Ramsay is?"

"Suicide," said Searle. "We found him just before I met you last. He had blown his brains out and left a typical note—poor chap: 'Reporter Reaps Ruin—Rum Ruins Ramsay!' "

They were silent for a moment.

"He was in on it from the beginning, of course?" asked Swift.

"Yes. He was the contact man. He actually switched the cigarettes. He faked an attack upon himself to divert suspicion."

Swift sighed. "Man, but I feel sleepy!"

"Effect of the drug. We've been living rapidly, perhaps more than a year in the last few hours. It's gone out of our lives."

"A year in a day," laughed the girl.

Swift caught her eye.

"Then I've known you a year, Louise," he said.

Her answering smile contained no trace of offense.

"We can call it that, Art."

"A heck of a fast worker," said Searle. "That goldarned scientist doesn't need to have anyone pep him up with a lot of extracts to make him work fast!"

All three joined in a laugh as the truck with its strange load swung to a stop before the *Star* office, the biggest scoop in a half century delivered at the very door of the newspaper.

ERLE STANLEY GARDNER

The Mezzotint

by M. R. James

Some time ago I believe I had the pleasure of telling you the story of an adventure which happened to a friend of mine by the name of Dennistoun, during his pursuit of objects of art for the museum of Cambridge.

He did not publish his experiences very widely upon his return to England; but they could not fail to become known to a good many of his friends, and among others to the gentleman who at that time presided over an art museum at another university. It was to be expected that the story should make a considerable impression on the mind of a man whose vocation lay in lines similar to Dennistoun's, and that he should be eager to catch at any explanation of the matter which tended to make it seem improbable that he should ever be called upon to deal with so agitating an emergency. It was, indeed, somewhat consoling to him to reflect that he was not expected to acquire ancient MSS for his institution; that was the business of the Shelburnian Library. The authorities of that institution might, if they pleased, ransack obscure corners of the Continent for such matters. He was glad to be obliged at the moment to confine his attention to enlarging the already unsurpassed collection of English topographical drawings and engravings possessed by his museum. Yet, as it turned out, even a department so homely and familiar as this may have its dark corners, and to one of these Mr. Williams was unexpectedly introduced.

Those who have taken even the most limited interest in the acquisition of topographical pictures are aware that there is one London dealer whose aid is indispensable to their researches. Mr. J. W. Britnell publishes at short intervals very admirable catalogues of a large and constantly changing stock of engravings, plans, and old sketches of mansions, churches, and towns in England and Wales. These catalogues were, of course, the ABC of his subject to Mr. Williams: but as his museum already contained an enormous accumulation of topographical pictures, he was a regular, rather than a copious, buyer; and he rather looked to Mr. Britnell to fill up gaps in the rank and file of his collection than to supply him with rarities.

Now, in February of last year there appeared upon Mr. Williams's desk at the museum a catalogue from Mr. Britnell's emporium, and accompanying it was a typewritten communication from the dealer himself. This letter ran as follows:'

Dear Sir,
We beg to call your attention to No. 978 in our accompanying catalogue, which we shall be glad to send on approval.
Your faithfully,
J. W. Britnell

To turn to No. 978 in the accompanying catalogue was with Mr. Williams (as he observed to himself) the work of a moment, and in the place indicated he found the following entry:

978.—*Unknown. Interesting mezzotint: View of a manor house, early part of the century. 15 by 10 inches; black frame.* £2 2s.

It was not specially exciting, and the price seemed high. However, as Mr. Britnell, who knew his business and his customer, seemed to set store by it, Mr. Williams wrote a postcard asking for the article to be sent on approval, along with some other engravings and sketches which appeared in the same catalogue. And so he passed without much excitement of anticipation to the ordinary labors of the day.

A parcel of any kind always arrives a day later than you expect it, and that of Mr. Britnell proved, as I believe the right phrase goes, no exception to the rule. It was delivered at the museum by the afternoon post of Saturday, after Mr. Williams had left his work, and it was accordingly brought round to his rooms in college by the attendant, in order that he might not have to wait over Sunday before looking through it and returning such of the contents as he did not propose to keep. And here he found it when he came in to tea, with a friend.

The only item with which I am concerned was the rather large, black-framed mezzotint of which I have already quoted the short description given in Mr. Britnell's catalogue. Some more details of it will have to be given, though I cannot hope to put before you the look of the picture as

M.R. JAMES

clearly as it is present to my eye. Very nearly the exact duplicate of it may be seen in a good many old inn parlors, or in the passages of undisturbed country mansions at the present moment. It was a rather indifferent mezzotint, and an indifferent mezzotint is, perhaps, the worst form of engraving known. It presented a full-face view of a not very large manor house of the last century, with three rows of plain sashed windows with rusticated masonry about them, a parapet with balls or vases at the angles, and a small portico in the center. On either side were trees, and in front a considerable expanse of lawn. The legend "A. W. F. sculpsit" was engraved on the narrow margin; and there was no further inscription. The whole thing gave the impression that it was the work of an amateur. What in the world Mr. Britnell could mean by affixing the price of £2 2s. to such an object was more than Mr. Williams could imagine. He turned it over with a good deal of contempt; upon the back was a paper label, the left hand half of which had been torn off. All that remained were the ends of two lines of writing; the first had the letters—*ngley Hall*; the second—*ssex*.

It would, perhaps, be just worthwhile to identify the place represented, which he could easily do with the help of a gazetteer, and then he would send it back to Mr. Britnell, with some remarks reflecting upon the judgment of that gentleman.

He lighted the candles, for it was now dark, made the tea, and supplied the friend with whom he had been playing golf (for I believe the authorities of the university I write of indulge in that pursuit by way of relaxation); and tea was taken to the accompaniment of a discussion which golfing persons can imagine for themselves, but which the conscientious writer has no right to inflict upon any nongolfing persons.

The conclusion arrived at was that certain strokes might have been better, and that in certain emergencies neither player had experienced that amount of luck which a human being has a right to expect. It was now that the friend—let us call him Professor Binks—took up the framed engraving, and said:

"What's this place, Williams?"

"Just what I am going to try to find out," said Williams, going to the shelf for a gazetteer. "Look at the back. Somethingley Hall, either in Sussex or Essex. Half the name's gone, you see. You don't happen to know it, I suppose?"

"It's from that man Britnell, I suppose, isn't it?" said Binks. "Is it for the museum?"

"Well, I think I should buy it if the price was five shillings," said Williams, "but for some unearthly reason he wants two guineas for it. I can't conceive why. It's a wretched engraving, and there aren't even any figures to give it life."

"It's not worth two guineas, I should think," said Binks, "but I don't think it's so badly done. The moonlight seems rather good to me; and I should have thought there *were* figures, or at least a figure, just on the edge in front."

"Let's look," said Williams. "Well, it's true the light is rather cleverly given. Where's your figure? Oh, yes! Just the head, in the very front of the picture."

And indeed there was—hardly more than a black blot on the extreme edge of the engraving—the head of a man or woman, a good deal muffled up, the back turned to the spectator, and looking towards the house.

Williams had not noticed it before.

"Still," he said, "though it's a cleverer thing than I thought, I can't spend two guineas of museum money on a picture of a place I don't know."

Professor Binks had his work to do, and soon went; and very nearly up to Hall time Williams was engaged in a vain attempt to identify the subject of his picture. "If the vowel before the *ng* had only been left, it would have been easy enough," he thought, "but as it is, the name may be anything from Guestingley to Langley, and there are many more names ending like this than I thought; and this rotten book has no index of terminations."

Hall in Mr. Williams's college was at seven. It need not be dwelt upon; the less so as he met there colleagues who had been playing golf during the afternoon, and words with which we have no concern were freely bandied across the table—merely golfing words, I would hasten to explain.

I suppose an hour or more to have been spent in what is called common room after dinner. Later in the evening some few retired to Williams's rooms, and I have little doubt that whist was played and tobacco smoked. During a lull in these operations Williams picked up the mezzotint from the table without looking at it, and handed it to a person mildly interested in art, telling him where it had come from, and the other particulars which we already know.

The gentleman took it carelessly, looked at it, then said, in a tone of

M.R. JAMES

some interest:

"It's really a very good piece of work, Williams; it has quite a feeling of the romantic period. The light is admirably managed, it seems to me, and the figure, though it's rather too grotesque, is somehow very impressive."

"Yes, isn't it?" said Williams, who was just then busy giving whisky and soda to others of the company, and was unable to come across the room to look at the view again.

It was by this time rather late in the evening, and the visitors were on the move. After they went Williams was obliged to write a letter or two and clear up some odd bits of work. At last, some time past midnight, he was disposed to turn in, and he put out his lamp after lighting his bedroom candle. The picture lay face upwards on the table where the last man who looked at it had put it, and it caught his eye as he turned the lamp down. What he saw made him very nearly drop the candle on the floor, and he declares now that if he had been left in the dark at that moment he would have had a fit. But, as that did not happen, he was able to put down the light on the table and take a good look at the picture. It was indubitable—rankly impossible, no doubt, but absolutely certain. In the middle of the lawn in front of the unknown house there was a figure where no figure had been at five o'clock that afternoon. It was crawling on all fours towards the house, and it was muffled in a strange black garment with a white cross on the back.

I do not know what is the ideal course to pursue in a situation of this kind. I can only tell you what Mr. Williams did. He took the picture by one corner and carried it across the passage to a second set of rooms which he possessed. There he locked it up in a a drawer, sported the doors of both sets of rooms, and retired to bed; but first he wrote out and signed an account of the extraordinary change which the picture had undergone since it had come into his possession.

Sleep visited him rather late; but it was consoling to reflect that the behavior of the picture did not depend upon his own unsupported testimony. Evidently the man who had looked at it the night before had seen something of the same kind as he had, otherwise he might have been tempted to think that something gravely wrong was happening either to his eyes or his mind. This possibility being fortunately precluded, two matters awaited him on the morrow. He must take stock of the picture very carefully, and call in a witness for the purpose, and he must make a determined effort to ascertain what house it was that was represented. He would therefore ask his neighbor Nisbet to breakfast with him, and he would subsequently spend a morning over the gazetteer.

Nisbet was disengaged, and arrived about nine thirty. His host was not quite dressed, I am sorry to say, even at this late hour. During breakfast nothing was said about the mezzotint by Williams, save that he had a picture on which he wished for Nisbet's opinion. But those who are familiar with university life can picture for themselves the wide and delightful range of subjects over which the conversation of two Fellows of Canterbury College is likely to extend during a Sunday morning breakfast. Hardly a topic was left unchallenged, from golf to lawn tennis. Yet I am bound to say that Williams was rather distraught; for his interest naturally centered in that very strange picture which was now reposing, face downwards, in the drawer in the room opposite.

The morning pipe was at last lighted, and the moment had arrived for which he looked. With very considerable—almost tremulous—excitement, he ran across, unlocked the drawer, and, extracting the picture—still face downwards—ran back, and put it into Nisbet's hands.

"Now," he said, "Nisbet, I want you to tell me exactly what you see in that picture. Describe it, if you don't mind, rather minutely. I'll tell you why afterwards."

"Well," said Nisbet, "I have here a view of a country house—English, I presume—by moonlight."

"Moonlight? You're sure of that?"

"Certainly. The moon appears to be on the wane, if you wish for details, and there are clouds in the sky."

"All right. Go on. I'll swear," added Williams in an aside, "there was no moon when I saw it first."

"Well, there's not much more to be said," Nisbet continued. "The house has one—two—three rows of windows, five in each row, except at the bottom, where there's a porch instead of the middle one, and—"

"But what about figures?" said Williams with marked interest.

"There aren't any," said Nisbet; "but—"

"What! No figure on the grass in front?"

"Not a thing."

"You'll swear to that?"

"Certainly I will. But there's just one other thing."

"What?"

"Why, one of the windows on the ground floor—left of the door—is open."

"Is it really so? My goodness! he must have got in," said Williams, with great excitement; and he hurried to the back of the sofa on which Nisbet was sitting, and, catching the picture from him, verified the matter for himself.

It was quite true. There was no figure, and there was the open window. Williams, after a moment of speechless surprise, went to the writing table and scribbled for a short time. Then he brought two papers to Nisbet, and asked him first to sign one—it was his own description of the picture, which you have just heard—and then to read the other which was Williams's statement written the night before.

"What can it all mean?" said Nisbet.

"Exactly," said Williams. "Well, one thing I must do—or three things, now I think of it, I must find out from Garwood"—this was his last night's visitor—" what he saw, and then I must get the thing photographed before it goes further, and then I must find out what the place is."

"I can do the photographing myself," said Nisbet, "and I will. But, you know, it looks very much as if we were assisting at the working out of a tragedy somewhere. The question is, has it happened already, or is it going to come off? You must find out what the place is. Yes," he said, looking at the picture again, "I expect you're right: he has got in. And if I don't mistake there'll be the devil to pay in one of the rooms upstairs."

"I'll tell you what," said Williams: "I'll take the picture across to old Green" (this was the senior Fellow of the College, who had been bursar for many years). "It's quite likely he'll know it. We have property in Essex and Sussex, and he must have been over the two counties a lot in his time."

"Quite likely he will," said Nisbet; "but just let me take my photograph first. But look here, I rather think Green isn't up today. He wasn't in Hall last night, and I think I heard him say he was going down for the Sunday."

"That's true, too," said Williams; "I know he's gone to Brighton. Well, if you'll photograph it now, I'll go across to Garwood and get his statement, and you keep an eye on it while I'm gone. I'm beginning to think two guineas is not a very exorbitant price for it now."

In a short time he had returned, and brought Mr. Garwood with him. Garwood's statement was to the effect that the figure, when he had seen it, was clear of the edge of the picture, but had not got far across the lawn. He remembered a white mark on the back of its drapery, but could not have been sure it was a cross. A document to this effect was then drawn up and signed, and Nisbet proceeded to photograph the picture.

"Now what do you mean to do?" he said. "Are you going to sit and watch it all day?"

"Well, no, I think not," said Williams. "I rather imagine we're meant to see the whole thing. You see, between the time I saw it last night and this morning there was time for lots of things to happen, but the creature only got into the house. It could easily have got through its business in the time and gone to its own place again; but the fact of the window being open, I think, must mean that it's in there now. So I feel quite easy about leaving it. And besides, I have a kind of idea that it wouldn't change much, if at all, in the daytime. We might go out for a walk this afternoon, and come in to tea, or whenever it gets dark. I shall leave it out on the table here, and sport the door. My skip can get in, but no one else."

The three agreed that this would be a good plan; and, further, that if they spent the afternoon together they would be less likely to talk about the business to other people; for any rumor of such a transaction as was going on would bring the whole of the Phasmatological Society about their ears.

We may give them a respite until five o'clock.

At or near that hour the three were entering Williams's staircase. They were at first slightly annoyed to see that the door of his rooms was unsported; but in a moment it was remembered that on Sunday the skips came for orders an hour or so earlier than on weekdays. However, a surprise was awaiting them. The first thing they saw was the picture leaning up against a pile of books on the table, as it had been left, and the next thing was Williams's skip, seated on a chair opposite, gazing at it with undisguised horror. How was this? Mr. Filcher (the name is not my own invention) was a servant of considerable standing, and set the standard of etiquette to all his own college and to several neighboring ones, and nothing could be more alien to his practice than to be found sitting on his master's chair, or appearing to take any particular notice of his master's furniture or pictures. Indeed, he seemed to feel this himself. He started violently when the three men were in the room, and got up with a marked effort. Then he said:

"I ask your pardon, sir, for taking such a freedom as to set down."

M.R. JAMES

"Not at all, Robert," interposed Mr. Williams. "I was meaning to ask you sometime what you thought of that picture."

"Well, sir, of course I don't set up my opinion again yours, but it ain't the pictur I should 'ang where my little girl could see it, sir."

"Wouldn't you, Robert? Why not?"

"No, sir. Why, the pore child, I recollect once she see a Door Bible, with picturs not 'alf what that is, and we 'ad to set up with her three or four nights afterwards, if you'll believe me; and if she was to ketch a sight of this skelinton here, or whatever it is, carrying off the pore baby, she would be in a taking. You know 'ow it is with children; 'ow nervish they git with a little thing and all. But what I should say, it don't seem a right pictur to be laying about, sir, not where anyone that's liable to be startled could come on it. Should you be wanting anything this evening, sir? Thank you, sir."

With these words the excellent man went to continue the round of his masters, and you may be sure the gentlemen whom he left lost no time in gathering round the engraving. There was the house, as before, under the waning moon and the drifting clouds. The window that had been open was shut, and the figure was once more on the lawn: but not this time crawling cautiously on hands and knees. Now it was erect and stepping swiftly, with long strides, towards the front of the picture. The moon was behind it, and the black drapery hung down over its face so that only hints of that could be seen, and what was visible made the spectators profoundly thankful that they could see no more than a white domelike forehead and a few straggling hairs. The head was bent down, and the arms were tightly clasped over an object which could be dimly seen and identified as a child, whether dead or living it was not possible to say. The legs of the appearance alone could be plainly discerned, and they were horribly thin.

From five to seven the three companions sat and watched the picture by turns. But it never changed. They agreed at last that it would be safe to leave it, and that they would return after Hall and await further developments.

When they assembled again, at the earliest possible moment, the engraving was there, but the figure was gone, and the house was quiet under the moonbeams. There was nothing for it but to spend the evening over gazetteers and guidebooks. Williams was the lucky one at last, and perhaps he deserved it. At eleven thirty P.M. he read from Murray's *Guide to Essex* the following lines:

16½ miles, Anningley. The church has been an interesting building of Norman date, but was extensively classicized in the last century. It contains the tomb of the family of Francis, whose mansion, Anningley Hall, a solid Queen Anne house, stands immediately beyond the churchyard in a park of about eighty acres. The family is now extinct, the last heir having disappeared mysteriously in infancy in the year 1802. The father, Mr. Arthur Francis, was locally known as a talented amateur engraver in mezzotint. After his son's disappearance he lived in complete retirement at the Hall, and was found dead in his studio on the third anniversary of the disaster, having just completed an engraving of the house, impressions of which are of considerable rarity.

This looked like business, and, indeed, Mr. Green on his return at once identified the house as Anningley Hall.

"Is there any kind of explanation of the figure, Green?" was the question which Williams naturally asked.

"I don't know, I'm sure, Williams. What used to be said in the place when I first knew it, which was before I came up here, was just this: old Francis was always very much down on these poaching fellows, and whenever he got a chance he used to get a man whom he suspected of it turned off the estate, and by degrees he got rid of them all but one. Squires could do a lot of things then that they daren't think of now. Well, this man that was left was what you find pretty often in that country—the last remains of a very old family. I believe they were lords of the manor at one time. I recollect just the same thing in my own parish."

"What, like the man in *Tess o' the D'Urbervilles*," Williams put in.

"Yes, I dare say; it's not a book I could ever read myself. But this fellow could show a row of tombs in the church there that belonged to his ancestors, and all that went to sour him a bit; but Francis, they said, could never get at him—he always kept just on the right side of the law—until one night the keepers found him at it in a wood right at the end of the estate. I could show you the place now; it marches with some land that used to belong to an uncle of mine. And you can imagine there was a row; and this man Gawdy (that was the name, to be sure—Gawdy; I thought I should get it—Gawdy), he was unlucky enough, poor chap!, to shoot a keeper. Well, that was what Francis wanted, and grand juries—you know what they would have been then—and poor Gawdy was strung up in double-quick time; and I've been shown the place he was

M.R. JAMES

buried in, on the north side of the church—you know the way in that part of the world: anyone that's been hanged or made away with themselves, they bury them that side. And the idea was that some friend of Gawdy's—not a relation, because he had none, poor devil!, he was the last of his line; kind of *spes ultima gentis*—must have planned to get hold of Francis's boy and put an end to *his* line, too. I don't know—it's rather an out-of-the-way thing for an Essex poacher to think of—but, you know, I should say now it looks more as if old Gawdy had managed the job himself. Booh! I hate to think of it! Have some whisky, Williams!"

The facts were communicated by Williams to Dennistoun, and by him to a mixed company, of which I was one, and the Sadducean Professor of Ophiology another. I am sorry to say that the latter, when asked what he thought of it, only remarked: "Oh, those Bridgeford people will say anything"—a sentiment which met with the reception it deserved.

I have only to add that the picture is now in the Ashleian Museum; that it has been treated with a view to discovering whether sympathetic ink has been used in it, but without effect; that Mr. Britnell knew nothing of it save that he was sure it was uncommon; and that, though carefully watched, it has never been known to change again.

The Peregrine

by Clark Howard

The road gang prisoners were working toward the center of a thick briar patch, attacking it from two sides with spades and hoes. The tangled jungle was so dense it would take weeks to clear. The briars, treacherous with thorns, were waist high, so that despite the burning Florida sun the men labored clad in denim jackets and harness gloves. They worked in pairs, at intervals of fifteen feet. Conley, as usual, worked with the old man, Beever.

It was Beever who found the peregrine.

"Look there," he said, grinning his toothless grin, "a baby chicken hawk."

Conley glanced cursorily where the old man was pointing, then snapped his eyes back when he fully realized what he had seen.

"Chicken hawks is bad for farmers," Beever observed. He raised his hoe a few inches to kill it.

"Don't," Conley said urgently. "That isn't a chicken hawk."

"I know a chicken hawk when I see one." Beever moved closer to his prey.

"Don't do it," Conley said evenly, his words now a warning.

Beever stopped and squinted curiously at him. "What's the matter with you? If that there ain't a chicken hawk, I'd like to know what it is."

"I'll tell you what it is," Conley said quietly, his eyes frozen on the bird lying snarled in the thicket. "It's a female peregrine. A falcon."

Conley glanced at the wooden guard shack a hundred yards away. Tevis, the road gang guard, sat on a chair in the shade, cradling a double-barreled shotgun across his knees. Fifty feet from the shack a long length of chain was stretched out in the dust. The chain was known as the Deadline; no prisoner was allowed to step beyond the chain when approaching the shack.

"Keep working," Conley said to the old man. "Watch Tevis and warn

CLARK HOWARD

me if he gets curious."

Conley moved behind and around Beever and inched his way toward the trapped peregrine. The bird fluttered its free wing nervously and opened wide its knifelike hooked beak. Round agate eyes, fluid with fear, watched every move Conley made.

"Easy, bird," Conley whispered in a soothing voice, "easy now." He drew a wrinkled handkerchief from his pocket and folded it lengthwise in eights. "Nice little falcon, nice baby."

When he was close enough he reached quickly and looped the thick fold of white over the peregrine's head, blindfolding it. The bird fell motionless at once and lay calmly in its briar trap.

"Give me a shoelace," Conley whispered to Beever. The old man's toothless mouth opened to protest, but the cold seriousness of Conley's face, the tightened lips and almost wild eyes, made him reconsider. Beever quickly pulled a lace from one hightopped prison brogan and tossed it to the ground near Conley. The younger man snatched it up and wound it snugly but not tightly around the handkerchief, securing it with an easily removable knot.

"Lie easily now, falcon," he whispered, moving back beside Beever. "How's Tevis doing?" he asked the old man.

"Ain't moved," Beever said. "What'd you do to that there—what'd you call it?"

"Peregrine," Conley said softly. "A peregrine falcon. I blindfolded it. When a falcon can't see, it dozes and rests. I don't want it to hurt its wing until I can untangle it from the thorns." Conley glanced up at Tevis now and saw that the guard was gazing off in another direction. "Listen," he said urgently to Beever, "when we break for the morning water ration, I want you to get me a piece of rawhide. I'll wander toward the Deadline and attract Tevis's attention. While he's watching me, you snatch a strip off the water bag lashing."

"How'm I gonna cut it?" Beever whined. "I don't have a knife."

"Use the head of the nail it's hanging on," Conley said impatiently.

"I don't know if I can."

"Listen, old man," Conley hissed "how would you like to get out of this pesthole?"

"Get out?" Beever said dumbly. "Sure. Sure, I would but—"

"Then do what I tell you, and a month from now you'll be eating steak and mushrooms in New Orleans." Conley paused for a moment, then shrugged his shoulders. "Of course, if you'd rather stay here and finish your time, I'll find somebody else to throw in with me. Just say so, that's all."

Conley turned and went back to work. Beever stared curiously as the younger man resumed his attack on the thicket. Steak and mushrooms in a month; the mere thought made his mouth water. 'Course, he'd have to get some new teeth first.

The old man grabbed up his hoe and moved quickly to catch up with Conley.

"Don't get so uppity," he grinned, showing his gums. "I'll get you the rawhide."

Conley nodded and grunted something inaudible. Beever fell in beside him and the two men worked in silence for the rest of the morning.

That afternoon, Conley used the rawhide strip to fashion a jess, a shackle-like contrivance that kept the falcon's legs too close together for it to fly, with a long, narrow loop trailing behind for leashing purposes. With the falcon thus fettered, Conley carefully and gently untangled its trapped wing from the briars. He examined the bird for injury and was pleased to find none. Smiling, he fed the falcon half the bologna from his noon sandwich, and put it to rest in a clearing he had hoed out.

"We're lucky," he said to Beever, falling in beside him again, "it's a young one."

"Where do you figure it come from?" the old man asked.

"Probably fell out of a migratory flock," Conley said. Beever squinted a frown.

"A what?"

Conley looked at the old man with unconcealed distaste. "Don't you know *anything*? Look, peregrines breed way up north, in eastern Canada. You've heard of Canada, I presume?"

"Course," Beever said stiffly.

"All right," Conley went on. "When it starts getting cold up there, they fly in groups down the coast to Central America. That's called migrating."

"I seen wild geese flying south," Beever allowed, "but I never seen no birds like that before."

"You never will, either. The peregrine, my ignorant friend, is a most exceptional bird. It flies higher than the naked eye can see. It glides about four times as fast as any human can run. And when one of them spots a prey and dives, it shoots down at about two hundred miles an hour."

"How come you know so much about it?" Beever asked, almost hostile in the face of Conley's superior knowledge.

"I've been around, old man," Conley said mysteriously. "I've seen places, done things that couldn't even be imagined by you and the rest of the dirt farmers and poolroom hoodlums in this filthy gang."

"What are you doing here then," Beever asked arrogantly. "if you're so much better than we are?"

"I am here," Conley said icily, "because a little plan of mine fell through just after a very wealthy, and very gullible, Miami widow had turned over a considerable sum of money for me to, ah—invest for her. An unfortunate stroke of the worst kind of luck, without which, my toothless comrade, I would have been spared this somewhat less than satisfying association with you—" Conley glanced around at the other dirty, sweating convicts, "and your peers."

"Sorry we ain't up to your standards," Beever remarked snidely.

The two men again worked in surly silence for the next few hours. At the midafternoon break, Conley smuggled two inches of water back to the falcon and watched it drink greedily, all the while stroking its sleek black feathers and gently running two fingertips over its flat, smooth crown.

"Nice girl," he cooed, "nice little falcon."

The next morning, sitting on a truckbed while they bumped along the twenty miles to their job, Beever leaned over and whispered in Conley's ear.

"I sneaked a chunk of pork fat for the bird," he said, showing Conley a folded scrap of sack paper with grease rings spotting it. Conley glared at him for an instant before slapping the paper from the old man's hand. Beever's mouth fell open in surprise as he watched the precious piece of meat fly off to the side of the road.

"You fool!" Conley hissed. "If I catch you feeding that bird, I'll strangle you!"

"I was just trying to help," Beever snorted.

"When I want your help, I'll ask for it! I don't want that falcon to eat anything—*anything*, you understand?—except that putrid bologna they feed us in the field at noon."

"That was a good chunk of meat," Beever complained.

"Oh, shut up!" Conley snarled. "You could have ruined the whole scheme with that filthy piece of pork!" He rolled his eyes upward in exasperation. "What I wouldn't give," he muttered loudly enough for Beever to hear, "to have you replaced by a reasonably intelligent eight-year-old."

When they got to the briar field and were unshackled from the truckbed and issued their hoes and spades, Conley made his way quickly to the area he and Beever had worked in the previous day. He found the peregrine where he had left it, still comfortably blindfolded and jessed.

"Hello, baby bird," Conley cooed, stealing a moment to caress the falcon's crown before lining up with Beever to begin the day's labor.

The sun came early that morning and beat down mercilessly on the convicts, its relentless heat drenching them with sweat and darkening their scratchy denim. As the discomfort of the sun increased, seemingly so did the treachery of the thorns that curved as long as three inches to their brutal points; that jabbed at and sometimes penetrated the harness gloves, pricking open the toughest of callouses, sending a message of sharp pain all the way through wrist and forearm to elbow. Dust, grimy and gritty, rose from the hoe slashes and spade thrusts, settling on parched lips and wet eyelids, clinging like resin. The briar patch was misery personified; a daily hell.

At the morning water break, Conley had Beever smuggle an inch of water back for the falcon, while the water he himself was able to steal he kept in reserve, under a flat rock to prevent its turning to mud from the dust, to give to the bird the last thing before the truck took them back to the prison camp.

"I want half of the bologna from your noon sandwich, too," Conley told the old man, "to feed our little winged friend before we go back tonight."

"Working in this heat on half rations ain't going to be easy," Beever grumbled, scratching his grizzled, dirty face. Conley glared at him.

"How much of your sentence do you still have left to do?" he asked sharply.

"Little better'n three years, I reckon. Why?"

"Well now, wouldn't you rather eat half rations at noon for a month, than full rations for the next three years? I mean, surely you have *that* much sense, Beever."

"Listen," the old man snapped, "I'm getting tired of you always telling me I'm stupid! Don't forget, slicker, it was me that found the bird in the first place!"

172   CLARK HOWARD

"Oh, yes," Conley said lightly, "and you didn't even know what it was. Why, you were so dumb you were going to kill it!"

"Yeah, well it was me that got the rawhide to tie it up, and it's me that helps sneak water and food back to it, an' me that watches Tevis and does the work for both of us while you're down on your knees talking to that damn perry-whatever-it-is—"

"All right, all right," Conley said urgently, "calm down, you fool, before Tevis hears you."

"There you go again!" Beever said in outrage. "You just called me a fool."

"Tevis is going to hear you." Conley hissed nervously.

"I don't care if he does!" Beever's voice grew louder and the convicts on both sides of them paused to see what was the trouble. "We's both convicts here," Beever continued to rant, "both working this here same patch of ground, and I'm getting powerful tired of your high and mighty ways. I'm good as you are, you hear me!"

"All right, Beever, all right," Conley was pleading now as he noticed the fat guard looking their way curiously, the sun gleaming off the polished stock of his scattergun.

"Say it then!" Beever demanded. "Say I'm good as you are!"

"You are," Conley said tightly, forcing the words from his throat, "you're as good as I am, old boy. Now will you please calm down before we both—"

The dreaded shrill of an unscheduled whistle pierced the still, clammy air.

"You two!" a thick voice shouted at them. Every convict in the line had turned to face the big road gang guard sitting in the shade beyond the Deadline. "You two there," he pointed the shotgun at Conley and Beever, "get over here!"

The two prisoners threw down their tools and doubletimed across the cleared area to the Deadline. With their toes even with the strip of chain, their hands behind their necks, they stood awaiting the pleasure of their vigilant keeper.

"What's the argument all about, children?" Tevis asked in mock sweetness, his fat lips curled in a cruel smile.

Conley swallowed down a dry throat, trying desperately to think of something to say. Beever, who had been on road gangs before, spoke up at once.

"I said it was my turn to hoe," he lied to Tevis, "and his turn to spade. He said it wasn't."

"That so?" Tevis asked Conley.

"Yes, sir," Conley said quickly.

"Well now," Tevis grinned sadistically, "we can't have no disharmony like that when we're supposed to be doing our work, now can we? It'll distract all the other children out there. Looks like teacher will have to decide. You—" he pointed at Conley, "will hoe, and you, old man, will spade. Can you remember that?"

"Yes, sir," Conley and Beever said in unison.

"All right then, get on back out there."

They turned and started trotting back toward the briars. Before they were halfway there, Tevis blew the whistle again and called them back.

"I near forgot," he said pleasantly. "Drop your gloves there at the Deadline. You two can work with your bare hands for the rest of the day. How do you like that?"

The two prisoners shucked their gloves. They doubletimed back to their tools, hearing Tevis's nasty chuckle behind them, thinking of the thorns and the bloody hands they would have that night.

Later, after the noon break, after Conley had fed the falcon, Beever apologized. "I reckon it was my fault," he allowed meekly. "You just got me riled."

"Forget it," Conley told him shortly.

"You shouldn't rile me like that."

"I won't any more," Conley promised soberly, feeling another thorn jab into his knuckle. He looked over at Beever and the old man grinned his toothless grin in silent friendship. Conley smiled back at him.

You filthy old scum, Conley thought, still smiling.

During the three weeks that followed, Conley treated the captured peregrine like a newborn prince. When the blindfold was removed, the falcon became nervous and angry, hissing frantically and spreading its razorlike talons threateningly; but Conley, with infinite, controlled patience, plied the bird with bits of bologna and soft, soothing words, until, after a few days, it let the convict feed it by hand instead of using a bramble twig. Progress was nerve-wrackingly slow, primarily because Conley could snatch only brief, stolen moments away from the watchful eye of Tevis, the guard; but gradually those moments brought results as a hesitant but definite change took place in the peregrine's personality.

174   CLARK HOWARD

"I can't see how you do it," Beever confessed, awed by Conley's quiet relentlessness in the bird's training.

"With any other kind of peregrine, I probably wouldn't be able to," Conley admitted in a rare moment of civility, "but we are triply fortunate in that this particular peregrine is a falcon, a female, and a young one to boot. Falcons are the easiest of all to train, and young ones are easier still. Being female, they like to have their food given to them without working for it; and being young, they haven't yet learned to seek out their own food when it isn't given to them."

Beever shook his head, not understanding, and Conley patiently explained it again in the most elementary language he could muster. He exercised an iron control over his personal distaste and carefully avoided losing his temper with the old man again. He needed Beever for the time being, and did not want to risk jeopardizing their relationship by offending him just now in any way.

Slowly, day in and day out, Conley continued to subject the peregrine to his own will; feeding it, caressing it, whispering to it, using the blindfold now only when the bird grew nervous from lack of flying. Soon the falcon began stirring in anticipation when it picked up Conley's scent as the convicts arrived for work.

It came to know by instinct when it was time for the morning water, the bologna at noon, the second watering at three o'clock, and the last feeding before the road gang left at night. It came to depend on Conley as its source of existence, its life.

"How come you won't let it eat nothin' but baloney?" Beever wanted to know.

"I'm making it an addict," Conley told him. "I'm conditioning its body solely to bologna; after a while that's all it will crave, because it won't remember what anything else tastes like. It won't know any other food but bologna."

"What good's that going to do?" Beever asked, puzzled.

"You'll see," Conley promised, "when the time is right."

The day came when Conley was convinced that the peregrine was ready. The young falcon could now detect the scent of bologna a hundred feet away; it was adjusted to two rations daily of the pungent meat; and the only friend it knew in the world was Conley. The time for which Conley had waited so long had arrived.

Conley stopped feeding the falcon. "We're almost ready," he told

Beever. "I think it's time we talked about the money, don't you?"

"What money?" Beever said innocently.

"The money you have rolled up in the seam of your shirt," Conley said matter-of-factly. "You aren't going to lie to me about it, are you, us being partners and all?"

Beever eyed Conley warily. "How much you reckon I got?" he challenged.

"I haven't the vaguest idea," Conley admitted. "However much it is, though, I want half of it."

"You ain't even told me yet how we're going to get out," the old man complained. "When do I hear?"

Conley stopped working and wiped the sweat from his neck. "All right, you're entitled to know. Stand up for a minute and take a look around." Conley waited, still stooped over his spade handle, while Beever did as instructed. When the old convict had resumed working position, Conley began to explain.

"We're out here twenty miles from the camp, you and I and the other prisoners, with one guard. That one guard has complete control over us as a group because he has a shotgun and sits behind a Deadline. There's no way to rush him because the moment any one of us or any group of us crosses the Deadline, he can shoot us. With the two barrels on that blaster of his, he can easily cut down ten men at medium range. So there's no possibility in the world of rushing him, right?"

"I reckon," Beever acquiesced.

"All right. Now suppose we could get Tevis out of the way sometime around noon? If we could run away from here at noon, what kind of chance would we have of escaping?"

"Good chance," the old man said. "We'd have a five hour headstart before the truck comes to take us back. The main highway's 'bout an hour from here. If we was lucky enough to get a ride the first hour or so after we got to the highway, we could prob'ly be across the line in Alabama 'fore they even started looking for us."

"Good," Conley said eagerly. "You give me half the money you've got hoarded up," he offered, "and lead the way to the highway, and I'll take care of Tevis so we can get away."

"How?" said Beever. "With that there bird?"

"Exactly."

"When?"

CLARK HOWARD

"The day after tomorrow."

"What if it don't work?" Beever said skeptically.

"It will," Conley assured him, "it will."

Beever squinted his eyes against the sun and speculated the proposition, his gummy mouth gaping open in thought. "I'll take you to the highway," he said craftily, "and we'll divide the money there."

Now it was Conley's turn to ponder. He eyed the old man suspiciously, turning over in his mind all the possibilities of the situation. He did not have much choice in the matter, he concluded. Besides, he was reasonably certain he could handle the old man.

"All right," he said finally, "it's a deal."

The falcon, in its rawhide jess, moved around the briar patch irritably, scratching at the hard-packed dirt, pecking at thorn roots, occasionally hissing quietly but angrily.

"What's the matter with it?" Beever asked. Conley grinned.

"It didn't get fed at noon. It's hungry."

Beever paused in his work for a moment. "If you didn't feed the bird," he asked flatly, "where's the half baloney sandwich I give you?"

"Oh, that," Conley said lightly, picking his teeth with a long thorn, "I was going to give it back to you but I accidentally dropped it in the dirt. I knew a well bred person like yourself wouldn't want to eat dirty food, so I threw it away."

Beever glared at Conley as the younger man bent to resume working. That's two pieces of meat you done me out of, slicker, he thought hatefully.

"Anyway," Conley went on, "you can keep your whole sandwich from now on; the falcon won't be eating any more."

The next day the peregrine was totally indignant. It hissed and spat, ruffled its pointed wings at Conley's scent and chewed furiously at the rawhide shackle that kept it grounded. Late in the day, after the bird had missed its fourth feeding, Conley had to blindfold it again to keep it from injuring itself.

"I pity Tevis tomorrow," he told Beever ominously that night.

On the day of the break, Conley and Beever worked close together. They whispered the morning long about what the afternoon might bring.

"They's gonna be cons all over the woods," Beever predicted. "We won't be the onliest ones taking off."

"No, but we'll be the first to go," Conley said. "The others will be too surprised to do anything very quickly. We'll have a good enough headstart." He turned and looked thoughtfully at the toothless old man. "You never did tell me how much money we have," he reminded.

"I ain't gonna lie to you, son," Beever said, grinning, "us being together in this. We got twenty dollars."

Conley nodded. "That ought to at least buy us some cheap clothes so we can get rid of these dirty things we're wearing."

They worked in silence for a while, both glancing back at Tevis from time to time, and at the now terribly hungry, terribly angry falcon, then up at the burning sphere of sun that today seemed to move so much more slowly toward its summit. The morning dragged; to Conley it seemed hours before Beever nudged him and whispered urgently.

"There he goes. It's time!"

Tevis, the guard, got up from his chair at exactly twelve o'clock, as was his daily custom. He cradled the shotgun under one arm, dragged a burlap bag from the shack and slung it over his shoulder. He blew his whistle loudly, a signal for the convicts to stand up straight so he could see them all and count them. When he had determined that none of them was close enough to endanger him, he walked over to the Deadline and put the bag down. From it he took a long loaf of prison bread and a brown-wrapped slab of sliced bologna. He spread the burlap out and put the food on it.

Conley and Beever, and now several other prisoners, watched intently as the falcon glided, unseen by the guard, in a slow circle above where Tevis stood. Only seconds before, when Tevis turned toward the shack for the bag of food, Conley had released the peregrine and thrown it into the air toward the guard shack. Now the starving bird was on the wing again, free to seek its own food; and the heavy summer air, to the falcon's extraordinary sense of smell, was thick with the scent of bologna.

Tevis was bent over the burlap when the falcon dived. It broke its dive only a few feet from the guard's head, its wings cutting the air silently and lowering it like a helicopter. Its talons sank deeply into the back of Tevis's neck. The guard screamed in horror, dropping the shotgun from its cradle.

Conley and Beever broke ranks and ran.

"How much farther to the highway?" Conley asked, leaning against a tree deep in the swampy woods, panting for breath, with the road gang four miles and fifty minutes behind them.

CLARK HOWARD

"Not far," Beever gasped. The old man was sprawled out on the damp marshy grass, his head propped up on a rotting log, chest heaving. " 'Bout a mile, I reckon."

"Straight ahead?" asked Conley. Beever glanced at him suspiciously. "More or less," he answered slowly.

"Let's get going then." Conley sucked in a last deep breath and pushed away from the tree. "You lead the way."

Beever dragged himself up and started forward. He had taken only three steps when Conley swooped up a smooth hand-sized rock from beside the tree and smashed it against the top of Beever's skull. The old man dropped limply to the ground. The dirty grey hair on the back of his head began to change slowly to crimson.

"There, you dirty old bum," Conley muttered to himself, rolling the limp form over and quickly ripping open the shirt seam. The money was rolled tightly, cigarette fashion, and had been slipped into the seam through a tiny slit at one end. Conley unrolled the bills and smoothed them out, counting as he did so. There were four ten dollar bills.

"Why you filthy old cheat!" Conley said outragedly. "You were going to take advantage of me!"

He paused only an instant to kick Beever's still body as hard as he could, then ran off into the marsh, grumbling indignantly at the thought of the old man's dishonor.

Pushing through the brush and slimy wet vines, Conley bore a course as near directly straight as he could determine. The grass under his feet grew mushy, causing his heavy prison brogans to slide precariously. Twice he slipped to his knees, cursing angrily at the slick residue left on his trouser legs. Once he saw a viper, black and threatening, and jumped back in horror, falling on his back in a thick, muddy bog and cursing furiously when some of the foul slush splashed up onto his face. Still he pushed on, clutching Beever's money in one fist.

It seemed to him that a very long time had passed since he had left the dead old man; much more time than should have been required to cover the last mile to the highway. He began to wonder if Beever had lied to him, and spent several minutes cursing his late dishonest partner again.

Soon a tight fear trickled into his mind and gave rise to the terrible suspicion that he might be lost. He stopped, wiping his face with the dry part of one sleeve. Glancing around, he saw that every direction looked the same, thick with vines, wet scrub, reeds, strange noises, and fore-

THE PEREGRINE

boding. He shivered.

In the wake of near panic came inspiration. Conley turned his face skyward. Some of the trees seemed to be very tall—that one over there, for instance; if he could climb to its top, surely he could see the highway.

He shoved the money deep into a pocket and grasped the green, strange-feeling moss of a low branch. Pulling himself up, he went from limb to limb, pausing on each to peer out over the marshes for a hopeful sight of the highway. Or a road, a shack—anything!

Halfway up the tree, a rotten limb broke. Conley dropped like dead weight, one shoulder careening him off a lower limb and throwing his body out away from the tree. His mind froze in terror at the thought of hitting the ground from such a height.

He landed on one side in a soft, thick bog and struggled frantically to his feet to keep from submerging in the muck. Uncontrollably he laughed, relief surging through him. *Made it—made it—made it!* he thought gleefully. He forced his legs forward in the thick, muddy scum.

Suddenly something flew past his face, frighteningly close. Conley leaped back and tried to see what it was. It came again, from behind, actually brushing his head this time. He jumped sideways in fright.

Then he saw the peregrine.

Conley could feel the color drain from his face, leaving him white with fear. *It remembers!* he thought. *I stopped feeding it, and it remembers!*

The falcon dived again, straight at his face. Conley pushed back away from it, stumbling awkwardly in the treacherous bog. The peregrine streaked past him, climbed, circled, dived again—and again and again. Always from the front it came now, head on, and each time Conley was forced to back away from it, each time leaning his body farther into the thick bog, until its demanding mass claimed his waist—his chest—his throat—

CLARK HOWARD

Anachron

by Damon Knight

The body was never found. And for that reason alone, there was no body to find.

It sounds like inverted logic—which, in a sense, it is—but there's no paradox involved. It was a perfectly orderly and explicable event, even though it could only have happened to a Castellare.

Odd fish, the Castellare brothers. Sons of a Scots-Englishwoman and an expatriate Italian, born in England, educated on the Continent, they were at ease anywhere in the world and at home nowhere.

Nevertheless, in their middle years, they had become settled men. Expatriates like their father, they lived on the island of Ischia, off the Neapolitan coast, in a palace—*quattrocento,* very fine, with peeling cupids on the walls, a multitude of rats, no central heating, and no neighbors.

They went nowhere; no one except their agents and their lawyers came to them. Neither had ever married. Each, at about the age of thirty, had given up the world of people for an inner world of more precise and more enduring pleasures. Each was an amateur—a fanatical, compulsive amateur.

They had been born out of their time.

Peter's passion was virtu. He collected relentlessly, it would not be too much to say savagely; he collected as some men hunt big game. His taste was catholic, and his acquisitions filled the huge rooms of the palace and half the vaults under them—paintings, statuary, enamels, porcelain, glass, crystal, metalwork. At fifty, he was a round little man with small, sardonic eyes and a careless patch of pinkish goatee.

Harold Castellare, Peter's talented brother, was a scientist. An amateur scientist. He belonged in the nineteenth century, as Peter was a throwback to a still earlier epoch. Modern science is largely a matter of teamwork and drudgery, both impossible concepts to a Castellare. But Harold's intelligence was in its own way as penetrating and original as a Newton's or a Franklin's. He had done respectable work in physics and electronics, and had even, at his lawyer's insistence, taken out a few patents. The income from these, when his own purchases of instruments and equipment did not consume it, he gave to his brother, who accepted it without gratitude or rancor.

Harold, at fifty-three, was spare and shrunken, sallow and spotted, with a bloodless, melancholy countenance; on his upper lip grew a neat hedge of pink-and-salt mustache, the companion piece and antithesis of his brother's goatee.

On a certain May morning, Harold had an accident.

Goodyear dropped rubber on a hot stove; Archimedes took a bath; Becquerel left a piece of uranium ore in a drawer with a photographic plate. Harold Castellare, working patiently with an apparatus which had so far consumed a great deal of current without producing anything more spectacular than some rather unusual corona effects, sneezed convulsively and dropped an ordinary bar magnet across two charged terminals.

Above the apparatus a huge, cloudy bubble sprang into being.

Harold, getting up from his instinctive crouch, blinked at it in profound astonishment. As he watched, the cloudiness abruptly disappeared and he was looking *through* the bubble at a section of tesselated flooring that seemed to be about three feet above the real floor. He could also see the corner of a carved wooden bench, and on the bench a small, oddly shaped stringed instrument.

Harold swore fervently to himself, made agitated notes, and then began to experiment. He tested the sphere cautiously with an electroscope, with a magnet, with a Geiger counter. Negative. He tore a tiny bit of paper from his notepad and dropped it toward the sphere. The paper disappeared; he couldn't see where it went.

Speechless, Harold picked up a meter stick and thrust it delicately forward. There was no feeling of contact; the rule went into and through the bubble as if the latter did not exist. Then it touched the stringed instrument, with a solid click. Harold pushed. The instrument slid over the edge of the bench and struck the floor with a hollow thump and jangle.

Staring at it, Harold suddenly recognized its tantalizingly familiar shape.

Recklessly he let go the meter stick, reached in and picked the fragile thing out of the bubble. It was solid and cool in his fingers. The varnish was clear, the color of the wood glowing through it. It looked as if it might

DAMON KNIGHT

have been made yesterday.

Peter owned one almost exactly like it, except for preservation—a viola d'amore of the seventeenth century.

Harold stooped to look through the bubble horizontally. Gold and rust tapestries hid the wall, fifty feet away, except for an ornate door in the center. The door began to open; Harold saw a flicker of umber. Then the sphere went cloudy again. His hands were empty; the viola d'amore was gone. And the meter stick, which he had dropped inside the sphere, lay on the floor at his feet.

"Look at that," said Harold simply.

Peter's eyebrows went up slightly. "What is it, a new kind of television?"

"No, no. Look here." The viola d'amore lay on the bench, precisely where it had been before. Harold reached into the sphere and drew it out.

Peter started. "Give me that." He took it in his hands, rubbed the smoothly finished wood. He stared at his brother. "By God and all the saints," he said. "Time travel."

Harold snorted impatiently. "My dear Peter, 'time' is a meaningless word taken by itself, just as 'space' is."

"But, barring that, time travel."

"If you like, yes."

"You'll be quite famous."

"I expect so."

Peter looked down at the instrument in his hands. "I'd like to keep this, if I may."

"I'd be very happy to let you, but you can't."

As he spoke, the bubble went cloudy; the viola d'amore was gone like smoke.

"There, you see?"

"What sort of devil's trick is that?"

"It goes back. . . . Later you'll see. I had that thing out once before, and this happened. When the sphere became transparent again, the viola was where I had found it."

"And your explanation for this?"

Harold hesitated. "None. Until I can work out the appropriate mathematics—"

"Which may take you some time. Meanwhile, in layman's language—"

Harold's face creased with the effort and interest of translation. "Very roughly, then—I should say it means that events are conserved. Two or three centuries ago—"

"Three. Notice the sound holes."

"Three centuries ago, then, at this particular time of day, someone was in that room. If the viola were gone, he or she would have noticed the fact. That would constitute an alteration of events already fixed; therefore it doesn't happen. For the same reason, I conjecture, we can't see into the sphere, or—" he probed at it with a fountain pen—"I thought not—or reach into it to touch anything; that would also constitute an alteration. And anything we put into the sphere while it is transparent comes out again when it becomes opaque. To put it very crudely, we cannot alter the past."

"But it seems to me that we did alter it. Just now, when you took the viola out, even if no one of that time saw it happen."

"This," said Harold, "is the difficulty of using language as a means of exact communication. If you had not forgotten all your calculus . . . However. It may be postulated (remembering of course that everything I say is a lie, because I say it in English) that an event which doesn't influence other events is not an event. In other words—"

"That, since no one saw you take it, it doesn't matter whether you took it or not. A rather dangerous precept, Harold; you would have been burned at the stake for that at one time."

"Very likely. But it can be stated in another way or, indeed, in an infinity of ways which only seem to be different. If someone, let us say God, were to remove the moon as I am talking to you, using zero duration, and substitute an exact replica made of concrete and plaster of Paris, with the same mass, albedo, and so on as the genuine moon, it would make no measurable difference in the universe as we perceive it—and therefore we cannot certainly say that it hasn't happened. Nor, I may add, does it make any difference whether it has or not."

" 'When there's no one about on the quad,' " said Peter.

"Yes. A basic and, as a natural consequence, a meaningless problem of philosophy. Except," he added, "in this one particular manifestation."

He stared at the cloudy sphere. "You'll excuse me, won't you, Peter? I've got to work on this."

"When will you publish, do you suppose?"

"Immediately. That's to say, in a week or two."

"Don't do it till you've talked it over with me, will you? I have a notion about it."

Harold looked at him sharply. "Commercial?"

"In a way."

"No," said Harold. "This is not the sort of thing one patents or keeps secret, Peter."

"Of course. I'll see you at dinner, I hope?"

"I think so. If I forget, knock on the door, will you?"

"Yes. Until then."

"Until then."

At dinner, Peter asked only two questions.

"Have you found any possibility of changing the time your thing reaches—from the seventeenth century to the eighteenth, for example, or from Monday to Tuesday?"

"Yes, as a matter of fact. Amazing. It's lucky that I had a rheostat already in the circuit; I wouldn't dare turn the current off. Varying the amperage varies the time set. I've had it up to what I think was Wednesday of last week—at any rate, my smock was lying over the workbench where I left it, I remember, Wednesday afternoon. I pulled it out. A curious sensation, Peter—I was wearing the same smock at the time. And then the sphere went opaque and of course the smock vanished. That must have been myself, coming into the room."

"And the future?"

"Yes. Another funny thing, I've had it forward to various times in the near future, and the machine itself is still there, but nothing's been done to it—none of the things I'm thinking I might do. That might be because of the conservation of events, again, but I rather think not. Still farther forward there are cloudy areas, blanks; I can't see anything that isn't in existence now, apparently, but here, in the next few days, there's nothing of that.

"It's as if I were going away. Where do you suppose I'm going?"

Harold's abrupt departure took place between midnight and morning. He packed his own grip, it would seem, left unattended, and was seen no more. It was extraordinary, of course, that he should have left at all, but the details were in no way odd. Harold had always detested what he called "the tyranny of the valet." He was, as everyone knew, a most independent man.

On the following day Peter made some trifling experiments with the time-sphere. From the sixteenth century he picked up a scent bottle of Venetian glass; from the eighteenth, a crucifix of carved rosewood; from the nineteenth, when the palace had been the residence of an Austrian count and his Italian mistress, a hand-illuminated copy of De Sade's *La Nouvelle Justine,* very curiously bound in human skin.

They all vanished, naturally, within minutes or hours—all but the scent bottle. This gave Peter matter for reflection. There had been half a dozen flickers of cloudiness in the sphere just futureward of the bottle; it ought to have vanished, but it hadn't. But then, he had found it on the floor near a wall with quite a large rat hole in it.

When objects disappeared unaccountably, he asked himself, was it because they had rolled into rat holes, or because some time fisher had picked them up when they were in a position to do so?

He did not make any attempt to explore the future. That afternoon he telephoned his lawyers in Naples and gave them instructions for a new will. His estate, including his half of the jointly owned Ischia property, was to go to the Italian government on two conditions: (1) that Harold Castellare should make a similar bequest of the remaining half of the property and (2) that the Italian government should turn the palace into a national museum to house Peter's collection, using the income from his estate for its administration and for futher acquisitions. His surviving relatives—two cousins in Scotland—he cut off with a shilling each.

He did nothing more until after the document had been brought out to him, signed, and witnessed. Only then did he venture to look into his own future.

Events were conserved, Harold had said—meaning, Peter very well understood, events of the present and future as well as of the past. But was there only one pattern in which the future could be fixed? Could a result exist before its cause had occurred?

The Castellare motto was *Audentes fortuna juvat*—into which Peter, at the age of fourteen, had interpolated the word *"prudentesque"*: "Fortune favors the bold—and the prudent."

Tomorrow: no change; the room he was looking at was so exactly like this one that the time-sphere seemed to vanish. The next day: a cloudy blur. And the next, and the next . . .

Opacity, straight through to what Peter judged, by the distance he had

DAMON KNIGHT

moved the rheostat handle, to be ten years ahead. Then, suddenly, the room was a long marble hall filled with display cases.

Peter smiled wryly. If you were Harold, obviously you could not look ahead and see Peter working in your laboratory. And if you were Peter, equally obviously, you could not look ahead and know whether the room you saw was an improvement you yourself were going to make, or part of a museum established after your death, eight or nine years from now, or . . .

No. Eight years was little enough, but he could not even be sure of that. It would, after all, be seven years before Harold could be declared legally dead. . . .

Peter turned the vernier knob slowly forward. A flicker, another, a long series. Forward faster. Now the flickering melted into a grayness; objects winked out of existence and were replaced by others in the showcases; the marble darkened and lightened again, darkened and lightened, darkened and remained dark. He was, Peter judged, looking at the hall as it would be some five hundred years in the future. There was a thick film of dust on every exposed surface; rubbish and the carcass of some small animal had been swept carelessly into a corner.

The sphere clouded.

When it cleared, there was an intricate trail of footprints in the dust, and two of the showcases were empty.

The footprints were splayed, trifurcate, and thirty inches long.

After a moment's deliberation Peter walked around the workbench and leaned down to look through the sphere from the opposite direction. Framed in the nearest of the four tall windows was a scene of picture-postcard banality: the sun-silvered bay and the foreshortened arc of the city, with Vesuvio faintly fuming in the background. But there was something wrong about the colors, even grayed as they were by distance.

Peter went and got his binoculars.

The trouble was, of course, that Naples was green. Where the city ought to have been, a rankness had sprouted. Between the clumps of foliage he could catch occasional glimpses of gray-white that might equally well have been boulders or the wreckage of buildings. There was no movement. There was no shipping in the harbor.

But something rather odd was crawling up the side of the volcano. A rust-orange pipe, it appeared to be, supported on hairline struts like the legs of a centipede, and ending without rhyme or reason just short of the top.

While Peter watched, it turned slowly blue.

One day farther forward: now all the display cases had been looted; the museum, it would seem, was empty.

Given, that in five centuries the world, or at any rate the department of Campania, has been overrun by a race of Somethings, the human population being killed or driven out in the process; and that the conquerors take an interest in the museum's contents, which they have accordingly removed.

Removed where, and why?

This question, Peter conceded, might have a thousand answers, nine hundred and ninety-nine of which would mean that he had lost his gamble. The remaining answer was: to the vaults, for safety.

With his own hands Peter built a hood to cover the apparatus on the workbench and the sphere above it. It was unaccustomed labor; it took him the better part of two days. Then he called in workmen to break a hole in the stone flooring next to the interior wall, rig a hoist, and cut the power cable that supplied the time-sphere loose from its supports all the way back to the fuse box, leaving him a single flexible length of cable more than a hundred feet long. They unbolted the workbench from the floor, attached casters to its legs, lowered it into the empty vault below, and went away.

Peter unfastened and removed the hood. He looked into the sphere.

Treasure.

Crates, large and small, racked in rows into dimness.

With pudgy fingers that did not tremble, he advanced the rheostat. A cloudy flicker, another, a leaping blur of them as he moved the vernier faster—and then there were no more, to the limit of the time-sphere's range.

Two hundred years, Peter guessed—A.D. 2700 to 2900 or thereabout—in which no one would enter the vault. Two hundred years of "unliquidated time."

He put the rheostat back to the beginning of that uninterrupted period. He drew out a small crate and prized it open.

Chessmen, ivory with gold inlay, Florentine, fourteenth century. Superb.

Another, from the opposite rack.

T'ang figurines, horses and men, ten to fourteen inches high. Priceless.

The crates would not burn, Tomaso told him. He went down to the kitchen to see, and it was true. The pieces lay in the roaring stove untouched. He fished one out with a poker; even the feathery splinters of the unplaned wood had not ignited.

It made a certain extraordinary kind of sense. When the moment came for the crates to go back, any physical scrambling that had occurred in the meantime would have no effect; they would simply put themselves together as they had been before, like Thor's goats. But burning was another matter; burning would have released energy that could not be replaced.

That settled one paradox, at any rate. there was another that nagged at Peter's orderly mind. If the things he took out of that vault, seven hundred-odd years in the future, were to become part of the collection bequeathed by him to the museum, preserved by it, and eventually stored in the vault for him to find—then precisely where had they come from in the first place?

It worried him. Peter had learned in life, as his brother had in physics, that one never gets anything for nothing.

Moreover, this riddle was only one of his perplexities, and that not among the greatest. For another example, there was the obstinate opacity of the time-sphere whenever he attempted to examine the immediate future. However often he tried it, the result was always the same: a cloudy blank, all the way forward to the sudden unveiling of the marble gallery.

It was reasonable to expect the sphere to show nothing at times when he himself was going to be in the vault, but this accounted for only five or six hours out every twenty-four. Again, presumably, it would show him no changes to be made by himself, since foreknowledge would make it possible for him to alter his actions. But he laboriously cleared one end of the vault, put up a screen to hide the rest and made a vow—which he kept—not to alter the clear space or move the screen for a week. Then he tried again—with the same result.

The only remaining explanation was that sometime during the next ten years something was going to happen which he would prevent if he could; and the clue to it was there, buried in that frustrating, unbroken blankness.

As a corollary, it was going to be something which he *could* prevent if only he knew what it was . . . or even when it was supposed to happen. The event in question, in all probability, was his own death. Peter therefore hired nine men to guard him, three to a shift—because one man alone could not be trusted, two might conspire against him, whereas three, with the very minimum of effort, could be kept in a state of mutual suspicion. He also underwent a thorough medical examination, had new locks installed on every door and window, and took every other precaution ingenuity could suggest. When he had done all these things, the next ten years were as blank as before.

Peter had more than half expected it. He checked through his list of safeguards once more, found it good, and thereafter let the matter rest. He had done all he could; either he would survive the crisis or he would not. In either case, events were conserved; the time-sphere could give him no forewarning.

Another man might have found his pleasure blunted by guilt and fear; Peter's was whetted to a keener edge. If he had been a recluse before, now he was an eremite; he grudged every hour that was not given to his work. Mornings he spent in the vault, unpacking his acquisitions; afternoons and evenings, sorting, cataloguing, examining and—the word is not too strong—gloating. When three weeks had passed in this way, the shelves were bare as far as the power cable would allow him to reach in every direction, except for crates whose contents were undoubtedly too large to pass through the sphere. These, with heroic self-control, Peter had left untouched.

And still he had looted only a hundredth part of that incredible treasure house. With grappling hooks he could have extended his reach by perhaps three or four yards, but at the risk of damaging his prizes; and in any case this would have been no solution but only a postponement of the problem. There was nothing for it but to go through the sphere himself and unpack the crates while on the other "side" of it.

Peter thought about it in a fury of concentration for the rest of the day. So far as he was concerned, there was no question that the gain would be worth any calculated risk; the problem was how to measure the risk and if possible reduce it.

Item: He felt a definite uneasiness at the thought of venturing through that insubstantial bubble. Intuition was supported, if not by logic, at least by a sense of the dramatically appropriate. Now, if ever, would be the

DAMON KNIGHT

time for his crisis.

Item: Common sense did not concur. The uneasiness had two symbols. One was the white face of his brother Harold just before the water closed over it; the other was a phantasm born of those gigantic, splayed footprints in the dust of the gallery. In spite of himself, Peter had often found himself trying to imagine what the creatures that made them must look like, until his visualization was so clear that he could almost swear he had seen them.

Towering monsters they were, with crested ophidian heads and great unwinking eyes; and they moved in a strutting glide, nodding their heads, like fantastic barnyard fowl.

But, taking these premonitory images in turn: first, it was impossible that he should ever be seriously inconvenienced by Harold's death. There were no witnesses, he was sure; he had struck the blow with a stone; stones also were the weights that had dragged the body down, and the rope was an odd length Peter had picked up on the shore. Second, the three toed Somethings might be as fearful as all the world's bogies put together, it made no difference, he could never meet them.

Nevertheless, the uneasiness persisted. Peter was not satisfied; he wanted a lifeline. When he found it, he wondered that he had not thought of it before.

He would set the time-sphere for a period just before one of the intervals of blankness. That would take care of accidents, sudden illnesses, and other unforeseeable contingencies. It would also insure him against one very real and not at all irrational dread: the fear that the mechanism which generated the time-sphere might fail while he was on the other side. For the conservation of events was not a condition created by the sphere but one which limited its operation. No matter what happened, it was impossible for him to occupy the same place-time as any future or past observer; therefore, when the monster entered that vault, Peter would not be there any more.

There was, of course, the scent bottle to remember. Every rule has its exception; but in this case, Peter thought, the example did not apply. A scent bottle could roll into a rat hole; a man could not.

He turned the rheostat carefully back to the last flicker of grayness; past that to the next, still more carefully. The interval between the two, he judged, was something under an hour: excellent.

His pulse seemed a trifle rapid, but his brain was clear and cool. He thrust his head into the sphere and sniffed cautiously. The air was stale and had a faint, unpleasant odor, but it was breathable.

Using a crate as a stepping stool, he climbed to the top of the workbench. He arranged another crate close to the sphere to make a platform level with its equator. And seven and a half centuries in the future, a third crate stood on the floor directly under the sphere.

Peter stepped into the sphere, dropped, and landed easily, legs bending to take the shock. When he straightened, he was standing in what to all appearances was a large circular hole in the workbench; his chin was just above the top of the sphere.

He lowered himself, half squatting, until he had drawn his head through and stepped down from the crate.

He was in the future vault. The sphere was a brightly luminous thing that hung unsupported in the air behind him, its midpoint just higher than his head. The shadows it cast spread black and wedge-shaped in every direction, melting into obscurity.

Peter's heart was pounding miserably. He had an illusory stifling sensation, coupled with the idiotic notion that he ought to be wearing a diver's helmet. The silence was like the pause before a shout.

But down the aisles marched the crated treasures in their hundreds.

Peter set to work. It was difficult, exacting labor, opening the crates where they lay, removing the contents and nailing the crates up again, all without disturbing the positions of the crates themselves, but it was the price he had to pay for his lifeline. Each crate was in a sense a microcosm, like the vault itself—a capsule of unliquidated time. But the vault's term would end some fifty minutes from now, when crested heads nodded down these aisles; those of the crates' interiors, for all that Peter knew to the contrary, went on forever.

The first crate contained lacework porcelain; the second, shakudo sword hilts; the third, an exquisite fourth century Greek ornament in *repoussé* bronze, the equal in every way of the Siris bronzes.

Peter found it almost physically difficult to set the thing down, but he did so; standing on his platform crate in the future with his head projecting above the sphere in the present—like (again the absurd thought!) a diver rising from the ocean—he laid it carefully beside the others on the workbench.

Then down again, into the fragile silence and the gloom. The next crates were too large, and those just beyond were doubtful. Peter followed

DAMON KNIGHT

his shadow down the aisle. He had almost twenty minutes left: enough for one more crate, chosen with care, and an ample margin.

Glancing to his right at the end of the row, he saw a door. It was a heavy door, rivet-studded, with a single iron step below it. There had been no door there in Peter's time; the whole plan of the building must have been altered. *Of course!* he realized suddenly. If it had not, if so much as a single tile or lintel had remained of the palace as he knew it, then the sphere could never have let him see or enter this particular here-and-now, this—what would Harold have called it?—this nexus in space-time.

For if you saw any now-existing thing as it was going to appear in the future, you could alter it in the present-carve your initials in it, break it apart, chop it down—which was manifestly impossible, and therefore . . .

And therefore the first ten years were necessarily blank when he looked into the sphere, not because anything unpleasant was going to happen to him, but because in that time the last traces of the old palace had not yet been eradicated.

There was no crisis.

Wait a moment, though! Harold had been able to look into the near future. . . . But—of course—Harold had been about to die.

In the dimness between himself and the door he saw a rack of crates that looked promising. The way was uneven; one of the untidy accumulations of refuse that seemed to be characteristic of the Somethings lay in windrows across the floor. Peter stepped forward carefully—but not carefully enough.

Harold Castellare had had another accident—and again, if you choose to look at it in that way, a lucky one. The blow stunned him; the old rope slipped from the stones; flaccid, he floated where a struggling man might have drowned. A fishing boat nearly ran him down, and picked him up instead. He was suffering from a concussion, shock, exposure, asphyxiation, and was more than three quarters dead. But he was still alive when he was delivered, an hour later, to a hospital in Naples.

There were, of course, no identifying papers, labels or monograms in his clothing—Peter had seen to that—and for the first week after his rescue Harold was quite genuinely unable to give any account of himself. During the second week he was mending but uncommunicative, and at the end of the third, finding that there was some difficulty about gaining his release in spite of his physical recovery, he affected to regain his memory, gave a circumstantial but entirely fictitious identification and was discharged.

To understand this as well as all his subsequent actions, it is only necessary to remember that Harold was a Castellare. In Naples, not wishing to give Peter any unnecessary anxiety, he did not approach his bank for funds but cashed a check with an incurious acquaintance, and predated it by four weeks. With part of the money so acquired he paid his hospital bill and rewarded his rescuers. Another part went for new clothing and for four days' residence in an inconspicuous hotel, while he grew used to walking and dressing himself again. The rest, on his last day, he spent in the purchase of a discreetly small revolver and a box of cartridges.

He took the last boat to Ischia and arrived at his own front door a few minutes before eleven. It was a cool evening, and a most cheerful fire was burning in the central hall.

"Signor Peter is well, I suppose," said Harold, removing his coat.

"Yes, Signor Harold. He is very well, very busy with his collection."

"Where is he? I should like to speak to him."

"He is in the vaults, Signor Harold. But . . . "

"Yes?"

"Signor Peter sees no one when he is in the vaults. He has given strict orders that no one is to bother him, Signor Harold, when he is in the vaults."

"Oh, well," said Harold. "I daresay he'll see me."

It was a thing something like a bear trap, apparently, except that instead of two semicircular jaws it had four segments that snapped together in the middle, each with a shallow, sharp tooth. The pain was quite unendurable.

Each segment moved at the end of a thin arm, cunningly hinged so that the ghastly thing would close over whichever of the four triggers you stepped on. Each arm had a spring too powerful for Peter's muscles. The whole affair was connected by a chain to a staple solidly embedded in the concrete floor; it left Peter free to move some ten inches in any direction. Short of gnawing off his own leg, he thought sickly, there was very little he could do about it.

The riddle was, what could the thing possibly be doing here? There

DAMON KNIGHT

were rats in the vaults, no doubt, now as in his own time, but surely nothing larger. Was it conceivable that even the three-toed Somethings would set an engine like this to catch a rat?

Lost inventions, Peter thought irrelevantly, had a way of being rediscovered. Even if he suppressed the time-sphere during his lifetime and it did not happen to survive him, still there might be other time-fishers in the remote future—not here, perhaps, but in other treasure houses of the world. And that might account for the existence of this metal-jawed horror. Indeed, it might account for the vault itself—a better mantrap—except that it was all nonsense; the trap could only be full until the trapper came to look at it. Events, and the lives of prudent time-travelers, were conserved.

And he had been in the vault for almost forty minutes. Twenty minutes to go, twenty-five, thirty at the most, then the Somethings would enter and their entrance would free him. He had his lifeline; the knowledge was the only thing that made it possible to live with the pain that was the center of his universe just now. It was like going to the dentist, in the bad old days before procaine; it was very bad, sometimes, but you knew that it would end.

He cocked his head toward the door, holding his breath. A distant thud, another, then a curiously unpleasant squeaking, then silence.

But he had heard them. He knew they were there. It couldn't be much longer now.

Three men, two stocky, one lean, were playing cards in the passageway in front of the closed door that led to the vault staircase. They got up slowly.

"Who is he?" demanded the shortest one.

Tomaso clattered at him in furious Sicilian; the man's face darkened, but he looked at Harold with respect.

"I am now," stated Harold, "going down to see my brother."

"No, signor," said the shortest one positively.

"You are impertinent," Harold told him.

"Yes, signor."

Harold frowned. "You will not let me pass?"

"No, signor."

"Then go and tell my brother I am here."

The shortest one said apologetically but firmly that there were strict orders against this also; it would have astonished Harold very much if he had said anything else.

"Well, at least I suppose you can tell me how long it will be before he comes out?"

"Not long, signor. One hour, no more."

"Oh, very well, then," said Harold pettishly, turning half away. He paused. "One thing more," he said, taking the gun out of his pocket as he turned, "put your hands up and stand against the wall there, will you?"

The first two complied slowly. The third, the lean one, fired through his coat pocket, just like the gangsters in the American movies.

It was not a sharp sensation at all, Harold was surprised to find; it was more as if someone had hit him in the side with a cricket bat. The racket seemed to bounce interminably from the walls. He felt the gun jolt in his hand as he fired back, but couldn't tell if he had hit anybody. Everything seemed to be happening very slowly, and yet it was astonishingly hard to keep his balance. As he swung around he saw the two stocky ones with their hands half inside their jackets, and the lean one with his mouth open, and Tomaso with bulging eyes. Then the wall came at him and he began to swim along it, paying particular attention to the problem of not dropping one's gun.

As he weathered the first turn in the passageway the roar broke out afresh. A fountain of plaster stung his eyes; then he was running clumsily, and there was a bedlam of shouting behind him.

Without thinking about it he seemed to have selected the laboratory as his destination; it was an instinctive choice, without much to recommend it logically. In any case, he realized halfway across the central hall, he was not going to get there.

He turned and squinted at the passageway entrance; saw a blur move and fired at it. It disappeared. He turned again awkwardly, and had taken two steps nearer an armchair which offered the nearest shelter, when something clubbed him between the shoulderblades. One step more, knees buckling, and the wall struck him a second, softer blow. He toppled, clutching at the tapestry that hung near the fireplace.

When the three guards, whose names were Enrico, Alberto, and Luca, emerged cautiously from the passage and approached Harold's body, it was already flaming like a Viking's in its impromptu shroud; the dim horses and men and falcons of the tapestry were writhing and crisping

DAMON KNIGHT

into brilliance. A moment later an uncertain ring of fire wavered toward them across the carpet.

Although the servants came with fire extinguishers and with buckets of water from the kitchen, and although the fire department was called, it was all quite useless. In five minutes the whole room was ablaze; in ten, as windows burst and walls buckled, the fire engulfed the second story. In twenty, a mass of flaming timbers dropped into the vault through the hole Peter had made in the floor of the laboratory, utterly destroying the time-sphere apparatus and reaching shortly thereafter, as the authorities concerned were later to agree, an intensity of heat entirely sufficient to consume a human body without leaving any identifiable trace. For that reason alone, there was no trace of Peter's body to be found.

The sounds had just begun again when Peter saw the light from the time-sphere turn ruddy and then wink out like a snuffed candle.

In the darkness, he heard the door open.

Change for a Dollar

by Elijah Ellis

For the third time that morning John Brann reached the outward-bound end of his route. He turned the big city bus around and checked his watch. It was ten twenty-eight. He was two minutes ahead of schedule. Leaning back in his seat, he lit a cigarette and smoked in short, angry puffs. He had a bellyache, and no wonder.

As usual, his wife had undercooked his breakfast bacon and overcooked his eggs.

He wondered if that woman could do anything right. Ten years they'd been married, and she still couldn't cook a decent meal, much less keep house. The place usually looked like a pigsty. Brann had tried and tried to get his wife to improve, but it was hopeless.

Sure, she had a job, but the amount of money she brought in was hardly enough to pay the household bills, and it was certainly no excuse for her sloppiness.

"At least she could cook a man a decent breakfast," John Brann told the rows of empty seats behind him.

Still muttering, he started on the inward-bound leg of his route, stopping to pick up passengers on the way. There weren't many. It was a cold, gray winter morning, probably would start snowing soon. That was all he needed.

About eleven, he reached a stop in the out-at-the-elbows neighborhood between the north side residential area and the downtown business district. An old woman was at the stop, bundled up in a moth-eaten coat and woolen scarf. She waved a hand at the approaching bus.

"I see you, sister," Brann grumbled. He stopped the bus and levered open the front door.

The old woman took what seemed like five minutes to haul herself up the steps and into the bus. Then she took more time to fumble around in a shabby purse, and came out with a dollar bill.

Another time Brann might have given her just a dirty look and let it go at that, but this morning . . .

"The fare's twenty cents, lady," he said, ignoring the dollar bill.

The old woman's wrinkled face reflected confusion. She said, "I don't have change."

Brann sighed heavily, then reached for the changer hooked to his belt. He shucked out five dimes and ten nickels, dumped them into the old woman's trembling hands after taking the dollar.

As he had expected, the old woman scurried to an empty seat and sat down. She put the handful of change into her purse and fixed her gaze on the floor.

Brann said with exaggerated patience, "Lady. I told you. The fare is twenty cents. In here." He tapped the fare box on its stand beside his seat.

A passenger muttered, "Oh, for . . . "

The elderly woman blinked around in bewilderment. "What? What's that?"

John Brann waited. "Any time today, lady," he said.

In the seat just behind the confused old woman, a kid nervously cracked his knuckles. He was on his way to his first job interview. It had taken him several days to screw up his courage to the point of actually going. If he could just get that job, maybe—maybe at last he'd be able to break free of the suffocating indulgence of his mother.

Now that he was started, he didn't want any delays. Why the heck didn't that slob of a driver get the bus moving? For gosh sake. Impulsively he got up, a lanky kid with hornrimmed glasses and a sprinkle of acne marring his cheeks.

"I—I'll put the money in for you," he told the old woman.

She fumbled open her purse and with shaking fingers dug out two dimes, gave them to the kid. He walked forward, dropped the dimes into the fare box, and started back for his seat.

John Brann scowled. Anything he couldn't take, it was these smart-aleck punks. He suddenly tramped on the gas pedal. The big bus lurched forward.

The kid, caught by surprise, waved his arms while his stork-like legs carried him in a ludicrous shamble down the aisle between the rows of seats. He finally managed to get his balance and stop himself by grabbing the vertical metal pole by the rear door.

CHANGE FOR A DOLLAR

"Sorry about that," Brann called, while some of the passengers laughed. The kid ducked his head in an agony of embarrassment. He'd made a fool of himself, as usual. What had ever made him think he could . . .

He got off the bus at the first stop. He was going home. He crossed the street to catch a north-bound bus, not noticing the icy wind that whipped gritty dust and scraps of paper along the street, or the man who stood in a recessed doorway of a sleazy office building near the bus stop.

The man had a bony, beardstubbled face under a tangle of black hair that curled down over the collar of the ancient suit jacket he wore. A pair of dingy bluejeans and badly worn army combat boots completed his costume. He gave the kid a quick once-over. Should be good for a quarter, maybe even a half. He sidled from the doorway and crossed the walk to stand beside the kid.

"Cold, ain't it?" he said.

The kid didn't answer, or even look around.

"Say, I wonder if you could help a man out. You know, I'm goin' to see about a job, but I need to get a shave and—"

Now the kid slowly turned his head and looked at the panhandler. Another time he would have given the guy a quarter—whatever change he might have to spare. Another time; not now.

The kid began to speak, and out spewed every obscenity he'd ever heard, with a few he invented on the spot. The panhandler, startled, took a backward step, then abruptly turned and hurried away. He covered half a block before he got out of range of the kid's shouted invective. He stopped finally on the corner, and stared into a window of a pawnshop.

His eyes focused on his own shadowy reflection in the window. Did he really look like that? Until this moment he had never quite admitted to himself that he was a bum. He'd always held on to the idea that one of these days he was going to straighten up, get a steady job, but when a young kid felt free to talk to you like that . . . and the way the kid had looked at him, the angry scorn, the—contempt. That was the word, contempt.

Shuddering, he raised a grimy hand, turned up the collar of his jacket against the wind. How he needed a drink, but the cheapest wine cost fifty cents and he had only a quarter.

He was a bum. That kid had made him realize that, once and for all. Too late to change; maybe it had always been too late. All right. That's the way it was. He thoughtfully fingered the rusty switchblade knife in

200   ELIJAH ELLIS

his pants pocket. He'd never pulled any rough stuff, but now was a good time to start. He was a bum; he'd act like a bum.

There was a little candy store around the corner, on the sidestreet. Probably no more than a couple bucks in its cash drawer, but that was all he needed, right now. It was a start. He hurried around the corner and into the musty store.

The owner of the store took one look at the whiskery, wild-eyed man who came in the front door, waving a knife. Then, with a sigh, he turned to the cash register and punched the "No Sale" button. He had been robbed four times in the past six months.

A minute later the bum rushed out of the store, clutching the knife in one hand, a couple of crumpled dollar bills in the other. The store owner watched him go, made no move to stop him, not for any lousy two dollars.

The bum plunged blindly into the street, heading for the mouth of an alley on the far side. He never saw the big, expensive car that bore down on him, and the driver of the car didn't see the bum—not until it was too late.

The driver, like the car, was big and expensive. He had a square-jawed face, a touch of distinguished gray at his temples, could have posed for man of distinction ads. He had a solvent business, a wife and three grown children, belonged to several exclusive clubs and was a power in the local chamber of commerce.

At the moment he was on his way for a midday visit to his mistress—perhaps his last visit, perhaps not. He couldn't quite decide. He had been considering the matter as he drove along the sidestreet toward the main traffic artery that led to the high-rent area where his mistress lived.

At the last split second he saw the figure plunge into the path of his car. The bum almost made it, but the left front fender caught him, sent him cartwheeling through the cold gray air to smash headfirst into the curb on the far side of the street, then lie still.

The driver of the car automatically braked to a stop. He looked back at the crumpled figure in the gutter. Then, in sudden panic, he tramped down on the gas pedal and sped away. There was no traffic on the sidestreet just then, and no pedestrian on the sidewalks, as far as he could see. Besides, the accident had not been his fault. The vital point, however, was that he simply could not be involved. A man in his position in the community . . .

CHANGE FOR A DOLLAR

201

At the intersection he hesitated only a moment before he turned south, toward the downtown business district. He would call his mistress from his club. Yes; tell her it was all over between them. Yes; send her a couple of hundred dollars—by mail—and that would be that.

As he drove, he took a handkerchief from his topcoat pocket and dabbed at the perspiration trickling down his ruggedly handsome, distinguished face. He felt a sudden flicker of anger. That bum, involving him—a man of his standing—in a sordid incident like this. It was intolerable. He had done exactly the right thing, driving away from the scene; yes.

Back on the grimy sidestreet, a small crowd of people had sprung from nowhere to form a ring around the dead man sprawled in the gutter. The candy store owner, who had made a note of the license number of the hit-and-run car, was dialing the nearest police precinct station on his phone. He was, in almost all things, a cynically tolerant man, but a long time ago a hit-and-run driver had struck down his wife. The driver had never been caught, and his wife had never walked again.

Now he said into the phone, "Hello, police? I want to report a—murder."

The distinguished man parked in front of his club and went inside. He didn't notice that the left front headlight of his car was broken, and several pieces of the glass were missing. He was too intent on his errand. He headed for the phone booth in the lobby and made his call. Another time he would have handled the matter with tact and good taste; another time, not now.

In the living room of a luxurious apartment high in a luxurious building a couple of miles to the north, a woman slammed down the telephone and stood glaring at it.

"Just like that," she said bitterly. "Well—the same to you, buster, and many of them."

She stormed into the kitchen and poured herself a jolt of imported scotch. She needed it. The nerve of that guy . . .

Downing her drink, she poured another. Carrying the glass, she followed a familiar path into the bedroom, and stood in front of the full-length mirror there.

She was a blonde—natural blonde, and you better believe it—and if the tiny wrinkles around her eyes were beginning to show a bit, and if she was beginning to sag a bit and really needed a girdle to hold in the bulges, so what? She still had it. She was still—she was—

ELIJAH ELLIS

"I'm thirty-five years old," she admitted to herself.

The way he had talked to her on the phone: cool and distant and completely—uninterested; making it all too clear that she had never been anything to him but a—convenience.

She leaned forward, giving her expertly madeup face a close scrutiny. Thirty-five . . . in a business where thirty-five was just one step this side of the boneyard.

Shaking her head wildly, she hurried to a closet, pulled out a coat trimmed with mink, slung it about her shoulders and half-ran out of the apartment. Maybe a brisk walk would help. Yeah, and maybe turning back the clock ten years would help. Only it didn't work that way.

If he'd given her a reason—his wife, pressure of business—any kind of good reason for calling it quits. But he hadn't! Just that cold dismissal, and didn't that in itself make the reason clear? Thirty-five!

She walked up one street and down the next, not knowing or caring, not even aware that snow had begun to fall from the gray gloom overhead; not a soft snow, but icy pellets driven along the deserted streets by the wind.

Finally she felt the cold and looked around. She must have walked a mile or more. There was a second-rate neighborhood drugstore on the corner. Second-rate—maybe she'd better start getting used to second-rate. At least she could have coffee and get warm. She reached the drugstore, went inside, and sat down on a stool near the front of the soda fountain counter.

The waitress, a thin, flat-chested woman with frowsy hair and dumb, cow-like eyes, came wearily toward her. She stared at the waitress and thought, *There I am, in a few weeks, a few months*. Fear surged through her body—and anger.

"Coffee," she snapped at the waitress.

The waitress turned to a coffee urn, drew a cup, and brought it to the counter. A little of the coffee slopped over into the chipped saucer under the cup.

The blonde glared at the slatternly waitress. With an irritated shrug, she reached for the sugar dispenser. The waitress plodded away. She had forgotten to give the blonde a spoon, or cream.

"You," the blonde said. Her voice rose, "You! Don't you serve cream with your coffee? And maybe a spoon?"

"Ma'am?" the waitress said, her cow-eyes blinking.

The manager of the drugstore looked up from a display case he was restocking on the far side of the store, and frowned. Now what? Slowly he moved toward the soda fountain.

"Don't 'ma'am' me," the blonde cried. She knew she was acting silly, making something of nothing, but she didn't care. Right now, this moment, she wanted to hit out at someone—anyone. She shrilled, "What kind of lousy place is this, anyway?"

The waitress blinked. "Ma'am? I don't—"

"What's the difficulty?" the manager asked. He ran an eye over the blonde, noted the expensive coat, the well-kept face. He knew class when he saw it.

The blonde got off the counter stool, whirled toward the door. "I didn't come in here to be insulted!"

"I'm sure there's been a—a misunderstanding," the manager said, following her, dry-washing his soft pale hands. "Please—" But the woman was gone, slamming out the door into the thickening snow, leaving behind only the rich aroma of her perfume.

For a few seconds the manager stared after her, then turned and looked around the store. There were no customers just now. Finally his eyes settled on the woman behind the counter.

"What happened?" he snapped. "What did you do?"

"Noth—nothing," the woman stammered. "I don't know. She asked for coffee, and all of a sudden she—"

"And you forgot to give her cream," the manager broke in. "And then got smart with her when she asked—"

"No! I didn't do anything." The waitress lifted her hands helplessly. Her face turned a mottled pink.

The manager looked at the wall clock. A quarter after one, and the woman behind the soda fountain was due to go off duty at two. . . . As scarce as customers were in this weather, the manager knew he could handle the soda fountain until the other waitress came on.

He nodded his head thoughtfully. For days now, he'd been looking for a good reason to fire this dame. She was too ugly and too slow for the job. He'd never liked her. Also, he thought he knew where he could find a girl who would work the morning shift for five dollars a day, instead of the six dollars he'd been paying this one.

He nodded again, decisively, then said crisply, "I'm sorry, Martha, but I'm going to have to let you go. If there's anything the store will not

ELIJAH ELLIS

tolerate, it's rudeness to our customers."

"But I—"

"No. I'll make out your check, and you can leave right now. And don't expect to be paid for the full day, not after the way you insulted that lady."

The waitress, Martha, opened her mouth, then shut it again. It had all happened too fast for her. She didn't think she'd insulted the lady, but—

A few minutes later Martha left the drugstore. There was a bus stop on the corner. She waited under the canopy in front of the store, watching the snow come down. She shivered inside her thin cloth coat, tightened the scarf around her head. She waited, wondering how she was ever going to explain to her husband why she'd lost her job when she didn't know why, herself. Her husband would probably . . .

The bus loomed out of the snow, stopped, and she stepped inside, grateful for the warmth. She dropped two dimes in the fare box—she was careful always to have the exact change for the bus; her husband had taught her that—then she took a seat back toward the rear.

Her husband! At least she had a couple of hours before he would get home from work, before she had to tell him she had lost her job. What would he say? She shook her head in dumb misery. She knew what he would say.

She left the bus at the stop nearest her home, plodded through the deepening snow for the final block and arrived trembling and breathless. Inside, she headed straight for the kitchen and put on water for tea.

She looked around the kitchen. The breakfast dishes were piled in the sink. She must remember to wash them, tidy up the house generally, make the bed, empty the garbage, run the sweeper over the living room rug, maybe.

That would please her busband.

Martha took off her coat and folded it over the back of a chair at the kitchen table. First, though, she'd have some tea—and consider what, how, she was going to tell him.

A little after four, John Brann keyed open the front door and tramped into his house. It had been a lousy day; lousy. Driving a city bus was hard work in the best of weather. On a day like this, it was sheer—

A clattering sound from the kitchen interrupted his sour thoughts. Then his wife's voice, "John?"

He walked into the kitchen. "What're you doing?"

Martha was at the sink, hastily finishing the last of the dirty dishes. She hadn't realized how late it was getting. She gave her husband a strained smile.

He ignored it, went back into the hall to take off and hang up his overcoat and bus driver's cap. While he did, he looked along the dusty hallway into the living room. It was a mess; magazines and last night's papers scattered around. Wouldn't that woman ever learn!

Martha nervously put away the washed dishes, then dried her hands on the dish towel and carefully hung the towel on its rack over the sink.

Her husband returned. He jerked out a chair and sat down, lit a cigarette and smoked it in short, angry puffs. Martha shrunk into herself. If only she'd had time to tidy up the house—

"I don't know," John Brann said, not looking at her. "I work like a dog all day. Then I come home and what do I find? House looks like a—a pigsty. It ain't like you didn't have the time to keep the place halfway decent."

Martha folded her arms across her chest, shivering.

Brann went on, and on.

Martha was used to it, of course. She should be, after all these years—and, in a way, she had to admit her husband was right. Yet this time some alien thing stirred deep within her brain. She looked inward and saw the angry face of that blonde woman, shrilling at her, and the sly face of the store manager as he fired her.

Brann kept talking, a monologue of complaints, his voice rumbling on and on like an endless train. Martha stared at his broad back, at the close-clipped, bristly hair on the back of his neck.

The thing within her stirred again, began to gnaw at the edges of her conscious mind.

Brann sat at the table, smoking another cigarette, intent only on what he was saying.

Martha turned to a drawer and opened it. Slowly she took a heavy butcher knife from the drawer. She didn't know why—only that the gnawing thing in her brain was telling her to. She raised the knife, looked at its shiny ten inch blade.

"And another thing," John Brann said.

Martha took a step toward him. The thing inside her suddenly screamed, *Now!*

The knife cut a glittering arc through the air and then its blade sank

ELIJAH ELLIS

deep into John Brann's back. He gave one loud grunt and fell forward across the table. Then his big body slid to the side and down, and he landed on the floor on his back, the lower half of his right leg still resting across the seat of the chair.

Martha looked at the body on the floor. It didn't move. She breathed, "John?"

The items in Brann's right-hand trousers pocket began to trickle out, thumping and tinkling on the kitchen floor: a small pocketknife, a key ring, some coins.

"John?" Martha said, wonderingly. Then she stared at the little heap of things that had fallen from the upended trousers pocket. There was a dime, two quarters, another dime, and still another. And four nickels. A dollar's worth of change, exactly.

Martha went to the window and looked out. She said over her shoulder, "John, you'll get your uniform all dusty, lying there."

She stared out at the snow sifting down from the gray winter sky. She stared and stared, while the window frosted over and the light dimmed, and faded into darkness.

Rest in Pieces

by W.T. Quick

Just as Jonny Calvert closed the door, the bomb popped out of thin air and said, "You didn't think it would be that easy, did you?"

Jonny's eyes bugged at the deadly titanium canister. It looked like an antique home-vac, but it wasn't. He froze for a moment. Then his brain clicked over and he tried a shaky smile. "You've got the wrong guy," he said.

"Are you Jonny Calvert?"

"No."

The bomb paused for a moment. "Yes, you are. Your brain waves match those given to me," it said matter-of-factly.

"Oh."

"Also, the money you stole from Bingle the Bookie is in that styrofoam container you're trying to hide."

"You mean this?" He raised the bag he'd been stuffing down his pants.

"Yes. Four hundred eighty-six thousand dollars. Yesterday's receipts."

Jonny shrugged. "Not quite. I spent the night in a hotel and had breakfast."

The bomb was silent. Jonny tried to remember everything he'd ever heard about robot killer-bombs. First, they were expensive. Bingle must've been really angry to go to such lengths. Unless—if Bingle was a syndicate front? Possible. The old Mafia was now a legal corporation. It paid its taxes as promptly as General Solar or U. S. Satellite, but it wasn't above hiding a bit of revenue like anybody else.

"Who hired you?" Jonny asked.

"I can't answer that," the bomb replied.

Jonny remembered something else. "Okay, how long do I have, and how much do I need?"

"I'm a four-hour bomb. My dismissal fee is five million dollars."

Jonny studied his reflection in the bomb's mirrored side. A shade over

W.T. QUICK

six feet. Two hundred muscular pounds. A charming, little-boy face, the kind that made women instantly want to mother him. Dark, curly hair. Quavering hands and a tongue licking nervously over wet lips.

"Five million bucks? That's ten times what I stole."

"You admit it, then?"

He felt like a kid who'd made a stupid mistake at checkers. "Um—ah—well, yes. Sure I stole it. Bingle doesn't pay very well." He inhaled sharply. "Five *million*, you say? I couldn't raise that much if my life depended on it."

"It does," the bomb assured him.

A sour ball began to throb in Jonny's gut. It didn't seem real. Probably it wasn't. They just wanted their money back and that would be the end of it. And maybe not. The thought set his teeth jittering, but he managed to say, "Does the escape clause apply?"

"Of course." The bomb sounded offended. "If, in four hours, you find a way to survive, then the contract is void."

It wasn't a very hopeful ray. "How much time is left?"

"Three hours, fifty-two minutes, twenty seconds."

Jonny bolted for the door. The bomb didn't mind. Once keyed to his brain pattern, it could follow him anywhere.

"Binnie, you got to help me. Here's the money back, almost every cent. I'll pay the rest, I swear it. Now, *please,* call off your dogs."

Binnie Bingle looked at the pile of bills on his desk. Then he raised his sad brown eyes and stared into Jonny's terrified blue ones. Bingle's perfume smelled like lilies. "I'd like to, Jonny, but I can't."

"What do you mean, you can't?"

"It's out of my hands," he said gently.

"Oh, no, Binnie, you aren't saying—"

"Yes. I didn't contract the hit. The organization did. It doesn't like theft—at least when its money is involved."

"No. Binnie, call them. Tell them I brought it back. Something. Please, Binnie."

The older man blinked. He glanced at the bomb squatting next to Johnny's foot. "How much time is left on that thing?" he asked nervously.

"Three hours, one minute, seventeen seconds," the bomb said.

"Oh." Bingle sounded relieved. "Well, you're a pretty likable kid, for a thief," he said. "Okay, I'll call." He activated his desk hush-phone and punched buttons.

Jonny tried to read Bingle's lips, but had no luck. He waited, smelling the sourness of his own sweat, tasting salt on his chewed lips. The bookie finished talking and looked up.

"Well?" Jonny asked.

A film of moisture glinted on Bingle's shiny skull. "I'm sorry, kid. No luck. They said something about setting an example. I didn't push. You don't push people like them."

"Yeah. Murderers," Jonny said bitterly. "I don't suppose you've got five million you'd like to lend me, Binnie?"

"Son, I don't have five thousand. No, don't look at me that way. I gave you a job and you stole from me. Nobody twisted your arm."

Jonny bowed his head contritely. "I know, but I never thought—"

"That's the problem. You never thought." Bingle's eyes twitched toward the bomb. "Look, I did what I could. But that thing gives me the shivers. How about you moving on?"

"You don't even care!"

"Did you care when you robbed me?"

Jonny's face twisted angrily. "I don't know why I bothered to return the money!"

Bingle's smile was knowing. "Because you thought you had to," he said. He pointed at the door. "Goodbye, Jonny. Been nice knowing you."

Jonny sat near a port station and ticked off point after hopeless point. The bomb perched on the bench beside him. In less than three hours it would detonate an implosion-shielded blast that would destroy everything within four meters. There was no escape he could think of. The bomb was equipped with transporters, both personal and remote. It could hook into the brain pattern of a human and shift him out of danger. It could hook into Jonny and, though not allowed to port him, could follow him anywhere.

Jonny remembered a guy who thought he'd found a weakness in the primary injunction against damaging anybody but the intended victim. He managed to get himself locked in a bank vault with several innocent bystanders. When the time came, the bomb simply ported everybody else out of the vault and then blew up. Some of the bettors over at Bingle's used to say they were spending "the old Fred," who was the guy that hadn't been so smart. He shuddered.

210   W.T. QUICK

"You're going to kill me," he said wonderingly. He still couldn't grasp it. "Over a lousy half million, you're going to blow me up into bloody little pieces."

"I am an efficient mechanism," the bomb said proudly.

"It's not fair!"

The bomb didn't reply.

The police wouldn't help. Since the mob was legal, the cops looked the other way at anything involving its internal affairs. Who cared what crooks, legal or not, did to each other? As long as nobody else got hurt, they wouldn't interfere. Besides, the injunctions, as well as the escape clause with its implicit possibility of avoiding the blast, gave them a moral out as well. If somebody couldn't buy or think his way out of the death sentence, maybe he deserved to die.

"I don't suppose you can be destroyed?" Jonny asked.

"Of course I can," the bomb said.

"Mind telling me how?"

"Lasers. Concussion. Heat. Pressure."

"Would it do me any good?"

"Possibly," the bomb admitted. "You'd have to be very fast. In case of attack, my detonation reflex is in the low nanoseconds."

A nanosecond. One billionth of a second. "Well, fry that," Jonny said.

For a while he sat and stared into the middle distance. He tasted bile in his mouth. The heat of the sun on the pavement brought the smell of cooking asphalt. Unseeing, he listened to the scuff of transient footsteps as strollers swept past, saw the bomb, and shied suddenly away. It made Jonny feel as if he were already dead, removed from human concern or help. He imagined the unpleasant sensation of dirt clods falling onto his face. Seconds dripped by.

Finally he looked up. "It's not fair," he said again.

The bomb gleamed noiselessly, metal blazing.

"I'm going to die." There was resignation in his voice, but something cold and dangerous grew there as well.

"How much time?" he asked.

"Two hours, fourteen minutes, nine seconds," the bomb told him.

"That's enough," Jonny said. He got up and stalked purposefully away.

Binnie Bingle's furry black eyebrows tried to crawl up his naked forehead like twin caterpillars when he recognized his visitor. Jonny almost laughed out loud.

"You!" Bingle blurted.

"Me," Jonny said, as he seated himself before Bingle's cluttered desk. His eyes glittered brightly.

Bingle licked thin, liverish lips. "What do you want? I already told you—"

"Shut up, Binnie," Jonny said.

"Shut up! Listen, you small-time—"

Jonny hauled out the antique .38-caliber revolver, a memento from his father. He pointed the ugly little weapon at the bookie's nose. "I said shut up."

Bingle shut up. A faint tic began to dance below his left eye.

"I got to thinking," Jonny said. "I'm pretty smart, you know. One of the best at the old con. That's how I've always made my living." He gestured at the bomb. "But I couldn't figure out how to con my way out of *that*."

Dark patches appeared on the armpits of Bingle's white loungesuit. Usually dapper, he now looked as disheveled as his office. His jaw quivered. "And so . . . ?" he asked.

"I'm going to die, Binnie. I decided I'd like company. You got elected," Jonny said simply.

"You're crazy!"

"Maybe."

"That thing will port me out before it explodes. Remember Fred?"

"By that time you'll have several holes in you. It won't help. It can only port someone away from its own blast."

Bingle was sweating visibly. The astringent odor, mixed with the flowery sweetness of his perfume, was overwhelming. His sallow face leaped and jumped minutely. "Jonny, why me? You think I can help? Sure. I'll try. I'll call again." He reached for his phone.

"No, don't touch that!"

"Why? Maybe I can do some good." Bingle's eyes were pleading.

"You know better. You said those guys don't push. If they want me five million bucks' worth of dead, the loss of a small-time bookie"—he relished returning the insult—"won't matter much. Will it?"

Bingle's narrow shoulders sagged. "No."

Jonny stared at the scrawny old man. Somehow this didn't feel right. He extended the pistol.

W.T. QUICK

"Jonny, I got a wife. Two kids. I say again, why me?"

"Why not? You set me up for this."

"I didn't! Sure, I had to report it, but *they* let the contract. I got no control, you know that."

The gun wavered, then steadied again. "I can't get at them. You'll have to do."

Every trembling line of the bookie's body expressed abject terror. Still, his voice held the lingering taste of rebellion. "Yeah, you'll do it," he said bitterly. "You're rotten enough. But it still ain't fair."

Jonny's finger tightened on the trigger.

Not fair? For the very first time in his life Jonny knew what was going on in another man's mind. It sickened him.

He lowered the gun. Then he got up and placed it on Bingle's desk. "You're right, Binnie," he said. "It isn't fair. None of it is." He paused, searching Bingle's ravaged face. "I'm a liar, a cheat, a thief. I don't think becoming a murderer will help anything.

Bingle remained absolutely still.

Jonny smiled. "I'm sorry, Binnie. Goodbye." Then he turned and walked out of the office.

The bookie stared at the closed door for several seconds. Then he said, "Goodbye, Jonny. I'm sorry, too."

For a while Jonny wandered in the sunlight. To his numbed mind, death seemed unavoidable. Something tickled his unconscious. Sure. Why not? Maybe he couldn't do anything for himself, but there might be a way to help the next victim. Perhaps his death, unlike his life, could mean something. He thought about it. Finally, he had a plan.

He ported out to the bay. He watched the choppy water for a few minutes. Then he walked onto the bridge. Fifty years before, it had carried thousands of cars in and out of the city. Now it held the homes and gardens of the rich. They liked the view. About halfway across he found what he was looking for. He had to pick two locks and climb a safety fence. Finally he reached the partially hidden ladder which ran straight up one of the mighty towers. He started to climb.

It was a simple plan. The top of the bridge was the highest, most visible place in the city. His climb would be noticed. Suicides often chose the bridge. At the top, in the eyes of thousands of people, the bomb would kill him. Perhaps the public would no longer tolerate murder if it had to watch the process.

He kept on climbing. The wind whipped at him. Far below, tiny figures gathered. Their upturned faces were indistinct white blobs. They waved and pointed. Good.

The top of the tower was about a meter square. A massive cable snaked up and over. Jonny sat down and looked out over the city, his back to the giant steel rope. He let his feet dangle over the edge. The breeze was cool and laden with salt.

"How much time?" he asked.

"Five minutes, twelve seconds," the bomb said.

Down below, someone began to climb the ladder after him. A helicam from one of the TV stations buzzed by, then hovered several meters away. Jonny ignored it all. For a space, he tilted his head up to the bright blue sky. Seagulls wheeled past, calling their forlorn, lost cries. The cable felt rough against his back. The air tasted sparkling and new. The sun shone warmly down.

"Ten seconds," the bomb said. "Nine . . . eight . . . seven—"

A worried face appeared at the top of the ladder. "Go away!" Jonny said urgently. He heard a sharp click from the bomb. The face disappeared.

"Five . . . four . . . three . . . "

How alive he felt! Every muscle in his body tensed in primal reflex. *Please, let it do some good,* he prayed.

A timeless moment.

"Congratulations, Jonny Calvert," the bomb said.

Slowly, Jonny felt his muscles un-kink. "What?" he said after a while.

"I'm unable to detonate. You've survived. The contract is void."

Another pause. "I don't understand," Jonny said. He began to look around.

"I'm not allowed to damage any human but you. Yet, I can only port humans away from my own blast area, as I did a few moments ago. My analysis of the structure we are on indicates that my detonation would cut one of its main support cables. The structure would collapse and hundreds of humans would be damaged."

Jonny stared at the ugly little canister. If it had features, it would look puzzled. Helplessly, he began to laugh.

"My manufacturers will pay a sizable amount for your silence. There

214   W.T. QUICK

are other bombs. It will take time to switch production to a new device."

Jonny rose to shaky knees. "Stupid hunk of tin," he said. "There's no secret to keep. It's all on film." He gestured toward the hovering heli-cam. "But even if it weren't, you could keep your payoff. I don't need blood money. I'm not a killer."

As his feet touched the ladder he felt the wind on his face like a bene-diction, and realized he was no longer a lot of other things, either.

Whistling, he began the long climb down.

Lot No. 249

by Arthur Conan Doyle

Of the dealings of Edward Bellingham with William Monkhouse Lee, and of the cause of the great terror of Abercrombie Smith, it may be that no absolute and final judgment will ever be delivered. It is true that we have the full and clear narrative of Smith himself, and such corroboration as he could look for from Thomas Styles the servant, from the Reverend Plumptree Peterson, Fellow of Old's, and from such other people as chanced to gain some passing glance at this or that incident in a singular chain of events. Yet, in the main, the story must rest upon Smith alone, and the most will think that it is more likely that one brain, however outwardly sane, has some subtle warp in its texture, some strange flaw in its workings, than that the path of Nature has been overstepped in open day in so famed a center of learning and light as the University of Oxford. Yet when we think how narrow and how devious this path of Nature is, how dimly we can trace it, for all our lamps of science, and how from the darkness which girds it round great and terrible possibilities loom ever shadowly upwards, it is a bold and confident man who will put a limit to the strange by-paths into which the human spirit may wander.

In a certain wing of what we will call Old College in Oxford there is a corner turret of an exceeding great age. The heavy arch which spans the open door has bent downwards in the center under the weight of its years, and the grey, lichen-blotched blocks of stone are bound and knitted together with withes and strands of ivy, as though the old mother had set herself to brace them up against wind and weather. From the door a stone stair curves upward spirally, passing two landings, and terminating in a third one, its steps all shapeless and hollowed by the tread of so many generations of the seekers after knowledge. Life has flowed like water down this winding stair, and, waterlike, has left these smooth-worn grooves behind it. From the long-gowned, pedantic scholars of Plantagenet days down to the young bloods of a later age, how full and strong had been that tide of young, English life. And what was left now of all those hopes, those strivings, those fiery energies, save here and there in some old-world churchyard a few scratches upon a stone, and perchance a handful of dust in a mouldering coffin? Yet here were the silent stair and the grey, old wall, with bend and saltire and many another heraldic device still to be read upon its surface, like grotesque shadows thrown back from the days that had passed.

In the month of May, in the year 1884, three young men occupied the sets of rooms which opened on to the separate landings of the old stair. Each set consisted simply of a sitting room and of a bedroom, while the two corresponding rooms upon the ground floor were used, the one as a coal cellar, and the other as the living-room of the servant, or scout, Thomas Styles, whose duty it was to wait upon the three men above him. To right and to left was a line of lecture rooms and of offices, so that the dwellers in the old turret enjoyed a certain seclusion, which made the chambers popular among the more studious undergraduates. Such were the three who occupied them now—Abercrombie Smith above, Edward Bellingham beneath him, and William Monkhouse Lee upon the lowest story.

It was ten o'clock on a bright, spring night, and Abercrombie Smith lay back in his armchair, his feet upon the fender, and his briar-root pipe between his lips. In a similar chair, and equally at his ease, there lounged on the other side of the fireplace his old school friend Jephro Hastie. Both men were in flannels, for they had spent their evening upon the river, but apart from their dress no one could look at their hard-cut, alert faces without seeing that they were open-air men—men whose minds and tastes turned naturally to all that was manly and robust. Hastie, indeed, was stroke of his college boat, and Smith was an even better oar, but a coming examination had already cast its shadow over him and held him to his work, save for the few hours a week which health demanded. A litter of medical books upon the table, with scattered bones, models, and anatomical plates, pointed to the extent as well as the nature of his studies, while a couple of single-sticks and a set of boxing gloves above the mantelpiece hinted at the means by which, with Hastie's help, he might take his exercise in its most compressed and least-distant form. They knew each other very well—so well that they could sit now in that soothing silence which is the very highest development of companionship.

"Have some whisky," said Abercrombie Smith at last between two cloudbursts. "Scotch in the jug and Irish in the bottle."

"No, thanks. I'm in for the sculls. I don't liquor when I'm training. How about you?"

"I'm reading hard. I think it best to leave it alone."

Hastie nodded, and they relapsed into a contented silence.

"By the way, Smith," asked Hastie, presently, "have you made the acquaintance of either of the fellows on your stair yet?"

"Just a nod when we pass. Nothing more."

"Hum! I should be inclined to let it stand at that. I know something of them both. Not much, but as much as I want. I don't think I should take them to my bosom if I were you. Not that there's much amiss with Monkhouse Lee."

"Meaning the thin one?"

"Precisely. He is a gentlemanly little fellow. I don't think there is any vice in him. But then you can't know him without knowing Bellingham."

"Meaning the fat one?"

"Yes, the fat one. And he's a man whom I, for one, would rather not know."

Abercrombie Smith raised his eyebrows and glanced across at his companion.

"What's up, then?" he asked. "Drink? Cards? Cad? You used not to be censorious."

"Ah! you evidently don't know the man, or you wouldn't ask. There's something damnable about him—something reptilian. My gorge always rises at him. I should put him down as a man with secret vices—an evil liver. He's no fool, though. They say that he is one of the best men in his line that they have ever had in the college."

"Medicine or classics?"

"Eastern languages. He's a demon at them. Chillingworth met him somewhere above the second cataract last long, and he told me that he just prattled to the Arabs as if he had been born and nursed and weaned among them. He talked Coptic to the Copts, and Hebrew to the Jews, and Arabic to the Bedouins, and they were all ready to kiss the hem of his frock-coat. There are some old hermit Johnnies up in those parts who sit on rocks and scowl and spit at the casual stranger. Well, when they saw this chap Bellingham, before he had said five words they just lay down on their bellies and wriggled. Chillingworth said that he never saw anything like it. Bellingham seemed to take it as his right, too, and strutted

218   ARTHUR CONAN DOYLE

about among them and talked down to them like a Dutch uncle. Pretty good for an undergrad. of Old's, wasn't it?"

"Why do you say you can't know Lee without knowing Bellingham?"

"Because Bellingham is engaged to his sister Eveline. Such a bright little girl, Smith! I know the whole family well. It's disgusting to see that brute with her. A toad and a dove, that's what they always remind me of."

Abercrombie Smith grinned and knocked his ashes out against the side of the grate.

"You show every card in your hand, old chap," said he. "What a prejudiced, green-eyed, evil-thinking old man it is! You have really nothing against the fellow except that."

"Well, I've known her ever since she was as long as that cherry-wood pipe, and I don't like to see her taking risks. And it is a risk. He looks beastly. And he has a beastly temper, a venomous temper. You remember his row with Long Norton?"

"No; you always forget that I am a freshman."

"Ah, it was last winter. Of course. Well, you know the towpath along by the river. There were several fellows going along it, Bellingham in front, when they came on an old market woman coming the other way. It had been raining—you know what those fields are like when it has rained—and the path ran between the river and a great puddle that was nearly as broad. Well, what does this swine do but keep the path, and push the old girl into the mud, where she and her marketings came to terrible grief. It was a blackguard thing to do, and Long Norton, who is as gentle a fellow as ever stepped, told him what he thought of it. One word led to another, and it ended in Norton laying his stick across the fellow's shoulders. There was the deuce of a fuss about it, and it's a treat to see the way in which Bellingham looks at Norton when they meet now. By Jove, Smith, it's nearly eleven o'clock!"

"No hurry. Light your pipe again."

"Not I. I'm supposed to be in training. Here I've been sitting gossiping when I ought to have been safely tucked up. I'll borrow your skull, if you can share it. Williams has had mine for a month. I'll take the little bones of your ear, too, if you are sure you won't need them. Thanks very much. Never mind a bag, I can carry them very well under my arm. Good night, my son, and take my tip as to your neighbor."

When Hastie, bearing his anatomical plunder, had clattered off down the winding stair, Abercrombie Smith hurled his pipe into the wastepaper basket, and drawing his chair nearer to the lamp, plunged into a formidable, green-covered volume, adorned with great, colored maps of that strange, internal kingdom of which we are the hapless and helpless monarchs. Though a freshman at Oxford, the student was not so in medicine, for he had worked for four years at Glasgow and at Berlin, and this coming examination would place him finally as a member of his profession. With his firm mouth, broad forehead, and clear-cut, somewhat hard-featured face, he was a man who, if he had no brilliant talent, was yet so dogged, so patient, and so strong that he might in the end overtop a more showy genius. A man who can hold his own among Scotchmen and North Germans is not a man to be easily set back. Smith had left a name at Glasgow and at Berlin, and he was bent now upon doing as much at Oxford, if hard work and devotion could accomplish it.

He had sat reading for about an hour, and the hands of the noisy carriage clock upon the side table were rapidly closing together upon the twelve, when a sudden sound fell upon the student's ear—a sharp, rather shrill sound, like the hissing intake of a man's breath who gasps under some strong emotion. Smith laid down his book and slanted his ear to listen. There was no one on either side or above him, so that the interruption came certainly from the neighbor beneath—the same neighbor of whom Hastie had given so unsavory an account. Smith knew him only as a flabby, pale-faced man of silent and studious habits, a man whose lamp threw a golden bar from the old turret even after he had extinguished his own. This community in lateness had formed a certain silent bond between them. It was soothing to Smith when the hours stole on towards dawning to feel that there was another so close who set as small a value upon his sleep as he did. Even now, as his thoughts turned towards him, Smith's feelings were kindly. Hastie was a good fellow, but he was rough, strong-fibered, with no imagination or sympathy. He could not tolerate departures from what he looked upon as the model type of manliness. If a man could not be measured by a public school standard, then he was beyond the pale with Hastie. Like so many who are themselves robust, he was apt to confuse the constitution with the character, to ascribe to want of principle what was really a want of circulation. Smith, with his stronger mind, knew his friend's habit, and made allowance for it now as his thoughts turned towards the man beneath him.

There was no return of the singular sound, and Smith was about to turn

ARTHUR CONAN DOYLE

to his work once more, when suddenly there broke out in the silence of the night a hoarse cry, a positive scream—the call of a man who is moved and shaken beyond all control. Smith sprang out of his chair and dropped his book. He was a man of fairly firm fiber, but there was something in this sudden, uncontrollable shriek of horror which chilled his blood and pringled in his skin. Coming in such a place and at such an hour, it brought a thousand fantastic possibilities into his head. Should he rush down, or was it better to wait? He had all the national hatred of making a scene, and he knew so little of his neighbor that he would not lightly intrude upon his affairs. For a moment he stood in doubt and even as he balanced the matter there was a quick rattle of footsteps upon the stairs, and young Monkhouse Lee, half-dressed and as white as ashes, burst into his room.

"Come down!" he gasped. "Bellingham's ill."

Abercrombie Smith followed him closely downstairs into the sitting room which was beneath his own, and intent as he was upon the matter in hand, he could not but take an amazed glance around him as he crossed the threshold. It was such a chamber as he had never seen before—a museum rather than a study. Walls and ceiling were thickly covered with a thousand strange relics from Egypt and the East. Tall, angular figures bearing burdens or weapons stalked in an uncouth frieze round the apartments. Above were bull-headed, stork-headed, cat-headed, owl-headed statues, with viper-crowned, almond-eyed monarchs, and strange, beetle-like deities cut out of the blue Egyptian lapis lazuli. Horus and Isis and Osiris peeped down from every niche and shelf, while across the ceiling a true son of old Nile, a great, hanging-jawed crocodile, was slung in a double noose.

In the center of this singular chamber was a large, square table, littered with papers, bottles, and the dried leaves of some graceful, palm-like plant. These varied objects had all been heaped together in order to make room for a mummy case, which had been conveyed from the wall, as was evident from the gap there, and laid across the front of the table. The mummy itself, a horrid, black, withered thing, like a charred head on a gnarled bush, was lying half out of the case, with its claw-like hand and bony forearm resting upon the table. Propped up against the sarcophagus was an old, yellow scroll of papyrus, and in front of it, in a wooden armchair, sat the owner of the room, his head thrown back, his widely opened eyes directed in a horrified stare to the crocodile above him, and his blue, thick lips puffing loudly with every expiration.

"My God! he's dying!" cried Monkhouse Lee, distractedly.

He was a slim, handsome young fellow, olive-skinned and dark-eyed, of a Spanish rather than of an English type, with a Celtic intensity of manner which contrasted with the Saxon phlegm of Abercrombie Smith.

"Only a faint, I think," said the medical student. "Just give me a hand with him. You take his feet. Now on to the sofa. Can you kick all those little wooden devils off? What a litter it is! Now he will be all right if we undo his collar and give him some water. What has he been up to at all?"

"I don't know. I heard him cry out. I ran up. I know him pretty well, you know. It is very good of you to come down."

"His heart is going like a pair of castanets," said Smith, laying his hand on the breast of the unconscious man. "He seems to me to be frightened all to pieces. Chuck the water over him! What a face he has got on him!"

It was indeed a strange and most repellent face, for color and outline were equally unnatural. It was white, not with the ordinary pallor of fear, but with an absolutely bloodless white, like the under side of a sole. He was very fat, but gave the impression of having at some time been considerably fatter, for his skin hung loosely in creases and folds, and was shot with a meshwork of wrinkles. Short, stubbly brown hair bristled up from his scalp, with a pair of thick, wrinkled ears protruding at the sides. His light grey eyes were still open, the pupils dilated and the balls projecting in a fixed and horrid stare. It seemed to Smith as he looked down upon him that he had never seen Nature's danger signals flying so plainly upon a man's countenance, and his thoughts turned more seriously to the warning which Hastie had given him an hour before.

"What the deuce can have frightened him so?" he asked.

"It's the mummy."

"The mummy? How, then?"

"I don't know. It's beastly and morbid. I wish he would drop it. It's the second fright he has given me. It was the same last winter. I found him just like this, with that horrid thing in front of him."

"What does he want with the mummy, then?"

"Oh, he's a crank, you know. It's his hobby. He knows more about these things than any man in England. But I wish he wouldn't! Ah, he's beginning to come to."

A faint tinge of color had begun to steal back into Bellingham's ghastly cheeks, and his eyelids shivered like a sail after a calm. He clasped and

ARTHUR CONAN DOYLE

unclasped his hands, drew a long, thin breath between his teeth, and suddenly jerking up his head, threw a glance of recognition around him. As his eyes fell upon the mummy, he sprang off the sofa, seized the roll of papyrus, thrust it into a drawer, turned the key, and then staggered back on to the sofa.

"What's up?" he asked. "What do you chaps want?"

"You've been shrieking out and making no end of a fuss," said Monkhouse Lee. "If our neighbor here from above hadn't come down, I'm sure I don't know what I should have done with you."

"Ah, it's Abercrombie Smith," said Bellingham, glancing up at him. "How very good of you to come in! What a fool I am! Oh, my God, what a fool I am!"

He sank his head on to his hands, and burst into peal after peal of hysterical laughter.

"Look here! Drop it!" cried Smith, shaking him roughly by the shoulder.

"Your nerves are all in a jangle. You must drop these little midnight games with mummies, or you'll be going off your chump. You're all on wires now."

"I wonder," said Bellingham, "whether you would be as cool as I am if you had seen—"

"What then?"

"Oh, nothing. I meant that I wonder if you could sit up at night with a mummy without trying your nerves. I have no doubt that you are quite right. I dare say that I have been taking it out of myself too much lately. But I am all right now. Please don't go, though. Just wait for a few minutes until I am quite myself."

"The room is very close," remarked Lee, throwing open the window and letting in the cool night air.

"It's balsamic resin," said Bellingham. He lifted up one of the dried palmate leaves from the table and frizzled it over the chimney of the lamp. It broke away into heavy smoke wreaths, and a pungent, biting odor filled the chamber. "It's the sacred plant—the plant of the priests," he remarked. "Do you know anything of Eastern languages, Smith?"

"Nothing at all. Not a word."

The answer seemed to lift a weight from the Egyptologist's mind.

"By the way," he continued, "how long was it from the time that you ran down, until I came to my senses?"

"Not long. Some four or five minutes."

"I thought it could not be very long," said he, drawing a long breath. "But what a strange thing unconsciousness is! There is no measurement to it. I could not tell from my own sensations if it were seconds or weeks. Now that gentleman on the table was packed up in the days of the eleventh dynasty, some forty centuries ago, and yet if he could find his tongue, he would tell us that this lapse of time has been but a closing of the eyes and a reopening of them. He is a singularly fine mummy, Smith."

Smith stepped over to the table and looked down with a professional eye at the black and twisted form in front of him. The features, though horribly discolored, were perfect, and two little nut-like eyes still lurked in the depths of the black, hollow sockets. The blotched skin was drawn tightly from bone to bone, and a tangled wrap of black, coarse hair fell over the ears. Two thin teeth, like those of a rat, overlay the shrivelled lower lip. In its crouching position, with bent joints and craned head, there was a suggestion of energy about the horrid thing which made Smith's gorge rise. The gaunt ribs, with their parchment-like covering, were exposed, and the sunken, leaden-hued abdomen, with the long slit where the embalmer had left his mark; but the lower limbs were wrapped round with coarse, yellow bandages. A number of little clove-like pieces of myrrh and of cassia were sprinkled over the body, and lay scattered on the inside of the case.

"I don't know his name," said Bellingham, passing his hand over the shrivelled head. "You see the outer sarcophagus with the inscriptions is missing. Lot 249 is all the title he has now. You see it printed on his case. That was his number in the auction at which I picked him up."

"He has been a very pretty sort of fellow in his day," remarked Abercrombie Smith.

"He has been a giant. His mummy is six feet seven in length, and that would be a giant over there, for they were never a very robust race. Feel these great, knotted bones, too. He would be a nasty fellow to tackle."

"Perhaps these very hands helped to build the stones into the pyramids," suggested Monkhouse Lee, looking down with disgust in his eyes at the crooked, unclean talons.

"No fear. This fellow has been pickled in natron, and looked after in the most approved style. They did not serve hodsmen in that fashion. Salt or bitumen was enough for them. It has been calculated that this sort of thing cost about seven hundred and thirty pounds in our money. Our

ARTHUR CONAN DOYLE

friend was a noble at the least. What do you make of that small inscription near his feet, Smith?"

"I told you that I know no Eastern tongue."

"Ah, so you did. It is the name of the embalmer, I take it. A very conscientious worker he must have been. I wonder how many modern works will survive four thousand years?"

He kept on speaking lightly and rapidly, but it was evident to Abercrombie Smith that he was still palpitating with fear. His hands shook, his lower lip trembled, and look where he would, his eye always came sliding round to his gruesome companion. Through all his fear, however, there was a suspicion of triumph in his tone and manner. His eyes shone, and his footstep, as he paced the room, was brisk and jaunty. He gave the impression of a man who has gone through an ordeal, the marks of which he still bears upon him, but which has helped him to his end.

"You're not going yet?" he cried, as Smith rose from the sofa. At the prospect of solitude, his fears seemed to crowd back upon him, and he stretched out a hand to detain him.

"Yes, I must go. I have my work to do. You are all right now. I think that with your nervous system you should take up some less morbid study."

"Oh, I am not nervous as a rule; and I have unwrapped mummies before."

"You fainted last time," observed Monkhouse Lee.

"Ah, yes, so I did. Well, I must have a nerve tonic or a course of electricity. You are not going, Lee?"

"I'll do whatever you wish, Ned."

"Then I'll come down with you and have a shakedown on your sofa. Good night, Smith. I am so sorry to have disturbed you with my foolishness."

They shook hands, and as the medical student stumbled up the spiral and irregular stair he heard a key turn in a door, and the steps of his two new acquaintances as they descended to the lower floor.

In this strange way began the acquaintance between Edward Bellingham and Abercrombie Smith, an acquaintance which the latter, at least, had no desire to push further. Bellingham, however, appeared to have taken a fancy to his rough-spoken neighbor, and made his advances in such a way that he could hardly be repulsed without absolute brutality.

Twice he called to thank Smith for his assistance, and many times afterwards he looked in with books, papers, and such other civilities as two bachelor neighbors can offer each other. He was, as Smith soon found, a man of wide reading, with catholic tastes and an extraordinary memory. His manner, too, was so pleasing and suave that one came, after a time, to overlook his repellent appearance. For a jaded and wearied man he was no unpleasant companion, and Smith found himself, after a time, looking forward to his visits, and even returning them.

Clever as he undoubtedly was, however, the medical student seemed to detect a dash of insanity in the man. He broke out at times into a high, inflated style of talk which was in contrast with the simplicity of his life.

"It is a wonderful thing," he cried, "to feel that one can command powers of good and of evil—a ministering angel or a demon of vengeance." And again, of Monkhouse Lee, he said,—"Lee is a good fellow, an honest fellow, but he is without strength or ambition. He would not make a fit partner for a man with a great enterprise. He would not make a fit partner for me."

At such hints and innuendoes stolid Smith, puffing solemnly at his pipe, would simply raise his eyebrows and shake his head, with little interjections of medical wisdom as to earlier hours and fresher air.

One habit Bellingham had developed of late which Smith knew to be a frequent herald of a weakening mind. He appeared to be forever talking to himself. At late hours of the night, when there could be no visitor with him, Smith could still hear his voice beneath him in a low, muffled monologue, sunk almost to a whisper, and yet very audible in the silence. This solitary babbling annoyed and distracted the student, so that he spoke more than once to his neighbor about it. Bellingham, however, flushed up at the charge, and denied curtly that he had uttered a sound; indeed, he showed more annoyance over the matter than the occasion seemed to demand.

Had Abercrombie Smith had any doubt as to his own ears he had not to go far to find corroboration. Tom Styles, the little wrinkled manservant who had attended to the wants of the lodgers in the turret for a longer time than any man's memory could carry him, was sorely put to it over the same matter.

"If you please, sir," said he, as he tidied down the top chamber one morning, "do you think Mr. Bellingham is all right, sir?"

"All right, Styles?"

"Yes, sir. Right in his head, sir."

"Why should he not be, then?"

"Well, I don't know, sir. His habits has changed of late. He's not the same man he used to be, though I make free to say that he was never quite one of my gentlemen, like Mr. Hastie or yourself, sir. He's took to talkin' to himself something awful. I wonder it don't disturb you. I don't know what to make of him, sir."

"I don't know what business it is of yours, Styles."

"Well, I takes an interest, Mr. Smith. It may be forward of me, but I can't help it. I feel sometimes as if I was mother and father to my young gentlemen. It all falls on me when things go wrong and the relations come. But Mr. Bellingham, sir. I want to know what it is that walks about his room sometimes when he's out and when the door's locked on the outside."

"Eh? you're talking nonsense, Styles."

"Maybe so, sir; but I heard it more'n once with my own ears."

"Rubbish, Styles."

"Very good, sir. You'll ring the bell if you want me."

Abercrombie Smith gave little heed to the gossip of the old manservant, but a small incident occurred a few days later which left an unpleasant effect upon his mind, and brought the words of Styles forcibly to his memory.

Bellingham had come up to see him late one night, and was entertaining him with an interesting account of the rock tombs of Beni Hassan in Upper Egypt, when Smith, whose hearing was remarkably acute, distinctly heard the sound of a door opening on the landing below.

"There's some fellow gone in or out of your room," he remarked.

Bellingham sprang up and stood helpless for a moment, with the expression of a man who is half-incredulous and half-afraid.

"I surely locked it. I am almost positive that I locked it," he stammered. "No one could have opened it."

"Why, I hear someone coming up the steps now," said Smith.

Bellingham rushed out through the door, slammed it loudly behind him, and hurried down the stairs. About half-way down Smith heard him stop, and thought he caught the sound of whispering. A moment later the door beneath him shut, a key creaked in a lock, and Bellingham, with beads of moisture upon his pale face, ascended the stairs once more, and re-entered the room.

"It's all right," he said, throwing himself down in a chair. "It was that fool of a dog. He had pushed the door open. I don't know how I came to forget to lock it."

"I didn't know you kept a dog," said Smith, looking very thoughtfully at the disturbed face of his companion.

"Yes, I haven't had him long. I must get rid of him. He's a great nuisance."

"He must be, if you find it so hard to shut him up. I should have thought that shutting the door would have been enough, without locking it."

"I want to prevent old Styles from letting him out. He's of some value, you know, and it would be awkward to lose him."

"I am a bit of a dog-fancier myself," said Smith, still gazing hard at his companion from the corner of his eyes. "Perhaps you'll let me have a look at it."

"Certainly. But I am afraid it cannot be tonight; I have an appointment. Is that clock right? Then I am a quarter of an hour late already. You'll excuse me, I am sure."

He picked up his cap and hurried from the room. In spite of his appointment, Smith heard him re-enter his own chamber and lock his door upon the inside.

This interview left a disagreeable impression upon the medical student's mind. Bellingham had lied to him, and lied so clumsily that it looked as if he had desperate reasons for concealing the truth. Smith knew that his neighbor had no dog. He knew, also, that the step which he had heard upon the stairs was not the step of an animal. But if it were not, then what could it be? There was old Styles's statement about the something which used to pace the room at times when the owner was absent. Could it be a woman? Smith rather inclined to the view. If so, it would mean disgrace and expulsion to Bellingham if it were discovered by the authorities, so that his anxiety and falsehoods might be accounted for. And yet it was inconceivable that an undergraduate could keep a woman in his rooms without being instantly detected. Be the explanation what it might, there was something ugly about it, and Smith determined, as he turned to his books, to discourage all further attempts at intimacy on the part of his soft-spoken and ill-favored neighbor.

But his work was destined to interruption that night. He had hardly caught up the broken threads when a firm, heavy footfall came three steps at a time from below, and Hastie, in blazer and flannels, burst into the room.

"Still at it!" said he, plumping down into his wonted armchair. "What a chap you are to stew! I believe an earthquake might come and knock Oxford into a cocked hat, and you would sit perfectly placid with your books among the ruins. However, I won't bore you long. Three whiffs of baccy, and I am off."

"What's the news, then?" asked Smith, cramming a plug of bird's-eye into his briar with his forefinger.

"Nothing very much. Wilson made seventy for the freshmen against the eleven. They say that they will play him instead of Buddicomb, for Buddicomb is clean off color. He used to be able to bowl a little, but it's nothing but half-volleys and long hops now."

"Medium right," suggested Smith, with the intense gravity which comes upon a 'varsity man when he speaks of athletics.

"Inclining to fast, with a work from leg. Comes with the arm about three inches or so. He used to be nasty on a wet wicket. Oh, by the way, have you heard about Long Norton?"

"What's that?"

"He's been attacked."

"Attacked?"

"Yes, just as he was turning out of the High Street, and within a hundred yards of the gate of Old's."

"But who—"

"Ah, that's the rub! If you said 'what,' you would be more grammatical. Norton swears that it was not human, and, indeed, from the scratches on his throat, I should be inclined to agree with him."

"What, then? Have we come down to spooks?"

Abercrombie Smith puffed his scientific contempt.

"Well, no; I don't think that is quite the idea, either. I am inclined to think that if any showman has lost a great ape lately, and the brute is in these parts, a jury would find a true bill against it. Norton passes that way every night, you know, about the same hour. There's a tree that hangs low over the path—the big elm from Rainy's garden. Norton thinks the thing dropped on him out of the tree. Anyhow, he was nearly strangled by two arms, which, he says, were as strong and as thin as steel bands. He saw nothing; only those beastly arms that tightened and tightened on him. He yelled his head nearly off, and a couple of chaps came running, and the thing went over the wall like a cat. He never got a fair sight of it the whole time. It gave Norton a shake up, I can tell you. I tell him it has been as good as a change at the seaside for him."

"A garrotter, most likely," said Smith.

"Very possibly. Norton says not; but we don't mind what he says. The garrotter had long nails, and was pretty smart at swinging himself over walls. By the way, your beautiful neighbor would be pleased if he heard about it. He had a grudge against Norton, and he's not a man, from what I know of him, to forget his little debts. But hallo, old chap, what have you got in your noodle?"

"Nothing," Smith answered curtly.

He had started in his chair, and the look had flashed over his face which comes upon a man who is struck suddenly by some unpleasant idea.

"You looked as if something I had said had taken you on the raw. By the way, you have made the acquaintance of Master B. since I looked in last, have you not? Young Monkhouse Lee told me something to that effect."

"Yes; I know him slightly. He has been up here once or twice."

"Well, you're big enough and ugly enough to take care of yourself. He's not what I should call exactly a healthy sort of Johnny, though no doubt, he's very clever, and all that. But you'll soon find out for yourself. Lee is all right; he's a very decent little fellow. Well, so long, old chap! I row Mullins for the vice-chancellor's pot on Wednesday week, so mind you come down, in case I don't see you before."

Bovine Smith laid down his pipe and turned stolidly to his books once more. But with all the will in the world, he found it very hard to keep his mind upon his work. It would slip away to brood upon the man beneath him, and upon the little mystery which hung round his chambers. Then his thoughts turned to this singular attack of which Hastie had spoken, and to the grudge which Bellingham was said to owe the object of it. The two ideas would persist in rising together in his mind, as though there were some close and intimate connection between them. And yet the suspicion was so dim and vague that it could not be put down in words.

"Confound the chap!" cried Smith, as he shied his book on pathology across the room. "He has spoiled my night's reading, and that's reason enough, if there were no other, why I should steer clear of him in the future."

For ten days the medical student confined himself so closely to his studies that he neither saw nor heard anything of either of the men beneath him. At the hours when Bellingham had been accustomed to visit him, he took care to sport his oak, and though he more than once heard a knocking at his outer door, he resolutely refused to answer it. One afternoon, however, he was descending the stairs when, just as he was passing it, Bellingham's door flew open, and young Monkhouse Lee came out with his eyes sparkling and a dark flush of anger upon his olive cheeks. Close at his heels followed Bellingham, his fat, unhealthy face all quivering with malignant passion.

"You fool!" he hissed. "You'll be sorry."

"Very likely," cried the other. "Mind what I say. It's off! I won't hear of it!"

"You've promised, anyhow."

"Oh, I'll keep that! I won't speak. But I'd rather little Eva was in her grave. Once for all, it's off. She'll do what I say. We don't want to see you again."

So much Smith could not avoid hearing, but he hurried on, for he had no wish to be involved in their dispute. There had been a serious breach between them, that was clear enough, and Lee was going to cause the engagement with his sister to be broken off. Smith thought of Hastie's comparison of the toad and the dove, and was glad to think that the matter was at an end. Bellingham's face when he was in a passion was not pleasant to look upon. He was not a man to whom an innocent girl could be trusted for life. As he walked, Smith wondered languidly what could have caused the quarrel, and what the promise might be which Bellingham had been so anxious that Monkhouse Lee should keep.

It was the day of the sculling match between Hastie and Mullins, and a stream of men were making their way down to the banks of the Isis. A May sun was shining brightly, and the yellow path was barred with the black shadows of the tall elm trees. On either side the grey colleges lay back from the road, the hoary old mothers of minds looking out from their high, mullioned windows at the tide of young life which swept so merrily past them. Black-clad tutors, prim officials, pale, reading men, brown-faced, straw-hatted young athletes in white sweaters or many-colored blazers, all were hurrying towards the blue, winding river which curves through the Oxford meadows.

Abercrombie Smith, with the intuition of an old oarsman, chose his position at the point where he knew that the struggle, if there were a struggle, would come. Far off he heard the hum which announced the start, the gathering roar of the approach, the thunder of running feet, and the shouts of the men in the boats beneath him. A spray of half-clad, deep-breathing runners shot past him, and craning over their shoulders, he saw Hastie pulling a steady thirty-six while his opponent, with a jerky forty, was a good boat's length behind him. Smith gave a cheer for his friend, and pulling out his watch, was starting off again for his chambers, when he felt a touch upon his shoulder, and found that young Monkhouse Lee was beside him.

"I saw you there," he said, in a timid, deprecating way. "I wanted to speak to you, if you could spare me a half hour. This cottage is mine. I share it with Harrington of King's. Come in and have a cup of tea."

"I must be back presently," said Smith. "I am hard on the grind at present. But I'll come in for a few minutes with pleasure. I wouldn't have come out only Hastie is a friend of mine."

"So he is of mine. Hasn't he a beautiful style? Mullins wasn't in it. But come into the cottage. It's a little den of a place, but it is pleasant to work in during the summer months."

It was a small, square, white building, with green doors and shutters, and a rustic trellis-work porch, standing back some fifty yards from the river's bank. Inside, the main room was roughly fitted up as a study—deal table, unpainted shelves with books, and a few cheap oleographs upon the wall. A kettle sang upon a spirit-stove, and there were tea things upon a tray on the table.

"Try that chair and have a cigarette," said Lee. "Let me pour you out a cup of tea. It's so good of you to come in, for I know that your time is a good deal taken up. I wanted to say to you that, if I were you, I should change my rooms at once."

"Eh?"

Smith sat staring with a lighted match in one hand and his unlit cigarette in the other.

"Yes; it must seem very extraordinary, and the worst of it is that I cannot give my reasons, for I am under a solemn promise—a very solemn promise. But I may go so far as to say that I don't think Bellingham is a very safe man to live near. I intend to camp out here as much as I can for a time."

"Not safe! What do you mean?"

"Ah, that's what I mustn't say. But do take my advice and move your

232   ARTHUR CONAN DOYLE

rooms. We had a grand row today. You must have heard us, for you came down the stairs."

"I saw that you had fallen out."

"He's a horrible chap, Smith. That is the only word for him. I have had doubts about him ever since that night when he fainted—you remember, when you came down. I taxed him today, and he told me things that made my hair rise, and wanted me to stand in with him. I'm not straight-laced, but I am a clergyman's son, you know, and I think there are some things which are quite beyond the pale. I only thank God that I found him out before it was too late, for he was to have married into my family."

"This is all very fine, Lee," said Abercrombie Smith curtly. "But either you are saying a great deal too much or a great deal too little."

"I give you a warning."

"If there is real reason for warning, no promise can bind you. If I see a rascal about to blow a place up with dynamite no pledge will stand in my way of preventing him."

"Ah, but I cannot prevent him, and I can do nothing but warn you."

"Without saying what you warn me against."

"Against Bellingham."

"But that is childish. Why should I fear him, or any man?"

"I can't tell you. I can only entreat you to change your rooms. You are in danger where you are. I don't even say that Bellingham would wish to injure you. But it might happen, for he is a dangerous neighbor just now."

"Perhaps I know more than you think," said Smith, looking keenly at the young man's boyish, earnest face. "Suppose I tell you that someone else shares Bellingham's rooms."

Monkhouse Lee sprang from his chair in uncontrollable excitement. "You know, then?" he gasped.

"A woman."

Lee dropped back again with a groan.

"My lips are sealed," he said. "I must not speak."

"Well, anyhow," said Smith, rising, "it is not likely that I should allow myself to be frightened out of rooms which suit me very nicely. It would be a little too feeble for me to move out all my goods and chattels because you say that Bellingham might in some unexplained way do me an injury. I think that I'll just take my chance, and stay where I am, and as I see that it's nearly five o'clock, I must ask you to excuse me."

He bade the young student adieu in a few curt words, and made his way homeward through the sweet spring evening, feeling half-ruffled, half-amused, as any other strong, unimaginative man might who has been menaced by a vague and shadowy danger.

There was one little indulgence which Abercrombie Smith always allowed himself, however closely his work might press upon him. Twice a week, on the Tuesday and the Friday, it was his invariable custom to walk over to Farlingford, the residence of Dr. Plumptree Peterson, situated about a mile and a half out of Oxford. Peterson had been a close friend of Smith's elder brother, Francis, and as he was a bachelor, fairly well-to-do, with a good cellar and a better library, his house was a pleasant goal for a man who was in need of a brisk walk. Twice a week, then, the medical student would swing out there along the dark country roads and spend a pleasant hour in Peterson's comfortable study, discussing, over a glass of old port, the gossip of the 'varsity or the latest developments of medicine or of surgery.

On the day which followed his interview with Monkhouse Lee, Smith shut up his books at a quarter past eight, the hour when he usually started for his friend's house. As he was leaving his room, however, his eyes chanced to fall upon one of the books which Bellingham had lent him, and his conscience pricked him for not having returned it. However repellent the man might be, he should not be treated with discourtesy. Taking the book, he walked downstairs and knocked at his neighbor's door. There was no answer; but on turning the handle he found that it was unlocked. Pleased at the thought of avoiding an interview, he stepped inside, and placed the book with his card upon the table.

The lamp was turned half down, but Smith could see the details of the room plainly enough. It was all much as he had seen it before—the frieze, the animal-headed gods, the hanging crocodile, and the table littered over with papers and dried leaves. The mummy case stood upright against the wall, but the mummy itself was missing. There was no sign of any second occupant of the room, and he felt as he withdrew that he had probably done Bellingham an injustice. Had he a guilty secret to preserve, he would hardly leave his door open so that all the world might enter.

The spiral stair was as black as pitch, and Smith was slowly making his way down its irregular steps, when he was suddenly conscious that something had passed him in the darkness. There was a faint sound, a whiff of air, a light brushing past his elbow, but so slight that he could scarcely be certain of it. He stopped and listened, but the wind was rustling among the ivy outside, and he could hear nothing else.

"Is that you, Styles?" he shouted.

There was no answer, and all was still behind him. It must have been a sudden gust of air, for there were crannies and cracks in the old turret. And yet he could almost have sworn that he heard a footfall by his very side. He had emerged into the quadrangle, still turning the matter over in his head, when a man came running swiftly across the smooth-cropped lawn.

"Is that you, Smith?"

"Hullo, Hastie!"

"For God's sake come at once! Young Lee is drowned! Here's Harrington of King's with the news. The doctor is out. You'll do, but come along at once. There may be life in him."

"Have you brandy?"

"No."

"I'll bring some. There's a flask on my table."

Smith bounded up the stairs, taking three at a time, seized the flask, and was rushing down with it, when, as he passed Bellingham's room, his eyes fell upon something which left him gasping and staring upon the landing.

The door, which he had closed behind him, was now open, and right in front of him, with the lamp light shining upon it, was the mummy case. Three minutes ago it had been empty. He could swear to that. Now it framed the lank body of its horrible occupant, who stood, grim and stark, with his black, shrivelled face towards the door. The form was lifeless and inert, but it seemed to Smith as he gazed that there still lingered a lurid spark of vitality, some faint sign of consciousness in the little eyes which lurked in the depths of the hollow sockets. So astounded and shaken was he that he had forgotten his errand, and was still staring at the lean, sunken figure when the voice of his friend below recalled him to himself.

"Come on, Smith!" he shouted. "It's life and death, you know. Hurry up! Now, then," he added, as the medical student reappeared, "let us do a sprint. It is well under a mile, and we should do it in five minutes. A human life is better worth running for than a pot."

Neck and neck they dashed through the darkness, and did not pull up until panting and spent, they had reached the little cottage by the river.

Young Lee, limp and dripping like a broken water plant, was stretched upon the sofa, the green scum of the river upon his black hair, and a fringe of white foam upon his leaden-hued lips. Beside him knelt his fellow student, Harrington, endeavoring to chafe some warmth back into his rigid limbs.

"I think there's life in him," said Smith, with his hand to the lad's side. "Put your watch glass to his lips. Yes, there's dimming on it. You take one arm, Hastie. Now work it as I do, and we'll soon pull him round."

For ten minutes they worked in silence, inflating and depressing the chest of the unconscious man. At the end of that time a shiver ran through his body, his lips trembled, and he opened his eyes. The three students burst out into an irrepressible cheer.

"Wake up, old chap. You've frightened us quite enough."

"Have some brandy. Take a sip from the flask."

"He's all right now," said his companion Harrington. "Heavens, what a fright I got! I was reading here, and he had gone out for a stroll as far as the river, when I heard a scream and a splash. Out I ran, and by the time I could find him and fish him out, all life seemed to have gone. Then Simpson couldn't get a doctor, for he has a game leg, and I had to run, and I don't know what I'd have done without you fellows. That's right, old chap. Sit up."

Monkhouse Lee had raised himself on his hands, and looked wildly about him.

"What's up?" he asked. "I've been in the water. Ah, yes; I remember." A look of fear came into his eyes, and he sank his face into his hands.

"How did you fall in?"

"I didn't fall in."

"How then?"

"I was thrown in. I was standing by the bank, and something from behind picked me up like a feather and hurled me in. I heard nothing, and I saw nothing. But I know what it was, for all that."

"And so do I," whispered Smith.

Lee looked up with a quick glance of surprise.

"You've learned, then?" he said. "You remember the advice I gave you?"

"Yes, and I begin to think that I shall take it."

"I don't know what the deuce you fellows are talking about," said Hastie, "but I think, if I were you, Harrington, I should get Lee to bed

ARTHUR CONAN DOYLE

at once. It will be time enough to discuss the why and the wherefore when he is a little stronger. I think, Smith, you and I can leave him alone now. I am walking back to college; if you are coming in that direction, we can have a chat."

But it was little chat that they had upon their homeward path. Smith's mind was too full of the incidents of the evening, the absence of the mummy from his neighbor's rooms, the step that passed him on the stair, the reappearance—the extraordinary, inexplicable reappearance of the grisly thing—and then this attack upon Lee, corresponding so closely to the previous outrage upon another man against whom Bellingham bore a grudge. All this settled in his thoughts, together with the many little incidents which had previously turned him against his neighbor, and the singular circumstances under which he was first called in to him. What had been a dim suspicion, a vague, fantastic conjecture, had suddenly taken form, and stood out in his mind as a grim fact, a thing not to be denied. And yet, how monstrous it was! how unheard of! how entirely beyond all bounds of human experience. An impartial judge, or even the friend who walked by his side, would simply tell him that his eyes had deceived him, that the mummy had been there all the time, that young Lee had tumbled into the river as any other man tumbles into a river, and the blue pill was the best thing for a disordered liver. He felt that he would have said as much if the positions had been reversed. And yet he could swear that Bellingham was a murderer at heart, and that he wielded a weapon such as no man had ever used in all the grim history of crime.

Hastie had branched off to his rooms with a few crisp and emphatic comments upon his friend's unsociability, and Abercrombie Smith crossed the quadrangle to his corner turret with a strong feeling of repulsion for his chambers and their associations. He would take Lee's advice, and move his quarters as soon as possible, for how could a man study when his ear was ever straining for every murmur or footstep in the room below? He observed, as he crossed over the lawn, that the light was still shining in Bellingham's window, and as he passed up the staircase the door opened, and the man himself looked out at him. With his fat, evil face he was like some bloated spider fresh from the weaving of his poisonous web.

"Good evening," said he. "Won't you come in?"

"No," cried Smith fiercely.

"No? You are as busy as ever? I wanted to ask you about Lee. I was sorry to hear that there was a rumor that something was amiss with him." His features were grave, but there was the gleam of a hidden laugh in his eyes as he spoke. Smith saw it, and he could have knocked him down for it.

"You'll be sorrier still to hear that Monkhouse Lee is doing very well, and is out of all danger," he answered. "Your hellish tricks have not come off this time. Oh, you needn't try to brazen it out. I know all about it."

Bellingham took a step back from the angry student, and half-closed the door as if to protect himself.

"You are mad," he said. "What do you mean? Do you assert that I had anything to do with Lee's accident?"

"Yes," thundered Smith. "You and that bag of bones behind you; you worked it between you. I tell you what it is, Master B., they have given up burning folk like you, but we still keep a hangman, and, by George! if any man in this college meets his death while you are here, I'll have you up, and if you don't swing for it, it won't be my fault. You'll find that your filthy Egyptian tricks won't answer in England."

"You're a raving lunatic," said Bellingham.

"All right. You just remember what I say, for you'll find that I'll be better than my word."

The door slammed, and Smith went fuming up to his chamber, where he locked the door upon the inside, and spent half the night in smoking his old briar and brooding over the strange events of the evening.

Next morning Abercrombie Smith heard nothing of his neighbor, but Harrington called upon him in the afternoon to say that Lee was almost himself again. All day Smith stuck fast to his work, but in the evening he determined to pay the visit to his friend Dr. Peterson upon which he had started the night before. A good walk and a friendly chat would be welcome to his jangled nerves.

Bellingham's door was shut as he passed, but glancing back when he was some distance from the turret, he saw his neighbor's head at the window outlined against the lamplight, his face pressed apparently against the glass as he gazed out into the darkness. It was a blessing to be away from all contact with him, if but for a few hours, and Smith stepped out briskly, and breathed the soft spring air into his lungs. The half moon lay in the west between two Gothic pinnacles, and threw upon the silvered street a dark tracery from the stonework above. There was a brisk breeze, and light, fleecy clouds drifted swiftly across the sky. Old's was on the very border of the town, and in five minutes Smith found himself beyond the houses and between the hedges of a May-scented, Oxfordshire lane. It was a lonely and little-frequented road which led to his friend's house. Early as it was, Smith did not meet a single soul upon his way. He walked briskly along until he came to the avenue gate, which opened into the long, gravel drive leading up to Farlingford. In front of him he could see the cosy, red light of the windows glimmering through the foliage. He stood with his hand upon the iron latch of the swinging gate, and he glanced back at the road along which he had come. Something was coming swiftly down it.

It moved in the shadow of the hedge, silently and furtively, a dark, crouching figure, dimly visible against the black background. Even as he gazed back at it, it had lessened its distance by twenty paces, and was fast closing upon him. Out of the darkness he had a glimpse of a scraggy neck, and of two eyes that will ever haunt him in his dreams. He turned, and with a cry of terror he ran for his life up the avenue. There were the red lights, the signals of safety, almost within a stone's-throw of him. He was a famous runner, but never had he run as he ran that night.

The heavy gate had swung into place behind him but he heard it dash open again before his pursuer. As he rushed madly and wildly through the night, he could hear a swift, dry patter behind him, and could see, as he threw back a glance, that this horror was bounding like a tiger at his heels, with blazing eyes and one stringy arm out-thrown. Thank God, the door was ajar. He could see the thin bar of light which shot from the lamp in the hall. Nearer yet sounded the clatter from behind. He heard a hoarse gurgling at his very shoulder. With a shriek he flung himself against the door, slammed and bolted it behind him, and sank half-fainting on to the hall chair.

"My goodness, Smith, what's the matter?" asked Peterson, appearing at the door of his study.

"Give me some brandy."

Peterson disappeared, and came rushing out again with a glass and a decanter.

"You need it," he said, as his visitor drank off what he poured out for him. "Why, man, you are as white as a cheese."

Smith laid down his glass, rose up, and took a deep breath.

"I am my own man again now," said he. "I was never so unmanned before. But, with your leave, Peterson, I will sleep here tonight, for I don't think I could face that road again except by daylight. It's weak, I know, but I can't help it."

Peterson looked at his visitor with a very questioning eye.

"Of course you shall sleep here if you wish. I'll tell Mrs. Burney to make up the spare bed. Where are you off to now?"

"Come up with me to the window that overlooks the door. I want you to see what I have seen."

They went up to the window of the upper hall whence they could look down upon the approach to the house. The drive and the fields on either side lay quiet and still, bathed in the peaceful moonlight.

"Well, really, Smith," remarked Peterson, "it is well that I know you to be an abstemious man. What in the world can have frightened you?"

"I'll tell you presently. But where can it have gone? Ah, now, look, look! See the curve of the road just beyond your gate."

"Yes, I see; you needn't pinch my arm off. I saw someone pass. I should say a man, rather thin, apparently, and tall, very tall. But what of him? And what of yourself? You are still shaking like an aspen leaf."

"I have been within hand-grip of the devil, that's all. But come down to your study, and I shall tell you the whole story."

He did so. Under the cheery lamplight with a glass of wine on the table beside him, and the portly form and florid face of his friend in front, he narrated, in their order, all the events, great and small, which had formed so singular a chain, from the night on which he had found Bellingham fainting in front of the mummy case until this horrid experience of an hour ago.

"There now," he said as he concluded, "that's the whole, black business. It is monstrous and incredible, but it is true."

Dr. Plumptree Peterson sat for some time in silence with a very puzzled expression upon his face.

"I never heard of such a thing in my life, never!" he said at last. "You have told me the facts. Now tell me your inferences."

"You can draw your own."

"But I should like to hear yours. You have thought over the matter, and I have not."

"Well, it must be a little vague in detail, but the main points seem to me to be clear enough. This fellow Bellingham, in his Eastern studies, has got hold of some infernal secret by which a mummy—can be tem-

ARTHUR CONAN DOYLE

porarily brought to life. He was trying this disgusting business on the night when he fainted. No doubt the sight of the creature moving had shaken his nerve, even though he had expected it. You remember that almost the first words he said were to call out upon himself as a fool. Well, he got more hardened afterwards, and carried the matter through without fainting. The vitality which he could put into it was evidently only a passing thing, for I have seen it continually in its case as dead as this table. He has some elaborate process, I fancy, by which he brings the thing to pass. Having done it, he naturally bethought him that he might use the creature as an agent. It has intelligence and it has strength. For some purpose he took Lee into his confidence; but Lee, like a decent Christian, would have nothing to do with such a business. Then they had a row, and Lee vowed that he would tell his sister of Bellingham's true character. Bellingham's game was to prevent him, and he nearly managed it, by setting this creature of his on his track. He had already tried its powers upon another man—Norton—towards whom he had a grudge. It is the merest chance that he has not two murders upon his soul. Then, when I taxed him with the matter, he had the strongest reasons for wishing to get me out of the way before I could convey my knowledge to anyone else. He got his chance when I went out, for he knew my habits and where I was bound for. I have had a narrow shave, Peterson, and it is mere luck you didn't find me on your doorstep in the morning. I'm not a nervous man as a rule, and I never thought to have the fear of death put upon me as it was tonight."

"My dear boy, you take the matter too seriously," said his companion. "Your nerves are out of order with your work, and you make too much of it. How could such a thing as this stride about the streets of Oxford, even at night, without being seen?"

"It has been seen. There is quite a scare in the town about an escaped ape, as they imagine the creature to be. It is the talk of the place."

"Well, it's a striking chain of events. And yet, my dear fellow, you must allow that each incident in itself is capable of a more natural explanation."

"What! even my adventure of tonight?"

"Certainly. You come out with your nerves all unstrung, and your head full of this theory of yours. Some gaunt, half-famished tramp steals after you, and seeing you run, is emboldened to pursue you. Your fears and imagination do the rest."

"It won't do, Peterson; it won't do."

'And again, in the instance of your finding the mummy case empty, and then a few moments later with an occupant, you know that it was lamp light, that the lamp was half turned down, and that you had no special reason to look hard at the case. It is quite possible that you may have overlooked the creature in the first instance."

"No, no; it is out of the question."

"And then Lee may have fallen into the river, and Norton been garrotted. It is certainly a formidable indictment that you have against Bellingham; but if you were to place it before a police magistrate, he would simply laugh in your face."

"I know he would. That is why I mean to take the matter into my own hands.

"Eh?"

"Yes; I feel that a public duty rests upon me, and, besides, I must do it for my own safety, unless I choose to allow myself to be hunted by this beast out of the college, and that would be a little too feeble. I have quite made up my mind what I shall do. And first of all, may I use your paper and pens for an hour?"

"Most certainly. You will find all that you want upon that side table."

Abercrombie Smith sat down before a sheet of foolscap, and for an hour, and then for a second hour his pen travelled swiftly over it. Page after page was finished and tossed aside while his friend leaned back in his armchair, looking across at him with patient curiosity. At last, with an exclamation of satisfaction, Smith sprang to his feet, gathered his papers up into order, and laid the last one upon Peterson's desk.

"Kindly sign this as a witness," he said.

"A witness? Of what?"

"Of my signature, and of the date. The date is the most important. Why, Peterson, my life might hang upon it."

"My dear Smith, you are talking wildly. Let me beg you to go to bed."

"On the contrary, I never spoke so deliberately in my life. And I will promise to go to bed the moment you have signed it."

"But what is it?"

"It is a statement of all that I have been telling you tonight. I wish you to witness it."

"Certainly," said Peterson, signing his name under that of his companion. "There you are! But what is the idea?"

"You will kindly retain it, and produce it in case I am arrested."

"Arrested? For what?"

"For murder. It is quite on the cards. I wish to be ready for every event. There is only one course open to me, and I am determined to take it."

"For Heaven's sake, don't do anything rash!"

"Believe me, it would be far more rash to adopt any other course. I hope that we won't need to bother you, but it will ease my mind to know that you have this statement of my motives. And now I am ready to take your advice and to go to roost, for I want to be at my best in the morning."

Abercrombie Smith was not an entirely pleasant man to have as an enemy. Slow and easy-tempered, he was formidable when driven to action. He brought to every purpose in life the same deliberate resoluteness which had distinguished him as a scientific student. He had laid his studies aside for a day, but he intended that the day should not be wasted. Not a word did he say to his host as to his plans, but by nine o'clock he was well on his way to Oxford.

In the High Street he stopped at Clifford's, the gunmaker's, and bought a heavy revolver, with a box of central-fire cartridges. Six of them he slipped into the chambers, and half-cocking the weapon, placed it in the pocket of his coat. He then made his way to Hastie's rooms, where the big oarsman was lounging over his breakfast, with the *Sporting Times* propped up against the coffee pot.

"Hullo! What's up?" he asked. "Have some coffee?"

"No, thank you. I want you to come with me, Hastie, and do what I ask you."

"Certainly, my boy."

"And bring a heavy stick with you."

"Hullo!" Hastie stared. "Here's a hunting crop that would fell an ox."

"One other thing. You have a box of amputating knives. Give me the longest of them."

"There you are. You seem to be fairly on the war trail. Anything else?"

"No; that will do." Smith placed the knife inside his coat, and led the way to the quadrangle. "We are neither of us chickens, Hastie," said he. "I think I can do this job alone, but I take you as a precaution. I am going to have a little talk with Bellingham. If I have only him to deal with, I won't, of course, need you. If I shout, however, up you come, and lam out with your whip as hard as you can lick. Do you understand?"

"All right. I'll come if I hear you bellow."

"Stay here, then. I may be a little time, but don't budge until I come down."

"I'm a fixture."

Smith ascended the stairs, opened Bellingham's door, and stepped in. Bellingham was seated behind his table, writing. Beside him, among his litter of strange possessions, towered the mummy case, with its sale number 249 still stuck upon its front, and its hideous occupant stiff and stark within it. Smith looked very deliberately round him, closed the door, and then, stepping across to the fireplace, struck a match and set the fire alight. Bellingham sat staring, with amazement and rage upon his bloated face.

"Well, really now, you make yourself at home," he gasped.

Smith sat himself deliberately down, placing his watch upon the table, drew out his pistol, cocked it, and laid it in his lap. Then he took the long amputating knife from his bosom, and threw it down in front of Bellingham.

"Now, then," said he, "just get to work and cut up that mummy."

"Oh, is that it? said Bellingham with a sneer.

"Yes, that is it. They tell me that the law can't touch you. But I have a law that will set matters straight. If in five minutes you have not set to work, I swear by the God who made me that I will put a bullet through your brain!"

"You would murder me?"

Bellingham had half-risen, and his face was the color of putty.

"Yes."

"And for what?"

"To stop your mischief. One minute has gone."

"But what have I done?"

"I know and you know."

"This is mere bullying."

"Two minutes are gone."

"But you must give reasons. You are a madman—a dangerous madman. Why should I destroy my own property? It is a valuable mummy."

"You must cut it up, and you must burn it."

"I will do no such thing."

"Four minutes are gone."

Smith took up the pistol and he looked towards Bellingham with an inexorable face. As the second hand stole round, he raised his hand, and

ARTHUR CONAN DOYLE

the finger twitched upon the trigger.

"There! there! I'll do it!" screamed Bellingham.

In frantic haste he caught up the knife and hacked at the figure of the mummy, ever glancing round to see the eye and the weapon of his terrible visitor bent upon him. The creature crackled and snapped under every stab of the keen blade. A thick, yellow dust rose up from it. Spices and dried essences rained down upon the floor. Suddenly, with a rending crack, its backbone snapped asunder, and it fell, a brown heap of sprawling limbs, upon the floor.

"Now into the fire! said Smith.

The flames leaped and roared as the dried and tinderlike debris was piled upon it. The little room was like the stoke-hole of a steamer and the sweat ran down the faces of the two men; but still the one stooped and worked, while the other sat watching him with a set face. A thick, fat smoke oozed out from the fire, and a heavy smell of burned resin and singed hair filled the air. In a quarter of an hour a few charred and brittle sticks were all that was left of Lot No. 249.

"Perhaps that will satisfy you," snarled Bellingham, with hate and fear in his little grey eyes as he glanced back at his tormentor.

"No; I must make a clean sweep of all your materials. We must have no more devil's tricks. In with all these leaves! They may have something to do with it."

"And what now?" asked Bellingham, when the leaves also had been added to the blaze.

"Now the roll of papyrus which you had on the table that night. It is in that drawer, I think."

"No, no," shouted Bellingham. "Don't burn that! Why, man, you don't know what you do. It is unique; it contains wisdom which is nowhere else to be found."

"Out with it!"

"But look here, Smith, you can't really mean it. I'll share the knowledge with you. I'll teach you all that is in it. Or, stay, let me only copy it before you burn it!"

Smith stepped forward and turned the key in the drawer. Taking out the yellow, curled roll of paper, he threw it into the fire, and pressed it down with his heel. Bellingham screamed, and grabbed at it; but Smith pushed him back and stood over it until it was reduced to a formless, grey ash.

"Now, Master B.," said he, "I think I have pretty well drawn your teeth. You'll hear from me again, if you return to your old tricks. And now good morning, for I must go back to my studies."

And such is the narrative of Abercrombie Smith as to the singular events which occurred in Old College, Oxford, in the spring of '84. As Bellingham left the university immediately afterwards, and was last heard of in the Sudan, there is no one who can contradict his statement. But the wisdom of men is small, and the ways of Nature are strange, and who shall put a bound to the dark things which may be found by those who seek for them?

ARTHUR CONAN DOYLE

Play a Game of Cyanide

by Jack Ritchie

"**C**hildren," Miss Wicker commanded, "tell the detective where you hid the cyanide."

But Ronnie and Gertrude simply smiled up at me and said nothing.

I held one of the sodium cyanide pellets between thumb and forefinger. It was cloudy white in color and approximately one and one quarter inches in diameter. "They all look like this, children, but they aren't candy. They definitely are not candy and they are not meant to be eaten."

"Ronnie and Gertrude are wretched, evil children," Miss Wicker declared firmly.

Their mother, Mrs. Randall flushed, but she said nothing.

Originally there had been nine of the pellets. We had recovered four from the grounds outside and another concealed in a toy train in this room. But four of the pellets still remained unaccounted for.

"Are you really a detective?" Ronnie asked. He was seven and younger than his sister.

"Yes. Now Ronnie, where have you children hidden the poison?"

"Where's your partner?"

"I don't have a partner."

"Why not?"

"I'm a detective-lieutenant. Detective-lieutenants don't have partners."

"Why not?"

I had the impulse to strangle.

"Because they're mean and nobody will work with them."

We were in the children's playroom. It was by far the gloomiest and most remote room in the large Victorian house.

I turned to their mother. "Can't you do anything about them?"

Mrs. Randall was a pale frightened woman. "I'm sure they'll tell you in time, lieutenant. But now they're in one of their stubborn spells and nobody can get them to do anything."

"Bad blood," Miss Wicker said. "Their father was a salesman."

Gertrude was almost nine. The pilot light of mischief danced in her blue eyes. "We live on bread and water."

Miss Wicker glared at her. "I provide you and your mother with a roof over your heads. You ought to be grateful."

"The bread is moldy," Ronnie said. "And sometimes the water has salt in it."

My men were outside searching the grounds again. They had been through the house, too, but without success.

I forced a smile. "Come now, children, we've been at this for over two hours."

"What are they good for?" Ronnie asked.

"For cleaning jewelry. Seems odd that cyanide should be used for that, but it's a fact."

"We don't have jewelry," Gertrude said. "But Aunt Agnes has."

Miss Wicker's eyes narrowed. "Have you been prying again?"

I realized now that I had made a tactical error, but I hadn't wanted to alarm the household unless it was absolutely necessary. I had ordered the grounds searched first and the children had evidently watched from the windows and decided that we were playing a delightful new game.

My smile was beginning to pain me. "That was really very clever of you children to hide a pellet in the toy train. Which one of you did that?"

"You'll never find out," Ronnie said smugly. "We wiped off the fingerprints."

I sighed. "I think the time has come for a good all-around spanking."

Miss Wicker heartily agreed, but an uncharacteristic firmness came into Mrs. Randall's face. "No," she said. "You will not touch the children."

I rubbed the back of my neck. "We'll have to search them."

Ronnie broke into a grin. "I'm clean."

Why didn't Ronnie's mother give him a haircut, I wondered irritably. He looked as though he were wearing a combed helmet.

"I'll wait until a policewoman comes," Gertrude said demurely.

She was blonde and tricky-smiled and would undoubtedly cause a great deal of trouble during the course of her life.

"I will search Ronnie," I said. "And your mother will search you."

We found nothing.

"Why don't you search Aunt Agnes?" Ronnie asked.

Miss Wicker bristled. "I do not have the pellets."

JACK RITCHIE

"I wouldn't trust nobody if I was a good detective," Ronnie said.

I had the temptation to give the boy a haircut myself. I studied the grin on his face and a thought descended. Little boys simply do not keep their hair combed. Not for two hours at a stretch.

"Ronnie," I said firmly. "Come here!" And when he hesitated, I added. "Right this minute! And bring your head."

I found another one of the pellets.

The little fiend had Scotch-taped it to his skull and combed his hair over it.

I forced myself to beam. "That was very ingenious of you, Ronnie. Now tell Uncle James where the other three pellets are."

"You're not my uncle."

I approached the problem from a tangent. "How would you two like some ice cream?"

A conference of glances united them. They would love it.

"Fine. And I'll see that you get all the ice cream you can eat just as soon as you tell me where the rest of the cyanide is."

They rejected the offer.

"I'll give you a dollar each," I said desperately.

Ronnie was not swayed. "We're holding out for a million dollars."

"I'll make it two dollars each. That's almost a million."

"No, it isn't. I can count up to a hundred and I know."

I found myself pacing the floor. The grounds surrounding the house were extensive. We knew that the pellets had been thrown over the wall near the gatehouse, but the children had been playing in that area when we arrived. Now the poison could be anywhere and it might take weeks before we found it all.

"Are you positive there were nine pellets?" Miss Wicker asked.

"Absolutely."

Miss Wicker thought and frowned. "Why would anyone want to steal them?"

"The thief didn't know what he was stealing. He just emptied the jeweler's safe and put everything in a bag. Later when he parked at the curb outside your grounds to examine his loot, he discovered the pellets. In a fit of exasperation, he threw them over your wall."

Mrs. Randall was shocked. "On these grounds? What a horrible man."

"He didn't know what they were. When we caught him, he still had everything from the safe but the pellets. But he did remember where he had thrown them."

Gertrude looked up at me. "Would you read us a story, Uncle James?"

"I am *not* your Uncle James," I snapped. But then I caught myself and smiled. "What would you like me to read?"

The children came to an agreement on *Lennie, the Giraffe with the Short Neck*. Mercifully, it was short.

I closed the book. "And now, children, where are those cyanide pellets?"

Ronnie blinked. "We didn't promise anything."

I had always regarded the Children's Crusade as a great tragedy. I was not quite so certain now. "Children, do you know what a tacit agreement is?"

They didn't.

"A tacit agreement is one in which two parties agree upon something without actually putting it into words or writing it down. Now why do you think I read that revol—that story to you?"

Ronnie grinned. "You thought that we'd tell you where the poison is."

I nodded. "Now would I have read the story if I hadn't expected you to do just that?"

"I guess not."

"But you let me read it anyway, didn't you? You didn't stop me?"

He admitted the fact.

"So, in effect, because you let me read the story we entered into a mutual agreement—a tacit agreement—that you would tell me where the pellets are. Now wouldn't your conscience bother you if you didn't tell me?"

"No."

"Ronnie," his mother said. "I don't think you're being nice. You really ought to tell Uncle James where they are."

Ronnie didn't agree.

"Just one?" Mrs. Randall coaxed. "Just where one itsy bitsy pellet is. That won't hurt you, now will it?"

The children had a whispered consultation and then Ronnie came forward. "All right. Just one. I threw it on the roof. Maybe it's in the rain gutter."

I went outside where Sergeant Davies was supervising the search.

He scratched his head. "We haven't turned up any more."

"Have you ever thought of looking up?"

"Up?"

"Yes," I snapped. "On the roof. In the rain gutters. Check the chimney, too."

His head must have itched again. "I never thought of that."

"Of course not," I said irritably. "You're just an adult."

I went back into the house and rubbed my hands. "Well, children, shall I read you another story?"

"No," Ronnie said definitely. "We don't want no more tacit agreements."

"It's time for your nap now," Mrs. Randall said.

I glared at her. "Nobody closes an eye until I find the rest of that cyanide."

But Mrs. Randall was uncompromising. "The children are tired. They will have their nap."

Miss Wicker left the room, but I stayed. I found an adult chair and sat down.

Mrs. Randall opened a sofa-bed and the children lay down. She read them a story—*Stanley, the Station Wagon*—and then adjusted the venetian blinds.

She tiptoed across the room and sat down beside me. "Aren't they sweet?"

Sergeant Davies came into the room. He saw the children drifting off to sleep and lowered his voice to a whisper. "I found another pellet. It was in the rain gutter."

"Well, good for you. Did you search the chimney, too?"

"Do I have to?"

"Get back up there."

"I'll get my suit all dirty."

"Davies," I said patiently. "After all, you *are* a sergeant. You outrank everybody out there."

He brightened. "That's right. I'll send Travers down the chimney."

When he was gone, I turned to Mrs. Randall. "Your husband . . . ?"

"He died two years ago." Mrs. Randall sighed. "He left no money and so we came to my aunt's place to live."

I thought about Miss Wicker and the general atmosphere of this place. "There was no place else to go?"

"No. Aunt Agnes is the only relative I have. And then, too, she's alone in the world and I thought . . . " She hesitated. "Well, I thought about going to work first and then I decided against it. I think a mother should be with her children, no matter how difficult things might get."

It was quiet in the room and after a while I nodded myself.

"Pellet."

I sat up. "Did you just hear somebody say 'pellet' ?"

"That was Ronnie. We had cottage cheese and chives for lunch. He always talks in his sleep when he has that."

I left my chair and went to the sofa-bed. Ronnie's eyes were closed and he breathed gently.

"Don't wake him up," Mrs. Randall whispered.

"That was the last thing I had in mind." I sat down beside Ronnie and waited. He said nothing more.

I prompted him softly. "You were talking about a pellet, Ronnie."

But Ronnie slept. Evidently he hadn't eaten enough cottage cheese and chives to speak further.

"Ronnie," I whispered, "when you wake you will tell me where the pellets are. Do you understand? When you wake you will tell me where the pellets are. When you—"

"What in heaven's name are you doing now?" Mrs. Randall demanded.

"I'm trying post-hypnotic suggestion." I leaned closer to Ronnie. "When you wake you will—"

"Stop that!" Mrs. Randall commanded. "I will not have you tampering with Ronnie's little mind!"

I sighed and got off my knees. Perhaps it wouldn't have worked anyway.

After a half an hour the children began stirring.

"Children," I said sternly. "I've had enough of this."

"First let them have their graham crackers and milk," Mrs. Randall said. "Would you like some milk too, lieutenant?"

I wasn't thinking about milk when I said, "About three fingers."

I waited impatiently while the children indulged in their food orgy.

Those two remaining pellets had to be somewhere. The grounds had been searched. The house had been searched. The children had been searched. I was even willing to search myself if that would do any . . .

The thought that struck me was frightening.

Mrs. Randall was alarmed. "Are you ill, lieutenant?"

Certainly I was perspiring. Those little monsters couldn't have had the gall, the unmitigated nerve, the satanic imagination to—

But they had.

JACK RITCHIE

I found another pellet.

It was in the cuff of my trousers.

I recovered from that slowly. At least now only one pellet remained to be found. I thought I might attack the problem by the process of canny elimination.

I smiled. "Children, your little game is over. I know where that last pellet is."

They were dubious.

"Yes, sir," I said, almost bubbling. "It's outside on the grounds."

Ronnie laughed with the delight of superior knowledge. "Oh, no, it isn't. It's in the house."

Gertrude favored him with a fierce frown.

I had outwitted the little imp. "A slip of the tongue," I said quickly. "I really meant to say that I know the pellet is inside the house and it's—" I divided the house into two sections. "It's on this floor."

But they weren't taken in this time. Their silence was infuriating.

Mrs. Randall smiled. "They're such intelligent children."

I glared at her. "Whose side are you on?"

"The law's, of course," she said hastily. "But can't we be sportsmen?"

Anyway, I had established the fact that the last pellet was in the house. I would have to call the search detail back inside and have it go over the building again.

Gertrude seemed to read my mind. "You'll never find it."

I had that feeling, too.

"Let's march," Ronnie said.

I looked at Mrs. Randall.

"Sometimes I play the piano," she explained. "And the children march around in a circle. They wear paper hats and blow horns and beat drums."

I dug into the reservoir of my courage. "I'll join them."

The children regarded me with justified suspicion.

Frankly, I had hoped to lure them into another tacit agreement, but I could see that such a thing wouldn't work this time. On the other hand, I had just committed myself and possibly the children might be antagonized if I backed out now. I created a smile. "This is on the house. I've always wanted to go around in circles."

"We'll have to close the door and put a carpet against the bottom of the door," Gertrude said. "Aunt Agnes doesn't like us to make noise. We plug the keyhole, too."

When that was done, Mrs. Randall played the upright piano. The children and I marched. Really a stupid business.

The door opened and Sergeant Davies almost tripped over the carpet. He froze in his tracks when he saw me.

I stopped blowing my horn and put it behind my back. "Well? What the devil do you want?"

He swallowed. "Travers didn't find anything in the chimney."

"Of course not," I snapped. "The last pellet is somewhere inside the house."

"The last pellet? Then you found another one of them? Where was it?"

I flushed. "Never mind that."

"I'll bring the boys in here," Davies said eagerly, "and we'll really tear the place apart this time."

"No," I said. "I'm taking care of this myself." I was not in the best of tempers. "Why are you standing there like that and gawking? Get back outside and search!"

"But you just said the pellet's in the house."

"I don't care what I said. Get out!" Another thought touched my mind. "Davies!"

He had been almost out the door, but he stopped.

"Davies, if you breathe one word . . . "

He shook his head almost sorrowfully. "I won't tell a soul what I just seen. They wouldn't believe me anyway."

When he was gone, we readjusted the carpet at the door and resumed marching.

After a while Mrs. Randall stopped playing. "I think that's enough for today, children. The lieutenant is winded."

I sat down gratefully and pondered my next move.

The scream that floated down upon us pierced through our sound-insulated room.

Mrs. Randall's hand went to her mouth. "That's Aunt Agnes. I'm sure she must be in her room. It's the first one at the head of the stairs."

I pulled open the door and dashed up to the second floor.

Miss Wicker lay gasping on the thick rug, her eyes wide with fright and pain and coming death.

I kneeled over her for a moment and then went to the phone. I dialed for an ambulance, but Miss Wicker was dead before I completed the call.

I put down the phone and looked down at her. A teacup lay just beyond

JACK RITCHIE

the tips of her fingers.

My eyes went to the side table—to the silver tea service, to the thin slices of lemon on a saucer, and to the sugar bowl.

The sugar bowl.

Mrs. Randall and her two children stood in the doorway.

Gertrude looked up at her mother. "Now we won't have to put the rug in front of the door any more, will we, Mommy?"

We had been looking for a pellet. But it wasn't a pellet any more. Someone had crushed it into a powder and . . .

Gertrude?

Or was it Ronnie?

He had a peculiar little smile on his face.

Or Mrs. Randall?

There was something about her eyes . . .

Or all three of them?

I had the tired feeling that I would never know.

A Kind of Murder

by Larry Niven

"**Y**ou are constantly coming to my home!" he shouted. "You never think of calling first. Whatever I'm doing, suddenly you're there. And where the hell do you keep getting keys to my door?"

Alicia didn't answer. Her face, which in recent years had taken on a faint resemblance to a bulldog's, was set in infinite patience as she relaxed at the other end of the couch. She had been through this before, and she waited for Jeff to get it over with.

He saw this, and the dinner he had not quite finished settled like lead in his belly. "There's not a club I belong to that you aren't a member, too. Whoever I'm with, you finagle me into introducing you. If it's a man, you try to make him, and if he isn't having any you get nasty. If it's a woman, there you are like a ghost at the feast. The discarded woman. It's a drag," he said. He wanted a more powerful word, but he couldn't think of one that wouldn't sound overdramatic, silly.

She said, "We've been divorced six years. What do you care who I sleep with?"

"I don't like looking like your pimp!"

She laughed.

The acid was rising in his throat. "Listen," he said, "why don't you give up one of the clubs? W-we belong to *four*. Give one up. Any of them." *Give me a place of refuge*, he prayed.

"They're my clubs too," she said with composure. "*You* change clubs."

He'd joined the Lucifer Club four years ago, for just that reason. She'd joined, too. And now the words clogged in his throat, so that he gaped like a fish.

There were no words left. He hit her.

He'd never done that before. It was a full-arm swing, but awkward because they were trying to face each other on the couch. She rode with the slap, then sat facing him, waiting.

It was as if he could read her mind. *We've been through this before, and it never changes anything. But it's your tantrum.* He remembered later that she'd said that to him once, those same words, and she'd looked just like that: patient, implacable.

The call reached Homicide at eight thirty-six P.M., July 20, 2019. The caller was a round-faced man with straight black hair and a stutter. "My ex-wife," he told the desk man. "She's dead. I just got home and f-found her like this. S-someone seems to have hit her with a c-cigarette box."

Hennessey (Officer-Two) had just come on for the night shift. He took over. "You just got home? You called immediately?"

"That's right. C-c-could you come right away?"

"We'll be there in ten seconds. Have you touched anything?"

"No. Not her, and not the box."

"Have you called the hospital?"

His voice rose. "No. She's *dead.*"

Hennessey took down his name—Walters—and booth number and hung up. "Linc, Fisher, come with me. Torrie, will you call the City Hospital and have them send a copter?" If Walters hadn't touched her he could hardly be sure she was dead.

They went through the displacement booth one at a time, dialing and vanishing. For Hennessey it was as if the Homicide Room vanished as he dialed the last digit, and he was looking into a porch light.

Jeffrey Walters was waiting in the house. He was medium-sized, a bit overweight, his light brown hair going thin on top. His paper business suit was wrinkled. He wore an anxious, fearful look—which figured, either way, Hennessey thought.

And he'd been right. Alicia Walters was dead. From her attitude she had been sitting sideways on the couch when something crashed into her head, and she had sprawled forward. A green cigarette box was sitting on the glass coffee table. It was bloody along one edge, and the blood had marked the glass.

The small, bloody, beautifully-marked green malachite box could have done it. It would have been held in the right hand, swung full-armed. One of the detectives used chalk to mark its position on the table, then nudged it into a plastic bag and tied the neck.

Walters had sagged into a reading chair as if worn out. Hennessey approached him. "You said she was your ex-wife?"

"That's right. She didn't give up using her married name."

"What was she doing here, then?"

"I don't know. We had a fight earlier this evening. I finally threw her out and went back to the Sirius Club. I was half afraid she'd just follow me back, but she didn't. I guess she let herself back in and waited for me here."

"She had a key?"

Walters' laugh was feeble. "She always had a key. I've had the lock changed twice. It didn't work. I'd come home and find her here. 'I just wanted to talk,' she'd say." He stopped abruptly.

"That doesn't explain why she'd let someone else in."

"No. She must have, though, mustn't she? I don't know why she did that."

The ambulance helicopter landed in the street outside. Two men entered with a stretcher. They shifted Alicia Walters' dead body to the stretcher, leaving a chalk outline Fisher had drawn earlier.

Walters watched through the picture window as they walked the stretcher into the portable JumpShift unit inside of the copter. They closed the hatch, tapped buttons in a learned rhythm on a phone dial set in the hatch. When they opened the hatch to check, it was empty. They closed it again and boarded the copter.

Walters said, "You'll do an autopsy immediately, won't you?"

"Of course. Why do you ask?"

"Well . . . it's possible I might have an alibi for the time of the murder."

Hennessey laughed before he could stop himself. Walters looked puzzled and affronted.

Hennessey didn't explain. But later—as he was leaving the station house for home and bed—he snorted. "Alibi," he said. "Idiot."

The displacement booths had come suddenly. One year, a science-fiction writer's daydream. The next year, 1992, an experimental reality. Teleportation. Instantaneous travel. Another year and they were being used for cargo transport. Two more, and the passenger displacement booths were springing up everywhere in the world.

By luck and the laws of physics, the world had had time to adjust. Teleportation obeyed the Laws of Conservation of Energy and Conservation of Momentum. Teleporting uphill took an energy input to match the gain in potential energy going downhill—and it was over a decade before JumpShift Inc. learned how to compensate for that effect. Tele-

LARRY NIVEN

portation over great distances was even more heavily restricted by the Earth's rotation.

Let a passenger flick too far west, and the difference between his momentum and the Earth's would smack him down against the floor of the booth. Too far east, and he would be flung against the ceiling. Too far north or south, and the Earth would be rotating faster or slower; he would flick in moving sideways, unless he had crossed the equator.

But cargo and passengers could be displaced betwen points of equal longitude and opposite latitude. Smuggling had become impossible to stop. There was a point in the South Pacific to correspond to any point in the United States, most of Canada, and parts of Mexico.

Smuggling via the displacement booths was a new crime. The Permanent Floating Riot Gangs were another. The booths would allow a crowd to gather with amazing rapidity. Practically any news broadcast could start a flash crowd. And with the crowds the pickpockets and looters came flicking in.

When the booths were new, many householders had taken to putting their booths in the living rooms or entrance halls. That had stopped fast, after an astounding rash of burglaries. These days only police stations and hospitals kept their booths indoors.

For twenty years the booths had not been feasible over distances greater than ten miles. If the short-distance booths had changed the nature of crime, what of the long-distance booths? They had been in existence only four years. Most were at what had been airports, being run by what had been airline companies. Dial three numbers and you could be anywhere on Earth.

Flash crowds were bigger and more frequent.

The alibi was as dead as the automobile.

Smuggling was cheaper. The expensive, illegal transmission booths in the South Pacific were no longer needed. Cutthroat competition had dropped the price of smack to something the Mafia wouldn't touch.

And murder was easier; but that was only part of the problem. There was a new *kind* of murder going around.

Hank Lovejoy was a tall, lanky man with a lantern jaw and a ready smile. The police had found him at his office—real estate—and he had agreed to come immediately.

"There were four of us at the Sirius Club before Alicia showed up," he said. "Me, and George Larimer, and Jeff Walters, and Jennifer—wait a minute—Lewis. Jennifer was over at the bar, and we'd, like, asked her to join us for dinner. You know how it is in a continuity club: you can talk to anyone. We'd have picked up another girl sooner or later."

Hennessey said, "Not two?"

"Oh, George is a monogamist. His wife is eight months pregnant, and she didn't want to come, but George just doesn't. He's not fay or anything, he just doesn't. But Jeff and I were both sort of trying to get Jennifer's attention. She was loose, and it looked likely she'd go home with one or the other of us. Then Alicia came in."

"What time was that?"

"Oh, about six fifteen. We were already eating. She came up to the table, and we all kind of waited for Jeff to introduce her and ask her to sit down, she being his ex-wife, after all." Lovejoy laughed. "George doesn't really understand about Jeff and Alicia. Me, I thought it was funny."

"What do you mean?"

"Well, they've been divorced about six years, but it seems he just can't get away from her. Couldn't I mean," he said, remembering. Remembering that good old Jeff *had* gotten away from her, because someone had smashed her skull.

Hennessey was afraid Lovejoy would clam up. He played stupid. "I don't get it. A divorce is a divorce, isn't it?"

"Not when it's a quote friendly divorce unquote. Jeff's a damn fool. I don't think he gave up sleeping with her, not right after the divorce. He wouldn't live with her, but every so often she'd, well, she'd seduce him, I guess you'd say. He wasn't used to being alone, and I guess he got lonely. Eventually he must have given that up, but he still couldn't get her out of his hair.

"See, they belonged to all the same clubs and they knew all the same people, and as a matter of fact they were both in routing and distribution software; that was how they met. So if she came on the scene while he was trying to do something else, there she was, and he had to introduce her. She probably knew the people he was dealing with, if it was business. A lot of business gets done at the continuity clubs. And she wouldn't go away. I thought it was funny. It worked out fine for me, last night."

"How?"

"Well, after twenty minutes or so it got through to us that Alicia wasn't

LARRY NIVEN

going to go away. I mean, we were eating dinner, and she wasn't, but she wanted to talk. When she said something about waiting and joining us for dessert, Jeff stood up and suggested they go somewhere to talk. She didn't look too pleased, but she went."

"What do you suppose he wanted to talk about?"

Lovejoy laughed. "Do I read minds without permission? He wanted to tell her to bug off, of course! But he was gone half an hour, and by the time he came back, Jennifer and I had sort of reached a decision. And George had this benign look he gets, like, *Bless you my children.* He doesn't play around himself, but maybe he likes to think of other couples getting together. Maybe he's right; maybe it brightens up the marriage bed."

"Jeff came back alone?"

"That he did. He was nervous, jumpy. Friendly enough; I mean, he didn't get obnoxious when he saw how it was with me and Jennifer. But he was sweating, and I don't blame him."

"What time was this?"

"Seven twenty."

"Dead on?"

"Yeah."

"Why would you remember a thing like that?"

"Well, when Jeff came back he wanted to know long he'd been gone. So I looked at my watch. Anyway, we stayed another fifteen minutes and then Jennifer and I took off."

Hennessey asked, "Just how bad were things between Jeff and Alicia?"

"Oh, they didn't *fight* or anything. It was just—funny. For one thing, she's kind of let herself go since the divorce. She used to be pretty. Now she's gone to seed. Not many men chase her these days, so she has to do the chasing. Some men like that."

"Do you?"

"Not particularly. I've spent some nights with her, if that's what you're asking. I just like variety. I'm not a heartbreaker, man; I run with girls who like variety, too."

"Did Alicia?"

"I think so. The trouble was, she slept with a lot of guys Jeff introduced her to. He didn't like that. It made him look bad. And once she played nasty to a guy who turned her down, and it ruined a business deal."

"But they didn't fight."

"No. Jeff wasn't the type. Maybe that's why they got divorced. She was just someone he couldn't avoid. We all know people like that."

"After he came back without Alicia, did he leave the table at any time?"

"I don't think so. No. He just sat there, making small talk. Badly."

George Larimer was a writer of articles, one of the few who made good money at it. He lived in Arizona. No, he didn't mind a quick trip to the police station, he said emphasizing the *quick*. Just let him finish this paragraph . . . and he breezed in five minutes later.

"Sorry about that. I just couldn't get the damn wording right. This one's for *Viewer's Digest,* and I have to explain drop ship technology for morons without talking down to them or the minimal viewer won't buy it. What's the problem?"

Hennessey told him.

His face took on an expression Hennessey recognized: like he ought to be feeling something, and he was trying, honest. "I just met her that night," he said. "Dead. Well."

He remembered that evening well enough. "Sure, Jeff Walters came back about the time we were finishing coffee. We had brandy with the coffee, and then Hank and, uh, Jennifer left. Jeff and I sat and played dominoes over scotch and sodas. You can do that at the Sirius, you know. They keep game boxes there, and they'll move up side tables at your elbows so you can have drinks or lunch."

"How did you do?"

"I beat him. Something was bothering him; he wasn't playing very well, I thought he wanted to talk, but he wouldn't talk about whatever was bugging him."

"His ex-wife?"

"Maybe. Maybe not. I'd only just met her, and she seemed nice enough. And she seemed to like Jeff."

"Yeah. Now, Jeff left with Alica. How long were they gone?"

"Half an hour, I guess. And he came back without her."

"What time?"

"Quarter past seven or thereabouts. Ask Hank, I don't wear a watch." He said this with a certain pride. A writer doesn't need a watch; he sets his own hours. "As I said, we had dessert and coffee and then played dominoes for an hour, maybe a little less. Then I had to go home to see how my wife was getting along in my absence."

"While you were having dessert and coffee and playing dominoes, did Jeff Walters leave the table at any time?"

"Well, we switched tables to set up the game." Larimer shut his eyes to think. He opened them. "No, he didn't go to the bathroom or anything."

"Did you?"

"No. We were together the whole time, if that's what you want to know."

Hennessey went out for lunch after Larimer left. Returning, he stepped out of the Homicide Room booth just ahead of Officer-One Fisher, who had spent the morning at Alicia Walters' place.

Alicia had lived in the mountains, within shouting distance of Lake Arrowhead. Property in that area was far cheaper than property around the lake itself. The high rent district in the mountains is near streams and lakes. Her own water supply had come from a storage tank kept filled by a small JumpShift unit.

Fisher was hot and sweaty and breathing hard, as if he had been working. He dropped into a chair and wiped his forehead and neck. "There wasn't much point in going," he said. "We found what was left of a bacon and tomato sandwich sitting on a placemat. Probably her last meal. She wasn't much of a housekeeper. Probably wasn't making much money, either."

"How so?"

"All her gadgetry is old enough to be going to pieces. Her Dustmaster skips corners and knocks things off tables. Her chairs and couches are all blow-ups, inflated plastic. Cheap, but they have to be replaced every so often, and she didn't. Her displacement booth must be ten years old. She should have replaced it, living in the mountains."

"No roads in that area?"

"Not near her house, anyway. In remote areas like that they move the booths in by helicopter, then bring the components for the house out through the booth. If her booth broke down she'd have had to hike out, unless she could find a neighbor at home, and her neighbors aren't close. I like that area," Fisher said suddenly. "There's elbow room."

"She should have made good money. She was in routing and distribution of software." Hennessey pondered. "Maybe she spent all her time following her ex-husband around."

The autopsy report was waiting on his desk. He read through it.

Alicia Walters had indeed been killed by a single blow to the side of the head, almost certainly by the malachite box. Its hard corner had crushed her skull around the temple. Malachite is a semiprecious stone, hard enough that no part of it had broken off in the wound; but there was blood, and traces of bone and brain tissue, on the box itself.

There was also a bruise on her check. *Have to ask Walters about that,* he thought.

She died about eight P.M., given the state of her body, including body temperature. Stomach contents indicated that she had eaten about five thirty P.M.: a bacon and tomato sandwich.

Hennessey shook his head. "I was right. He's still thinking in terms of alibis."

Fisher heard. "Walters?"

"Sure, Walters. Look: he came back to the Sirius Club at seven thirty, and he called attention to the time. He stayed until around eight thirty, to hear Larimer tell it, and he was always in someone's company. Then he went home, found the body, and called us. The woman was killed around eight, which is right in the middle of his alibi time. Give or take fifteen minutes for the lab's margin of error, and it's still an alibi."

"Then it clears him."

Hennessey laughed. "Suppose he did go to the bathroom. Do you think anyone would remember it? Nobody in the world has had an alibi for something since the JumpShift booths took over. You can be at a party in New York and kill a man in the California Sierras in the time it would take to go out for cigarettes. You can't use displacement booths for an alibi."

"You could be jumping to conclusions," Fisher pointed out. "So he's not a cop. So he reads detective stories. So someone murdered his wife in his own living room. *Naturally* he wants to know if he's got an alibi."

Hennessey shook his head.

"She didn't bleed a lot," said Fisher. "Maybe enough, maybe not. Maybe she was moved."

"I noticed that, too."

"Someone who knew she had a key to Walters' house killed her and dumped her there. He would have hit her with the cigarette box in the spot where he'd already hit her with something else."

Hennessey shook his head again. "It's not just Walters. It's a *kind* of

LARRY NIVEN

murder. We get more and more of these lately. People kill each other because they can't move away from each other. With the long distance booths everyone in the country lives next door to everyone else. You live a block away from your ex-wife, your mother-in-law, the girl you're trying to drop, the guy who lost money in your business deal and blames you. Any secretary lives next door to her boss, and if he needs something done in a hurry she's right there. God help the doctor if his patients get his home number. I'm not just pulling these out of the air. I can name you an assault rap for every one of these situations."

"Most people get used to it," said Fisher. "My mother used to flick in to visit me at work, remember?"

Hennessey grinned. He did. Fortunately she'd given it up. "It was worse for Walters," he said.

"It didn't really sound that bad. Lovejoy said it was a friendly divorce. So he was always running into her. So what?"

"She took away his clubs."

Fisher snorted. But Fisher was young. He had grown up with the short-distance booths.

For twenty years passenger teleportation had been restricted to short hops. People had had time to get used to the booths. And in those twenty years the continuity clubs had come into existence.

The continuity club was a guard against future shock. Its location . . . ubiquitous: hundreds of buildings in hundreds of cities, each building just like all the others, inside and out. Wherever a member moved in this traveling society, the club would be there. Today even some of the customers would be the same: everyone used the long-distance booths to some extent.

A man had to have some kind of stability in his life. His church, his marriage, his home, his club. Any man might need more or less stability than the next. Walters had belonged to *four* clubs . . . and they were no use to him if he kept meeting Alicia Walters there. And his marriage had broken up, and he wasn't a churchgoer, and a key to his house had been found in Alicia's purse. She should at least have left him his clubs.

Fisher spoke, interrupting his train of thought. "You've been talking about impulse murders, haven't you? Six years of not being able to stand his ex-wife and not being able to get away from her. So finally he hits her with a cigarette box."

"Most of them are impulse murders, yes."

"Well, this wasn't any impulse murder. Look at what he had to do to bring it about. He'd have had to ask her to wait at home for him. Then make some excuse to get away from Larimer, shift home, kill her *fast*, and get back to the Sirius Club before Larimer wonders where he's gone. Then he's got to hope Larimer will forget the whole thing. That's not just coldblooded, it's also stupid."

"Yeah. So far it's worked, though."

"Worked, hell. The only evidence you've got against Walters is that he had good reason to kill her. Listen, if she got on his nerves that much, she may have irritated some other people, too."

Hennessey nodded. "That's the problem, all right." But he didn't mean it the way Fisher did.

Walters had moved to a hotel until such time as the police were through with his house. Hennessey called him before going off duty.

"You can go home," he told him.

"That's good," said Walters. "Find out anything?"

"Only that your wife was murdered with that selfsame cigarette box. We found no sign of anyone in the house except her, and you." He paused, but Walters only nodded thoughtfully. He asked, "Did the box look familiar to you?"

"Oh, yes, of course. It's mine. Alicia and I bought it on our honeymoon, in Switzerland. We divided things during the divorce, and that went to me."

"All right. Now, just how violent was that argument you had?"

He flushed. "As usual. I did a lot of shouting, and she just sat there letting it go past her ears. It never did any good."

"Did you strike her?"

The flush deepened, and he nodded. "I've never done that before."

"Did you by any chance hit her with a malachite box?"

"Do I need a lawyer?"

"You're not under arrest, Mr. Walters. But if you feel you need a lawyer, by all means get one." Hennessey hung up.

He had asked to be put on the day shift today, in order to follow up this case. It was quitting time now, but he was reluctant to leave.

Officer-One Fisher had been eavesdropping. He said, "So?"

"He never mentioned the word *alibi*," said Hennessey. "Smart. He's not suppose to know when she was killed."

266   LARRY NIVEN

"You're still sure he did it."

"Yeah. But getting a conviction is something else again. We'll find more people with more motives. And all we've got is the laboratory." He ticked items off his fingers. "No fingerprints on the box. No blood on Walters or any of his clothes, unless he had paper clothes and ditched 'em. No way of proving Walters let her in or gave her the key . . . though I wonder if he really had that much trouble keeping her out of the house.

"We'd be asking a jury to believe that Walters left the table and Larimer forgot about it. Larimer says no. Walters is pretty sure to get the benefit of the doubt. She didn't bleed much; a good defense lawyer is bound to suggest that she was moved from somewhere else."

"It's possible."

"She wasn't dead until she was hit. Nothing in the stomach but food. No drugs or poisons in the bloodstream. She'd have had to be killed by someone who"—he ticked them off—"knew she had Walters' key; knew Walters' displacement booth number; and knew Walters wouldn't be home. Agreed?"

"Maybe. How about Larimer or Lovejoy?"

Hennessey spread his hands in surrender. "It's worth asking. Larimer's alibi is as good as Walters', for all that's worth. And we've still got to interview Jennifer Lewis."

"Then again, a lot of people at the Sirius Club knew Walters. Some of them must have been involved with Alicia. Anyone who saw Walters halfway through a domino game would know he'd be stuck there for a while."

"True. Too true." Hennessey stood up. "Guess I'll be getting dinner."

Hennessey came out of the restaurant feeling pleasantly stuffed and torpid. He turned left toward the nearest booth, a block away.

The Walters case had haunted him all through dinner. Fisher had made a good deal of sense . . . but what bugged him was something Fisher hadn't said. Fisher hadn't said that Hennessey might be looking for easy answers.

Easy? If Walters had killed Alicia during a game of dominoes at the Sirius Club, then there wouldn't *be* any case until Larimer remembered. Aside from that, Walters would have been an idiot to try such a thing. Idiot, or desperate.

But if someone else had killed her, it opened a bag of snakes. Restrict it to members of the Sirius Club and how many were left? They'd both done business there. How many of Jeffrey Walters acquaintances had shared Alicia's bed? Which of them would have killed her, for reason or no reason? The trouble with sharing too many beds was that one's chance of running into a really bad situation was improved almost to certainty.

If Walters had done it, things became simpler.

But she hadn't bled much.

And Walters couldn't have had reason to move her body to his home. Where could he have killed her that would be worse than that?

Walters owned the murder weapon . . . no, forget that. She could have been hit with anything, and if she were in Walters' house fifteen seconds later she might still be breathing when the malachite box finished the job.

Hennessey slowed to a stop in front of the booth. Something Fisher *had* said, something had struck him funny. What was it?

"Her displacement booth must be ten years old—" That was it. The sight of the booth must have sparked the memory. And it *was* funny. How had he known?

JumpShift booths were all alike. They had to be. They all had to hold the same volume, because the air in the receiver had to be flicked back to the transmitter. When JumpShift improved a booth, it was the equipment they improved, so that the older booths could still be used.

Ten years old. Wasn't that—yes. The altitude shift. Pumping energy into a cargo, so that it could be flicked a mile or a hundred miles uphill, had been an early improvement. But a transmitter that could absorb the lost potential energy of a downhill shift had not become common until ten years ago.

Hennessey stepped in and dialed the police station.

Sergeant Sobel was behind the desk. "Oh, Fisher left an hour ago," he said. "Want his number?"

"Yes . . . no. Get me Alicia Walters' number."

Sobel got it for him. "What's up?"

"Tell you in a minute," said Hennessey, and flicked out.

It was black night. His ears registered the drop in pressure. His eyes adjusted rapidly, and he saw that there were lights in Alicia Walters' house.

He stepped out of the booth. Whistling, he walked a slow circle around it.

LARRY NIVEN

It was a JumpShift booth. What more was there to say? A glass cylinder with a rounded top, big enough for a tall man to stand upright and a meager amount of baggage to stand with him—or for a man holding a dead woman in his arms, clenching his teeth while he tried to free one finger for dialing. The machinery that made the magic was buried beneath the booth. The dial, a simple push-button phone dial. Even the long-distance booths looked just like this one, though the auxiliary machinery was far more complex.

"But he was sweating—" Had Lovejoy meant it literally?

Hennessey was smiling ferociously as he stepped back into the booth.

The lights of the Homicide Room flashed in his eyes. Hennessey came out tearing at his collar. Sweat started from every pore. Living in the mountains like that, Alicia should certainly have had her booth replaced. The room felt like a furnace, but it was his own body temperature that had jumped seven degrees in a moment. Seven degress of randomized energy, to compensate for the drop in potential energy between here and Lake Arrowhead.

Walters sat slumped, staring straight ahead of him. "She didn't understand and she didn't care. She was taking it like we'd been all through this before but we had to do it again and let's get it over with." He spoke in a monotone, but the nervous stutter was gone. "Finally I hit her. I guess I was trying to get her attention. She just took it and looked at me and waited for me to go on."

Hennessey said, "Where did the malachite box come in?"

"Where do you think? I hit her with it."

"Then it was hers, not yours."

"It was ours. When we broke up, she took it. Look, I don't want you to think I wanted to *kill* her. I wanted to scar her."

"To scare her?"

"No! To scar her!" His voice rose. "To leave a mark she'd remember every time she looked in a mirror, so she'd know I meant it, so she'd leave me alone! I wouldn't have cared if she sued. Whatever it cost, it would have been worth it. But I hit her too hard, too hard. I felt the crunch."

"Why didn't you report it?"

"But I did! At least, I tried. I picked her up in my arms and wrestled her out to the booth and dialed the Los Angeles Emergency Hospital. I don't know if there's any place closer, and I wasn't thinking too clear.

Listen, maybe I can prove this. Maybe an intern saw me in the booth. I flicked into the hospital, and suddenly I was broiling. Then I remembered that Alicia had an old booth, the kind that can't absorb a difference in potential energy."

"We guessed that much."

"So I dialed quick and flicked right out again. I had to go back to Alicia's for the malachite box and to wipe off the sofa, and my own booth *is* a new one, so I got the temperature shift again. God, it was hot. I changed suits before I went back to the club. I was still sweating."

"You thought that raising her temperature would foul up our estimate of when she died."

"That's right." Walter's smile was wan. "Listen, I did try to get her to a hospital. You'll remember that, won't you?"

"Yeah. But you changed your mind."

LARRY NIVEN

Confession

by Algernon Blackwood

The fog swirled slowly round him, driven by a heavy movement of its own, for of course there was no wind. It hung in poisonous thick coils and loops; it rose and sank; no light penetrated it directly from street lamp or motorcar, though here and there some big shop window shed a glimmering patch upon its evershifting curtain.

O'Reilly's eyes ached and smarted with the incessant effort to see a foot beyond his face. The optic nerve grew tired, and sight, accordingly, less accurate. He coughed as he shuffled forward cautiously through the choking gloom. Only the stifled rumble of crawling traffic persuaded him he was in a crowded city at all—this, and the vague outlines of groping figures, hugely magnified, emerging suddenly and disappearing again, as they fumbled along inch by inch towards uncertain destinations.

The figures, however, were human beings; they were real. That much he knew. He heard their muffled voices, now close, now distant, strangely smothered always. He also heard the tapping of innumerable sticks, feeling for iron railings or the curb. These phantom outlines represented living people. He was not alone.

It was the dread of finding himself *quite* alone that haunted him, for he was still unable to cross an open space without assistance. He had the physical strength, it was the mind that failed him. Midway the panic terror might descend upon him, he would shake all over, his will dissolve, he would shriek for help, run wildly—into the traffic probably—or, as they called it in his North Ontario home, "throw a fit" in the street before advancing wheels. He was not yet entirely cured, although under ordinary conditions he was safe enough, as Dr. Henry had assured him.

When he left Regent's Park by Tube an hour ago the air was clear, the November sun shone brightly, the pale blue sky was cloudless, and the assumption that he could manage the journey across London Town alone was justified. The following day he was to leave for Brighton for the week of final convalescence: this little preliminary test of his powers on a bright November afternoon was all to the good. Doctor Henry furnished minute instructions: "You change at Piccadilly Circus—without leaving the underground station, mind—and get out at South Kensington. You know the address of your V.A.D. friend. Have your cup of tea with her, then come back the same way to Regent's Park. Come back before dark—say six o'clock at latest. It's better." He had described exactly what turns to take after leaving the station, so many to the right, so many to the left; it was a little confusing, but the distance was short. "You can always ask. You can't possibly go wrong."

The unexpected fog, however, now blurred these instructions in a confused jumble in his mind. The failure of outer sight reacted upon memory. The V.A.D. besides had warned him that her address was "not easy to find the first time. The house lies in a backwater. But with your 'backwoods' instincts you'll probably manage it better than any Londoner!" She, too, had not calculated upon the fog.

When O'Reilly came up the stairs at South Kensington station, he emerged into such murky darkness that he thought he was still underground. An impenetrable world lay round him. Only a raw bite in the damp atmosphere told him he stood beneath an open sky. For some little time he stood and stared—a Canadian soldier, his home among clear brilliant spaces, now face to face for the first time in his life with that thing he had so often read about—a bad London fog. With keenest interest and surprise he "enjoyed" the novel spectacle for perhaps ten minutes, watching the people arrive and vanish, and wondering why the station lights stopped dead the instant they touched the street—then, with a sense of adventure—it cost an effort—he left the covered building and plunged into the opaque sea beyond.

Repeating to himself the directions he had received—first to the right, second to the left, once more to the left, and so forth—he checked each turn, assuring himself it was impossible to go wrong. He made correct if slow progress, until someone blundered into him with an abrupt and startling question: "Is this right, do you know, for South Kensington station?"

It was the suddenness that startled him; one moment there was no one, the next they were face to face, another, and the stranger had vanished into the gloom with a courteous word of grateful thanks. But the little shock of interruption had put memory out of gear. Had he already turned

ALGERNON BLACKWOOD

twice to the right, or had he not? O'Reilly realized sharply he had forgotten his memorized instructions. He stood still, making strenuous efforts at recovery, but each effort left him more uncertain than before. Five minutes later he was lost as hopelessly as any townsman who leaves his tent in the backwoods without blazing the trees to ensure finding his way back again. Even the sense of direction, so strong in him among his native forests, was completely gone. There were no stars, there was no wind, no smell, no sound of running water. There was nothing anywhere to guide him, nothing but occasional dim outlines, groping, shuffling, emerging, and disappearing in the eddying fog, but rarely coming within actual speaking, much less touching, distance. He was lost utterly; more, he was alone.

Yet not *quite* alone—the thing he dreaded most. There were figures still in his immediate neighborhood. They emerged, vanished, reappeared, dissolved. No, he was not quite alone. He saw these thickenings of the fog, he heard their voices, the tapping of their cautious sticks, their shuffling feet as well. They were real. They moved, it seemed, about him in a circle, never coming very close.

"But they're real," he said to himself aloud, betraying the weak point in his armor. "They're human beings right enough. I'm positive of that."

He had never argued with Dr. Henry—he wanted to get well; he had obeyed implicitly, believing everything the doctor told him—up to a point. But he had always had his own idea about these "figures," because, among them, were often enough his own pals from the Somme, Gallipoli, the Mespot horror, too. And he ought to know his own pals when he saw them! At the same time he knew quite well he had been "shocked," his being dislocated, half dissolved as it were, his system pushed into some lopsided condition that meant inaccurate registration. True. He grasped that perfectly. But, in that shock and dislocation, had he not possibly picked up another gear? Were there not gaps and broken edges, pieces that no longer dovetailed, fitted as usual, interstices, in a word? Yes, that was the word—interstices. Cracks, so to speak, between his perception of the outside world and his inner interpretation of these? Between memory and recognition? Between the various states of consciousness that usually dovetailed so neatly that the joints were normally imperceptible?

His state, he well knew, was abnormal, but were his symptoms on that account unreal? Could not these "interstices" be used by—others? When he saw his "figures," he used to ask himself: "Are not these the real ones, and the others—the human beings—unreal?"

This question now revived in him with a new intensity. Were these figures in the fog real or unreal? The man who had asked the way to the station, was he not, after all, a shadow merely?

By the use of his cane and foot and what of sight was left to him he knew that he was on an island. A lamppost stood up solid and straight beside him, shedding its faint patch of glimmering light. Yet there were railings, however, that puzzled him, for his stick hit the metal rods distinctly in a series. And there should be no railings round an island. Yet he had most certainly crossed a dreadful open space to get where he was. His confusion and bewilderment increased with dangerous rapidity. Panic was not far away.

He was no longer on an omnibus route. A rare taxi crawled past occasionally, a whitish patch at the window indicating an anxious human face; now and again came a van or cart, the driver holding a lantern as he led the stumbling horse. These comforted him, rare though they were. But it was the figures that drew his attention most. He was quite sure they were real. They were human beings like himself.

For all that, he decided he might as well be positive on the point. He tried one accordingly—a big man who rose suddenly before him out of the very earth.

"Can you give me the trail to Morley Place?" he asked.

But his question was drowned by the other's simultaneous inquiry in a voice much louder than his own.

"I say, is this right for the Tube station, d'you know? I'm utterly lost. I want South Ken."

And by the time O'Reilly had pointed the direction whence he himself had just come, the man was gone again, obliterated, swallowed up, not so much as his footsteps audible, almost as if—it seemed again—he never had been there at all.

This left an acute unpleasantness in him, a sense of bewilderment greater than before. He waited five minutes, not daring to move a step, then tried another figure, a woman this time, who, luckily, knew the immediate neighborhood intimately. She gave him elaborate instructions in the kindest possible way, then vanished with incredible swiftness and ease into the sea of gloom beyond. The instantaneous way she vanished was disheartening, upsetting: it was so uncannily abrupt and sudden. Yet she comforted him. Morley Place, according to her version, was not two hundred yards from where he stood. He felt his way forward, step by step, using his cane, crossing a giddy open space, kicking the curb with each boot alternately, coughing and choking all the time as he did so. "They were real, I guess, anyway," he said aloud. "They were both real enough all right. And it may lift a bit soon!" He was making a great effort to hold himself in hand. He was already fighting, that is. He realized this perfectly. The only point was—the reality of the figures. "It may lift now any minute," he repeated louder. In spite of the cold, his skin was sweating profusely.

But, of course, it did not lift. The figures, too, became fewer. No carts were audible. He had followed the woman's directions carefully, but now found himself in some byway, evidently, where pedestrians at the best of times were rare. There was dull silence all about him. His foot lost the curb, his cane swept the empty air, striking nothing solid, and panic rose upon him with its shuddering, icy grip. He was alone, he knew himself alone, worse still—he was in another open space.

It took him fifteen minutes to cross that open space, most of the way upon his hands and knees, oblivious of the icy slime that stained his trousers, froze his fingers, intent only upon feeling solid support against his back and spine again. It was an endless period. The moment of collapse was close, the shriek already rising in his throat, the shaking of the whole body uncontrollable, when—his outstretched fingers struck a friendly curb, and he saw a glimmering patch of diffused radiance overhead. With a great, quick effort he stood upright, and an instant later his stick rattled along an area railing. He leaned against it, breathless, panting, his heart beating painfully while the street lamp gave him the further comfort of its feeble gleam, the actual flame, however, invisible. He looked this way and that; the pavement was deserted. He was engulfed in the dark silence of the fog.

But Morley Place, he knew, must be very close by now. He thought of the friendly little V.A.D. he had known in France, of a warm bright fire, a cup of tea and a cigarette. One more effort, he reflected, and all these would be his. He pluckily groped his way forward again, crawling slowly by the area railings. If things got really bad again, he would ring a bell and ask for help, much as he shrank from the idea. Provided he had no more open spaces to cross, provided he saw no more figures emerging and vanishing like creatures born of the fog and dwelling within it as within their native element—it was the figures he now dreaded more than anything else, more than even the loneliness—provided the panic sense—

A faint darkening of the fog beneath the next lamp caught his eye and made him start. He stopped. It was not a figure this time, it was the shadow of the pole grotesquely magnified. No, it moved. It moved towards him. A flame of fire followed by ice flowed through him. It was a figure—close against his face. It was a woman.

The doctor's advice came suddenly back to him, the counsel that had cured him of a hundred phantoms:

"Do not ignore them. Treat them as real. Speak and go with them. You will soon prove their unreality then. And they will leave you . . ."

He made a brave, tremendous effort. He was shaking. One hand clutched the damp and icy area railing.

"Lost your way like myself, haven't you, ma'am?" he said in a voice that trembled. "Do you know where we are at all? Morley Place I'm looking for—"

He stopped dead. The woman moved nearer and for the first time he saw her face clearly. Its ghastly pallor, the bright, frightened eyes that stared with a kind of dazed bewilderment into his own, the beauty, above all, arrested his speech midway. The woman was young, her tall figure wrapped in a dark fur coat.

"Can I help you?" he asked impulsively, forgetting his own terror for the moment. He was more than startled. Her air of distress and pain stirred a peculiar anguish in him. For a moment she made no answer, thrusting her white face closer as if examining him, so close, indeed, that he controlled with difficulty his instinct to shrink back a little.

"Where am I?" she asked at length, searching his eyes intently. "I'm lost—I've lost myself. I can't find my way back." Her voice was low, a curious wailing in it that touched his pity oddly. He felt his own distress merging in one that was greater.

"Same here," he replied more confidently. "I'm terrified of being alone, too. I've had shellshock, you know. Let's go together. We'll find a way together—"

"Who are you?" the woman murmured, still staring at him with her big bright eyes, their distress, however, no whit lessened. She gazed at him as though aware suddenly of his presence.

He told her briefly. "And I'm going to tea with a V.A.D. friend in Morley Place. What's your address? Do you know the name of the street?"

ALGERNON BLACKWOOD

She appeared not to hear him, or not to understand exactly; it was as if she was not listening again.

"I came out so suddenly, so unexpectedly," he heard the low voice with pain in every syllable; "I can't find my way home again. Just when I was expecting him, too—" She looked about her with a distraught expression that made O'Reilly long to carry her in his arms to safety then and there. "He may be there now—waiting for me at this very moment—and I can't get back." And so sad was her voice that only by an effort did O'Reilly prevent himself putting out his hand to touch her. More and more he forgot himself in his desire to help her. Her beauty, the wonder of her strange bright eyes in the pallid face, made an immense appeal. He became calmer. This woman was real enough. He asked again the address, the street and number, the distance she thought it was. "Have you any idea of the direction, ma'am, any idea at all? We'll go together and—"

She suddenly cut him short. She turned her head as if to listen, so that he saw her profile a moment, the outline of the slender neck, a glimpse of jewels just below the fur.

"Hark! I hear him calling! I remember . . . !" And she was gone from his side into the swirling fog.

Without an instant's hesitation O'Reilly followed her, not only because he wished to help, but because he dared not be left alone. The presence of this strange, lost woman comforted him; he must not lose sight of her, whatever happened. He had to run, she went so rapidly, ever just in front, moving with confidence and certainty, turning right and left, crossing the street, but never stopping, never hesitating, her companion always at her heels in breathless haste, and with a growing terror that he might lose her any minute. The way she found her direction through the dense fog was marvellous enough, but O'Reilly's only thought was to keep her in sight, lest his own panic redescend upon him with its inevitable collapse in the dark and lonely street. It was a wild and panting pursuit, and he kept her in view with difficulty, a dim fleeting outline always a few yards ahead of him. She did not once turn her head, she uttered no sound, no cry; she hurried forward with unfaltering instinct. Nor did the chase occur to him once as singular; she was his safety, and that was all he realized.

One thing, however, he remembered afterwards, though at the actual time he no more than registered the detail, paying no attention to it—a definite perfume she left upon the atmosphere, one, moreover, that he knew, although he could not find its name as he ran. It was associated vaguely, for him, with something unpleasant, something disagreeable. He connected it with misery and pain. It gave him a feeling of uneasiness. More than that he did not notice at the moment, nor could he remember—he certainly did not try—where he had known this particular scent before.

Then suddenly the woman stopped, opened a gate and passed into a small private garden—so suddenly that O'Reilly, close upon her heels, only just avoided tumbling into her. "You've found it?" he cried. "May I come in a moment with you? Perhaps you'll let me telephone to the doctor?"

She turned instantly. Her face, close against his own, was livid.

"Doctor!" she repeated in an awful whisper. The word meant terror to her. O'Reilly stood amazed. For a second or two neither of them moved. The woman seemed petrified.

"Dr. Henry, you know," he stammered, finding his tongue again. "I'm in his care. He's in Harley Street."

Her face cleared as suddenly as it had darkened, though the original expression of bewilderment and pain still hung in her great eyes. But the terror left them, as though she suddenly forgot some association that had revived it.

"My home," she murmured. "My home is somewhere here. I'm near it. I must get back—in time—for him. I must. He's coming to me." And with these extraordinary words she turned, walked up the narrow path, and stood upon the porch of a two-story house before her companion had recovered from his astonishment sufficiently to move or utter a syllable in reply. The front door, he saw, was ajar. It had been left open.

For five seconds, perhaps for ten, he hesitated; it was the fear that the door would close and shut him out that brought the decision to his will and muscles. He ran up the steps and followed the woman into a dark hall where she had already preceded him, and amid whose blackness she now had finally vanished. He closed the door, not knowing exactly why he did so, and knew at once by an instinctive feeling that the house he now found himself in with this unknown woman was empty and unoccupied. In a house, however, he felt safe. It was the open streets that were his danger. He stood waiting, listening a moment before he spoke; and he heard the woman moving down the passage from door to door, repeating to herself in her low voice of unhappy wailing some words he

ALGERNON BLACKWOOD

could not understand:

"Where is it? Oh, where is it? I must get back . . ."

O'Reilly then found himself abruptly stricken with dumbness, as though, with these strange words, a haunting terror came up and breathed against him in the darkness.

"Is she after all a figure?" ran in letters of fire across his numbed brain. "Is she unreal—or real?"

Seeking relief in action of some kind he put out a hand automatically, feeling along the wall for an electric switch, and though he found it by some miraculous chance, no answering glow responded to the click.

And the woman's voice from the darkness: "Ah! Ah! At last I've found it. I'm home again—at last . . . !" He heard a door open and close upstairs. He was on the ground floor now—alone. Complete silence followed.

In the conflict of various emotions—fear for himself lest his panic should return, fear for the woman who had led him into this empty house and now deserted him upon some mysterious errand of her own that made him think of madness—in this conflict that held him a moment spellbound, there was a yet bigger ingredient demanding instant explanation, but an explanation that he could not find. Was the woman real or was she unreal? Was she a human being or a "figure"? The horror of doubt obsessed him with an acute uneasiness that betrayed itself in a return of that unwelcome inner trembling he knew was dangerous.

What saved him from a *crise* that must have had most dangerous results for his mind and nervous system generally, seems to have been the outstanding fact that he felt more for the woman than for himself. His sympathy and pity had been deeply moved; her voice, her beauty, her anguish and bewilderment, all uncommon, inexplicable, mysterious, formed together a claim that drove self into the background. Added to this was the detail that she had left him, gone to another floor without a word, and now, behind a closed door in a room upstairs, found herself face to face at last with the unknown object of her frantic search—with "it," whatever "it" might be. Real or unreal, figure or human being, the overmastering impulse of his being was that he must go to her.

It was this clear impulse that gave him decision and energy to do what he then did. He struck a match, he found a stump of candle, he made his way by means of this flickering light along the passage and up the carpetless stairs. He moved cautiously, stealthily, though not knowing why he did so. The house, he now saw, was indeed untenanted; dustsheets covered the piled-up furniture; he glimpsed, through doors ajar, pictures screened upon the walls, brackets draped to look like hooded heads. He went on slowly, steadily, moving on tiptoe as though conscious of being watched, noting the well of darkness in the hall below, the grotesque shadows that his movements cast on walls and ceiling. The silence was unpleasant, yet, remembering that the woman was "expecting" someone, he did not wish it broken. He reached the landing and stood still. Closed doors on both sides of a corridor met his sight, as he shaded the candle to examine the scene. Behind which of these doors, he asked himself, was the woman, figure or human being, now alone with "it"?

There was nothing to guide him, but an instinct that he must not delay sent him forward again upon his search. He tried a door on the right—an empty room, with the furniture hidden by dustsheets, and mattress rolled up on the bed. He tried a second door, leaving the first one open behind him, and it was, similarly, an empty bedroom. Coming out into the corridor again he stood a moment waiting, then called aloud in a low voice that yet woke echoes unpleasantly in the hall below: "Where are you? I want to help—which room are you in?"

There was no answer; he was almost glad he heard no sound, for he knew quite well that he was waiting really for another sound—the steps of him who was "expected." And the idea of meeting with this unknown third sent a shudder through him, as though related to an interview he dreaded with his whole heart, and must at all costs avoid. Waiting another moment or two, he noted that his candlestump was burning low, then crossed the landing with a feeling, at once of hesitation and determination, towards a door opposite to him. He opened it; he did not halt on the threshold. Holding the candle at arm's length, he went boldly in.

And instantly his nostrils told him he was right at last, for a whiff of the strange perfume, though this time much stronger than before, greeted him, sending a new quiver along his nerves. He knew now why it was associated with unpleasantness, with pain, with misery, for he recognized it—the odor of a hospital. In this room a powerful anesthetic had been used—and recently.

Simultaneously with smell, sight brought its message, too. On the large double bed behind the door on his right lay, to his amazement, the woman in the dark fur coat. He saw the jewels on the slender neck; but the eyes he did not see, for they were closed—closed too, he grasped at once, in death. The body lay stretched at full length, quite motionless. He ap-

ALGERNON BLACKWOOD

proached. A dark thin streak that came from the parted lips and passed downwards over the chin, losing itself then in the fur collar, was a trickle of blood. It was hardly dry. It glistened.

Strange it was perhaps that, while imaginary fears had the power to paralyze him, mind and body, this sight of something real had the effect of restoring confidence. The sight of blood and death, amid conditions often ghastly and even monstrous, was no new thing to him. He went up quietly, and with steady hand he felt the woman's cheek, the warmth of recent life still in its softness. The final cold had not yet mastered this empty form whose beauty, in its perfect stillness, had taken on the new strange sweetness of an unearthly bloom. Pallid, silent, untenanted, it lay before him, lit by the flicker of his guttering candle. He lifted the fur coat to feel for the unbeating heart. A couple of hours ago at most, he judged, this heart was working busily, the breath came through those parted lips, the eyes were shining in full beauty. His hand encountered a hard knob—the head of a long steel hat-pin driven through the heart up to its hilt.

He knew then which was the figure—which was the real and which the unreal. He knew also what had been meant by "it."

But before he could think or reflect what action he must take, before he could straighten himself even from his bent position over the body on the bed, there sounded through the empty house below the loud clang of the front door being closed. And instantly rushed over him that other fear he had so long forgotten—fear for himself. The panic of his own shaken nerves descended with irresistible onslaught. He turned, extinguishing the candle in the violent trembling of his hand, and tore headlong from the room.

The following ten minutes seemed a nightmare in which he was not master of himself and knew not exactly what he did. All he realized was that steps already sounded on the stairs, coming quickly nearer. The flicker of an electric torch played on the banisters, whose shadows ran swiftly sideways along the wall as the hand that held the light ascended. He thought in a frenzied second of police, of his presence in the house, of the murdered woman. It was a sinister combination. Whatever happened, he must escape without being so much as even seen. His heart raced madly. He darted across the landing into the room opposite, whose door he had luckily left open. And by some incredible chance, apparently, he was neither seen nor heard by the man who, a moment later, reached the landing, entered the room where the body of the woman lay, and closed the door carefully behind him.

Shaking, scarcely daring to breathe lest his breath be audible, O'Reilly, in the grip of his own personal terror, remnant of his uncured shock of war, had no thought of what duty might demand or not demand of him. He thought only of himself. He realized one clear issue—that he must get out of the house without being heard or seen. Who the newcomer was he did not know, beyond an uncanny assurance that it was *not* he whom the woman had "expected," but the murderer himself, and that it was the murderer, in his turn, who was expecting this third person. In that room with death at his elbow, a death he had himself brought about but an hour or two ago, the murderer now hid in waiting for his second victim. And the door was closed.

Yet any minute it might open again, cutting off retreat.

O'Reilly crept out, stole across the landing, reached the head of the stairs, and began, with the utmost caution, the perilous descent. Each time the bare boards creaked beneath his weight no matter how stealthily this weight was adjusted, his heart missed a beat. He tested each step before he pressed upon it, distributing as much of his weight as he dared upon the banisters. It was a little more than halfway down that, to his horror, his foot caught in a projecting carpet tack; he slipped on the polished wood, and only saved himself from falling headlong by a wild clutch at the railing, making an uproar that seemed to him like the explosion of a handgrenade in the forgotten trenches. His nerves gave way then, and panic seized him. In the silence that followed the resounding echoes he heard the bedroom door opening on the floor above.

Concealment was now useless. It was impossible, too. He took the last flight of stairs in a series of leaps, four steps at a time, reached the hall, flew across it, and opened the front door, just as his pursuer, electric torch in hand, covered half the stairs behind him. Slamming the door, he plunged headlong into the welcome, all-obscuring fog outside.

The fog had now no terrors for him, he welcomed its concealing mantle; nor did it matter in which direction he ran so long as he put distance between him and the house of death. The pursuer had, of course, not followed him into the street. He crossed open spaces without a tremor. He ran in a circle nevertheless, though without being aware he did so. No people were about, no single groping shadow passed him, no boom of traffic reached his ears, when he paused for breath at length against

ALGERNON BLACKWOOD

an area railing. Then for the first time he made the discovery that he had no hat. He remembered now. In examining the body, partly out of respect, partly perhaps unconsciously, he had taken it off and laid it—on the very bed.

It was there, a telltale bit of damning evidence, in the house of death. And a series of probable consequences flashed through his mind like lightning. It was a new hat fortunately; more fortunate still, he had not yet written name or initials in it; but the maker's mark was there for all to read, and the police would go immediately to the shop where he had bought it only two days before. Would the shop people remember his appearance? Would his visit, the date, the conversation be recalled? He thought it was unlikely; he resembled dozens of men; he had no outstanding peculiarity. He tried to think, but his mind was confused and troubled, his heart was beating dreadfully, he felt desperately ill. He sought vainly for some story to account for his being out in the fog and far from home without a hat. No single idea presented itself. He clung to the icy railings, hardly able to keep upright, collapse very near—when suddenly a figure emerged from the fog, paused a moment to stare at him, put out a hand and caught him, and then spoke.

"You're ill, my dear sir," said a man's kindly voice. "Can I be of any assistance? Come, let me help you." He had seen at once that it was not a case of drunkenness. "Come, take my arm, won't you? I'm a physician. Luckily, too, you are just outside my very house. Come in." And he half dragged, half pushed O'Reilly, now bordering on collapse, up the steps and opened the door with his latchkey.

"Felt ill suddenly—lost in the fog . . . terrified, but be all right soon, thanks awfully—" the Canadian stammered his gratitude, already feeling better. He sank into a chair in the hall, while the other put down a paper parcel he had been carrying, and led him presently into a comfortable room; a fire burned brightly; the electric lamps were pleasantly shaded; a decanter of whisky and a siphon stood on a small table beside a big armchair; and before O'Reilly could find another word to say the other had poured him out a glass and bade him sip it slowly, without troubling to talk till he felt better.

"That will revive you. Drink it slowly. You should never have been out a night like this. If you've far to go, better let me put you up—"

"Very kind, very kind, indeed," mumbled O'Reilly, recovering rapidly in the comfort of a presence he already liked and felt even drawn to.

CONFESSION

"No trouble at all," returned the doctor. "I've been at the front, you know. I can see what your trouble is—shellshock, I'll be bound."

The Canadian, much impressed by the other's quick diagnosis, noted also his tact and kindness. He had made no reference to the absence of a hat, for instance.

"Quite true," he said. "I'm with Dr. Henry, in Harley Street," and he added a few words about his case. The whisky worked its effect, he revived more and more, feeling better every minute. The other handed him a cigarette; they begn to talk about his symptoms and recovery; confidence returned in a measure, though he still felt badly frightened. The doctor's manner and personality did much to help, for there was strength and gentleness in the face, though the features showed unusual determination, softened occasionally by a sudden hint as of suffering in the bright, compelling eyes. It was the face, thought O'Reilly, of a man who had seen much and probably been through hell, but of a man who was simple, good, sincere. Yet not a man to trifle with; behind his gentleness lay something very stern. This effect of character and personality woke the other's respect in addition to his gratitude. His sympathy was stirred.

"You encourage me to make another guess," the man was saying, after a successful reading of the impromptu patient's state, "that you have had, namely, a severe shock quite recently, and"—he hesitated for the merest fraction of a second—"that it would be a relief to you," he went on, the skillful suggestion in the voice unnoticed by his companion, "it would be wise as well, if you could unburden yourself to—someone—who would understand." He looked at O'Reilly with a kindly and very pleasant smile. "Am I not right, perhaps?" he asked in his gentle tone.

"Someone who would understand," repeated the Canadian. "That's my trouble exactly. You've hit it. It's all so incredible."

The other smiled. "The more incredible," he suggested, "the greater your need for expression. Suppression, as you may know, is dangerous in cases like this. You think you have hidden it, but it bides its time and comes up later, causing a lot of trouble. Confession, you know"—he emphasized the word—"confession is good for the soul!"

"You're dead right," agreed the other.

"Now, if you can, bring yourself to tell it to someone who will listen and believe—to myself, for instance. I am a doctor, familiar with such things. I shall regard all you say as a professional confidence, of course; and, as we are strangers, my belief or disbelief is of no particular consequence. I may tell you in advance of your story, however—I think I can promise it—that I shall believe all you have to say."

O'Reilly told his story without more ado, for the suggestion of the skilled physician had found easy soil to work in. During the recital his host s⁻eyes never once left his own. He moved no single muscle of his body. His interest seemed intense.

"A bit tall, isn't it?" said the Canadian, when his tale was finished. "And the question is—" he continued with a threat of volubility which the other checked instantly.

"Strange, yes, but incredible, no," the doctor interrupted. "I see no reason to disbelieve a single detail of what you have just told me. Things equally remarkable, equally incredible, happen in all large towns, as I know from personal experience. I could give you instances." He paused a moment, but his companion, staring into his eyes with interest and curiosity, made no comment. "Some years ago, in fact," continued the other, "I knew of a very similar case—strangely similar."

"Really! I should be immensely interested—"

"So similar that it seems almost a coincidence. You may find it hard, in your turn, to credit it." He paused again, while O'Reilly sat forward in his chair to listen. "Yes," pursued the doctor slowly, "I think everyone connected with it is now dead. There is no reason why I should not tell it, for one confidence deserves another, you know. It happened during the Boer War—as long ago as that," he added with emphasis. "It is really a very commonplace story in one way, though very dreadful in another, but a man who has served at the front will understand and—I'm sure—will sympathize."

"I'm sure of that," offered the other readily.

"A colleague of mine, now dead, as I mentioned—a surgeon, with a big practice, married a young and charming girl. They lived happily together for several years. His wealth made her very comfortable. His consulting room, I must tell you, was some distance from his house—just as this might be—so that she was never bothered with any of his cases. Then came the war. Like many others, though much over age, he volunteered. He gave up his lucrative practice and went to South Africa. His income, of course, stopped; the big house was closed; his wife found her life of enjoyment considerably curtailed. This she considered a great hardship, it seems. She felt a bitter grievance against him. Devoid of imagination, without any power of sacrifice, a selfish type, she was yet a beautiful, attractive woman—and young. The inevitable lover came upon the scene to console her. They planned to run away together. He was rich. Japan they thought would suit them. Only, by some ill luck, the husband got wind of it and arrived in London just in the nick of time."

"Well rid of her," put in O'Reilly, "*I* think,"

The doctor waited a moment. He sipped his glass. Then his eyes fixed upon his companion's face somewhat sternly.

"Well rid of her, yes," he continued, "only he determined to make that riddance final. He decided to kill her—and her lover. You see, he loved her."

O'Reilly made no comment. In his own country this method with a faithless woman was not unknown. His interest was very concentrated. But he was thinking, too, as he listened, thinking hard.

"He planned the time and place with care," resumed the other in a lower voice, as though he might possibly be overheard. "They met, he knew, in the big house, now closed, the house where he and his young wife had passed such happy years during their prosperity. The plan failed, however, in an important detail—the woman came at the appointed hour, but without her lover. She found death waiting for her—it was a painless death. Then her lover, who was to arrive half an hour later, did not come at all. The door had been left open for him purposely. The house was dark, its rooms shut up, deserted; there was no caretaker even. It was a foggy night—just like this."

"And the other?" asked O'Reilly in a failing voice. "The lover—"

"A man did come in," the doctor went on calmly, "but it was not the lover. It was a stranger."

"A stranger?" the other whispered. "And the surgeon—where was he all the time?"

"Waiting outside to see him enter—concealed in the fog. He saw the man go in. Five minutes later he followed, meaning to complete his vengeance, his act of justice, whatever you like to call it. But the man who had come in was a stranger—he came in by chance—just as you might have done—to shelter from the fog—or—"

O'Reilly, though with a great effort, rose abruptly to his feet. He had an appalling feeling that the man facing him was mad. He had a keen desire to get outside, fog or no fog, to leave this room, to escape from the calm accents of this insistent voice. The effect of the whisky was still in his blood. He felt no lack of confidence. But words came to him with

ALGERNON BLACKWOOD

difficulty.

"I think I'd better be pushing off now, doctor," he said clumsily. "But I feel I must thank you very much for all your kindness and help." He turned and looked hard into the keen eyes facing him. "Your friend," he asked in a whisper, "the surgeon—I hope—I mean, was he ever caught?"

"No," was the grave reply, the doctor standing up in front of him, "he was never caught."

O'Reilly waited a moment before he made another remark. "Well," he said at length, but in a louder tone than before, "I think—I'm glad." He went to the door without shaking hands.

"You have no hat," mentioned the voice behind him. "If you'll wait a moment I'll get you one of mine. You need not trouble to return it." And the doctor passed him, going into the hall. There was a sound of tearing paper. O'Reilly left the house a moment later with a hat upon his head, but it was not till he reached the Tube station half an hour afterwards that he realized it was his own.

The Adventure of the Intarsia Box

by August Derleth

Solar Pons and I were at breakfast one fair morning only a week after our return from the country and the curious affair of the Whispering Knights, when the door below was thrown violently open and there was a rush of feet on the stairs that stopped short of our threshold. Pons looked up, his grey eyes intent, his whole lean figure taut with waiting.

"A young woman, agitated," he said, nodding. He flashed a glance at the clock. "Scarcely seven. It is surely a matter of some urgency to her. The hour has only now occurred to her. She hesitates. No, she is coming on."

The sound of footsteps was now scarcely audible, but they came on up the stairs. In a moment there was a faint, timorous tapping on the door to our quarters, and an equally timorous voice, asking beyond the door, "Mr. Pons? Mr. Solar Pons?"

"Pray play the gentleman, Parker," said Pons.

I sprang up and threw open the door.

A sandy-haired young woman not much over her middle twenties stood there, a package wrapped in a shawl pressed to her breast. She looked from one to the other of us with candid blue eyes, her full lower lip trembling uncertainly, a slow flush mounting her cheeks toward the scattering of freckles that bridged her nose and swept under her eyes. Then, with that unerring intuition that women especially seem to have, she fixed upon Pons.

"Mr. Pons! I hope I'm not intruding. I had to come. I had to do something. Uncle will do nothing—just wait for whatever is to happen. Oh, it's dreadful, Mr. Pons, dreadful!"

"Do come in, Miss . . . ?"

"I am Flora Morland of Morland Park, Mr. Pons. You may have heard of my uncle, Colonel Burton Morland?"

"Retired resident at Malacca," said Pons promptly. "But do compose

AUGUST DERLETH

yourself, Miss Morland. Let me take that box you're holding."

"No, no!" she cried, and pressed it momentarily closer to her body. Then she bit her lip and smiled weakly. "But that is why I came. Forgive me, Mr. Pons. You shall see for yourself—now."

She threw back the shawl and revealed a box, scarcely as large as a cigar box, make of *kamuning* wood. It was beautifully carved on the top and around on all sides, with curious figures, like a bas relief. It seemed obviously Oriental in design.

"Open it, Mr. Pons!" She shuddered a little. "I don't know how I could bear to have carried it all this way. I can't look again!"

Pons took the box gently from her. He pushed the breakfast dishes to one side and set the box on the table. He stood for a moment admiring its workmanship, while Miss Morland waited with an apprehensive tautness that was almost tangible in the room. Then he threw it open.

I fear I gasped. I do not know what I expected to see—a priceless jewel, perhaps?—a bibliophile's treasure?—something fitting to the exquisite box containing it. Certainly it was nothing I could have dreamed in my wildest imaginings! In the box lay a mummified human hand, severed at the wrist, affixed to the bottom of the box by two bands of white silk.

Pons's emotion showed only in his eyes, which lit up with quick interest. He touched the dried skin with the fingertips of one hand, while caressing the carved box with the other.

"Intarsia," murmured Pons. "An Italian art, Miss Morland. But this box would appear to be of Oriental origin; the subjects of the ornamentation are all Oriental. Would you care now to tell us how you came by it?"

He closed the box almost with regret, and, Miss Morland having taken the stuffed chair near the fireplace, came to stand against the mantel, filling his pipe with the detestable shag he smoked.

Miss Morland clasped her hands together. "I hardly know how to begin, Mr. Pons," she said.

"Let us start with this fascinating object you have brought us," suggested Pons.

"It was delivered to my uncle three days ago, Mr. Pons. I myself took it from the postman. It was mailed first class from Kuala Lumpur. My uncle was in his study that morning, and I took it in to him. I recall that his face darkened when he saw the package, but I supposed that it was only in wonder at who might have sent it. It was ten years ago that he left Malaya. He looked for some clue to its origin; there was no return address on the package. He began to take off its wrappings. I had turned away from him to put some books back on the shelves, when suddenly I heard him make a kind of explosive sound, and on the instant he slipped from his chair to the floor. He had swooned dead away. I ran over to him, of course, Mr. Pons—and that's how I came to see what was in the box. There was a little card, too—linen paper, I thought, Mr. Pons—I believe such details are important to you. On it was written in a flowing hand a single sentence: *I will come for you.*"

"The card is not now in the box," said Pons.

"I suppose my uncle removed it. I closed the box, Mr. Pons. I couldn't bear to look at what was in it. Then I brought my uncle around. I expected him to tell me what was in the box and what it all meant, but he said nothing—never a word. Seeing that the box was closed, he assumed that he had closed it before or as he fainted, and that I didn't know what was in it. Mr. Pons, I was deeply shocked by what was in the box, but I was even more profoundly disturbed by my uncle's failure to say anything at all of it to me. Since the day he received it, furthermore, he has been very busy, and everything he has done is in the way of putting his affairs in order."

"Did your uncle notify the police?"

"If so, I don't know of it, Mr. Pons."

Pons puffed reflectively on his pipe for a moment before he asked, "I take it you are an orphan and have been living with your uncle. For how long?"

"Ten years," she replied. "My mother died when I was very young, and my father five years after Uncle Burton returned from Malaya. He has been very kind to me. He has treated me as his own child."

"Your uncle is not married?"

"Uncle Burton was married at one time. I believe there was some cloud over the marriage. My father occasionally talked about my aunt in deprecatory terms, called her 'the Eurasian woman.' My cousin Nicholas, who spent the last five years of Uncle Burton's tenure with him in Malacca, also married a Eurasian woman. My aunt died before my uncle's return to England."

"Your cousin?"

"He returned with Uncle Burton. He's a barrister with offices in the City. His wife is the proprietress of a small, but I believe thriving, im-

AUGUST DERLETH

porting business in the Strand."

"Your cousin—Nicholas Morland, is it?"

"There were three brothers, Mr. Pons—my father, Nick's father, and Uncle Burton."

"Your cousin, I take it, was your uncle's assistant in Malacca?"

"Yes, Mr. Pons."

"How old is your uncle, Miss Morland?"

"Seventy."

"So he was fifty-five when he retired," mused Pons. "How long had he been the resident in Malacca?"

"Fifteen years. He went out there when he was forty. I never really knew him, Mr. Pons, until his return. I hadn't been born when he was sent out. But Uncle Burton seemed to be very fond of me from the moment he saw me, and it seemed only natural that he would invite me to live with him when Father died. Uncle Burton is very wealthy, he has many servants, and, though he is regarded by some of them as a martinet, they do stay, most of them. And he has a large and secluded home in Chipping Barnet. It seemed the most natural thing to do, to live with him. He sent me to school, and through a small private college. For my part, I am expected to play hostess whenever he has one of his small parties, which are attended chiefly by my cousin and his wife and some other ex-Colonials and their wives. I rather like that now, though I didn't at first. But my uncle is the soul of rectitude. He will tolerate no deviation from proper conduct, so there are never any social problems for me to deal with."

"Your uncle's heirs—who are they?"

Our client looked momentarily startled. "Why, I suppose Nick and I are his only heirs," she said. "I know nothing of his affairs, Mr. Pons. But there is no one else. All our relatives of my uncle's generation are dead, and Nick and I are the only ones of our generation. Nick has no children, so there is no coming generation, either." She took a deep breath and asked impulsively, "Mr. Pons, can you get to the bottom of this mystery? It troubles me very much to see Uncle Burton—well, preparing for death. That's what he's doing, Mr. Pons, it really is."

"Your uncle has no knowledge of your coming here, Miss Morland?"

"None. I left at dawn. He seldom rises before eight o'clock."

"Then you've not had breakfast, Miss Morland?"

"No, Mr. Pons."

THE ADVENTURE OF THE INTARSIA BOX 291

"Allow me!" Pons strode to the door, opened it, stuck his head out and called, "Mrs. Johnson, if you please!" He turned back to our client. "Pray give me a few minutes to ponder your problem, Miss Morland. In the meantime, Mrs. Johnson will be happy to prepare breakfast for you in her quarters. Will you not, Mrs. Johnson?" he asked of our longsuffering landlady as she appeared on the threshold.

"That I will, to be sure, Mr. Pons. If you'll come with me, Miss?"

Miss Morland, too surprised to protest, allowed herself to be led from the room by Mrs. Johnson.

The door had hardly closed behind them before Pons was once again at the box, opening it. I was drawn to his side.

"Is this not an unique warning indeed, Parker?" he asked.

"I have seldom seen anything as gruesome."

"It was intended to be. I submit that this severed hand must have a deep significance for our client's uncle. What do you make of it?"

I bent and peered closely at it, examining it as well as I could without disturbing it or removing it from the box. "A man's right hand," I said. "Of probably about forty, not much older, certainly. It is brown skinned, not only from age. Eurasian?"

"Native. See how beautifully kept the nails are! This man did little work. There are no observable calluses. The hand is smooth even to the fingertips. How long would you say this hand has been severed?"

"Without more scientific apparatus, I should think it impossible to say."

"Could it be as old, say, as Colonel Morland's tenure in Malacca?"

"I should think so. But what could it mean to Morland?"

"Ah, Parker, when we can answer that question we will know why it was sent to him." He smiled grimly. "I fancy it concerns some dark episode of his past. He retired at fifty-five. Is that not early?"

"His health, perhaps, demanded his retirement."

"Or his conduct."

"Miss Morland speaks of him as a model of rectitude."

"And as something of a martinet. Conduct in search of rectitude may be as reprehensible as its opposite." He touched the silk bands. "What do you make of these, Parker?"

"If I may venture a guess, white is the color of mourning in the Orient," I said.

"The bands are new," observed Pons.

"That is certainly elementary," I could not help saying. "I can think

AUGUST DERLETH

of several reasons why they should be. What puzzles me is the reason for being of the hand in the first place."

"I submit its owner kept it as long as he lived."

"Well, that's reasonable," I agreed. "It has been properly mummified. Are we to take it that the owner is not still alive?"

"If he were sufficiently attached to this appendage while he lived, would he so readily have sent it off?"

"Hardly."

"Unless it had a message to convey or an errand to perform."

"Absurd!"

"Yet it did convey a message to Colonel Morland. It may be gruesome, but surely not so much so as to cause a normal and healthy man to swoon at sight of it. It reminds me of that horrible little trifle of wizard lore known as the glory hand, the bewitched, animated hand of a dead man sent to perform its owner's wishes, even to murder."

"Superstitious claptrap!"

"Colonel Morland, at least, is convinced that his life is in danger, and that the threat to it emanates from Malaya. Let us just have a look at the ship's registry before our client returns to determine the number of ships that have docked from Malaya in the past few days."

We had time to search back five days before our client returned from Mrs. Johnson's quarters; during those five days no ship from Malaya had docked at England's ports, though a freighter, the *Alor Star,* was listed as due within twenty-four hours. At Miss Morland's entrance, Pons thrust the papers aside.

"Thank you, indeed, Mrs. Johnson," said Pons as our landlady turned at the threshold. "And now, Miss Morland, two or three questions occur to me. Pray be seated."

Our client, now somewhat more composed and less uncertain in her manner, took her former seat and waited expectantly.

"Miss Morland, when your uncle came around, did he say or do anything significant?" asked Pons.

"He didn't say a word," she answered. "He was very pale. He looked for the box and seemed relieved to find it closed. He picked it up at once. I asked him, 'Are you all right, Uncle?' He said, 'Just a trifle dizzy. You run along.' I left him, but, of course, I did watch to be sure he would be all right. He hurried straight to his bedroom with this box. He hid it there, for when he came out again in a few moments, he no longer carried it. He then locked himself in his study, and within two hours his solicitor came. He could only have sent for him, because Mr. Harris would certainly not otherwise have come to call at that hour."

"You evidently found the intarsia box, Miss Morland."

"My uncle has in his bedroom only a cabinet, a bureau, and an old sea chest which he fancied, and which had accompanied him on his journeys. He served a short term in the Royal Navy as a young man, before entering the foreign service. He acquired the chest at that time. I knew that the box had to be in one of those three places, and I found it carefully covered up in the chest while my uncle was closeted with Mr. Harris. Last night, about eleven o'clock, after he went to sleep, I slipped in and took the box so that I might be ready to come to you without the risk of waking Uncle Burton by taking the box this morning."

"Did your uncle mention the box to anyone?"

"I don't know, Mr. Pons. But I should think that, if he had spoken of it to Mr. Harris, he would have shown it to him. Yet Uncle Burton never left the study while Mr. Harris was in the house; so he could not have done so."

"I see. I think, then, Miss Morland, our only recourse is to ask your uncle the questions you cannot answer."

Our client's hand flew to her lips; an expression of dismay appeared in her eyes. "Oh, Mr. Pons," she cried, "I'm afraid of what Uncle Burton might say."

"Miss Morland, I believe your uncle's life to be in great jeopardy. This belief he evidently shares. He can do no more than refuse to see us, and he can certainly not take umbrage at your attempt to be of service to him."

Her hand fell back to her lap. "Well, that's true," she decided.

Pons looked at the clock. "It is now nine. We can take the Underground at Baker Street and be at Watford Junction within the hour. Let us leave the box, if you please."

Our client sat for but a moment, undecided. Then, pressing her lips determinedly together, she got to her feet. "Very well, Mr. Pons. My uncle can do no worse than give me the back of his tongue!"

As we drew near to the home of Colonel Morland in the cab we had taken at Watford Junction, Pons's face grew more grim. "I fear we are too late, Miss Morland," he said presently.

"Oh, Mr. Pons! Why do you say so?" cried our client.

AUGUST DERLETH

"No fewer than four police vehicles have passed us—two returning, two going our way," he answered. "I should be very much surprised not to find the police at Morland Park."

Miss Morland pressed a handkerchief to her lips.

Nor was Pons in error. Two police cars stood before the tall hedge that separated the parklike grounds which our client indicated as her uncle's home, and a constable stood on guard at the gate in the hedge.

"Young Mecker," murmured Pons at sight of him.

As the cab pulled up, Mecker stepped forward to wave it away. Then, his arm upraised, he recognized Pons getting out. His arm dropped.

"Mr. Pons!" he cried. "How could you have learned?" Then he caught sight of our client. "Could this be Miss Flora Morland?"

"It could be," said our client. "Please! Tell me what has happened?"

"Inspector Jamison has been looking for you, Miss Morland. Please come with me."

"Never mind, Mecker," interposed Pons. "We'll take her in."

"Very well, sir. Thank you, sir." He shook his head, frowning. "Dreadful business, sir, dreadful."

Our client stood for a moment, one hand on Pons's arm, trembling.

"I am afraid, Miss Morland," said Pons with unaccustomed gentleness, "that what your uncle feared has come to pass."

We went up a closely hedged walk arbored over with trees to a classically Georgian country house of two and a half stories. The front door was open to the warm summer morning; just inside it stood the portly figure of Inspector Seymour Jamison of Scotland Yard, talking with another constable. He turned abruptly at our entrance, frowning.

"Mr. Solar Pons, the private enquiry agent," he said heavily. "Do you smell these matters, Pons?" Then his eyes fell upon our client. "Aha! Miss Flora Morland. We've been looking for you, Miss Morland."

"Please! What has happened?" she beseeched him.

"You don't know?"

"I do not."

"Colonel Morland was found murdered in his bed this morning," said Jamison coldly. "The house was locked, no windows had been forced, and you were missing. I must ask you, Miss Morland, to come into the study with me."

"I should like to look into the bedroom, Jamison," said Pons.

"By all means. The photographer is there now, but he should be finished soon. Just down the hall, the third door on the left. Around the stairs."

Our client shot Pons a beseeching glance; he smiled reassuringly. Then she turned and went submissively with Inspector Jamison into the study, which was on the right.

Pons pushed past the police photographer into the late Colonel Moreland's bedroom. Before us lay a frightful scene. Colonel Morland, a tall, broad chested man, lay outspread on his back on his bed, a wavy Malay *kris* driven almost to the hilt into his heart. Most shocking of all—his right hand had been severed at the wrist and lay where it had fallen in a pool of blood on the carpet beside the bed. Gouts of blood had spattered the bed; a froth of blood had welled from the dead man's lips to color his thick mustache; and the wide staring eyes seemed still to wear an expression of the most utter horror.

The room was a shambles. Whoever had slain our client's uncle had torn it apart in search of something. The colonel's sea chest lay open, its contents strewn about. The drawers of the bureau, save for the very smallest at the top, had been pulled open and emptied, and the contents of the tall wardrobe-cabinet, even to the uppermost shelves, were banked about the hassock that stood before it. The sight was almost enough to unnerve a stronger man than I, and I marveled at Pons's cool, keen detachment as he looked searchingly upon the scene.

The photographer, having finished, departed.

"How long would you say he has been dead, Parker?" asked Pons.

I stepped around gingerly and made a cursory examination. "At least eight hours," I said, presently. "I should put it at between midnight and two o'clock—not before, and not very long after."

"Before our client left the house," murmured Pons.

He stood for a moment where he was. Then he stepped gingerly over to the bed and looked down at Colonel Morland's body.

"The *kris* does not appear to have been disturbed," he said, "which suggests that the murderer carried a second weapon solely for the purpose of severing his victim's hand!"

"A ritual weapon! I cried. "And carried away with him!"

Pons smiled lightly. "Cut with a single sweeping stroke, very cleanly," he observed.

He stepped away from the bed and began to move carefully among the objects strewn about, disturbing nothing. He went straight to the bureau, the top of which had evidently not been disturbed, for what I assumed to be the dead man's watch and wallet lay there. The wallet was the first object of Pons's attention; he picked it up and examined its contents.

"Twenty-seven pound notes," he murmured.

"So the object of this search could hardly have been money," I said.

Pons shook his head impatiently. "No, no, Parker—the murderer was looking for the intarsia box. The top of the bureau was not disturbed because, had it been there, the box would have been instantly apparent; nor have the top drawers been opened because they are not deep enough to hold the box."

He moved cautiously to the side of the bed, avoiding the pool of blood which had gushed from Colonel Morland's cleanly severed wrist. "The murderer must have stood just here," he said, and dropped to his knees to scrutinize the carpet intently. He was somewhat hampered by the presence of bloodstains, but I could see by the glint in his eyes that he had seen something of significance, however invisible it was to me, for he gave a small sound of satisfaction, as he picked something from the carpet just back from the edge of the great bed and put it into two of the little envelopes he always carried.

Just as he rose from his position, Inspector Jamison came into the room, wearing a patent glow of confidence.

"Nasty little job here, Pons," he said almost cheerfully. "You'll be sorry to learn I've sent Miss Morland off to the Yard to be put through it."

"Indeed," said Pons. "What admirable—and needlessly precipitate —dispatch! You have reason to think her involved?"

"My dear fellow," said Jamison patronizingly. "Consider. Every window and door of this house was locked. Only four people had keys—Colonel Morland, whose key is on his ring; his valet, who was his batboy in Malacca and who discovered his body; the housekeeper, and Miss Morland. All of their keys are in their possession. Nothing has been forced. Miss Morland, I am told by Mr. Harris, the colonel's counsel, stands to inherit sixty percent of a considerable estate, considerable even after the Crown duties."

"It does not seem to you significant that on so warm a night this house should have been locked up so tightly?" asked Pons.

"You're not having me on that, Pons," retorted Jamison, grinning. "We know all about that intarsia box. Morland was in fear for his life."

"You are suggesting then that Miss Morland slipped into the room, stabbed her uncle, cut off his right hand, searched the room until she turned up the box, and then made her way to Number 7B to enlist my services?"

"Hardly that. She is hardly strong enough to have driven that *kris* into him with such force."

"Hardly," agreed Pons dryly.

"But there is nothing to prevent her having hired an accomplice."

"And what motive could she possibly have had for cutting off her uncle's hand?" pressed Pons.

"What better way could be devised to confuse the investigation into the motive for so gruesome a crime?"

"And Miss Morland seems to you, after your conversation with her, the kind of young lady who could lend herself to such a crime?"

"Come, come, Pons. You have a softness for a pretty face," said Jamison.

"I submit that this would have been a most fantastic rigmarole to go through simply to inherit the wealth of a man who, by all the evidence, granted her every whim. No Jamison, it won't wash."

"That intarsia box—she tells me it is in your possession. We shall have to have it."

"Send round to 7B for it. But give me at least today with it, will you?"

"I'll send for it tomorrow."

"Tell me—you've questioned the servants, I suppose? Did anyone hear anything in the night?"

"Not a sound. And I may say that the dog, which habitually sleeps at the front door of the house, outside, never once was heard to bark. I need hardly tell you the significance of that."

"It suggests that the murderer entered . . . "

"Or was let in."

"By the back door."

Jamison's face reddened. He raised his voice. "It means that since the dog did nothing in the nighttime the murderer was known to him."

Pons clucked sympathetically. "You ought to stay away from Sir Arthur's stories, my dear chap. They have a tendency to vitiate your style."

"I suppose you will be telling us to look for a giant of a man who can charm dogs," said Jamison with heavy sarcasm.

"Quite the contrary. Look for a short, lithe man who, in this case at least, probably went barefooted." He turned and pointed to the scarcely visible hassock. "Only a man shorter than average would have had to use that hassock to look at the top shelves of the cabinet. The indentations

298   AUGUST DERLETH

in the carpet indicate that the hassock's usual position is over against the wall beside the cabinet."

Jamison's glance flashed to the hassock, and returned, frowning, to Pons.

"If you don't mind, Jamison, I'll just have a look around out in back. Then perhaps you could send us back to Watford Junction in one of the police cars."

"Certainly, Pons. Come along."

Jamison led the way out and around the stairs to a small areaway from which doors opened to the kitchen on the right, and a small storeroom on the left, and into the back yard. A maid and an elderly woman, manifestly the housekeeper, sat red-eyed at a table in the kitchen. Jamison hesitated, evidently of the opinion that Pons wished to speak with them, but Pons's interest was in the back door, where he crouched to look at the lock. He really inspected it.

"We've been all through that, Pons," said Jamison with an edge of impatience in his voice.

Pons ignored him. He opened the door, crouched to examine the sill, then dropped to his knees and, on all fours, crawled out to the recently reset flagstone walk beyond it. From one place he took up a pinch of soil and dropped it into one of his envelopes. At another he pointed wordlessly, beckoning to Inspector Jamison, who came and saw the unmistakable print of human toes.

Then Pons sprang up and went back into the house, Jamison and myself at his heels. He found a telephone directory, consulted it briefly, and announced that he was ready to leave, if Jamison would be kind enough to lend us a police car and driver.

Once again on the Underground, I asked Pons, "We're not going back to 7B?"

"No, Parker. I am delighted to observe how well you read me. I daresay we ought to lose no time discovering the secret of the intarsia box. Since Colonel Morland is dead, we shall have to ask Nicholas Morland whether he can explain it. You'll recall that he spent the last five years of his uncle's residency with him. He has an office in the Temple. I took the trouble to look him up in the directory before we left Morland Park."

"I followed the matter of the murderer's height readily enough," I said, "But how did you arrive at his being barefooted?"

"There were in the carpet beside the bed, just where a man might have stood to deliver the death blow, three tiny files of soil particles, in such a position as to suggest the imprint of toes. The soil was quite probably picked up among the flagstones."

"And, you know, Pons—Jamison has a point about the dog."

Pons smiled enigmatically. "The dog did nothing. Very well. Either he knew the murderer—or he didn't hear him, which is quite as likely. A barefooted man could travel with singular noiselessness. And Morland Park is a paradise for prowlers!" He looked at me, his eyes dancing. "Consider the severed hand. Since you are so busy making deductions, perhaps you have accounted for it."

"Now you press me," I admitted, "that seems to me the most elementary detail of all. I suggest that an indignity the late Colonel Morland committed in the past has now been visited upon him."

"Capital! Capital!" cried Pons. "You have only to keep this up, my dear fellow, and I can begin to think of retiring."

"You are making sport of me!" I protested.

"On the contrary. I could not agree with you more. There are one or two little points about the matter that trouble me, but I have no doubt these will be resolved in due time."

For the rest of the journey Pons rode in silent contemplation, his eyes closed, the thumb and forefinger of his right hand ceaselessly caressing the lobe of his ear. He did not open his eyes again until we came into Temple Station.

Nicholas Morland proved to be a somewhat frosty man in his early forties. He was dressed conservatively, but in clothes befitting his station. Save for the difference in years, he was not unlike his late uncle in appearance, with the same kind of mustache, the same outward thrust of the lips, the same bushy brows. His frosty mien was superficial, for it collapsed as he listened to Pons's concise summary of events, and little beads of perspiration appeared at his temples.

"We must rely upon you, Mr. Morland," concluded Pons, "to explain the significance of the intarsia box and its contents."

Morland came shakily to his feet and walked back and forth across his office, biting his lip. "It is something I had hoped never to have to speak about," he said at last. "Is it really necessary, Mr. Pons?"

"I assure you it is. Scotland Yard will expect to hear about it before the day is out. I am here in advance of their coming because I am acting in the interests of your cousin."

AUGUST DERLETH

"Of course. I quite understand. '

He took another turn or two about his office, and then sat down again, dabbing at his forehead with a handkerchief.

"Well, Mr. Pons, it is a matter that does not reflect at all well upon my late uncle," he began. "As Flora may perhaps have told you, Uncle Burton married an Eurasian woman, a very fine, very beautiful woman some ten years his junior—perhaps as much as fifteen, I cannot be sure, though I suspect my wife would know. I am sure you are aware that matters of moral conduct among the ethnically mixed peoples of the Federated States of Malaya are considered lax by British standards, and perhaps it was true that my aunt engaged in improper conduct with Bendarloh Ali, an uncle of my wife's, who belonged to one of the better native families in Malacca. My uncle thought he would lose face, and he set about to prevent it. My aunt died; there is some reason to believe that it was by poison at my uncle's hands. Her lover was arrested. Some valuable items belonging to my uncle were found in his home. He was accused of having stolen them, on no stronger evidence than their presence in his home, and he suffered the indignity of having his right hand cut off at the wrist. That is the sum total of the matter, sir."

"How long ago did this happen, Mr. Morland?"

"Only a month or two before he was sent home. The sultan of Malacca was outraged—though he had approved the punishment, he was later led to repudiate it—and demanded the recall of the resident. The governor really had no alternative but to relieve my uncle of his post."

"Over fifteen years, then. Does it seem likely that he would wait so long to take vengeance?"

"Not he, Mr. Pons. My uncle's victim died three months ago. I think it not inconsistent of the Malay character that his son might believe it incumbent upon him to avenge the honor of his house and the indignity done his father."

"I submit it would be an unnatural son who would separate his father's right hand from his remains," said Pons.

Morland shook his head thoughtfully. "Mr. Pons, I would tend to agree. There is this point to consider. The hand sent my uncle may *not* have been Bendarloh Ali's. Even if it were, I suppose the family represents that ethnic mixture so common in Malacca that no standard of conduct consistent with ancient Malay customs could be ascribed to it."

Pons sat for a few moments in contemplative silence. Then he said,

THE ADVENTURE OF THE INTARSIA BOX

301

"You are very probably aware that you and your cousin will share your uncle's estate."

"Oh, yes. There is no one else. We are a small family, and unless Flora marries, we will very likely die out entirely. Oh, there are distant cousins, but we have not been in touch for many years." He shrugged. "But it's a matter of indifference to me. My practice is quite sufficient for our needs, though I suppose my wife can find a use for what Uncle Burton may leave us, what with the constant innovations at her shop."

The telephone rang suddenly at Morland's elbow. He lifted it to his ear, said, "Morland here," and listened. When he put it down after but a brief period, he said, "Gentlemen, the police are on the way."

Pons got to his feet with alacrity. "One more question, Mr. Morland. Your relations with your uncle—were they friendly, tolerant, distant?"

"The three of us had dinner at Morland Park once a month, Mr. Pons," said Morland a little stiffly.

"Three?"

"My wife's cousin lives with us. Uncle Burton naturally would not exclude him."

"Thank you, sir."

We took our leave.

Outside, Pons strode purposefully along, some destination in mind, his eyes fixed upon an inner landscape. Within a few minutes we were once more on the Underground, and rode in silence unbroken by any word from Pons, until we reached Trafalgar Station and emerged to walk in the Strand.

"Pons," I cried finally, exasperated at his silence. "It's noon. What are we doing here?"

"Ah, patience, Parker, patience. The Strand is one of the most fascinating areas in the world. I mean to idle a bit and shop."

Within half an hour, Pons had exchanged his deerstalker for a conservative summer hat, leaving his deerstalker to be dispatched to our quarters by post; he had bought a light summer coat, which he carried loosely on his arm; and he had added a walking stick to his ensemble, all to my open-mouthed astonishment. He presented quite a different picture from that to which I had become accustomed in the years I had shared his quarters, and he offered no explanation of his purchases.

We continued in the Strand until we came to a small shop modestly proclaiming that antiques and imports were to be had.

"Ah, here we are," said Pons. "I beg you, Parker, keep your face frozen. You have an unhappy tendency to show your reactions on it."

So saying, he went into the shop.

A bell, tinkling in a back room, brought out a dapper, brownskinned man of indeterminate age. He came up to us and bowed. He looked little older than a boy, but he was not a boy. He smiled, flashing his white teeth, and said, "If it please you, gentlemen, I am here to serve you."

"Are you the proprietor?" asked Pons abruptly.

"No, sir. I am Ahmad. I work for Mrs. Morland."

"I am looking," said Pons, "for an intarsia box."

"Ah. Of any precise size?"

"Oh, so—and so," said Pons, describing the size of the intarsia box Miss Morland had brought to our quarters.

"Just so. One moment, if you please."

He vanished into the room to the rear, but came out in a very few moments carrying an intarsia box, which he offered to Pons.

"Seventeenth century Italian, sir. Genuine. I trust this is the box you would like."

"It is certainly exquisite work," said Pons. "But, no, it is not quite what I would like. The size is right. But I would like something with Oriental ornamentation."

"Sir, there are no antique intarsia boxes of Oriental manufacture," said Ahmad. "I am sorry."

"I'm not looking for an antique," said Pons. "I am, of course, aware that intarsia boxes were not made in the Orient before the eighteenth century."

Ahmad's pleasant face brightened. "Ah, in that case, sir, I may have something for you."

He vanished once more into the quarters to the rear of the shop.

When he came out this time he carried another intarsia box. With a triumphant smile, he gave it to Pons. Then he stood back to wait upon Pons's verdict.

Pons turned it over, examining it critically. He opened it, smelled it, caressed it with his fingers, and smiled. "Excellent!" he cried. "This will do very well, young man. What is its price?"

"Ten pounds, sir."

Pons paid for it without hesitation. "Pray wrap it with care. I should not like any of that beautifully wrought carving to be damaged, even scratched."

Ahmand beamed. "Sir, you like the intarsia?"

"Young man, I have some knowledge of these things," said Pons almost pontifically. "This is among the finest work of its kind I have been."

Ahmad backed away from Pons, bowing, his face glowing. He retired once again into the back room, from which presently came the sounds of rustling paper. In just under five minutes Ahmad reappeared and placed the carefully wrapped intarsia box in Pons's hands. He was still glowing with pleasure. Moreover, he had the air of bursting with something he wanted to say, which only decorum prevented his giving voice.

Pons strolled leisurely from the shop and away down the street. But, once out of sight of the shop, he moved with alacrity to hail a cab and gave the driver our Praed Street address.

"Did you not have the feeling that Ahmad wished to tell us something?" I asked when we were on our way.

"Ah, he told us everything," said Pons, his eyes glinting with good humor. "Ahmad is an artist in intarsia. I trust you observed the costly antiques offered in Mrs. Morland's shop?"

"I did indeed."

"It suggested nothing to you?"

"That her business is thriving, as Miss Morland told us." I reached over and tapped the package Pons held. "Did it not seem to you that this box is very much like Miss Morland's?"

Pons smiled. "Once the first box is turned out, the pattern is made. The rest come with comparative ease. They are probably identical, not only with each other, but with a score or more of others."

Back in our quarters, Pons carefully unwrapped the intarsia box he had bought and placed it beside our client's. Except for the fact that there was some difference in age between them, they were virtually identical. Pons examined the boxes with singular attention to detail, finding each smallest variation between them.

"Are they identical or not?" I asked finally.

"Not precisely. The box Miss Morland brought us is at least seventy-five years old; it may be a hundred. It is made of the same beautiful *kamuning* wood out of which the Malays fashion the hilts of their weapons. I trust you observed that the handle of the *kris* which killed Colonel Morland was of this same wood. It has been polished many times and waxed; there is actually some visible wearing away of the wood. The other

AUGUST DERLETH

is a copy of a box like this, made by a skilled artist. I suppose there is a demand for objects of this kind and I have no doubt they are to be had in all the shops which have imported pieces from the Orient for sale. Chinese boxes like this are most frequently in metal or ceramic; wood is more commonly in use from Japan down the coast throughout the Polynesians and Melanesians in the south Pacific." He dismissed the intarsia boxes with a gesture. "But now, let us see what we have from the late Colonel Morland's bedroom."

He crossed to the corner where he kept his chemistry apparatus and settled himself to examine the contents of the envelopes he had used at Morland Park. There were but three of them, and it was unlikely that they would occupy him for long. Since I had a professional call to make at two o'clock, I excused myself.

When I returned within the hour, I found Pons waiting expectantly.

"Ah, Parker," he cried, "I trust you are free for the remainder of the afternoon. I am expecting Jamison and together we may be able to put an end to Scotland Yard's harassing of our client."

"Did you learn anything at the slides?" I asked.

"Only confirmation of what I suspected. The particles of soil I found on the carpet beside the bed were identical with the soil around the flagstone, even to grains of limestone, of which the flagstones are made. There seems to be no doubt but that the soil was carried into the house by the bare toes of the murderer. Other than that, there was also just under the edge of the bed a tiny shaving of camphor wood, which is also commonly used by the Malays who work the jungle produce of that country."

"We are still tied to Colonel Morland's past," I said.

"We have never strayed from it," said Pons shortly. "But thus far in the course of the inquiry, unless Scotland Yard has turned up fingerprints on the handle of the *kris*, we have only presumptive, not convicting, evidence. It is all very well to know the identity of the murderer; the trick is to convict him. Ah, I hear a motor slowing down. That will be Jamison."

Within a moment a car door slammed below, and we heard Jamison's heavy tread on the stairs.

The inspector came into our quarters gingerly carrying a small package, which he surrendered to Pons with some relief. "Here it is, Pons," he said. "I had a little trouble getting the loan of it."

THE ADVENTURE OF THE INTARSIA BOX

"Capital!" cried Pons. He took the package and carried it to the intarsia box he had bought in the shop on the Strand. "I don't suppose you're armed, Jamison?"

"The tradition of the Yard," began Jamison ponderously.

"Yes, yes, I know," said Pons. "Parker, get my revolver."

I went into the bedroom and found Pons's weapon where he had last carelessly laid it down on the bureau.

"Give it to Jamison, will you?"

"I don't know what you're up to, Pons," said Jamison, with some obvious misgiving on his ruddy face. "P'raps that young woman's turned your head."

The contents of the inspector's package had vanished into the intarsia box, which Pons now took up, having resumed the garb he had bought in the Strand shops.

"Let us be off. I want to try an experiment, Jamison. Frankly, it is no more than that. It may succeed. It may not. We shall see."

Our destination was the antique and imports shop in the Strand, and all the way there Pons said nothing, only listened with a sardonic smile on his hawk-like features to Jamison's weighty discourse on the damning circumstances which made our client seem guilty of arranging her uncle's death.

As the police car approached the shop, Pons spoke for the first time to Constable Mecker, who was at the wheel. "Either stop short of the shop or drive past it, Mecker."

Mecker obediently stopped beyond the shop.

"Now, Jamison," said Pons brusquely, as we got out of the car, "hand on gun, and pray be ready. Try to look a little less like a policeman, that's a good fellow."

Pons led the way into the shop, carrying the carefully wrapped intarsia box he had bought only a few hours previously. An extraordinarily handsome Eurasian woman came forward to wait upon him. She was of indeterminate age. She could have been anywhere between twenty and forty, but certainly did not seem over thirty.

"What can I do for you, gentlemen?"

"The young man who waited on me this noon," said Pons, unwrapping the intarsia box as he spoke. "Is he here?"

She nodded, raised her voice to call, "Ahmad!" and stepped back.

Ahmad came out, a look of polite inquiry on his face. He recognized

Pons as his noon hour customer. His eyes fell to the box.

"Sir! You are disappointed?"

"In the beauty of the box, no," said Pons. "But the interior!"

Ahmad stepped lightly forward and took the box, discarding the wrappings. "We shall see," he said, bowing almost obsequiously.

Then he opened the intarsia box.

Instantly, a dramatic and frightening metamorphosis took place. Ahmad's smiling face altered grotesquely. Its mask of politeness washed away to reveal dark murderous features, suffused with sudden rage and fear. He dropped the intarsia box—and from it rolled the severed hand of Colonel Burton Morland! Simultaneously, he leaped backward with a feline movement, tore down from the wall behind him a scimitar-like *chenangka*, and turned threateningly upon Pons.

For scarcely a moment the scene held. Then Mrs. Morland began to waver, and I sprang forward to catch her as she fainted. At the same moment, Inspector Jamison drew his gun upon Ahmad.

"My compliments, inspector," said Pons. "You've just taken the murderer of Colonel Morland. I think," he added blandly, "if I were you I should take Mrs. Nicholas Morland along and question her about the profit motive in the death of her husband's uncle. I believe it almost certain that hers was the brain in which this devilish crime was conceived. Is the lady coming around, Parker?"

"In a few moments," I said.

"Call Mecker," said Jamison, finding his voice.

Pons stepped into the street and shouted for the constable.

"It was not alone the fact that no ship had docked recently from Malaya that made an avenger from the Orient unlikely," said Pons as we rode back to Praed Street on the Underground, "but the same aspect of the matter that so impressed Jamison. The murderer clearly had prior knowledge of Morland Park, something no newly arrived foreigner could have had, and he must have been someone who had ample opportunity to take an impression of the back door key, since he would prefer to enter by that door not guarded by the dog. Nothing in that house was disturbed, save Colonel Morland's room. Not a sound aroused anyone throughout the entry into the house and the commission of the crime.

"Yet it was evident that the murderer also had knowledge of the indignity done to Bendarloh Ali, Miss Morland had no such knowledge. Her cousin Nicholas had. Presumably, since his wife was of Bendarloh

Ali's family, and had been in Malacca at the time Ali was so brutally punished, she knew as much as her husband. It is not too much to conclude that her cousin, who was therefore also of Bendarloh Ali's family, knew the circumstances also. Ahmad, of course, is that cousin. Ahmad had been as frequent a visitor at Morland Park as his employer. He knew the grounds and the house. The shaving of camphor wood, as much a product of Malaya as *kamuning* wood, places Ahmad indisputably in the late Colonel Morland's bedroom.

"Manifestly, the preparations were made with great care. Mrs. Morland directed her relatives to send the hand of Bendarloh Ali to Colonel Morland in the intarsia box which she forwarded to Malay for that purpose. That the box had served as a model for Ahmad's carefully-wrought imitations did not seem to her important, since Ahmad had been instructed to bring the box back from Morland Park. Ahmad undoubtedly killed Colonel Morland to avenge the family honor after Bendarloh Ali died, but I think it inescapable that his desire for vengeance was planted and carefully nourished by Mrs. Nicholas Morland, whose real motive was not vengeance, but the control of the unlimited funds which would be at her disposal when her husband came into his share of his uncle's estate.

"One of our most sanguinary cases, Parker. And though we have taken the murderer, I suspect that the real criminal will go free to enjoy the expansion of her shop according to her plan. It is one of life's little ironies."

AUGUST DERLETH

A Question of Ethics

by James Holding

On this occasion, his contact in Rio was a man called simply Rodolfo. Perhaps Rodolfo had another name, but if so, Manuel Andradas did not know it. He was to meet Rodolfo in the Rua do Ouvidor on a corner by the flower market. While he waited, standing with his back against a building wall on the narrow sidewalk, he looked with admiration at a basket of purple orchids being offered for sale in a flower stall opposite. He wore his camera case slung prominently over his left shoulder.

Rodolfo, when he brushed past Manuel and murmured, "Follow," from the corner of his mouth, proved to be a nondescript, shabbily dressed man. Manuel followed him through the noonday crowd to a small cafe. There, over a cafezinho, they faced each other. Manuel kept his attention on his tiny cup of jet-black coffee. Rodolfo said, "Photographer, would you like a little trip?"

Manuel shrugged.

"To Salvador," Rudolfo said, "Bahia. A beautiful city."

"So I have heard. Is there a deadline?"

"No deadline. But as little delay, Photographer, as possible." Manuel was known to his contacts simply as The Photographer. He *was* a photographer, in truth. And a good one, too.

"The price?" And as he asked the question, Manuel lifted his muddy brown eyes to Rodolfo, and sipped delicately at his coffee.

"Three hundred thousand cruzeiros."

Manuel sucked in his breath. "Your principal must need the work done desperately," he ventured.

Rodolfo smiled, if you could call the oily lift of his lip a smile. "Perhaps," he said. "I do not know. Is it satisfactory?"

"Very generous, yes. Perfectly satisfactory. Expenses, of course, and a third of the price now?"

"*Va bem.*"

The man called Rodolfo idly scratched with a pencil stub on the back of the cafe menu, and turned it toward Manuel. On it, he had written a name and an address. Automatically, Manuel committed them to memory. Then he folded the menu and tore it into tiny pieces and dropped them into the pocket of his neat dark suit. He was frowning.

Watching his expression, Rodolfo said, "What's the matter?"

Manuel said with disapproval, "It's a woman."

Rodolfo laughed. "Business is business, isn't it?"

"I prefer men, that's all," Manuel said.

They rose after draining their coffee cups and turned out into the avenue. Rodolfo, when he shook hands, left a thick pad of currency in Manuel's hand.

Manuel stopped in an open street stall on his way back to his studio and drank a glass of cashew juice. It was better than coffee for settling the nerves, he believed.

Six days later, he went ashore at Bahia from a down-at-the-heels freighter that stopped there on its way north to take on a consignment of cocoa, hides, and castor beans.

Unwilling to invite attention, he walked from the landing place through the teeming traffic of the Baixa to one of the muncipal elevators he could see towering against the cliff above the lower town. The elevator lifted him quickly to the Alta and spewed him out into the municipal square of the upper town. From there, he had a magnificent view over the foliage of fire-red flamboyant trees to the harbor below him, with its lively shipping and quiet fortress.

In the shadowed lobby of the Palace hotel on Rua Chile, he registered for a room under his own name, Manuel Andradas. And for two days thereafter he behaved exactly as a photographer on assignment for a picture magazine might behave. With two cameras draped about him, he visited Bahia's places of interest, taking numerous photographs of everything from the elaborately carved facade of the Church of the Third Order to the Mondrian-like blue and tan egg-crate walls of the new Hotel Bahia. On the third day of his stay, having established for himself in the city the character of a harmless, innocent photographer, he set about his true business in Bahia.

About an hour after noon, he stuffed a pair of swimming shorts into his camera case with his cameras and left the hotel. He walked up Rua Chile

JAMES HOLDING

to the square where scores of buses were angled into parking slots, bearing with mechanical indifference the deluge of propaganda and music that cascaded upon him from loudspeakers placed around the plaza. He swung confidently aboard a bus that was labelled "Rio Vermelho and Amaralina" and took a seat at the rear, a sallow, fine-boned man of quite ordinary appearance except for disproportionately large hands and heavily muscled forearms. Not one among the vociferous, pushing passengers that soon filled the bus to overflowing gave him more than a passing glance.

Manuel closed his eyes and thought of the work ahead. He felt the bus start, heard the excited gabble of the passengers, but did not open his eyes. The name, now? He remembered it perfectly. Eunicia Camarra. Yes. The address? Amaralina, Bahia. Yes.

Eunicia Camarra. A woman. What was she, or what had she done, that somebody in Rio—his formless, nameless, unknown "customer" in Rio—should want her nullified? That was the word Manuel always used to himself: nullified. Was she a faithless mistress, perhaps? A woman who had spurned an offer of marriage? Three hundred thousand cruzeiros was a substantial sum. Perhaps a woman of whom his customer . . . also a woman? . . . was jealous?

Manuel, of course, never knew the truth about his assignments. After the job was done by whatever means seemed most appropriate and practical to Manuel, he never found out the true reason why his professional services had been required. And that was just as well. He preferred to remain emotionally uninvolved in his work. He did each job quietly and efficiently, and avoided becoming entangled in its moral or ethical ramifications.

He put Eunicia Camarra from his mind and opened his eyes. The bus went inland a little way, giving him brief glimpses of raw red earth, patchy gardens, lush tropical foliage. Then its route took the bus back within sight of the sea again, and he felt a cool ocean breeze, entering through the bus windows, begin to dry the slick of perspiration off his face.

At the Amaralina bus stop, he was deposited beside a thatched circular shelter house only a few yards from the beach. Directly before him stood a cafe, scrubbed clean of paint by the endless pummeling of wind and blown sand. It had an open terrace facing the beach. Nearby, a man with shiny white teeth smilingly sold coconuts to half a dozen schoolgirls, hacking off the top of the nuts for them with a machete so that they could drink the sweet milk.

The children's voices, gay with school-is-over-for-the-day spirits, rang merrily in Manuel's ears as he walked slowly past the cafe terrace and up the beach to a tumbledown bathing pavilion where he changed into his swimming trunks. Then he took his camera case and went out to the beach.

There were not many people about. He saw one couple lying in the sand behind some outcropping rocks, completely engrossed in each other. He saw a small knot of bathers off to his right, wading knee deep in the foaming surf and emitting shrill cries of pleasure. Far off to his left, he could see the buildings of Ondina hugging the sapphire bay. And before him, close to the water's edge, the same schoolgirls he had noticed buying coconuts were cavorting in the sand.

He went and sat on the sand near the children, cradling his camera case in his hands. The girls wore a simple blue and white school uniform, he saw, and were approximately of the same age . . . twelve or thirteen, perhaps. He smiled at them and greeted them gravely, *"Bons dias, senhoritas."* That was all. He didn't push himself forward. He was more subtle than that. When they returned his greeting, they saw the camera case in his hands. And at once, they evinced a lively interest in it, especially the blonde child who seemed to be the leader of the group.

She approached Manuel. "Is there a camera in that case?" she asked, "May we please see it? Will you take our picture? Are your photos in color? What kind of *pellicula* do you find most satisfactory, *senhor?* Will you show me how to adjust the lens so that I may take a photo also?"

This was said so breathlessly, so beguilingly, with such animated childish curiosity, that Manuel laughed in spite of himself and said, "Not quite so fast, senhorita, if you please! So many questions all at once! Yes, it contains a camera. Several of them. And yes, you may have a quick look at them, but be careful not to get any grains of sand in them." He held out the camera case and the children clustered around it, chattering and exclaiming. The little girl who had requested the privilege of seeing his camera opened the case.

"Wonder!" she said. "A Leica! It is very expensive, no? My grandmother has one." She delved deeper. "And a baby camera!" she exclaimed, holding up Manuel's Minox. "Such a small camera I have never seen."

Manuel sat quietly in the sand and let the children handle his equipment, keeping an eye on them to prevent damage, however. Then he

JAMES HOLDING

said, "I shall take a photo of you now, all in your school uniforms." They stood demurely together, smiling while he snapped their picture.

The blonde child said, "Will you send us the picture? My grandmother would like to see it."

"Certainly," Manuel said. "And I shall not charge you for it, though I am a professional photographer and get large sums for my work."

"Oh, thank you, senhor," the blonde girl said. Manuel nodded to her, realizing with satisfaction that he had now so ingratiated himself with these children that they would answer eagerly any questions he chose to ask them; questions about Amaralina, their homes, their neighbors, their parents' friends, even questions, no doubt, about a woman named Eunicia Camarra. But there was no hurry.

The blonde child said, "Are you going into the water, senhor? If so, we will care for your cameras while you bathe. No harm shall come to them." She appealed to her friends; they chorused agreement.

"Why not?" Manuel said. "If you will be so kind. *Muito obrigado.*" And in rising to enter the water, he made his first mistake. But he was hot and sweaty, and a swim would be welcome, even though he was not a good swimmer. And the girls would remain until he came back, because they would be watching his cameras for him.

"Have a care, there by the rocks," the blonde child said. "There is a strong current there."

He scarcely heard her. His mind was on other things. And only when he had plunged boldly into the water and stroked his way some distance out from shore did he fully comprehend what the child had said. Then it was almost too late. He felt himself in the grip of a force too powerful for even his big hands and muscled arms to resist. His head went under the water and he choked. And he thought, foolishly, how much better to remain hot and sweaty than to cool off at such a price. Then he couldn't think any more at all.

When he opened his eyes, the glaring blue of the sky hurt them. He was lying on his back in the sand. He felt weak, sick. And as he shifted his pained gaze, it centered on the skinny naked body of the blonde girl standing not far from him, about to drop her grubby uniform dress over her head to cover her wet skin. Near her, as his eyes turned, were two of the other schoolgirls, also engaged in slipping on their dresses over wet bodies. He made a choking, grunting sound and sat up suddenly.

The girls screamed and went on wriggling happily into their dresses. "Do not look, senhor!" the blonde child cried gaily. "We must first arrange our clothing! We have been swimming without suits." The other girls' laughing voices joined hers like the twittering of small parrots. Manuel shook his head to clear it, coughing water onto the sand. The little blonde girl was saying, "We warned you, senhor. There is a strong undertow. You paid no attention!" She scolded him gently, but he could tell that she was mightily pleased he had ignored her warning so that she and her friends might have the marvelous excitement of saving him from the sea. "We are all excellent swimmers," she continued chidingly, "because we live here in Amaralina. But you are not a good swimmer, senhor." She smiled at him. "But we pulled you out. Maria and Letitia and I." Scornfully she said, "The others ran away."

Now Manuel Andradas felt a wave of a very unfamiliar emotion sweep through him, and he said, "Senhoritas, I owe you my life. I am grateful. I thank you from my heart." They were embarrassed.

He looked at the blonde child, who was combing her fingers through her wet taffy-colored hair, and asked with a premonition of disaster, *"Come se chama?* What is your name?"

"Eunicia Camarra," she said. "What is yours?"

He sent the other children home with his thanks, but prevailed upon Eunicia to stay a little longer on the beach with him. "I wish to take your picture again," he explained. "Alone. To have a record of the lady who saved my life." And curiously enough, he found himself for the first time in his career regarding a proposed victim with something besides cold objectivity. He felt an unaccustomed lift of his heart when he looked at Eunicia—an emotion compounded of gratitude, admiration, liking and strangest of all, tenderness, almost as though she were his own child, he thought vaguely. At the end, after snapping her in a series of childish, charming poses, he said on an impulse, "Now show me how I looked when you pulled me from the water and dragged me onto the beach."

She laughed delightedly and flopped down like a rag doll on the sand. Her arms were disposed limply at her sides; her legs lay loosely asprawl; the closed eyes in her thin face were turned up to the sky; and her mouth gaped. She looked remarkably like a corpse. Manuel leaned over her then, and used his Minox to snap her like that.

And all the time, they were talking.

JAMES HOLDING

"Do you live here with your mother and father?" he asked.

"Oh, no, senhor Andradas, my mother and father are dead. I live with my grandmother, in that big house up there on the hill." She waved inland.

"I see. A big house, you say. Your grandmother is a rich woman, I suppose. Not likely to want you saving the life of a poor photographer."

She was indignant. "My grandmother is a great lady," she averred stoutly. "But of course, she is very rich, as you say. After all, when my grandfather was alive, was he not the greatest diamond merchant in Brazil?"

"Was he?"

"So my grandmother says."

"Then I am sure it is true. And you are alone there with your grandmother, eh?" He peered at her with his muddy eyes. "No brothers or sisters or relatives to keep you company?"

"None," she said sadly. Then she brightened. "But I have a half brother in Rio. He is an old man now, over thirty I believe, but he is my half brother nevertheless. His mother was the same as mine," she explained importantly. "But a different father, you see?"

Manuel was, in truth, beginning to see. "Your grandmother does not like your half brother?" he guessed.

"No. She says he is *malo*. A liar and a cheat and a disgrace to her family. My mother ran away and married when she was too young. And brother Luis was born then. I feel sorry for him, because his father is dead, like mine. I write to him sometimes, but I do not tell my grandmother."

"I can see that you might not want her to know," Manuel agreed gravely.

"Especially when she will not help him, even with money. And he asks her many times, I know. She refuses, always."

"Perhaps she will leave him some money in her will when she dies."

"Oh, no, she will not. I am to have it all. Luis will not get a penny, grandmother says, while anybody else is alive in the family. She has no patience with brother Luis, you see. Poor Luis. But I think he is quite nice. I shall go to Rio and visit him and do his cooking for him," she finished in a dreaming voice, "when grandmother gives me enough money."

"You've never seen him?"

"No. Only his picture. He sent me a picture in a letter last year, the one in which he asked whether Grandmother had softened toward him. And I sent him a picture of me when I answered. He's quite handsome, really."

"What is his name?" Manuel said.

"Luis Ferreira."

"Does he have a job?"

"Yes. He works in the office of the Aranha hotel."

After he had changed out of his swimming trunks in the pavilion, Manuel took Eunicia up to the cafe terrace and, with unaccustomed generosity, bought her a bottle of orange pop. She guzzled the pop energetically. Then she went home, saying her grandmother would be anxious if she didn't soon appear. Manuel said in parting, "I am very grateful, Eunicia. Perhaps I shall be able to do you a service in return."

Long after she had gone, he sat alone on the cafe terrace, crouching uncomfortably on a fixed pedestal seat beside a square slate table, and stared out across the beach at the foam-laced sea. He ordered three Cinzanos and drank them down rapidly, one after the other, wrestling with his unexpected problem. Three hundred thousand cruzeiros! The whole thing, he thought gloomily, had now come down simply to a question of ethics.

He wished he had a glass of cashew juice.

Manuel Andradas returned to Rio on the night plane that evening. He went from the airport directly to his studio, developed the Minox film he had exposed in Bahia, and carefully examined the tiny negatives with a magnifying glass before selecting one and making a blown up print of it. He called the anonymous telephone number that eventually put him in touch with the man called Rodolfo, and arranged to meet him again in the Rua do Ouvidor in the morning. Then he went to bed and slept dreamlessly.

Next day, he showed the print to the man called Rodolfo. "It was not a woman," he said with disapproval. "It was a child."

Rodolfo examined the photograph of Eunicia. It showed her lying limp and unquestionably dead on the beach at Amaralina. He nodded with satisfaction. "This should be adequate proof," he said. He kept looking at the picture. Then he smiled. "Even the young donkey sometimes loses its footing," he said sententiously. "May I keep this photograph? It will

JAMES HOLDING

be passed along to our principal. And if all is well, I shall meet you at the same place tomorrow afternoon at three."

He went off with Manuel's print. And at three the next afternoon, he met Manuel again near the flower market and paused only long enough to shake his hand and say, "Good work. Satisfactory." This time, he left an even thicker pad of currency in Manuel's hand than when first they had met.

Manuel pocketed the banknotes almost casually, and hailed a taxi. In it, he had himself driven to Copacabana Beach, where he descended about a block from the Aranha hotel on Avenida Atlantica. Dismissing the cab, he glanced appraisingly at the wide beach, peopled at this hour of the afternoon by bathers as numerous as ants on a dropped sugar cake. Then he entered the public telephone booth across the street, called the Aranha hotel, and was soon talking in a purposely muffled voice to Senhor Luis Ferreira, one of the hotel's bookkeepers.

All he said to him, however, was, "I have a message for you from Bahia, Senhor Ferreira. Meet me on the beach across from your hotel in ten minutes. By the kite-seller's stand." He waited for no reply, but hung up and left the booth.

Then he strolled up the beach toward the hotel, automatically picking his way between the thousands of sea and sun worshippers scattered on the sand. Near the small dark man who sold bird-kites to the children he stationed himself, an unnoticed member of the holiday crowd. From the corners of his eyes, he watched the hotel entrance.

Soon a slightly stooped young man with a receding chin and thinning blond hair, came out of the hotel door, dodged through the rushing traffic of the avenue to the beach, and approached the kite salesman. He paused there, looking with worried eyes at the people around him. The beach was crowded; any one of all those thousands could be the message-bringer from Bahia. He looked at his wrist watch, gauging the ten minutes Manuel had mentioned. And Manuel was sure, then, that this was Luis Ferreira, and none other . . . the half brother of Eunicia Camarra.

Manuel stepped quietly toward him through the hodge-podge of bathers. As he did so, he withdrew his hand from his pocket, and brought out with it, concealed in the palm, a truncated dart of the kind, with a long metal point, that is used to throw at a cork target. The dart had its point filed to a needle sharpness; half the wooden shaft had been cut off, so that the dart handle fitted easily into Manuel's hand with only a half inch of needle projecting. And on the needle's point was thickly smeared a dark, tarry substance.

Several customers were clustered around the kite seller. Four youths were playing beach ball three yards away. A fat man and a thin woman lay on the sand, almost at Ferreira's feet.

Approaching Ferreira, Manuel seemed to stumble over the outthrust foot of the fat sunbather. He staggered a bit, and his heavy boot came down with sickening force on the instep of Luis Ferreira. Manuel threw out his hands as though to catch himself. And in that act, the point of the dart entered deeply into Ferreira's wrist, just below his coat sleeve.

Ferreira did not notice. The prick of the needle was overlooked in the excruciating pain of his trodden instep. He jumped back and cursed. Manuel apologized for his clumsiness and walked on up the beach, losing himself in the crowd within seconds.

He neither hurried enough to be conspicuous, nor lagged enough to waste precious time. Nor did he look back. Not even when he left the beach after a few blocks and walked briskly down Avenida Atlantica toward the city's center did he so much as turn his head toward where he had left Ferreira. What need? He knew perfectly well what was happening back there.

Already the curare from the dart point would have completed its deadly work. Ferreira's body would be lying upon the beach, still unnoticed, perhaps, among all those reclining figures, but with the motor nerve endings in its striated muscles frozen and helpless, the beating of its heart soon to be forever stilled by the paralyzing drug. In three minutes or less, Ferreira would be dead. That was certain. And the blonde child of Bahia who had so strangely touched the long-dormant buds of affection in Manuel Andradas was safe from harm.

Manuel permitted himself a chuckle as he walked toward town. If someone saves your life, he thought, you owe them a life in return. And if someone pays for a death, you owe them a death for their money.

He smiled, his muddy brown eyes looking straight ahead.

This question of ethics, he thought, is not so difficult after all.

JAMES HOLDING

A Hint of Henbane

by Frederick Pohl and C.M. Kornbluth

I used to think that my wife systematically lied to me about her family, but one by one I met them and found her tales were all true. There was Uncle H—, for one. He earned his unprintable nickname on the day in 1937 when he said to the bank examiner, "Oh, H—!," walked right down to the depot, and got on a westbound train, never to return. He sounded like a wish-fulfillment myth, but two summers ago we drove through Colorado and looked him up. Uncle H—was doing fine; brown as a berry, and gave us bear ham out of his own smokehouse for lunch. And, just the way the story went, his shanty was papered with color comics from the Chicago Sunday *Tribune*.

Uncle Edgar, the salesman, was real, too. Sarah claimed that in 1942 he had sold a Wisconsin town the idea of turning over its municipal building to him so he could start a defense plant. Well, last year I visited him in his executive suite, which used to be the mayor's office. He had converted to roller skates. Whenever anyone hinted to him that he might start paying rent or taxes or something he would murmur quietly that he was thinking of moving plant and payroll to Puerto Rico, and then there would be no more hinting for a while.

Grandma and Grandpa were right off the cover of the *Saturday Evening Post*, rocking and dozing on the porch of their big house. Grandpa, if pressed, would modestly display his bullet scars from the Oklahoma land rush, and Sarah assured me that Grandma had some, too. Great-grandmother, pushing the century mark a couple of miles down the road, gloomily queened it over five hundred central Ohio acres from her dusty plush bedroom. She decided in '35 to take to her bed, and there she had stayed while suburban housing developments and shopping centers and drive-in movies encroached on the old farm and the money rolled in. Sarah had a grudging respect for her, though she had seen her will and her money was all going to a Baptist mission in Naples, Italy.

There was even, at last, a strained sort of peace between Sarah and her father. He came out of World War One with a D.S.C., a silver plate in his skull, and a warped outlook on civilian life. He was a bootlegger throughout most of the twenties. It made for an unpleasant childhood. When it was too late to do the children much good, the V.A. replaced his silver plate with a tantalum plate and he promptly enrolled in a theological seminary and wound up a Lutheran pastor in Southern California.

Sarah's attitude toward all the aforementioned is partly "judge not lest ye be judged" and partly "so what?," but of her cousin's husband, Bill Oestreicher, she said dogmatically: "He's a lousy so-and-so."

We used to see more of him than the rest of the family, as an unavoidable side effect of visiting Sarah's Cousin Claire, to whom he was married. Sarah was under some special indebtedness to Cousin Claire. I think Claire used to take her in during the rough spells with Dad.

On the way to meet them for the first time—they lived in Indiana, an easy drive from Detroit—Sarah told me: "Try to enjoy the scenery, because you won't enjoy Bill. Did I warn you not to lend him money or go into any kind of business deal with him?"

"You did."

"And another thing, don't talk to him about your own business. Uncle Edgar let him mail a couple of customers' statements for him, and Bill went to the customers offering to undercut Edgar's prices. There was great confusion for a month and Edgar lost two customers to the Japs. To this day Bill can't understand why Edgar won't talk to him any more."

"I'll come out fighting and protect my chin at all times."

"You'd better."

Claire was a dark, birdlike little woman with an eager-to-please air, very happy to see Sarah and willing to let some of it splash over onto me. She had just come from work. She was a city visiting nurse and wore a snappy blue cape and hat. Even after eight hours of helping a nineteen-year-old girl fight D.T.'s she was neat, every hair in place. I suspected a compulsion. She wore a large, incongruous costume-jewelry sort of ring which I concluded to be a dime-store anniversary present from good old Bill.

Bill's first words to me were: "Glad to meet you, Tommy. Tommy, how much money can you raise in a pinch?" I came out fighting. I've got an automotive upholstery business with a few good accounts. The Ford buyer could ruin me overnight by drawing a line through my name on his list, but until that happens I'm solvent. I concealed this from Bill. It was easy. At fifty-odd he was a fat infant. He was sucking on candy sourballs, and when he had crunched them up he opened a box of Cracker Jack. I never saw him when he wasn't munching, gulping, sucking. Beer, gum, chocolate, pretzels—he was the only person I ever saw who *lapped* pretzels—pencils, the earpieces of his hornrimmed glasses, the ends of his mustache. Slop, slurp, slop. With his mouth open.

Bill maneuvered me into the kitchen, sucked on a quartered orange and told me he was going to let me in on a can't-miss scrap syndicate which would buy army surplus and sell it right back to the government at full price. I told him no he wasn't.

His surprise was perfectly genuine. "What do you want to be like that for?" he asked, round-eyed, and went over it again with pencil and paper, sucking on the end of the pencil when he wasn't scribbling with it, and when I said no again he got angry.

"Tommy, what're you being so stupid for? Can't you see I'm just trying to give one of Claire's people a helping hand? Now *listen* this time, I haven't got all day."

Well, what can you do? I told him I'd think about it.

He shook my hand. Between chomps and slurps he said it was a wise decision; if I could pony up say five thousand we'd get under way with a rush; and had I thought of a second mortgage on my house?

"Let's celebrate it," he said. "Claire. *Claire, don't you hear me?*"

She popped in. "Case of beer," he said. He didn't even look at her.

"The beauty of this, Tommy, is it's air force money. Who's going to say no when the air force wants to buy something? Tommy, what about borrowing on your insurance?"

Cousin Claire came staggering up from the basement with a case of twenty-four bottles of beer. "Nice and cold," she panted. "From the north corner."

He said, "Giddadahere. Now the markup—" She fluttered out. He turned to the case of beer and his eyes popped. "How do you like that?" he asked me incredulously. "She didn't open any. She must have thought I wanted to *look* at beer."

"Well," I said, "you know." Martyred, he got a bottle opener from a drawer.

Driving back to Detroit I was in a state of shock for about twenty miles.

Finally I was able to ask Sarah: "*Why* in God's name did she marry him?"

She said helplessly: "I think it's because they won't let you be an old maid any more. She got middle-aged, then she got panicky, Bill turned up and they were married. He gets a job once in a while. His people are in politics. . . . She's still got her ring," Sarah said with pride.

"Huh?"

"The Charlier ring. Topaz signet—didn't you see it?"

"What about it?"

"Bill's been trying to get it away from her since they were married, but *I'm* going to get it next. It's family. It's a big topaz and it swivels. One side is plain and the other side has the Charlier crest and it's a poison ring."

I honked at a convertible that was about to pull out in front and kill us. "You'll hate me for this," I said, "but there aren't any poison rings. There never were."

"Nuts to you," she said, indignant. "I've opened it with my own little fingers. It comes apart in two little slices of topaz and there's a hollow for the poison."

"Not poison. Maybe a saint's relic, or a ladylike pinch of snuff. In the olden days they didn't have poisons that fitted into little hollows. You had to use *quarts* of what they had. Everything you've heard to the contrary is bunk because everybody used to think everybody else had powerful, subtle poisons. Now, of course, we've got all kinds—"

She wasn't listening. "Somebody unwisely told Bill that the Ford Museum offered Grandmother a thousand dollars for the ring. Ever since then he's been after her to sell it so he can 'put the money into business.' But she won't. . . . .She doesn't look well, Tommy." I spared a second from the traffic to glance at her. There were tears in her eyes.

A week later began a series of semi-literate, petulant letters from Cousin Bill.

He was, or said he was, under the impression that I had pledged my sacred word of honor to put up $30,000 and go in with him on the junk deal. I answered the first letter, trying to set him straight, and ignored the rest when I realized he couldn't be set straight. Not by me, not by anybody. The world was what he wanted it to be. If it failed him, he screamed and yelled at the world until it got back into line.

We saw them a couple of months later. He bore me no malice. He tried to get me to back a chain of filling stations whose gimmick would be a special brand of oil—filtered crankcase drainings, picked up for a song, dyed orange, and handsomely packaged. He took to using my company name as a credit reference, and I had my lawyer write him a letter, after which he took to using my lawyer's name as a credit reference. We saw him again and he still was not angry. Munching and slobbering and prying, he just didn't understand how I could be so stupid as not to realize that he wanted to help me. At every visit he was fatter and Claire was thinner.

He complained about it. Licking the drips off the side of an ice cream cone he said: "You ought to have more meat on your bones, the way the grocery bills run."

"Has it ever occurred to you," Sarah snapped, "that your wife might be a sick woman?"

Cousin Claire made shushing noises. Cousin Bill chewed the cone, looking at her. "No kidding," he said, licking his finger. "For god's sake, Claire. We got Blue Cross, Blue Shield, City Health, we been paying all these years, won't cost a nickel. What's the matter with you? You go get a checkup."

"I'll be all right," said Cousin Claire, buttering a slice of pound cake for her husband.

Afterwards I burst out: "All right, I'm not a doctor, I supply auto upholstery fabrics, but can't you get her into a hospital?"

Sarah was very calm. "I understand now. She knows what she's doing. In Claire's position—what would *you* do?"

I thought it over and said, "Oh," and after that drove very carefully. It occurred to me that we had something to live for, and that Cousin Claire obviously had not.

My wife phoned me at the office a few weeks later and she was crying. "The mail's just come. A letter from a nurse, a friend of Claire's. Bill's put her in the hospital."

"Well, Sarah, I mean, isn't that where she ought to—"

"No!" So that night we drove to Indiana and went directly to Claire's hospital room—her one-seventh of a room, that is. Bill had put her in a ward. But she was already dead.

We drove to their house, ostensibly to get a burial dress for Cousin Claire, perhaps really to knock Cousin Bill down and jump on his face. Sarah had seen the body. The ring was not on Claire's finger. It was not in the effects I checked out at the desk, either. "He took it," Sarah said.

"I know. Because she was three weeks dying, the floor nurse told me. And Claire told me she knew it was coming and she had hyoscine in the ring." So Sarah had her triumph after all; the ring had become a poison ring, for a sick, despairing woman's quick way out of disappointment and pain. "The lousy so-and-so," Sarah said. "Tommy, I want her buried with the ring."

I felt her trembling. Well, so was I. He had taken the ring from a woman too sick to protect herself and for the sake of a thousand lousy bucks and had cheated her out of her exit. I don't mean that. I'm a businessman. There is nothing lousy about a thousand bucks, but . . . I wanted to bury her with the ring, too.

No one answered the front door, and when we went around to the pantry and found it open we found out why. Bill was slumped in a kitchen chair facing us, a spilled bottle of beer tacky on the linoleum, a bag of pretzels open in front of him and his finger in his mouth. You know what hyoscine is? They used to get it from henbane before they learned to put it together in a test tube more cheaply. It was a good, well-considered substance for a nurse to put in her ring because it kills like *that*. Bill had not been able to resist taking the ring from her. And then he had not been able to resist putting it in his mouth.

FREDERICK POHL AND C.M. KORNBLUTH

The Cold Equations

by Tom Godwin

He was not alone.

There was nothing to indicate the fact but the white hand of the tiny gauge on the board before him. The control room was empty but for himself; there was no sound other than the murmur of the drives—but the white hand had moved. It had been on zero when the little ship was launched from the *Stardust*; now, an hour later, it had crept up. There was something in the supplies closet across the room, it was saying, some kind of a body that radiated heat.

It could be but one kind of a body—a living, human body.

He leaned back in the pilot's chair and drew a deep, slow breath, considering what he would have to do. He was an EDS pilot, inured to the sight of death, long since accustomed to it and to viewing the dying of another man with an objective lack of emotion, and he had no choice in what he must do. There could be no alternative—but it required a few moments of conditioning for even an EDS pilot to prepare himself to walk across the room and coldly, deliberately, take the life of a man he had yet to meet.

He would, of course, do it. It was the law, stated very bluntly and definitely in grim Paragraph L, Section 8, of Interstellar Regulations: *Any stowaway discovered in an EDS shall be jettisoned immediately following discovery.*

It was the law, and there could be no appeal.

It was a law not of men's choosing but made imperative by the circumstances of the space frontier. Galactic expansion had followed the development of the hyperspace drive and as men scattered wide across the frontier there had come the problem of contact with the isolated first-colonies and exploration parties. The huge hyperspace cruisers were the product of the combined genius and effort of Earth and were long and expensive in the building. They were not available in such numbers that small colonies could possess them. The cruisers carried the colonists to their new worlds and made periodic visits, running on tight schedules, but they could not stop and turn aside to visit colonies scheduled to be visited at another time; such a delay would destroy their schedule and produce a confusion and uncertainty that would wreck the complex interdependence between old Earth and the new worlds of the frontier.

Some method of delivering supplies or assistance when an emergency occurred on a world not scheduled for a visit had been needed and the Emergency Dispatch Ships had been the answer. Small and collapsible, they occupied little room in the hold of the cruiser; made of light metal and plastics, they were driven by a small rocket drive that consumed relatively little fuel. Each cruiser carried four EDS's and when a call for aid was received the nearest cruiser would drop into normal space long enough to launch an EDS with the needed supplies or personnel, then vanish again as it continued on its course.

The cruisers, powered by nuclear converters, did not use the liquid rocket fuel, but nuclear converters were far too large and complex to permit their installation in the EDS's. The cruisers were forced by necessity to carry a limited amount of the bulky rocket fuel and the fuel was rationed with care, the cruisers' computers determining the exact amount of fuel each EDS would require for its mission. The computers considered the course coördinates, the mass of the EDS, the mass of pilot and cargo; they were very precise and accurate and omitted nothing from their calculations. They could not, however, foresee, and allow for, the added mass of a stowaway.

The *Stardust* had received the request from one of the exploration parties stationed on Woden; the six men of the party already being stricken with the fever carried by the green *kala* midges and their own supply of serum destroyed by the tornado that had torn through their camp. The *Stardust* had gone through the usual procedure; dropping into normal space to launch the EDS with the fever serum, then vanishing again in hyperspace. Now, an hour later, the gauge was saying there was something more than the small carton of serum in the supplies closet.

He let his eyes rest on the narrow white door of the closet. There, just inside, another man lived and breathed and was beginning to feel assured that discovery of his presence would now be too late for the pilot to alter the situation. It *was* too late—for the man behind the door it was far later than he thought and in a way he would find terrible to believe.

TOM GODWIN

There could be no alternative. Additional fuel would be used during the hours of deceleration to compensate for the added mass of the stowaway; infinitesimal increments of fuel that would not be missed until the ship had almost reached its destination. Then, at some distance above the ground that might be as near as a thousand feet or as far as tens of thousands of feet, depending upon the mass of ship and cargo and the preceding period of deceleration, the unmissed increments of fuel would make their absence known; the EDS would expend its last drops of fuel with a sputter and go into whistling free fall. Ship and pilot and stowaway would merge together upon impact as a wreckage of metal and plastic, flesh and blood, driven deep into the soil. The stowaway had signed his own death warrant when he concealed himself on the ship; he could not be permitted to take seven others with him.

He looked again at the telltale white hand, then rose to his feet. What he must do would be unpleasant for both of them; the sooner it was over, the better. He stepped across the control room, to stand by the white door.

"Come out!" His command was harsh and abrupt above the murmur of the drive.

It seemed he could hear the whisper of a furtive movement inside the closet, then nothing. He visualized the stowaway cowering closer into one corner, suddenly worried by the possible consequences of his act and his self-assurance evaporating.

"I said *out!*"

He heard the stowaway move to obey and he waited with his eyes alert on the door and his hand near the blaster at his side.

The door opened and the stowaway stepped through it, smiling. "All right—I give up. Now what?"

It was a girl.

He stared without speaking, his hand dropping away from the blaster and acceptance of what he saw coming like a heavy and unexpected physical blow. The stowaway was not a man—she was a girl in her teens, standing before him in little white gypsy sandals with the top of her brown, curly head hardly higher than his shoulder, with a faint, sweet scent of perfume coming from her and her smiling face tilted up so her eyes could look unknowing and unafraid into his as she waited for his answer.

Now what? Had it been asked in the deep, defiant voice of a man he would have answered it with action, quick and efficient. He would have taken the stowaway's identification disk and ordered him into the air lock. Had the stowaway refused to obey, he would have used the blaster. It would not have taken long; within a minute the body would have been ejected into space—had the stowaway been a man.

He returned to the pilot's chair and motioned her to seat herself on the boxlike bulk of the drive-control units that sat against the wall beside him. She obeyed, his silence making the smile fade into the meek and guilty expression of a pup that has been caught in mischief and knows it must be punished.

"You still haven't told me," she said. "I'm guilty, so what happens to me now? Do I pay a fine, or what?"

"What are you doing here?" he asked. "Why did you stow away on this EDS?"

"I wanted to see my brother. He's with the government survey crew on Woden and I haven't seen him for ten years, not since he left Earth to go into government survey work."

"What was your destination on the *Stardust*?"

"Mimir. I have a position waiting for me there. My brother has been sending money home all the time to us—my father and mother and I—and he paid for a special course in linguistics I was taking. I graduated sooner than expected and I was offered this job on Mimir. I knew it would be almost a year before Gerry's job was done on Woden so he could come on to Mimir and that's why I hid in the closet, there. There was plenty of room for me and I was willing to pay the fine. There were only the two of us kids—Gerry and I—and I haven't seen him for so long, and I didn't want to wait another year when I could see him now, even though I knew I would be breaking some kind of a regulation when I did it."

I knew I would be breaking some kind of a regulation—in a way, she could not be blamed for her ignorance of the law; she was of Earth and had not realized that the laws of the space frontier must, of necessity, be as hard and relentless as the environment that gave them birth. Yet, to protect such as her from the results of their own ignorance of the frontier, there had been a sign over the door that led to the section of the *Stardust* that housed the EDS's; a sign that was plain for all to see and heed:

UNAUTHORIZED PERSONNEL
KEEP OUT!

"Does your brother know that you took passage on the *Stardust* for

Mimir?"

"Oh, yes. I sent him a spacegram telling him about my graduation and about going to Mimir on the *Stardust* a month before I left Earth. I already knew Mimir was where he would be stationed in a little over a year. He gets a promotion then, and he'll be based on Mimir and not have to stay out a year at a time on field trips, like he does now."

There were two different survey groups on Woden, and he asked, "What is his name?"

"Cross—Gerry Cross. He's in Group Two—that was the way his address read. Do you know him?"

Group One had requested the serum; Group Two was eight thousand miles away, across the Western Sea.

"No, I've never met him," he said, then turned to the control board and cut the deceleration to a fraction of a gravity; knowing as he did so that it could not avert the ultimate end, yet doing the only thing he could do to prolong that ultimate end. The sensation was like that of the ship suddenly dropping and the girl's involuntary movement of surprise half lifted her from the seat.

"We're going faster now, aren't we?" she asked. "Why are we doing that?"

He told her the truth.

"To save fuel for a little while."

"You mean, we don't have very much?"

He delayed the answer he must give her so soon to ask: "How did you manage to stow away?"

"I just sort of walked in when no one was looking my way," she said. "I was practicing my Gelanese on the native girl who does the cleaning in the ship's supply office when someone came in with an order for supplies for the survey crew on Woden. I slipped into the closet there after the ship was ready to go and just before you came in. It was an impulse of the moment to stow away, so I could get to see Gerry—and from the way you keep looking at me so grim, I'm not sure it was a very wise impulse.

"But I'll be a model criminal—or do I mean prisoner?"

She smiled at him again.

"I intended to pay for my keep on top of paying the fine. I can cook and I can patch clothes for everyone and I know how to do all kinds of useful things, even a little bit about nursing."

There was one more question to ask:

"Did you know what the supplies were that the survey crew ordered?"

"Why, no. Equipment they needed in their work, I supposed."

Why couldn't she have been a man with some ulterior motive? A fugitive from justice, hoping to lose himself on a raw new world; an opportunist, seeking transportation to the new colonies where he might find golden fleece for the taking; a crackpot, with a mission—

Perhaps once in his lifetime an EDS pilot would find such a stowaway on his ship; warped men, mean and selfish men, brutal and dangerous men—but never, before, a smiling, blue-eyed girl who was willing to pay her fine and work for her keep that she might see her brother.

He turned to the board and turned the switch that would signal the *Stardust*. The call would be futile but he could not, until he had exhausted that one vain hope, seize her and thrust her into the air lock as he would an animal—or a man. The delay, in the meantime, would not be dangerous with the EDS deceleration at fractional gravity.

A voice spoke from the communicator. "*Stardust*. Identify yourself and proceed."

"Barton, EDS 34G11. Emergency. Give me Commander Delhart."

There was a faint confusion of noises as the request went through the proper channels. The girl was watching him, no longer smiling.

"Are you going to order them to come back after me?" she asked.

The communicator clicked and there was the sound of a distant voice saying, "Commander, the EDS requests—"

"Are they coming back after me?" she asked again. "Won't I get to see my brother, after all?"

"Barton?" The blunt, gruff voice of Commander Delhart came from the communicator. "What's this about an emergency?"

"A stowaway," he answered.

"A stowaway?" There was a slight surprise to the question. "That's rather unusual—but why the 'emergency' call? You discovered him in time so there should be no appreciable danger, and I presume you've informed Ship's Records so his nearest relatives can be notified."

"That's why I had to call you, first. The stowaway is still aboard and the circumstances are so different—"

"Different?" the commander interrupted, impatience in his voice. "How can they be different? You know you have a limited supply of fuel; you also know the law, as well as I do: 'Any stowaway discovered in an

TOM GODWIN

EDS shall be jettisoned immediately following discovery.' "

There was the sound of a sharply indrawn breath from the girl. "*What does he mean?*"

"The stowaway is a girl."

"*What?*"

"She wanted to see her brother. She's only a kid and she didn't know what she was really doing."

"I see." All the curtness was gone from the commander's voice. "So you called me in the hope I could do something?" Without waiting for an answer he went on, "I'm sorry—I can do nothing. This cruiser must maintain its schedule; the life of not one person but the lives of many depend on it. I know how you feel but I'm powerless to help you. You'll have to go through with it. I'll have you connected with Ship's Records."

The communicator faded to a faint rustle of sound and he turned back to the girl. She was leaning forward on the bench, almost rigid, her eyes fixed wide and frightened.

"What did he mean, to go through with it? To jettison me . . . to go through with it—what did he mean? Not the way it sounded . . . he couldn't have. What did he mean . . . what did he really mean?"

Her time was too short for the comfort of a lie to be more than a cruelly fleeting delusion.

"He meant it the way it sounded."

"*No!*" She recoiled from him as though he had struck her, one hand half upraised as though to fend him off and stark unwillingness to believe in her eyes.

"It will have to be."

"No! You're joking—you're insane! You can't mean it!"

"I'm sorry." He spoke slowly to her, gently. "I should have told you before—I should have, but I had to do what I could first; I had to call the *Stardust*. You heard what the commander said."

"But you can't—if you make me leave the ship, I'll *die*."

"I know."

She searched his face and the unwillingness to believe left her eyes, giving way slowly to a look of dazed horror.

"You know?" She spoke the words far apart, numb and wonderingly.

"I know. It has to be like that."

"You mean it—you really mean it." She sagged back against the wall, small and limp like a little rag doll and all the protesting and disbelief gone. "You're going to do it—you're going to make me die?"

"I'm sorry," he said again. "You'll never know how sorry I am. It has to be that way and no human in the universe can change it."

"You're going to make me die and I didn't do anything to die for—I didn't *do* anything—"

He sighed, deep and weary. "I know you didn't, child. I know you didn't—"

"EDS." The communicator rapped brisk and metallic. "This is Ship's Records. Give us all information on subject's identification disk."

He got out of his chair to stand over her. She clutched the edge of the seat, her upturned face white under the brown hair and the lipstick standing out like a blood-red cupid's bow.

"*Now?*"

"I want your identification disk," he said.

She released the edge of the seat and fumbled at the chain that suspended the plastic disk from her neck with fingers that were trembling and awkward. He reached down and unfastened the clasp for her, then returned with the disk to his chair.

"Here's your data, Records: Identification Number T837—"

"One moment," Records interrupted. "This is to be filed on the gray card, of course?"

"Yes."

"And the time of the execution?"

"I'll tell you later."

"Later? This is highly irregular; the time of the subject's death is required before—"

He kept the thickness out of his voice with an effort. "Then we'll do it in a highly irregular manner—you'll hear the disk read, first. The subject is a girl and she's listening to everything that's said. Are you capable of understanding that?"

There was a brief, almost shocked, silence, then Records said meekly: "Sorry. Go ahead."

He began to read the disk, reading it slowly to delay the inevitable for as long as possible, trying to help her by giving her what little time he could to recover from her first horror and let it resolve into the calm of acceptance and resignation.

"Number T8374 dash Y54. Name: Marilyn Lee Cross. Sex: Female. Born: July 7, 2160. *She was only eighteen.* Height: 5–3. Weight: 110.

TOM GODWIN

Such a slight weight, yet enough to add fatally to the mass of the shell-thin bubble that was an EDS. Hair: Brown. Eyes: Blue. Complexion: Light. Blood Type: O. *Irrelevant data.* Destination: Port City, Mimir. *Invalid data—*"

He finished and said, "I'll call you later," then turned once again to the girl. She was huddled back against the wall, watching him with a look of numb and wondering fascination.

"They're waiting for you to kill me, aren't they? They want me dead, don't they? You and everybody on the cruiser want me dead, don't you?" Then the numbness broke and her voice was that of a frightened and bewildered child. "Everybody wants me dead and I didn't *do* anything. I didn't hurt anyone—I only wanted to see my brother."

"It's not the way you think—it isn't that way, at all," he said. "Nobody wants it this way; nobody would ever let it be this way if it was humanly possible to change it."

"Then why is it? I don't understand. Why is it?"

"This ship is carrying *kala* fever serum to Group One on Woden. Their own supply was destroyed by a tornado. Group Two—the crew your brother is in—is eight thousand miles away across the Western Sea and their helicopters can't cross it to help Group One. The fever is invariably fatal unless the serum can be had in time, and the six men in Group One will die unless this ship reaches them on schedule. These little ships are always given barely enough fuel to reach their destination and if you stay aboard your added weight will cause it to use up all its fuel before it reaches the ground. It will crash, then, and you and I will die and so will the six men waiting for the fever serum."

It was a full minute before she spoke, and as she considered his words the expression of numbness left her eyes.

"Is that it?" she asked at last. "Just that the ship doesn't have enough fuel?"

"Yes."

"I can go alone or I can take seven others with me—is that the way it is?"

"That's the way it is."

"And nobody wants me to have to die?"

"Nobody."

"Then maybe— Are you sure nothing can be done about it? Wouldn't people help me if they could?"

THE COLD EQUATIONS

"Everyone would like to help you but there is nothing anyone can do. I did the only thing I could do when I called the *Stardust*."

"And it won't come back—but there might be other cruisers, mightn't there? Isn't there any hope at all that there might be someone, somewhere, who could do something to help me?"

She was leaning forward a little in her eagerness as she waited for his answer.

"No."

The word was like the drop of a cold stone and she again leaned back against the wall, the hope and eagerness leaving her face. "You're sure—you *know* you're sure?"

"I'm sure. There are no other cruisers within forty light years; there is nothing and no one to change things."

She dropped her gaze to her lap and began twisting a pleat of her skirt between her fingers, saying no more as her mind began to adapt itself to the grim knowledge.

It was better so; with the going of all hope would go the fear; with the going of all hope would come resignation. She needed time and she could have so little of it. How much?

The EDS's were not equipped with hull-cooling units; their speed had to be reduced to a moderate level before entering the atmosphere. They were decelerating at .10 gravity; approaching their destination at a far higher speed than the computers had calculated on. The *Stardust* had been quite near Woden when she launched the EDS; their present velocity was putting them nearer by the second. There would be a critical point, soon to be reached, when he would have to resume deceleration. When he did so the girl's weight would be multiplied by the gravities of deceleration, would become, suddenly, a factor of paramount importance; the factor the computers had been ignorant of when they determined the amount of fuel the EDS should have. She would have to go when deceleration began; it could be no other way. When would that be—how long could he let her stay?

"How long can I stay?"

He winced involuntarily from the words that were so like an echo of his own thoughts. How long? He didn't know; he would have to ask the ship's computers. Each EDS was given a meager surplus of fuel to compensate for unfavorable conditions within the atmosphere and relatively little fuel was being consumed for the time being. The memory banks of

TOM GODWIN

the computers would still contain all data pertaining to the course set for the EDS; such data would not be erased until the EDS reached its destination. He had only to give the computers the new data; the girl's weight and the exact time at which he had reduced the deceleration to .10.

"Barton." Commander Delhart's voice came abruptly from the communicator, as he opened his mouth to call the *Stardust*. "A check with Records shows me you haven't completed your report. Did you reduce the deceleration?"

So the commander knew what he was trying to do.

"I'm decelerating at point ten," he answered. "I cut the deceleration at seventeen fifty and the weight is a hundred and ten. I would like to stay at point ten as long as the computers say I can. Will you give them the questions?"

It was contrary to regulations for an EDS pilot to make any changes in the course or degree of deceleration the computers had set for him but the commander made no mention of the violation, neither did he ask the reason for it. It was not necessary for him to ask; he had not become commander of an interstellar cruiser without both intelligence and an understanding of human nature. He said only: "I'll have that given the computers."

The communicator fell silent and he and the girl waited, neither of them speaking. They would not have to wait long; the computers would give the answer within moments of the asking. The new factors would be fed into the steel maw of the first bank and the electrical impulses would go through the complex circuits. Here and there a relay might click, a tiny cog turn over, but it would be essentially the electrical impulses that found the answer; formless, mindless, invisible, determining with utter precision how long the pale girl beside him might live. Then five little segments of metal in the second bank would trip in rapid succession against an inked ribbon and a second steel maw would spit out the slip of paper that bore the answer.

The chronometer on the instrument board read eighteen ten when the commander spoke again.

"You will resume deceleration at nineteen ten."

She looked toward the chronometer, then quickly away from it. "Is that when . . . when I go?" she asked. He nodded and she dropped her eyes to her lap again.

THE COLD EQUATIONS   335

"I'll have the course corrections given you," the commander said. "Ordinarily I would never permit anything like this but I understand your position. There is nothing I can do, other than what I've just done, and you will not deviate from these new instructions. You will complete your report at nineteen ten. Now—here are the course corrections."

The voice of some unknown technician read them to him and he wrote them down on the pad clipped to the edge of the control board. There would, he saw, be periods of deceleration when he neared the atmosphere when the deceleration would be five gravities—and at five gravities, one hundred ten pounds would become five hundred fifty pounds.

The technician finished and he terminated the contact with a brief acknowledgment. Then, hesitating a moment, he reached out and shut off the communicator. It was eighteen thirteen and he would have nothing to report until nineteen ten. In the meantime, it somehow seemed indecent to permit others to hear what she might say in her last hour.

He began to check the instrument readings, going over them with unnecessary slowness. She would have to accept the circumstances and there was nothing he could do to help her into acceptance; words of sympathy would only delay it.

It was eighteen twenty when she stirred from her motionlessness and spoke.

"So that's the way it has to be with me?"

He swung around to face her. "You understand now, don't you? No one would ever let it be like this if it could be changed."

"I understand," she said. Some of the color had returned to her face and the lipstick no longer stood out so vividly red. "There isn't enough fuel for me to stay; when I hid on this ship I got into something I didn't know anything about and now I have to pay for it."

She had violated a man-made law that said KEEP OUT but the penalty was not for men's making or desire and it was a penalty men could not revoke. A physical law had decreed: *h amount of fuel will power an EDS with a mass of m safely to its destination*; and a second physical law had decreed: *h amount of fuel will not power an EDS with a mass of m plus x safely to its destination*.

EDS's obeyed only physical laws and no amount of human sympathy for her could alter the second law.

"But I'm afraid. I don't want to die—not now. I want to live and nobody is doing anything to help me; everybody is letting me go ahead and acting just like nothing was going to happen to me. I'm going to die and nobody *cares*."

"We all do," he said. "I do and the commander does and the clerk in Ship's Records; we all care and each of us did what little he could to help. It wasn't enough—it was almost nothing—but it was all we could do."

"Not enough fuel—I can understand that," she said, as though she had not heard his own words. "But to have to die for it. *Me*, alone—"

How hard it must be for her to accept the fact. She had never known danger of death; had never known the environments where the lives of men could be as fragile and fleeting as sea foam tossed against a rocky shore. She belonged on gentle Earth, in that secure and peaceful society where she could be young and gay and laughing with the others of her kind; where life was precious and well-guarded and there was always the assurance that tomorrow would come. She belonged in that world of soft winds and a warm sun, music and moonlight and gracious manners and not on the hard, bleak frontier.

"How did it happen to me so terribly quickly? An hour ago I was on the *Stardust*, going to Mimir. Now the *Stardust* is going on without me and I'm going to die and I'll never see Gerry and Mama and Daddy again—I'll never see anything again."

He hesitated, wondering how he could explain it to her so she would really understand and not feel she had, somehow, been the victim of a reasonlessly cruel injustice. She did not know what the frontier was like; she thought in terms of safe, secure Earth. Pretty girls were not jettisoned on Earth; there was a law against it. On Earth her plight would have filled the newscasts and a fast black Patrol ship would have been racing to her rescue. Everyone, everywhere, would have known of Marilyn Lee Cross and no effort would have been spared to save her life. But this was not Earth and there were no Patrol ships; only the *Stardust*, leaving them behind at many times the speed of light. There was no one to help her, there would be no Marilyn Lee Cross smiling from the newscasts tomorrow. Marilyn Lee Cross would be but a poignant memory for an EDS pilot and a name on a gray card in Ship's Records.

"It's different here; it's not like back on Earth," he said. "It isn't that no one cares; it's that no one can do anything to help. The frontier is big and here along its rim the colonies and exploration parties are scattered so thin and far between. On Woden, for example, there are only sixteen men—sixteen men on an entire world. The exploration parties, the survey crews, the little first-colonies—they're all fighting alien environments, trying to make a way for those who will follow after. The environments fight back and those who go first usually make mistakes only once. There is no margin of safety along the rim of the frontier; there can't be until the way is made for the others who will come later, until the new worlds are tamed and settled. Until then men will have to pay the penalty for making mistakes with no one to help them because there is no one *to* help them."

"I was going to Mimir," she said. "I didn't know about the frontier; I was only going to Mimir and *it's* safe."

"Mimir is safe but you left the cruiser that was taking you there."

She was silent for a little while. "It was all so wonderful at first; there was plenty of room for me on this ship and I would be seeing Gerry so soon. . . . I didn't know about the fuel, didn't know what would happen to me—"

Her words trailed away and he turned his attention to the viewscreen, not wanting to stare at her as she fought her way through the black horror of fear toward the calm gray of acceptance.

Woden was a ball, enshrouded in the blue haze of its atmosphere, swimming in space against the background of star-sprinkled dead blackness. The great mass of Manning's Continent sprawled like a gigantic hourglass in the Eastern Sea with the western half of the Eastern Continent still visible. There was a thin line of shadow along the right-hand edge of the globe and the Eastern Continent was disappearing into it as the planet turned on its axis. An hour before the entire continent had been in view, now a thousand miles of it had gone into the thin edge of shadow and around to the night that lay on the other side of the world. The dark blue spot that was Lotus Lake was approaching the shadow. It was somewhere near the southern edge of the lake that Group Two had their camp. It would be night there, soon, and quick behind the coming of night the rotation of Woden on its axis would put Group Two beyond the reach of the ship's radio.

He would have to tell her before it was too late for her to talk to her brother. In a way, it would be better for both of them should they not do so but it was not for him to decide. To each of them the last words would be something to hold and cherish, something that would cut like the blade of a knife yet would be infinitely precious to remember, she for her own brief moments to live and he for the rest of his life.

He held down the button that would flash the grid lines on the view-screen and used the known diameter of the planet to estimate the distance the southern tip of Lotus Lake had yet to go until it passed beyond radio range. It was approximately five hundred miles. Five hundred miles; thirty minutes—and the chronometer read eighteen thirty. Allowing for error in estimating, it could not be later than nineteen five that the turning of Woden would cut off her brother's voice.

The first border of the Western Continent was already in sight along the left side of the world. Four thousand miles across it lay the shore of the Western Sea and the Camp of Group One. It had been in the Western Sea that the tornado had originated, to strike with such fury at the camp and destroy half their prefabricated buildings, including the one that housed the medical supplies. Two days before, the tornado had not existed; it had been no more than great gentle masses of air out over the calm Western Sea. Group One had gone about their routine survey work, unaware of the meeting of air masses out at sea, unaware of the force the union was spawning. It had struck their camp without warning; a thundering, roaring destruction that sought to annihilate all that lay before it. It had passed on, leaving the wreckage in its wake. It had destroyed the labor of months and had doomed six men to die and then, as though its task was accomplished, it once more began to resolve into gentle masses of air. But for all its deadliness, it had destroyed with neither malice nor intent. It had been a blind and mindless force, obeying the laws of nature, and it would have followed the same course with the same fury had men never existed.

Existence required Order and there was order; the laws of nature, irrevocable and immutable. Men could learn to use them but men could not change them. The circumference of a circle was always pi times the diameter and no science of Man would ever make it otherwise. The combination of chemical A with chemical B under condition C invariably produced reaction D. The law of gravitation was a rigid equation and it made no distinction between the fall of a leaf and the ponderous circling of a binary star system. The nuclear conversion process powered the cruisers that carried men to the stars; the same process in the form of a nova would destroy a world with equal efficiency. The laws *were*, and the universe moved in obedience to them. Along the frontier were arrayed all the forces of nature and sometimes they destroyed those who were fighting their way outward from Earth. The men of the frontier had long ago learned the bitter futility of cursing the forces that would destroy them, for the forces were blind and deaf; the futility of looking to the heavens for mercy, for the stars of the galaxy swung in their long, long sweep of two hundred million years, as inexorably controlled as they by the laws that knew neither hatred nor compassion. The men of the frontier knew—but how was a girl from Earth to fully understand? *H amount of fuel will not power an EDS with a mass of m plus x safely to its destination.* To himself and her brother and parents she was a sweet-faced girl in her teens; to the laws of nature she was x, the unwanted factor in a cold equation.

She stirred again on the seat. "Could I write a letter? I want to write to Mama and Daddy and I'd like to talk to Gerry. Could you let me talk to him over your radio there?"

"I'll try to get him," he said.

He switched on the normal-space transmitter and pressed the signal button. Someone answered the buzzer almost immediately.

"Hello. How's it going with you fellows now—is the EDS on its way?"

"This isn't Group One; this is the EDS," he said. "Is Gerry Cross there?"

"Gerry? He and two others went out in the helicopter this morning and aren't back yet. It's almost sundown, though, and he ought to be back right away—in less than an hour at the most."

"Can you connect me through to the radio in his 'copter?"

"Huh-uh. It's been out of commission for two months—some printed circuits went haywire and we can't get any more until the next cruiser stops by. Is it something important—bad news for him, or something?"

"Yes—it's very important. When he comes in get him to the transmitter as soon as you possibly can."

"I'll do that; I'll have one of the boys waiting at the field with a truck. Is there anything else I can do?"

"No, I guess that's all. Get him there as soon as you can and signal me."

He turned the volume to an inaudible minimum, an act that would not affect the functioning of the signal buzzer, and unclipped the pad of paper from the control board. He tore off the sheet containing his flight instructions and handed the pad to her, together with the pencil.

TOM GODWIN

"I'd better write to Gerry, too," she said as she took them. "He might not get back to camp in time."

She began to write, her fingers still clumsy and uncertain in the way they handled the pencil and the top of it trembling a little as she poised it between words. He turned back to the viewscreen, to stare at it without seeing it.

She was a lonely little child, trying to say her last goodbye, and she would lay out her heart to them. She would tell them how much she loved them and she would tell them to not feel badly about it, that it was only something that must happen eventually to everyone and she was not afraid. The last would be a lie and it would be there to read between the sprawling uneven lines; a valiant little lie that would make the hurt all the greater for them.

Her brother was of the frontier and he would understand. He would not hate the EDS pilot for doing nothing to prevent her going; he would know there had been nothing the pilot could do. He would understand, though the understanding would not soften the shock and pain when he learned his sister was gone. But the others, her father and mother—they would not understand. They were of Earth and they would think in the manner of those who had never lived where the safety margin of life was a thin, thin line—and sometimes not at all. What would they think of the faceless, unknown pilot who had sent her to her death?

They would hate him with cold and terrible intensity but it really didn't matter. He would never see them, never know them. He would have only the memories to remind him; only the nights to fear, when a blue-eyed girl in gypsy sandals would come in his dreams to die again—

He scowled at the viewscreen and tried to force his thoughts into less emotional channels. There was nothing he could do to help her. She had unknowingly subjected herself to the penalty of a law that recognized neither innocence nor youth nor beauty, that was incapable of sympathy or leniency. Regret was illogical—and yet, could knowing it to be illogical ever keep it away?

She stopped occasionally, as though trying to find the right words to tell them what she wanted them to know, then the pencil would resume its whispering to the paper. It was eighteen thirty-seven when she folded the letter in a square and wrote a name on it. She began writing another, twice looking up at the chronometer as though she feared the black hand might reach its rendezvous before she had finished. It was eighteen forty-five when she folded it as she had done the first letter and wrote a name and address on it.

She held the letters out to him. "Will you take care of these and see that they're enveloped and mailed?"

"Of course." He took them from her hand and placed them in a pocket of his gray uniform shirt.

"These can't be sent off until the next cruiser stops by and the *Stardust* will have long since told them about me, won't it?" she asked. He nodded and she went on. "That makes the letters not important in one way but in another way they're very important—to me, and to them."

"I know. I understand, and I'll take care of them."

She glanced at the chronometer, then back to him. "It seems to move faster all the time, doesn't it?"

He said nothing, unable to think of anything to say, and she asked, "Do you think Gerry will come back to camp in time?"

"I think so. They said he should be in right away."

She began to roll the pencil back and forth between her palms. "I hope he does. I feel sick and scared and I want to hear his voice again and maybe I won't feel so alone. I'm a coward and I can't help it."

"No," he said, "you're not a coward. You're afraid, but you're not a coward."

"Is there a difference?"

He nodded. "A lot of difference."

"I feel so alone. I never did feel like this before; like I was all by myself and there was nobody to care what happened to me. Always, before, there was Mama and Daddy there and my friends around me. I had lots of friends, and they had a going-away party for me the night before I left."

Friends and music and laughter for her to remember—and on the viewscreen Lotus Lake was going into the shadow.

"Is it the same with Gerry?" she asked. "I mean, if he should make a mistake, would he have to die for it, all alone and with no one to help him?"

"It's the same with all along the frontier; it will always be like that so long as there is a frontier."

"Gerry didn't tell us. He said the pay was good and he sent money home all the time because Daddy's little shop just brought in a bare living but he didn't tell us it was like this."

"He didn't tell you his work was dangerous?"

TOM GODWIN

"Well—yes. He mentioned that, but we didn't understand. I always thought danger along the frontier was something that was a lot of fun; an exciting adventure, like in the three-D shows." A wan smile touched her face for a moment. "Only it's not, is it? It's not the same at all, because when it's real you can't go home after the show is over."

"No," he said. "No, you can't."

Her glance flicked from the chronometer to the door of the air lock then down to the pad and pencil she still held. She shifted her position slightly to lay them on the bench beside her, moving one foot out a little. For the first time he saw that she was not wearing Vegan gypsy sandals but only cheap imitations; the expensive Vegan leather was some kind of grained plastic, the silver buckle was gilded iron, the jewels were colored glass. *Daddy's little shop just brought in a bare living*—She must have left college in her second year, to take the course in linguistics that would enable her to make her own way and help her brother provide for her parents, earning what she could by part-time work after classes were over. Her personal possessions on the *Stardust* would be taken back to her parents—they would neither be of much value nor occupy much storage space on the return voyage.

"Isn't it—" She stopped, and he looked at her questioningly. "Isn't it cold in here?" she asked, almost apologetically. "Doesn't it seem cold to you?"

"Why, yes," he said. He saw by the main temperature gauge that the room was at precisely normal temperature. "Yes, it's colder than it should be."

"I wish Gerry would get back before it's too late. Do you really think he will, and you didn't just say so to make me feel better?"

"I think he will—they said he would be in pretty soon." On the viewscreen Lotus Lake had gone into the shadow but for the thin blue line of its western edge and it was apparent he had overestimated the time she would have in which to talk to her brother. Reluctantly, he said to her, "His camp will be out of radio range in a few minutes; he's on that part of Woden that's in the shadow"—he indicated the viewscreen—"and the turning of Woden will put him beyond contact. There may not be much time left when he comes in—not much time to talk to him before he fades out. I wish I could do something about it—I would call him right now if I could."

"Not even as much time as I will have to stay?"

"I'm afraid not."

"Then—" She straightened and looked toward the air lock with pale resolution. "Then I'll go when Gerry passes beyond range. I won't wait any longer after that—I won't have anything to wait for."

Again there was nothing he could say.

"Maybe I shouldn't wait at all. Maybe I'm selfish—maybe it would be better for Gerry if you just told him about it afterward."

There was an unconscious pleading for denial in the way she spoke and he said, "He wouldn't want you to do that, to not wait for him."

"It's already coming dark where he is, isn't it? There will be all the long night before him, and Mama and Daddy don't know yet that I won't ever be coming back like I promised them I would. I've caused everyone I love to be hurt, haven't I? I didn't want to—I didn't intend to."

"It wasn't your fault," he said. "It wasn't your fault at all. They'll know that. They'll understand."

"At first I was so afraid to die that I was a coward and thought only of myself. Now, I see how selfish I was. The terrible thing about dying like this is not that I'll be gone but that I'll never see them again; never be able to tell them that I didn't take them for granted; never be able to tell them I knew of the sacrifices they made to make my life happier, that I knew all the things they did for me and that I loved them so much more than I ever told them. I've never told them any of those things. You don't tell them such things when you're young and your life is all before you—you're so very afraid of sounding sentimental and silly.

"But it's so different when you have to die—you wish you had told them while you could and you wish you could tell them you're sorry for all the little mean things you ever did or said to them. You wish you could tell them that you didn't really mean to ever hurt their feelings and for them to only remember that you always loved them far more than you ever let them know."

"You don't have to tell them that," he said. "They will know—they've always known it."

"Are you sure?" she asked. "How can you be sure? My people are strangers to you."

"Wherever you go, human nature and human hearts are the same."

"And they will know what I want them to know—that I love them?"

"They've always known it, in a way far better than you could ever put in words for them."

344   TOM GODWIN

"I keep remembering the things they did for me, and it's the little things they did that seem to be the most important to me, now. Like Gerry—he sent me a bracelet of fire-rubies on my sixteenth birthday. It was beautiful—it must have cost him a month's pay. Yet, I remember him more for what he did the night my kitten got run over in the street. I was only six years old and he held me in his arms and wiped away my tears and told me not to cry, that Flossy was gone for just a little while, for just long enough to get herself a new fur coat and she would be on the foot of my bed the very next morning. I believed him and quit crying and went to sleep dreaming about my kitten coming back. When I woke up the next morning, there was Flossy on the foot of my bed in a brand-new white fur coat, just like he had said she would be.

"It wasn't until a long time later that Mama told me Gerry had got the pet-shop owner out of bed at four in the morning and, when the man got mad about it, Gerry told him he was either going to go down and sell him the white kitten right then or he'd break his neck."

"It's always the little things you remember people by; all the little things they did because they wanted to do them for you. You've done the same for Gerry and your father and mother; all kinds of things that you've forgotten about but that they will never forget."

"I hope I have. I would like for them to remember me like that."

"They will."

"I wish—" She swallowed. "The way I'll die—I wish they wouldn't ever think of that. I've read how people look who die in space—their insides all ruptured and exploded and their lungs out between their teeth and then, a few seconds later, they're all dry and shapeless and horribly ugly. I don't want them to ever think of me as something dead and horrible, like that."

"You're their own, their child and their sister. They could never think of you other than the way you would want them to; the way you looked the last time they saw you."

"I'm still afraid," she said. "I can't help it, but I don't want Gerry to know it. If he gets back in time, I'm going to act like I'm not afraid at all and—"

The signal buzzer interrupted her, quick and imperative.

"Gerry!" She came to her feet. "It's Gerry, now!"

He spun the volume control knob and asked: "Gerry Cross?"

"Yes," her brother answered, an undertone of tenseness to his reply.

"The bad news—what is it?"

She answered for him, standing close behind him and leaning down a little toward the communicator, her hand resting small and cold on his shoulder.

"Hello, Gerry." There was only a faint quaver to betray the careful casualness of her voice. "I wanted to see you—"

"Marilyn!" There was sudden and terrible apprehension in the way he spoke her name. "What are you doing on that EDS?"

"I wanted to see you," she said again. "I wanted to see you, so I hid on this ship—"

"You *hid* on it?"

"I'm a stowaway. . . . I didn't know what it would mean—"

"*Marilyn!*" It was the cry of a man who calls hopeless and desperate to someone already and forever gone from him. "What have you done?"

"I . . . it's not—" Then her own composure broke and the cold little hand gripped his shoulder convulsively. "Don't, Gerry—I only wanted to see you; I didn't intend to hurt you. Please, Gerry, don't feel like that—"

Something warm and wet splashed on his wrist and he slid out of the chair, to help her into it and swing the microphone down to her own level.

"Don't feel like that— Don't let me go knowing you feel like that—"

The sob she had tried to hold back choked in her throat and her brother spoke to her. "Don't cry, Marilyn." His voice was suddenly deep and infinitely gentle, with all the pain held out of it. "Don't cry, sis—you mustn't do that. It's all right, honey—everything is all right."

"I—" Her lower lip quivered and she bit into it. "I didn't want you to feel that way—I just wanted us to say goodbye because I have to go in a minute."

"Sure—sure. That's the way it'll be, sis. I didn't mean to sound the way I did." Then his voice changed to a tone of quick and urgent demand. "EDS—have you called the *Stardust*? Did you check with the computers?"

"I called the *Stardust* almost an hour ago. It can't turn back, there are no other cruisers within forty light years, and there isn't enough fuel."

"Are you sure that the computers had the correct data—sure of everything?"

"Yes—do you think I could ever let it happen if I wasn't sure? I did

346   TOM GODWIN

everything I could do. If there was anything at all I could do now, I would do it."

"He tried to help me, Gerry." Her lower lip was no longer trembling and the short sleeves of her blouse were wet where she had dried her tears. "No one can help me and I'm not going to cry any more and everything will be all right with you and Daddy and Mama, won't it?"

"Sure—sure it will. We'll make out fine."

Her brother's words were beginning to come in more faintly and he turned the volume control to maximum. "He's going out of range," he said to her. "He'll be gone within another minute."

"You're fading out, Gerry," she said. "You're going out of range. I wanted to tell you—but I can't now. We must say goodbye so soon—but maybe I'll see you again. Maybe I'll come to you in your dreams with my hair in braids and crying because the kitten in my arms is dead; maybe I'll be the touch of a breeze that whispers to you as it goes by; maybe I'll be one of those gold-winged larks you told me about, singing my silly head off to you; maybe, at times, I'll be nothing you can see but you will know I'm there beside you. Think of me like that, Gerry; always like that and not—the other way."

Dimmed to a whisper by the turning of Woden, the answer came back: "Always like that, Marilyn—always like that and never any other way."

"Our time is up, Gerry—I have to go, now. Good—" Her voice broke in mid-word and her mouth tried to twist into crying. She pressed her hand hard against it and when she spoke again the words came clear and true:

"Goodbye, Gerry."

Faint and ineffably poignant and tender, the last words came from the cold metal of the communicator:

"Goodbye, little sister—"

She sat motionless in the hush that followed, as though listening to the shadow-echoes of the words as they died away, then she turned away from the communicator, toward the air lock, and he pulled down the black lever beside him. The inner door of the air lock slid swiftly open, to reveal the bare little cell that was waiting for her, and she walked to it.

She walked with her head up and the brown curls brushing her shoulders, with the white sandals stepping as sure and steady as the fractional gravity would permit and the gilded buckles twinkling with little lights of blue and red and crystal. He let her walk alone and made no move to help her, knowing she would not want it that way. She stepped into the air lock and turned to face him, only the pulse in her throat to betray the wild beating of her heart.

"I'm ready," she said.

He pushed the lever up and the door slid its quick barrier between them enclosing her in black and utter darkness for her last moments of life. It clicked as it locked in place and he jerked down the red lever. There was a slight waver to the ship as the air gushed from the lock, a vibration to the wall as though something had bumped the outer door in passing, then there was nothing and the ship was dropping true and steady again. He shoved the red lever back to close the door on the empty air lock and turned away, to walk to the pilot's chair with the slow steps of a man old and weary.

Back in the pilot's chair he pressed the signal button of the normal-space transmitter. There was no response; he had expected none. Her brother would have to wait through the night until the turning of Woden permitted contact through Group One.

It was not yet time to resume deceleration and he waited while the ship dropped endlessly downward with him and the drives purred softly. He saw that the white hand of the supplies closet temperature gauge was on zero. A cold equation had been balanced and he was alone on the ship. Something shapeless and ugly was hurrying ahead of him, going to Woden where its brother was waiting through the night, but the empty ship still lived for a little while with the presence of the girl who had not known about the forces that killed with neither hatred nor malice. It seemed, almost, that she still sat small and bewildered and frightened on the metal box beside him, her words echoing hauntingly clear in the void she had left behind her:

I didn't do anything to die for—I didn't do anything—